## Praise for the Moonlight Harbor novels by Sheila Roberts

"A masterful blend of comedic timing with characters you believe in and want good things for.... A wonderful summer read for anyone who wants to enjoy a well told story."            —*MBR Bookwatch* on *Sand Dollar Lane*

"Roberts proves again why she is the premier purveyor of small-town, feel-good romance. Love, laughter, and even a few tears are deftly integrated into the book's multithreaded plot as Jenna, her family, and her friends navigate life's challenges with hope and heart."
            —*Booklist* on *Sunset on Moonlight Beach*

"What better place to start over than Moonlight Harbor, where new friendships and new beginnings await?... Moonlight Harbor is a great place to lose yourself for a few hours and *Beachside Beginnings* is an empowering, heart-tugging way to do it."            —*The Romance Dish*

"In her latest superbly crafted addition to her Moonlight Harbor series, Roberts skillfully and sensitively incorporates the fears and challenges women facing abuse must overcome into an empowering tale of hope and change. This sweetly romantic, emotionally enriching small-town tale is simply charming in every way."            —*Booklist* on *Beachside Beginnings*

"Small-town politics, meddling townsfolk, and gossip with a mean-girl vibe keep the things upbeat in an irresistible story that will have readers wondering until the conclusion.... Lighthearted and full of colorful, quirky characters and surf-side warmth, this latest foray into Roberts's picturesque coastal world is sheer delight and will appeal to romance and women's fiction fans alike."
            —*Library Journal* on *The Summer Retreat*

# SHEILA ROBERTS

## Mermaid Beach

mira

ISBN-13: 978-0-7783-3354-8

Mermaid Beach

Copyright © 2023 by Roberts Ink LLC

This is a work of fiction. Names, characters, places and incidents are either the
product of the author's imagination or are used fictitiously. Any resemblance
to actual persons, living or dead, businesses, companies, events or locales is
entirely coincidental.

For questions and comments about the quality of this book, please contact us
at CustomerService@Harlequin.com.

Mira
22 Adelaide St. West, 41st Floor
Toronto, Ontario M5H 4E3, Canada
www.Harlequin.com

**Printed in Lithuania**

MIX
Paper | Supporting
responsible forestry
FSC® C021394

To Candy and Chuck and Denise and Dwight,
the Nashville gang

# Mermaid Beach

# One

When you were a Mermaid, how could you not be inspired to paint mermaids? "But is it too cutesy?" Bonnie Brinks asked her boss and friend, Realtor Lucy Holmes, who owned Beach Dream Homes with her husband Brody.

Bonnie worked part-time at the office, filling in as needed, helping their full-time staff as their business continued to grow. This day Lucy had come over for a rare girls' afternoon relaxation break on Bonnie's back deck. Complete with treats from Sunshine Bakery, of course. (One should share sugar addictions.)

Lucy was probably the wrong person to ask. She was in awe of Bonnie's artistic leanings.

"I think it's brilliant," Lucy said. "And so unlike any kind of mermaid paintings you normally see. It's whimsical."

Bonnie studied her mermaids. One was older and had a few wrinkles and only the tiniest hint of crepey skin on her mermaid arms. Bonnie had left her neck crepe-free. The painting was a gift, after all. And instead of long hair, this mermaid's was short and white, spiked and tipped with green. A perfect match for Bonnie's mom, Loretta, who was

the drummer for The Mermaids, the all-girl band she and
Bonnie had started back when Bonnie's daughter was finishing up college. Mermaid Loretta was sitting on top of a
rock jutting out of the sea, holding a leopard print martini
glass, and was laughing uproariously, head thrown back,
at something the mermaid sitting next to her was saying.
The mermaid with her was also enjoying a fancy drink and
just happened to look a lot like Bonnie, with long auburn
hair falling in waves past her shoulders. Both mermaids
had green eyes, like Bonnie and Loretta. And both mermaids had starfish covering the tips of their breasts—perky
breasts, which were not true to life any more than the barely
aging skin. But Bonnie wasn't into realism.

"Your mom's going to love it. It's the perfect birthday
present," Lucy said. "And I'm jealous. I want a mermaid
of my own."

"I just did this for Mom because I wanted to give her
something fun for hitting sixty-five. It's kind of a landmark
birthday and she's not looking forward to it."

"They do get harder the higher you go," said Lucy. "I'm
sure in no hurry to hit fifty."

"You got a ways to go," Bonnie said consolingly. Fifty
was in her future, too, but far enough around the corner
that she couldn't see it making faces at her yet.

"Honestly, I don't know why you've kept this talent hidden," Lucy said.

"Maybe because I'm not Van Gogh."

"Which is why you have both your ears. Come on, I
know you have more. I want to see. Please, please, please."

"All right. But they're really nothing. Painting's just what
I do for fun."

"Yeah, yeah, like your photography, which is amazing,"
Lucy said, motioning to the piece Bonnie had gotten en-

larged and framed and then hung over her fireplace. "That is just so cool with the beach grass close up and beach and water in the background. And that tanker in the distance, all blurry and ghostlike. By the way, I had another offer just the other day for the one you gave me of the birds in flight at sunset."

"That was a lucky shot," Bonnie said, as she led the way to her small artist studio.

"There is such a thing as skill," Lucy told her. "You have so many artistic gifts."

"Much good they do me," Bonnie said with a snort. She wasn't a starving artist. More like a perpetually dieting one, getting by but hardly getting rich.

"They'd probably do you a lot of good if you pursued them in earnest," Lucy said.

Bonnie shook her head and frowned. "Now you sound like my mother."

Loretta never tired of reminding Bonnie how talented she was. She'd spent years after Bonnie returned home after her Nashville crash trying to convince her to not give up, to get back in there and fight to make her dreams come true. She still had a tendency to slip into stage mother mode.

Bonnie wasn't interested. She'd learned the hard way that dreams could quickly turn into nightmares. She was much happier living her small but hurt-free life in Moonlight Harbor, enjoying beach walks, taking pictures, playing local gigs. Every once in a while, someone would talk about the danger of a tsunami hitting the Washington State coast and taking out the little town, but Bonnie would rather risk a tsunami than revisit the emotional upheaval she'd experienced once upon a heartbreak in Music City.

"I'll take that as a compliment," Lucy said. "I love your mom."

"So do I," said Bonnie. "Even when she's making me nuts with this latest man she's found. She hardly knows him but she's already envisioning them living happily ever after in her condo and taking Mediterranean cruises during the winter."

"It could happen. You never know where you're going to find love," said Lucy. "Look at Brody and me. From real estate rivals to partners for life."

"A nice, happy ending," Bonnie said. "And good for you, cause they're harder to find than four-leaf clovers."

She opened the door to the room where three paintings, two finished, one almost complete, sat propped against a wall. In one a mermaid with dark hair and deep bronze skin perched on the bow of a boat, leaning over and kissing a red-nosed old man in dungarees and a well-worn T-shirt who was holding a beer bottle in one hand and a fishing pole in another. He wore a goofy smile and his eyes were closed as he savored the moment. Another picture captured two mermaids, both tan with flaxen hair streaked with green, enjoying a little tea party on a rock by the sea. A small red-checked cloth had been placed on the rock and on it was a blue teapot and plate of cookies. Each mermaid held a blue teacup. The final painting was mostly done and showed a pale mermaid with light red hair sitting on the bow of yet another rowboat, playing the guitar and singing for a hunky-looking man lounging in the stern. He wore board shorts and no shirt and he was ripped.

"Is this you?" Lucy said, pointing to it. "She looks a lot like you."

"Hardly," Bonnie said, unwilling to admit she'd painted the thing under the influence of self-pity. It happened. Once in a while when she watched a romantic movie. Especially right around the time of the CMA awards. "Last I checked there were no gorgeous men our age moving to Moonlight Harbor."

"People are moving here all the time. Or have you forgotten how many houses we've sold in the last year?"

Bonnie shrugged. "Families, retired couples. This isn't exactly Mecca for single men in their forties."

"We have a few single men here over the age of thirty," Lucy reminded her.

Bonnie cocked an eyebrow. "And which of them should I pick? Seth Waters's beer-gut buddy? Or how about Annie's ex, the deadbeat dad? Of course, I could expand my horizons and go out with Jeffrey Hooverman."

Lucy held up a hand. "Okay, okay. You made your point. But the town is growing, with new people coming here all the time. You never know." She returned her attention to the pictures. "So, which one of these are you going to sell me?"

"None," Bonnie said firmly.

Lucy frowned.

"If I did something for you it would need to be tailor made."

"Okay, tailor make me one. I'm commissioning you."

"I'll make you one for your birthday."

"That's not until June. That's months away."

"Art takes time," Bonnie said.

"Okay, okay, I can wait. With anticipation," Lucy added. She checked her smart watch. "I'd better get going. I have to show the Millers' house at four and with all the kids coming down for the weekend I need to get to the store and stock up on food."

"You guys are coming to The Drunken Sailor tonight?"

"Of course. The girls are looking forward to practicing their line dance steps."

One of Moonlight Harbor's favorite night spots, The

Drunken Sailor offered great pub food and had a long bar for patrons to belly up to. Two carved wood lady pirates, complete with pirate hats and boobs almost spilling out of their pirate vests greeted guests when they came in and many a man, whether a sailor or not, took selfies with them.

To balance things out, the owner had recently imported two manly pirates, one of them dark and swashbuckling, standing with one foot on a treasure chest, the other, an older specimen who'd lost his swash, seated on a chair and waiting for the cute young tourists to put on his hat and rub his bald head.

In addition to its wooden greeters, the place had pool tables, darts and a big wooden dance floor and offered line dancing lessons every Sunday afternoon, followed by dancing in the evening. Whether on a Sunday evening or a Friday night that dance floor was always full.

The Mermaids had, over the last few months, become the house band, graduating from playing weddings and occasionally at local Elks and Eagles club events. The Drunken Sailor was a nice gig—Friday and Saturday nights, which left the rest of the week free for Bonnie to help Lucy and her husband with their growing real estate empire and work on her own creative projects.

"I'll see you there then," she said to Lucy.

Bonnie did, indeed, see Lucy and Brody at The Drunken Sailor that night, along with Lucy's daughter and Brody's son, who had gotten married, as well as Brody's daughter. Brody had never been one to get lured out onto the dance floor until Lucy came on the scene. He still refused to participate in the line dancing, but when The Mermaids sang "Neon Moon" he was out there with Lucy, doing the cowboy cha-cha along with everyone else.

The song was a crowd favorite, but it wasn't one of Bonnie's. Singing about broken dreams and watching all those happy couples circling the floor tended to make her grumpy and that night was no different. They finished the song and went into the next one she'd scheduled in the set. "Before He Cheats." Ah, much better.

Pete Long, loyal patron and token stubble-chinned Ancient Mariner, came up to the bandstand after they finished and were about to start the next song.

"I don't know why you have to keep playin' that mean song," he said to Bonnie.

"Because I like it," she replied.

He frowned at her. "I got a request."

"Don't tell me, let me guess. 'Crazy.'"

He nodded. "Yeah, how'd you know?"

"Because you always request that song after we sing 'Before He Cheats.'"

"'Cause any woman who'd wreck a perfectly good car has gotta be nuts," Pete said. "Anyway, that song's a classic and you sing it good. It was Edie's favorite," he added.

Edie Patterson, one of Moonlight Harbor's grand dames, and the love of the scruffy old dude's life, was no longer with them. He missed her like, well, like crazy, and he spent a lot of time dragging Bonnie's mom, Loretta, down Memory Lane with him, cornering her during a band break at least once a week.

Bonnie always obliged him when he requested the song, even though that one wasn't a favorite, either. But she could really pour herself into it. She knew about the craziness of thinking love could be enough to hold a man.

"Okay, you got it, Pete. But first we have to play a fast song and get everybody moving. Okay?"

"Okay," he said and slouched off back to the bar, hands in the pockets of his faded jeans.

"Now, everybody, I hope you got your boots fired up 'cause we're gonna rock this place," Bonnie said into her mike, which brought out several whoops from some of the louder patrons.

She turned to Loretta, who was looking fine in her black skinny jeans and spangly, jade green top. "Count us off, Mom."

Loretta lifted the drumsticks over her head and hit them together in fast 4/4 time, showing off arms fit enough to be the envy of every senior citizen in town.

Their young bass player, Gina, hit the first note on the bass and walked down, accompanied by Bonnie's daughter, Avril, on the rhythm guitar and Bonnie went into the guitar riff she'd created. The song was one she'd written and it always got people up dancing.

The dancers recognized the intro and charged the dance floor, lining up to do the Tush Push. They were going at it by the time Bonnie began to sing.

"Get off your chair, get on the floor and shake your booty. You gotta start this party, so get out there and do your duty. Bring it on, bring it on, bring it on—bring on the moves. Come on, come on, come on, everybody's watchin' you. Oh, yeah."

It was true. The dance floor was a mass of fast-moving bodies, everyone smiling. At the bar, male onlookers watched appreciatively as Lucy Holmes and her daughter and stepdaughter shook their butts and shuffled back and forth along with Courtney Greer, who owned Beach Babes Boutique. Moira King from Waves Salon, who kept Loretta's hair looking stylish and mermaid worthy, was out there also, as well as Jenna Waters, proud owner of the Driftwood

Inn while her husband, Seth, watched from their table. Jenna's sister Celeste was right next to her, rocking a new pair of cowgirl boots, and beside her was their friend Tyrella, who owned the hardware store. The song could have been written for Tyrella. She had the moves to show off. Brody's son, Declan, and Moira's husband, Victor King, were dancing as well, but it was the women who were stealing the show, with their joy and confidence.

*Go, girls*, thought Bonnie as she watched them. The song was such a crowd-pleaser. Too bad the only crowd who'd ever hear it would be patrons of a small-town pub.

*Don't go there.*

She obediently veered away from the thought. It was the lament of every failed songwriter and damn it, she wasn't going to lament. She wasn't a failure. Not totally.

She moved into the chorus, her daughter, the one good thing that had come out of her time in Nashville, joining her on harmony. "Party on, yeah, yeah, party on. Keep it all goin', goin' on till dawn. Party on, yeah show 'em what you got. Your boots are burning down the floor. You're red hot."

So was she as she went into her guitar solo, letting the strings scream. Making music like this, being spot-on and with the crowd into it, it was the musician's equivalent of a runner's high.

She did another verse and chorus, then went into the bridge, which ramped everything up and ended in a vocal scream. The drinkers at the bar and the dancers all got into it and screamed with her, and people started singing along as they went through the last chorus. Loretta took them out with a bang and everyone clapped and hooted.

Bonnie's heart was beating as fast as the drums had been and her hairline was damp with sweat in spite of her sleeveless turquoise top with the fringed neckline. It may have been cold outside but it was hot in The Drunken Sailor.

"We killed," said Loretta from her seat at the drums.

Yeah, they did. "Okay, y'all," Bonnie said to the crowd.

Y'all. As if she was still in Nashville. Even after so many years away, she slipped back into that Southern thing when she was on stage and high on the music.

"We got a request," she continued. "This one's for Pete." She didn't have to tell her band what song they were going to sing. They all knew and slowed it down for the Patsy Cline classic.

After that they went into Lady A's "Need You Now." And then Bonnie needed a break. She loved country music but many of those songs had a way of wringing her out. Time for a Diet Coke.

It would be regular Coke for Avril, 7-Up for Gina, and tonic water for Loretta. Nobody drank when the band was performing. No drugs, either, legal or otherwise. Not that any of them did drugs. But that would have been the rule for whomever Bonnie was playing with. She'd played in enough bands where musicians got sloppy when under the influence. She still remembered the bass player in one of the cover bands she was in, falling off the stage after one too many whiskey shots.

The two younger band members, both over twenty-one, made a beeline for the bar. Loretta stopped to flirt with Pete, as usual. "Just giving the guy a little ego boost," she liked to say, but Bonnie suspected that boosting thing was a two-way street.

Avril was temporarily waylaid by a hefty twentysomething man with dark hair and a bird's nest of a beard. Bonnie could swear she saw drool glistening on that beard. But Avril had the situation well under control even before her man, Kenny, a six-foot tank, got there to put a stop to the stranger hitting on her. She got her drink and they headed for the band table.

Bonnie herself was almost to the bar when her biggest fan, Jeffrey Hooverman, waylaid her. "Bonnie, let me buy you a drink."

"Thanks, Jeffrey, but remember? I don't drink when I'm working."

"Okay, I'll buy your soda pop."

"You don't need to. They're on the house for the band."

"Some fries then? Onion rings?"

"No, I'm good. Thanks," she said and picked up her pace.

He did, too, his soft belly swinging as he went. "Nobody does 'Crazy' like you."

Hmm. There was a good song hook. Bonnie filed it away for future use.

"The song, I mean," he hastened to add.

"Thanks, Jeffrey. That's sweet of you."

"You know, that offer of dinner still stands," he said.

She nodded. "I know. But I'd be wasting your money."

"Being with you would never be a waste," he said earnestly.

"Aww, you don't want to hang out with me," Bonnie said. "Sally Farnham's come out again tonight. You probably can't tell from where you're sitting, but from the bandstand I can see her looking at you."

He followed her gaze to where a slightly pudgy woman with Betty Boop lips and hair dyed violet was looking at them. She gave a little wave and Jeffrey half lifted a hand in response.

"Not my type," he said.

"What is your type?" Bonnie asked. Bad idea. The last thing she wanted to know was Jeffrey Hooverman's type.

"I like 'em younger. Frisky."

Of course he did. Because Jeffrey was delusional. He was probably close to sixty with a balding scalp, trying desperately to hold on to the few hairs he had left. Plus he had the build of a jellyfish and the personality to match. Jeffrey was a nice man, but he wasn't a temptation, especially for a woman who wasn't looking for a man. Ever. She'd been there, done that, bought the T-shirt, took it back.

"Well, Jeffrey, you might want to rethink that. Did you know that a woman doesn't reach her sexual peak until her fifties?"

Jeffrey blinked at such frankness. Then his expression turned thoughtful. "You don't say."

"And poor Sally has been all alone for the last three years. I bet she could use some consoling." Yep, she had him now.

Jeffrey's thoughtful moment disappeared. "Well, there's plenty of men her age here. When can I take you to dinner?"

"Jeffrey, stop already," Bonnie said firmly. "Get in touch with your inner white knight and go buy Sally a drink."

Jeffrey went away, pouting, and returned to his seat at the bar next to Pete Long, who was talking to Loretta. The two hot bachelors of Moonlight Harbor.

"I see Jeffrey was after you again," Loretta said to Bonnie when she finally joined the others at the band table.

"You're such a man magnet, Mom," teased Avril.

If ever there was a man magnet, it was her daughter, with her long, dark hair. She had the same green eyes as Bonnie, but she had her father's tall, lean body and olive complexion and his patrician nose and generous lips. Would he ever recognize her if he saw her?

No need to worry about that. Avril didn't know who her father was and she would not be going to Nashville. Bonnie had explained the music facts of life to Avril at a young age, and anyway, between her job, her boyfriend and the band she was firmly rooted in Moonlight Harbor.

"We know who the man magnet in the family is," Bonnie said, making Kenny frown.

Avril frowned, too. "Don't remind me."

"I thought it was sweet that those boys in your high school choir made up a song for you," Loretta said.

"Kind of creepy," said Gina.

Loretta chuckled. "Reminds me of myself when I was your age. You know who Tony Arata really wrote 'The Dance' for," she said to Kenny.

"Yes, Garth Brooks," said Bonnie.

"But he was inspired by me," Loretta insisted.

"No shit," Kenny said, impressed.

Loretta Brinks, a legend in her own mind. Bonnie rolled her eyes.

Loretta caught her. "It's true," she insisted. "Ah, that's the magic of Nashville."

"Black magic," Bonnie muttered.

"It's never too late. You go back wiser, stronger and you find the magic," Loretta said, looking pointedly at her.

"Mom, do you have any idea how hard it is to make it in this day and age?" Bonnie snapped. Honestly, how many times had they had this conversation or some variation of it?

"You can still make connections," Loretta insisted.

"It's not like it was in the golden eighties," Bonnie argued. "Things were changing even when I was there, thanks to people pirating songs. Now it's even harder to make it. You have to be more than a talent. You have to be a media pro with thousands and thousands of followers on Twitter and Instagram and TikTok. And if you don't have a label buying those followers for you, you get nowhere. You can't make an appointment to go in and see a publisher and play them your songs like you could in your day, either."

Loretta squirmed in her seat. "I never said it was easy."

"And you're hardly in a position to talk. You tried and look where it didn't get you." Okay, that had been a cheap shot and Bonnie regretted her words the moment they were out of her mouth.

Loretta narrowed her eyes and pointed a red acrylic nail at her daughter. "I traded fame for true love. I gave it up for your father because I knew if I didn't my career would break us up and I loved him too much. He was the light of my life and..." Her words trailed off and the tears began to leak out. "Oh, darn it all, now my mascara's running. I should have bought waterproof." She stood up and marched away from the table, leaving an awkward silence behind her.

Bonnie could feel her daughter's accusing gaze. "My bad," she said.

"You should let Glamma have her memories," Avril scolded, "even if they are exaggerated."

Bonnie sighed and went after her mother.

She found Loretta in the women's bathroom, sniffling and dabbing at her face. Their mirror reflections exchanged looks, one apologetic, one accusing.

"Mom," Bonnie began.

Loretta held up a hand to stop her. "Don't say a word."

"I need to. I'm sorry I was a snot."

Loretta looked away. "I'm sorry you got hurt. I'm sorry your dreams didn't come true. You had something special." She turned to face her daughter. "You still do," she said earnestly. "You have a gift, Bonnie."

"I use it. Right here."

"Avril has that gift, too."

"She's perfectly happy in Moonlight Harbor," Bonnie insisted. "She's got a good job as a teacher and a nice man."

"Ho hum," scoffed Loretta. "She wants to fly and you know it. You can't keep her wings clipped forever."

"And you can't try to push her out of the nest by romanticizing that life," Bonnie countered. "I know you wanted more for yourself, for me. I know you wanted me to be the star you could have been, but it didn't work out that way."

"You gave up. I would have come down and helped take care of Avril."

"I didn't want that." Great. Now her voice was rising. She took a deep breath. "Mom, let's not do this." They'd had those discussions enough when she first came back to Washington, beaten and emotionally bruised. They'd resurfaced with the first band Bonnie joined and again when Avril won a local vocal competition in high school. Her daughter's burgeoning interest in music and songwriting when she went to college brought back the same old song again but Bonnie had been able to talk sense into her daughter, get her to see the wisdom of teaching music instead of trying to get famous playing it.

"Because you have unresolved issues, and you know it," Loretta said.

"I don't."

Loretta cocked an eyebrow. "No? Then tell me, why did we form this band?"

"For Avril." Scratch the itch, keep her home—a twofer.

"And why were you in three different bands back when we lived in Seattle? Avril was just a kid then. You weren't doing it for her."

"Okay, so I had to play. I got to play. Shit, Mom. Are we going to keep having this conversation till the end of time?"

"I'm not the one who started it," Loretta said, and left the bathroom.

"You could have fooled me," Bonnie grumbled, and followed her.

Break time was over. The two oldest Mermaids put their show faces back on, got on the bandstand and rocked it, with Bonnie singing every favorite dance standard from "Here for the Party" to "Footloose."

As always, they worked in one of Avril's songs, "What I Really Want." It was a love song, but, after her conversation with her mother, it left Bonnie worried about what she knew her daughter really wanted. She wished Avril wasn't so talented, wished she'd never met up with that online songwriting group. Wished Avril would stop encouraging her grandmother to reminisce about Nashville. It wasn't Music City. It was the land of broken dreams.

Avril didn't need that kind of heartache. She had the perfect life, right where she was. Their band was top-notch, she had a good job and was with a man who adored her. What more could a woman want out of life?

The set ended and the last call for drink orders came. Sally Farnham had long ago given up on seeing any action and gone home. It was time to pack up the guitars and leave. Happily, now that The Mermaids were the house band, the drum set and all the sound equipment stayed put.

Bonnie was ready to go home and stay put. She'd paired her jeans with the red heels that always made her feel sexy and her feet were not happy with her. A bad deal all around. Feeling sexy and having someone to go home to were two different things and the shoes had been a waste of comfort.

The patrons began drifting out, but Jeffrey Hooverman was still on hand to tell Bonnie how great she'd sounded.

"You could have been a star," he told her.

Her mood had been sliding into the mudhole ever since her conversation with her mother and she was feeling cranky. It was all she could do not to invite Jeffrey to take a nice walk on the beach and into the water, right over his head.

She managed a polite, "Thanks," because that was what you did. You kept the patrons happy.

"You're off now. You could have a drink," he said.

"It was last call ten minutes ago. The bar's closed, Jeffrey."

"I got some beer at my house."

"And to think you could have had someone sharing it with you right now if you'd just picked up on Sally's signals," Bonne said.

He did his old man version of a pout. "She's not on my wavelength."

"I'm sorry, Jeffrey, but I'm not, either." Bonnie shut her guitar case, picked it up and made for the door, where her mother was waiting.

"Someday you're gonna come to your senses," he called after her.

"Did that twenty-two years ago," she muttered, and kept walking.

"You still mad at me?" Loretta asked as they walked out together.

"I haven't decided. You still mad at me?"

"I'm too tired." Loretta linked their arms. "You know you love me."

"Yes, Loretta Lynn 2.0, I do. But that doesn't mean I have to like you 24-7."

"What a wicked thing to say to your dear, old mother," Loretta scolded teasingly.

"There is nothing old about you."

"Remember that and don't put any candles on my birthday cake."

"Who says you're getting a cake?" Bonnie taunted.

And just like that they were pals again. Enough so that, when they got into Bonnie's SUV, Loretta could say, "I just want to see Avril have the best life ever."

"So do I," Bonnie said, *and that's right here.*

"I want the same for you, too, daughter. I don't want you to get to my age and have regrets."

"I won't," Bonnie assured her.

"You shouldn't be wasting your talent."

"It's not wasted if people enjoy it," Bonnie argued.

"And you shouldn't be going home alone at your age." Loretta continued, switching to a new theme.

Oh, boy, here was another familiar topic, Bonnie's non–love life. "Mom. Stop already. I'm perfectly happy."

"No one can be happy without love," Loretta insisted.

"Oh, my gosh! Are you trying to tell me you don't love me?"

Loretta pointed that same red-tipped finger at her. "Don't get smart."

"I'm already smart," Bonnie joked. "Quit worrying about me. You have enough to do just keeping track of your own love life."

"Very funny. And my life love life is doing fine, I'll have you know." She laid her head back and shut her eyes. "I am ready for bed," she said, putting an end to the conversation.

Loretta had gone through a series of men over the years looking for a Mr. Right to replace Bonnie's dead father. Bonnie had been cautioning her about this latest man she'd found online and the last thing Bonnie wanted to do was talk about him.

She dropped Loretta off at her beachfront condo, thinking it was just as well her mother had gotten her own place when she moved to the beach to be with Bonnie and Avril full-time, rather than moving in with her daughter. Bonnie didn't want to witness up close and personal whatever Loretta was up to with this new man. Not that she'd even had a glimpse of him yet.

Was it just her or was it odd that he hadn't made an effort to meet her? she thought as she went on to her own house on Sand Dollar Lane. Probably just her. She had a suspicious mind.

The porch light was on, the house waiting to welcome her. It was no mansion, but it had been plenty big enough to finish raising her daughter and she loved being on one of the town's many canals. She occasionally got in her kayak and did some paddling, but mostly she liked to sit on her deck on a warm weekday evening, with a homemade piña colada and watch the world go by, enjoying the sight of teens on paddle boards and people on party barges, taking a twilight cruise.

Watch the world go by. Was that all she was doing?

She shoved aside the thought, made herself a cup of mint tea, and unwound by streaming one of her favorite classic cop shows. Her life was just fine.

And plenty interesting. She liked working part-time for Lucy and her husband, Brody, enjoyed chatting with the customers and keeping the website updated with pictures of the various houses they listed for sale.

Monday and Tuesday went by quickly enough, maybe not with roller-coaster level thrills, but Bonnie could live with that. Safe was better than sorry.

Wednesday night was band practice night, and The Mermaids always met at her house. With both girls living in the town's one apartment building and Loretta in her condo, Bonnie's place offered the most freedom to make noise without disturbing the neighbors.

Loretta had just set up her compact practice drum set in the corner of Bonnie's living room and Bonnie and Avril were tuning their guitars when Gina slipped in wearing trendy jeans and boots and a jacket. She was blond and almost as striking as Avril.

Something was missing though. Her bass.

"Hi, guys. Sorry I'm late," she said, her eyes searching for someplace to look other than any of her band members' faces. Why was she looking guilty?

"No problem," Bonnie said. "Where's your bass?"

Gina opened her mouth. Hesitated. Not a good sign.

"Actually, I have some bad news. Well, it's not all bad," Gina amended. "Except it kind of is for you guys."

Bonnie had been in enough bands to know what was coming next.

# Two

"I'm quitting the band," Gina announced.

The shock nearly knocked Avril over. "What? Why?" she demanded.

She and Gina had been besties since high school, both singing in choir together, both vying for parts in the school musicals. They'd become big fans of Taylor Swift and vowed to take the music world by storm just like she had. Gina was going to become a star and Avril was going to write all her songs. So far neither had gotten any farther than Moonlight Harbor, with Gina working as a secretary for the local insurance agent and Avril teaching at Moonlight Harbor High. Taylor had signed her first music publishing deal at fourteen. They were way behind schedule.

"I'm moving," Gina said.

"Moving?" Avril echoed. "Where?"

Gina's eyes did a guilty sideways slide. "Nashville."

"Nashville! We were going to go together," Avril protested. Not anything she'd shared with her mother and now she could feel Mom's surprised stare burning into her. Her eyes did a sideways slide of their own.

"If I don't do it now I never will," Gina said. "I'm not

exactly going places doing what I'm doing. You, at least, are teaching music."

*Those who can't do teach.* The old saw came around and gave Avril a kick in the heart. Why was she directing choir and working with select groups who all wanted to go on TV talent shows and doing nothing to further her own dreams? She'd fallen in a rut, one her own mother had built for her.

It had been a comfortable enough rut. The band was fun. "A good way to build your chops," Mom had said.

But then Avril had started wanting more, yearning to play on a bigger stage, to write her songs for a larger audience. "You're not ready yet," Mom had said. And said. And said. Then it was, "Do you know how few people who go there ever make it big? Ever even make a living doing music?" Yep, some vote of confidence. Okay, so she wasn't Taylor Swift. But she could write.

"Of course, we wish you all the best," Mom told Gina.

Great. Gina got the vote. What was with that?

Not that Avril didn't want the best for her friend, but she was having trouble getting the words out of her mouth. Instead, she said, "You never told me."

"It was kind of sudden," Gina said. "Greg's moving there."

"The singer you met when you were in Seattle visiting your cousin?" Loretta asked, and Gina nodded.

"He wants to start a band and he wants me to play bass," she said.

Avril could feel the green-eyed monster chewing away at her soul. "I can't believe you're really going."

"We've been talking about it for how long?" Gina reminded her.

And now Gina was actually doing what Avril had only talked about doing for the last two years. Avril looked resentfully at her mom, who was the constant rain cloud over her parade, always discouraging her.

"Good for you," said Loretta. "You're only young once. Now's the time to chase your dream when you don't have anything keeping you here."

Not her best friend, obviously.

Okay, this was what Glamma called stinkin' thinkin'. Avril needed to be happy for Gina. At least one of them was really going for it.

"I know you're going to make it," she said to Gina, and hugged her.

"Thanks," said Gina, hugging her back. "When you're ready, you can come stay with me."

Avril was ready. She'd finish out the school year then tell her principal she wasn't coming back in the fall. It was now or never. "Count on it," she said.

"When are you leaving?" Glamma asked.

"I just gave notice today. I'm out of here in a week."

"Well, play with us this weekend and we'll have a send-off party for you," said Mom.

Gina nodded. "Okay. Uh, I'd better get going. I got a ton of stuff to do."

"See you Friday," said Mom.

"See you Friday," Gina echoed, and then she was gone.

"I can't believe she's doing it," Avril said. *Without me.*

"It's a good time. She's not with anyone special and she can find office work anywhere," said Glamma.

"I wish I was going with her," Avril said. Right now. Screw finishing the school year. Screw Moonlight Harbor. Screw…

"What about Kenny?" Mom said. "You'd just up and leave him?"

"Maybe he'd move with you," Glamma said, and Mom

gave her The Look, the one she always gave Avril's grandmother when Glamma talked in glowing terms about her
favorite city.

"He's a fisherman, Mom. There's no ocean in Tennes-
see," Mom said sternly. Then she focused the sternness on
Avril. "A hundred people a day move to Nashville. You
know how many of them make it?"

"How come you didn't say that to Gina?" Avril demanded.

"Gina's not my daughter. It's not my job to protect her."

"I'm not twelve anymore," Avril shot back. "You don't
have to protect me, either."

"What kind of mother would I be if I didn't?"

"A better one."

It was a shitty thing to say. Her mom had a been a great
mother, and Avril had enjoyed a happy life growing up at
the beach. But that little devil in the cowboy hat sitting on
her shoulder said, "Yeah, stick it to her."

Avril unplugged her guitar from her practice amp and
put it back in the case.

"Where are you going?" Mom demanded.

"We don't need to practice," Avril said, "and I need to
go think."

"Avril." Her mother's voice was soft and pleading.

*Let's get out of here*, said cowboy devil.

So they did.

"I guess no band practice tonight," Loretta said after a
moment of stunned silence.

"I guess not," Bonnie said, trying not to cry.

"You know she didn't mean that," Loretta told her.

Bonnie bit her lip and nodded. *What goes around comes
around*, she lectured herself, *and her own snottiness of
the other night as boomeranging back on her.* She went

in search of the chocolate wine she kept for an occasional treat. She certainly deserved a treat after what had just happened. Maybe she'd treat herself to the whole bottle, just like a character in a country song.

"Whatever you're having, I'll have some, too," Loretta said, and followed her into the kitchen.

Bonnie poured them each a glass, then stood at the kitchen counter and looked out. It was always windy at the beach, especially in late fall and winter. The canal could look like glass on a lovely summer morning. This November evening the wind was whipping along the water, pushing it forward, stirring it up.

"I'm losing control," Bonnie murmured and took a deep drink.

"Of her or you?" Loretta asked.

"Both."

Bonnie considered herself a pretty mellow person. Except for the times when "Drunken Dreams" played on the radio. But other than that, she was laid-back, easy to get along with. Until her mother or daughter pushed her buttons. It seemed like there was a lot of that going on lately.

Seeing Rance Jackson win a CMA award for entertainer of the year probably had something to do with her current mental state. Sometimes, even when you tried to ignore it, your past came around to mock you.

"Honey, she's her own person."

"Is she?" Bonnie countered. "How much of this dream is something you planted in her, Mom? She grew up hearing stories of you writing songs with Royce Porter and whooping it up at The Bluebird. Blowing up those couple of cuts I got on a CD like I'd accomplished something?"

"You had."

"They were nothing and went nowhere."

"You still get royalties."

"Yeah, I can live on those for half a day. And that whole thing about your mom knowing Loretta Lynn and naming you after her. You'd think we were country music royalty."

Loretta's comforting smile fell away, and she set down her glass. "Now, listen here, young lady. I've had enough of this out of you. I watched the CMA awards, too, and I know how you get this time of year. But I'm allowed my memories and I'm allowed to share. And your daughter is allowed to have her dreams and to pick her future. You don't get to control either of us. The only one you get to control is you, and you'd better master that or you're going to have a very unpleasant future. And your grandmother *did* know Loretta Lynn and I *was* named after her."

With that, she marched back into the living room and to the coat closet.

"Where are *you* going?" Bonnie demanded. How dare her mother leave her when she needed comforting?

And was in the middle of a tirade.

"Band practice is canceled," Loretta said, taking out her coat. "Drink your wine and put on a nice romantic comedy. You'll feel better in the morning."

"I doubt it," Bonnie shot back. "By morning I'll have a hangover cause I'm going to drink all of this chocolate wine. And your glass, too!"

Loretta was not one to be cheated out of the last word. "Pleasant dreams then."

Drunken dreams. Bonnie scowled and poured the whole bottle down the sink.

Avril texted Kenny the moment she walked in the door of her apartment. Come over.

Thought you had band practice, he texted back.

It's off for 2nite. Please come!!!

On my way.

It normally took him forty minutes to get from his place in Westhaven to hers in Moonlight Harbor. He was at her door in just under thirty.

She opened the door and threw herself into his arms. Fab, solid Kenny. This big guy with his rock-hard body and marshmallow heart had been her big love and number one fan for two years. They'd met when she and Gina had gone to Westhaven for their Pirate Days festival. They'd wandered onto the docks to check out the fishing boats and she'd wound up checking him out instead. No doubt about it, Kenny was the sweetest man on the planet.

"I need you," she said.

"You got me." He walked them over to the couch and settled her on his lap. "What's going on?"

"Gina's going to Nashville," she announced, and started crying.

"Oh, now, hey, how's that a bad thing?"

"She's going and I'm stuck here!"

"You're in the hottest band in Grays Harbor County. Everybody loves you and you get to do your own songs."

It should have been enough. Why wasn't it?

"And you've got me."

She had to smile at that. "Truth."

"And with Gina moving there, you can make trips down as much as you want, and you'll have a free place to stay. Best of both worlds, right?"

"It could be," she said thoughtfully.

He grinned. "You'll have Nashville for great music and me for great everything else."

"Good point," she said, smiling at him.

He smiled back and kissed her. "Feel better?" he asked.

"I'm getting there," she said, and kissed him again.

Okay, her life wasn't so bad. In fact, it was pretty good. Except was pretty good enough?

Visiting Nashville would be great but visiting made you a tourist. Living there made you a success, and, darn, she wanted that success. She wanted the excitement, the glamor, the super buzz of singing in studio sessions, of going to the CMAs and knowing everyone as peers instead of idols. She wanted to be writing songs with real Nashville songwriters and she wanted to sing her songs at The Bluebird Café. Instead she had...

School the next day. Two girls got in a fight right before choir, and in the process of trying to break it up she got socked in the eye. A lovely way to start the day.

It didn't get better. Shane Hawkins, a senior and star quarterback for the Moonlight Harbor High football team— nickname: the Hawk—was waiting for her in the cafeteria during first lunch period. She was leaving the lunch line with her tray and on her way to the teacher's lounge when he fell in step with her. It was like walking next to a water heater with legs.

"Hey, Miss B, are you chaperoning the Christmas Ball?"

"No." The principal had asked her, but she didn't want to be stuck at a kids' dance. The band's regular gig had given her the perfect out.

"You're breakin' my heart," he said, putting a hand to his water heater chest. "I bet you've got the moves on the floor."

"Chaperones don't do moves on the floor," she informed him.

"Mr. Childs does and that's scary. But I bet you can talk with your hips," he added with a leer.

She frowned and pointed a finger at him, like Glamma would do. "That is out of line."

He shrugged. "Just sayin'. You should come and dance with me."

"Sorry, my band will be playing. And besides, that wouldn't be appropriate," she said in her best grownup voice.

He shrugged. "You know, I graduate this year."

*Thank God.* "That's good."

"I'll be eighteen in May. Not a minor anymore."

Oh, boy. She knew where this was going.

"You're not that much older than me," he pressed.

Something of which she was well aware. Sometimes it was hard to keep order in her rowdier classes when she, herself, looked more like one of her students than their teacher.

"I'm enough older and I'm your teacher and the ice you're on now is so thin I can see the polar sharks," she said sternly. "Go eat lunch and find someone your own age to hit on."

He was unfazed. "You'll change your mind once I'm out of school."

"Shane, stop already. You're ruining my appetite."

He laughed, shrugged and strutted off like they'd come to some kind of agreement.

"Cheer up," said Millie Orwell, one of the seasoned teachers, when Avril told her what had happened. "That'll stop when you're older. After a certain age you become invisible."

Millie was still single at fifty-three. Her big excitement was looking for floats on the beach and doing puzzles. Avril didn't know whether to feel comforted or mildly depressed.

"I don't want to be invisible," she said. "I just don't want to be hit on by my students. It creeps me out."

"That needs to be reported. But he's harmless," Millie said, unconcerned. "And I've got to admit at this point I'd be happy if anything male hit on me."

Avril changed the subject.

Loretta got on Facebook to find that she had a friend request from one of her old friends from Queen Anne High in Seattle. Lawrence Fisher, former Grizzly fullback, had sung in choir with her, often eaten at her lunch table. They'd been pals but that was all. Loretta had already given her heart to a basketball star when Lawrence arrived at the school in their sophomore year. And then to a cute boy she'd met at the roller rink. And then…well, there'd been several and thens. Along with several breakups. Lawrence had always offered a shoulder to cry on.

They'd kept in touch for a few years after graduation, long enough to send wedding presents to each other. But they'd finally drifted apart, busy with their separate lives, him building his business making fly rods and fishing poles of all things, and her singing vocals in Nashville recording studios, trying to make it as a singer.

She'd never quite succeeded, she was sure because of love. She'd gotten married, and then her husband's rise in the company had required a move back north. Getting in touch with her inner Tammy Wynette, she'd stood by her man. After two miscarriages came the difficult pregnancy and her precious daughter, and Nashville stayed in the rearview mirror, the people she'd met and the fun she'd had surrounded by the mists of memory.

She liked the idea of reconnecting with her old pal, so she accepted his request and wrote on his wall. Grizzlies forever! Even though the school is no more, we're still standing.

She got a message from him an hour later. Loretta, I'm so glad I found you.

She smiled and replied. Wonderful to hear from you. How's Carol?

Lost her two years ago. Aneurysm.

How awful, she pecked out on her phone. I'm so sorry.

Me, too. Miss her a lot. How about you? How's Eddie?

Tears sprang to her eyes. Gone. It's been years but, of course, I still miss him terribly.

I'm sorry. Hard going on without our other halves, isn't it?

But we have to go on, she typed back. Thank God she'd found Marlon, who was helping her go on splendidly. And we can remember the good times.

She'd had a lot of them. More than many people ever got.

We can.

They chatted a little longer, then she finished with, Keep in touch.

Will do! he replied.

Of course, he probably wouldn't. People always said that, then got distracted. But it had been fun to hear from him.

She was still online when a call came in. Marlon! Hearing his ring tone goosed her heart with a happy thrill. "Well, hello there," she answered.

"Hello," said a rich male voice. "How's my beautiful mermaid today?"

"Just fine. And how's my favorite captain of industry?"

"Hardly that," Marlon said with a chuckle. "But all is well on the ship. In fact, it's so well, I was able to slip away. How do you feel about lunch at the Lake Quinault Lodge?"

"That place is charming," she said.

Nestled in the Olympic National Forest among Sitka spruce, Douglas fir and western red cedar, the large rustic lodge built in 1926 reeked of rustic elegance and offered visitors a chance to step back in time with its secluded setting. President Roosevelt had visited the lodge in 1936 and the elegant dining room was named after him. Loretta had gone there once a few years back for a girlfriend weekend with a couple of friends and had fallen in love with the place. She'd always wanted to go back, and as things continued to get serious with Marlon, found herself imagining honeymooning there.

"Could you meet me for lunch? I'm not far from there."

"I'd love to," she said.

"Great. I should be there in about half an hour."

"See you then."

She ended the call and hurried to her bedroom to pick out something country club casual. She finally chose black leggings and a black sweater, which she accented with a thin gold chain dangling a small gold *L*—a gift from her mother when she turned thirty—and a bangle that almost passed for gold. She finished the jewelry with the small gold hoops her husband had given her for a wedding present. Eddie wouldn't mind that she was wearing them to meet another man. She was sure he'd been up in heaven, rooting for her to find her way all these years.

The Roosevelt Room was dark wood vintage. The tables all wore white linen cloths and the view of the lake from the windows was beautiful. Not quite as breathtaking as the ocean view from her condo window but still pretty darned special.

The best view, however, was the dark-haired man waiting for her at one of the tables. He stood as she entered the room and smiled.

"I'm glad you could meet me," he said, taking her arm and kissing her cheek.

The touch of his lips on her cheek sent a thrill through her. "It's not that far from Moonlight Harbor."

"Which was why I thought you wouldn't mind the drive."

"I like driving," she said, "and I can certainly drive longer distances than this," she added, hoping he'd file that away and invite her to come see him in Seattle soon.

"These country roads can be dangerous," he said, and pulled out her chair.

"I'm not afraid of a little danger," she said. Their waiter appeared and poured wine for them. Pinot grigio, her favorite. "Anyway, my daughter can track me on my phone and make sure I'm getting where I need to go."

"A very good idea," he said, then chuckled. "I don't want that on my phone. My secretary would be watching my every move. As it is she hardly gives me a moment's peace."

Loretta had noticed that. He often turned off his phone when they were together.

"I hope you don't mind that I ordered for you. I really want you to try the mushroom polenta," he said.

"That sounds wonderful." She looked around. "Isn't this lovely?"

"A lovely setting for a lovely woman," he said. "I wish I didn't have to get back to the city. It would be great to stay here."

She'd been thinking the same thing. "I understand you can't just shirk your responsibilities on a whim."

"Sometimes I'd like to." He took her hand and kissed it, giving her a fresh jolt. "But at least I have you for a while. Now, tell me how things are going in Moonlight Harbor."

She took a sip of her wine, then filled him in on all the latest Mermaid drama.

"Family matters are never easy," he said when she'd finished.

"But normally my girls get along perfectly," she hurried to tell him, fearing he'd think they were a bunch of high-maintenance drama queens. Lately it seemed they were, but Marlon didn't need to know that.

Their food arrived. "Just a burger for you?" she asked. With all the interesting things on the menu it seemed an inferior choice.

"I happen to like burgers," he said.

And chicken. And sometimes simply fish and chips. Marlon didn't go overboard when ordering for himself. And never wanting to look like she was taking advantage, she usually chose the cheapest thing on the menu. Which was often comparable to what he was having. But if he liked burgers and fish and chips who was she to question his taste?

They were halfway through the meal when he reached in his pocket and took out his phone, which was vibrating. A frown half surfaced. He turned off the phone and returned it to his pocket.

"You don't need to take that?" she asked.

"My secretary. Yet again. I'll check in when we're done."

"Maybe it was important," Loretta suggested.

"It's always something when you run an IT company," he said.

She felt as if that something was eating at him even as he finished the rest of his hamburger. He smiled, he listened attentively, he admired the view and the lodge. Yes, it would be nice to stay there sometime. He was…almost there.

Perhaps he was preoccupied with thoughts of his terminally ill brother. "How's your brother doing?"

"What?"

"Your brother?"

"Oh, he's holding his own." He smiled at her. "That's what I love about you, Loretta. You care."

"Yes, I do," she said. Especially about him.

Which was why she found herself frustrated that she wasn't able to figure out what had pulled him out of the moment. It had to have something to do with that phone call.

"I should let you get back to work," she finally said.

He nodded. "I'm afraid duty calls. Can I walk you to your car?"

"Of course," she said.

He laid a fifty-dollar bill on the table, which she hoped would cover their meal and wine, then took her elbow and escorted her out of the room and then the lodge. At her car, he put his arms around her and kissed her.

"Every minute with you is like a diamond. Every one is priceless," he murmured, his breath tickling her ear.

"There will be more minutes," she said.

"Yes, there will," he assured her.

He waited until she was behind the wheel, then got in his own car. She thought he'd give her one final wave before leaving, but he drove off, the tender smile he'd worn for her replaced by a frown.

She sighed. "I know, Eddie," she said as if her dead husband was actually listening. "It's the price you pay for being with a businessman and being a future trophy wife." Okay, so she was a little old for that.

She could almost hear Eddie saying, *No you're not. You've still got it.*

Yes, she did. If only she had more time to share it with Marlon.


The rest of Avril's day was without incident, but she went home feeling out of sorts. She knew why.

"I was rotten to Mom," she confessed to Gina, as she helped her friend sort through her clothes to see which items were Nashville worthy.

It was a kind of pass the poop game the Brinks women played. At least when it came to the topic of music success. Glamma would irritate Mom, Mom would get poopy with Glamma, then Mom would pass the irritation on to Avril, who, in turn would give her a nice little handful of poop.

"You're never rotten to your mom," Gina said. "Should I take these or are they too touristy?" she asked, holding up a pair of shiny pink cowgirl boots with a rhinestone buckle.

Avril studied them. "Too touristy," she decided, then added with a grin, "You should leave them with me."

"Done," Gina said, handing them over.

"Really?"

"Really."

"I'll pay you."

Gina gave a snort of disgust. "Don't be a goof. Call it your fee for being my fashion consultant."

"Thanks," Avril said. She took off her shoes and tried them on, twisting her feet one way and another to admire the effect. "Oh, yeah. Sizzlin'." Her happiness over her acquisition was quickly smothered by her daughter guilt. "I was super mean."

"Well, then, you should give her a super apology."

"I should, but I kind of hate to 'cause it's like, I don't know, surrendering."

Gina was not tracking. "Surrendering what?"

"My future. Sometimes I think she wants me to stay a nobody. I mean, just because things didn't work out for her in Nashville."

"She had a couple of cuts on CDs. Doesn't she still get royalties?"

"Yeah. They're not a lot, but still." Avril shook her head. "If she'd stayed she'd have gotten a lot more. I don't get why she didn't. All she ever says is it wasn't worth the heartbreak."

"Maybe she doesn't want you to find your dad. He could still be there somewhere."

"She says he was just a tequila hookup. She doesn't even remember his name. So that's not it."

"Hard to imagine your mom ever having been that, uh…"

"I know," Avril said.

The wildest her mom ever got was an occasional glass of her favorite chocolate wine. She didn't date, didn't do much of anything except work and play in the band and hang out with Glamma. It wasn't exactly a thrill-packed life. It for sure wasn't the kind of life Avril wanted. Unlike her mother, she was going to do something with her talent.

"Maybe she doesn't want you to go because it's so far away. My mom's not real happy that I'm leaving. She's sure I'm gonna become a superstar and get into drugs. Or get divorced and remarried ten times."

"At least she's sure you're going to become a star," Avril said. She pulled a pale blue Western shirt from Gina's closet. "You should take this. It totally matches your eyes."

"You're right," Gina said and added it to her growing

stack of clothes. "I found a one-bedroom apartment, furnished, with a sofa bed in the living room. It'll be perfect for when you come down." She pulled it up on her phone and showed Avril. "Isn't it coco?"

It was cute. "I wish I was going with you right now," Avril said, forgetting her temporary contentment of the night before.

"I'll start making connections for us," Gina promised.

"Thanks. You're the best," Avril said.

Although she was making connections of her own. She hung out at Gina's a little longer, then went back to her own place for her six o'clock Zoom with her fellow songwriters. The group had started with six people two years earlier and was down to three—herself, a girl named Sarah who was in West Virginia, and a guy named Colton Gray. Colton was already living in Nashville, working for a tech company by day and writing songs and hitting various clubs by night. He was a connection. A hot one.

He was hosting and was already on and ready to let Avril into the meeting. "Hey there, Ocean Girl," he greeted her once her video was on and her sound was working. "How's the battle?"

Battle. Was he psychic? Did he know she'd been shitty to her mom?

No, he was just giving her his usual greeting.

"Okay," she said. "My friend Gina's leaving the band."

"Yeah?"

"She's moving to Nashville."

"No shit. So, when are you coming down?"

"Soon, I hope."

"You should. Your stuff's good."

"According to my mom it has to be better than good. It has to be great."

"Yeah, she's right. I think you could make it here though."

"Really?"

"Oh, yeah. Now at least if you want to come check it out you got two places to stay. Your friend and me."

Staying with Colton. If she wasn't with Kenny she'd be all over that. Unlike her, he was Viking blond with eyes as blue as a fjord and dimples set in a Noah Schnapp chin. He was the kind of man women wrote love songs about.

But she had Kenny. Sweet, strong Kenny, who had a superhero chin, shoulders broad enough to wear a cape and arms bulked up from hauling in fishing nets and lugging around other mysterious boat equipment. Kenny, who thought she was the most brilliant songwriter ever and who never got tired of listening to her sing. She loved Kenny and if she wanted to keep Kenny she was going to have to stay in Moonlight Harbor.

The thought left her feeling unsettled and grumpy. Hmm. What did that say about how much she loved Kenny?

"Sarah's here," said Colton.

A moment later, Sarah's face showed up on the screen. It wasn't a particularly beautiful face. It was long and her lips were thin. But it was a happy face, and what Sarah lacked in looks she more than made up for in talent.

"Hey, guys," she said. "What up?"

"Just BS'n', waiting on you," Colton said. "You been writing this week?"

"Of course," Sarah said. "You guys, I have the best idea for a Christmas song. I'm texting Santa."

"Is he giving it to you?" Colton asked.

"No, that's the hook."

"I like it," said Avril.

"Wanna hear what I got so far?" Sarah asked eagerly.

"Spill," Avril said.

She did. The song was fun and catchy, and got four thumbs-up from her fellow songwriters.

"What are you working on, Avril?" Colton asked.

After listening to Sarah's song, "I got nothing but crap," Avril said. Maybe she wasn't ready for the big-time yet.

"Let's hear your crap," Sarah said encouragingly.

"Next week," Avril said. "What have you got, Colton? Need help with anything?"

"I always need help," he said.

Avril was willing to bet there were plenty of women willing to give it to him. He'd talked about clubs he'd gone to and songwriters he'd met, but so far there'd been no mention of a girlfriend.

Not that it mattered. She wasn't looking for anyone. She had Kenny.

Colton played his song. It was full of clichés and boring phrases like, "I want you."

"I think you gotta come up with a more original way of saying that," Sarah told him after pointing out the phrase.

"Okay, how about 'I need you'?"

"It's a quarter after one," Avril began to sing, quoting the huge Lady A hit.

"Proves my point," he argued. "They say 'I need you.'"

"Yeah, but they preface it with something fresh," pointed out Avril. "How about, instead, a play on that whole need you thing? The more I drink the less I need you."

"Or the more I drink the more you stink," cracked Sarah, making Avril giggle and Colton smile.

"Or none of the above," Avril said. "Drinkin's been done a lot."

"It's all been done," Cody said with a frown and a sigh.

"That's what makes songwriting so exciting," Avril told him. "Coming up with new ways to say the same old thing."

"Yeah, it's an addiction," he said.

Which was probably why Avril ached to get to Nashville. If they were the addicts that city was their pusher. What addict only visited her pusher occasionally?

And yet there was Kenny.

They talked a little longer, then all said good-bye. Avril shut down her laptop, looked to where her guitar sat on its stand and frowned. She needed to figure out her life.

After she'd texted an apology to her mom.

# Three

It was going to be a fun weekend, just the kind Loretta liked. Friday was her birthday, and, although she wasn't looking forward to hitting sixty-five, she never turned down an opportunity to scrounge chocolate from her friends.

"Of course, birthdays are more than that," she said, as she sat at a table in Good Times Ice Cream Parlor with its owner, Nora Singleton. "At this point in life it's good to remember to be thankful that I'm still here and healthy. Although, of course, I'd prefer to go back in time and be here when I was young and my skin didn't feel like the Sahara."

She was starting to depress herself, so she took another drink of her hot chocolate. With extra whipped cream, of course, because what would hot chocolate be like without whipped cream? And you needed lots since the stuff closest to the drink melted instantly.

"You sure don't look like you're going to be sixty-five. More like fifty-five. I don't know how you stay so thin," Nora said.

"Drumming burns a lot of calories."

"Even when you do it on your mug," Nora teased.

Loretta stopped her tapping. "A silly habit, but it gives

my hands something to do. I haven't smoked in almost twenty years but once in a while my hands still want to look for a cigarette to enjoy with my drink. This keeps 'em out of trouble. Plus it keeps my fingers fit," she joked.

"You've got fit everything," Nora said, sounding a tiny bit jealous. She sighed. "I wish I could bring myself to go to the gym three times a week like you do, but I'm not into torture."

"You might find that you like it," Loretta told her. "It doesn't always feel good at the time, but you do feel great afterward."

"I'll take your word for it."

Loretta chuckled and changed the subject. "Are you going to help me celebrate my birthday?"

"Birthday?" Nora hedged.

"You don't have to play coy. I know Bonnie's planning something, even though she denies it."

Loretta suspected it would be a celebration at The Drunken Sailor and had invited Marlon Smith, her Mr. I-Finally-Got-It-Right to come to the beach for the weekend. He'd promised to move heaven and earth to come down.

"My lips are sealed."

"Which confirms it."

"But if there was a party, would this new fabulous man you're seeing be there?"

"That's the plan," Loretta said. "I'm hoping nothing comes up to prevent him coming."

Marlon's schedule was her only complaint about the man. Sometimes he had trouble getting away and had to cancel whatever plans they had at the last moment. It was frustrating. She wanted to show him off to her friends and she was anxious to introduce him to Bonnie and Avril.

If they were truly going to be a couple he needed to be

part of her life in Moonlight Harbor and she needed to be part of his in Seattle. She understood that between his business and obligation to his poor brother that he had to do a lot of schedule juggling, but surely he could juggle in time to meet the people who were important to her.

Her birthday was the weekend to do it. Everyone who mattered would be present to help her celebrate.

"Let's hope he makes it down here," said Nora, "because I want to meet him. He sure sounds like a keeper, coming all this way to take you to dinner every week."

If he could manage to come down once a week to take her to lunch or dinner he ought to be able to manage making it to her birthday party.

"All that wining and dining," Nora continued. "I'm jealous. And going to the Westhaven winery even. I hear the food at their restaurant there is five-star."

"It is," Loretta confirmed.

In addition to the winery, Marlon had taken her to the elegant restaurant at the Ocean Crest Resort as well as the casino in Quinault and The Porthole, the closest thing to upscale dining that Moonlight Harbor had to offer. The last time he'd planned to come take her out she'd suggested inviting Bonnie along and had been looking forward to him meeting her daughter, but he'd had to cancel coming down to see her at the last minute.

"Work," he'd said. "And I was looking forward to meeting your girl."

"She wants to meet you, too," Loretta had said. Although *inspect* might have been a more accurate verb.

"I suppose next he'll be inviting you to Seattle for a romantic weekend," Nora speculated.

"I doubt it. He says he doesn't want me to have to drive

all that way." Still, she hoped that at some point he'd invite her to come to Seattle.

"A little over a three-hour drive—it's not that far. After all, he makes it to come see you."

"He says I'm worth the trip down," Loretta said.

"That goes without saying. And midweek, no less. How does he manage to come down here in the middle of the week when he has a business to run?"

"He takes the time when he can find it."

"Then you'd think he'd be able to come down for a weekend."

"You'd think so, but Marlon often has to wine and dine people on the weekends. Business."

"Every weekend?"

"So far that's how it's worked out. Then, of course, there's his brother. Marlon helps the family out a lot and takes his brother to many of his doctor appointments."

"He sounds like a saint. But he also sounds pretty embedded in his life up there."

"Eventually that's going to change," said Loretta. "He wants to move here once he sells his company and retires."

"How far in the future is that?" Nora wanted to know.

"A couple of years, I think. He needs to build up the company more."

Nora nodded, took a thoughtful sip of her hot chocolate.

Loretta supposed Marlon's plans sounded a little nebulous, but she understood. Falling in love didn't mean all the pieces of your life fell instantly into place. Not at their age.

"It does say a lot that he'd willing to move here," Nora said.

"He says he wouldn't want to uproot me. Isn't that sweet?"

"It is. I swear, this man is too good to be true. You lucked out, girlfriend."

"I did."

"He does know it's your birthday on Friday, right?"

"Oh, yes."

"So he'll at least get down this weekend."

"That's the plan."

Nora gave her a teasing grin. "Does he know which birthday this is?"

"Of course. Fifty-nine."

Nora laughed and shook her head. "You little liar, you."

"I believe in honesty in relationships. But a woman can lie about her age. Anyway, it's a harmless fib. I'm only off by a few years."

"And how old is he?"

"Fifty-eight."

"Let's hope *he's* being honest," Nora teased.

A couple of middle-aged women came in, bundled in coats and probably looking for the same thing Loretta had been in search of. Nora downed the last of her drink and stood. "I'd better take care of my customers. See you Friday."

"At my party," Loretta said with a wink.

Nora refused to take the bait, simply smiling and giving her a little wave before taking her position behind the ice cream counter. No matter. Loretta knew what was going on, and she was looking forward to the celebration her daughter had cooked up.

She was ready. She had the perfect new skirt to wear—a double mesh midi skirt in caramel which would look great with her turquoise short-sleeved top. The Mermaids always wore some sort of top in a sea-related color, their nod to their band name. And the chunky black boots she'd ordered online had arrived the day before. She was going to look great.

Some people might have said the outfit was too young for her. But some people didn't know nothin'.

Loretta finished her drink, then stopped by the Beach Dream Homes office to fill her daughter in on what she'd gotten for their gift to Gina. Bonnie was at her desk when Loretta walked in, holding down the fort with the office manager, Missy Warren. Her bosses and their other agent, Taylor Marsh, were nowhere to be seen, probably out showing houses or trying to get a listing. Missy was on a phone call, but she managed to give Loretta a friendly wave.

Bonnie had been typing something into her computer, and, seeing her, Loretta felt a momentary twinge of guilt. She shouldn't have been bothering her daughter when she was working.

"Hi, Mom. What's up?" Bonnie greeted her.

"You're busy."

"I've got a minute."

Bonnie sounded like her usual mellow self again. Good. The post-CMA soul cramps were wearing off.

"I just wanted to let you know that I got Gina's band gift."

"What are we giving her?"

"A hundred-dollar Mastercard gift card so she can at least eat while she's finding her feet down there. It'll keep her in ramen for a while anyway."

"I remember all the care packages you sent to me when I was at Belmont," Bonnie said. "That's a good idea."

"I'm full of good ideas," said Loretta. "Sunshine Bakery's going to do a cake and put some cowboy boots on it."

"Perfect."

"A lot of cake to eat this weekend," Loretta said.

Bonnie half smiled. "You're fishing."

"I know you're up to something so you might as well tell me what."

"You'll just have to wait and see."

"Hopefully, Marlon's coming down this weekend to join in the fun." Envisioning him spending the weekend with her and finally getting to see her in action on the drums made her giddy.

"Good. It's about time I got to meet him."

Her daughter, the love guard.

"You don't need to worry. This one's a keeper." Finally, after years of searching for someone to take Eddie's place.

"Just remember, you don't need to rush into anything, Mom," said Bonnie, the queen of not rushing. No, make that not moving at all, which was sad and wrong if you asked Loretta. Not that Bonnie did.

Loretta, on the other hand, had had her share of relationships over the years, hoping to fill the void left after her husband died. Even though none had worked out yet, she didn't regret getting out there and trying.

Although Bonnie wasn't making it easy. She had a habit of giving the men Loretta dated an enthusiastic thumbs-down. With the last two, Loretta had to admit Bonnie had been right. One had become possessive. The other turned out to be too selfish. "He just wants you to cook for him, Mom," Bonnie had pointed out. When he'd suggested staying in on Valentine's Day and showed up with the steaks for Loretta to broil for them she'd decided her daughter was right. Cooking was okay once in a while, but expecting a woman to do it on Valentine's Day? It was a sign even Loretta could read.

"Don't rush into anything," one of her church friends, Estella Morgan, had counseled, sounding like a Bonnie Brinks echo. "At our age we're vulnerable."

Rushing? Who was rushing? Why did people keep saying that? And it was easy for Estella to offer advice. She'd been happily married for years, with someone to share a bed at night and drink coffee with in the morning. Married women had no clue what it was like to be a widow.

Anyway, Loretta had wised up when it came to men. She'd looked for red flags when Marlon showed up, and, unlike her previous love mistakes there'd been none. Not one of their dates had involved her having to cook. Marlon said he enjoyed eating out. And he always brought flowers or candy, so she knew he wasn't stingy. He was never rude or insulting or overbearing. In short, he was exactly the man she could see herself spending the rest of her life with.

He usually stayed at the Driftwood Inn, but not this visit. She had the guest room all made up and champagne in her fridge. Yes, happy birthday!

Friday afternoon Loretta was at Waves, getting her hair done, when she got Marlon's text.

Looks like I won't be able to join you this weekend, beautiful. Work. I'm sure sorry.

So much for moving heaven and earth. Her happy bubble burst with a painful pop. No special time with Marlon, no showing him off to her friends. No meeting her daughter. This was the birthday booby prize.

"*You're* sorry," she said to her phone. "I'm spending a fortune getting gorgeous all for nothing."

*No, not for nothing*, she told herself. She'd look great when The Mermaids played their weekend gig. And she was going to have fun no matter what.

Sorry you have to miss out, she texted back, determined not to be a text brat.

I'll make it up to you, he promised.

Of course he would. But darn.

Come Friday night The Drunken Sailor was packed, not only with the regulars, but with the many people Loretta had become friends with over the years. The band table was piled high with cards and presents, including the mermaid painting Bonnie had done for her. Loretta had been delighted. The painting was charming, and the fact that her daughter had done it made it priceless.

Arthur Cork, owner of the town's art gallery and purveyor of gorgeous hand-crafted jewelry, was on hand to give her a pair of shell-shaped earrings and to rave over the painting. He wanted to know if Bonnie had more, and to see someone raving over her daughter's talent was an even better present. His interest was a bonus birthday present.

"It's about time someone started appreciating at least one of your talents," she said to Bonnie after the foolish girl fobbed him off. "You should take advantage of it."

"Never mind that. Check out your cake," Bonnie said, pointing to the neighboring table where a giant cake with chocolate frosting and a huge bouquet of red frosting roses sat.

The *Happy Birthday, Loretta* written on it conveniently made no mention of her age. Her daughter was such a smart woman.

"Here's to you, Loretta," said Madison, the young hipster who was working the bar. She filled Loretta's glass with her usual tonic water and slid it over. "When I grow up I want to be you."

"Don't grow up then, cause I'm not," Loretta said. "I'm

going to stay young forever." She'd done the grown-up thing, raising her daughter, mourning her man at fifty. That was enough grown-up-ness for her. "Forever young," she belted, singing a line from one of her favorite songs. Yes, a song for every occasion.

Pete Long, who had been hanging around the bandstand a lot the last couple of months, fell in step with her as she started to make her rounds of the tables of friends who'd shown up to help her celebrate. He was carrying a square pink envelope, probably a birthday card, which he could have left on the gift table.

Poor Pete had been at loose ends ever since his girl-friend, Edie Patterson, died. He loved to reminisce, and Loretta was happy to be a listening ear. And flirt a little, just to make them both feel good about themselves. But lately she'd gotten the impression that Pete was wanting to move beyond simply reminiscing. He probably wasn't more than six or seven years older than Loretta, but that made him too old in her book.

"You look good tonight, Loretta, old girl," he said.

"Old? Excuse me?" She raised a disapproving eyebrow.

He held up a hand. "I didn't mean anything bad. I used to call Edie that all the time."

"Edie was old. I'm not," Loretta snapped.

"Well, you ain't exactly young," he pointed out. "And there ain't nothing wrong with being old."

Unless you were a woman. Then men walked right past you, heading for the sweet, young things. Well, Loretta was having none of that. Thank heaven she'd met Marlon.

"I don't want to hear one word about being old tonight," she informed Pete.

"Okay, okay. I don't know why you women get your knickers in a knot over your age."

"You men are the ones who knot them," she said.

"Sorry," he muttered. He held out the card. "Here. Happy birthday. You're probably not gonna like this card but I thought it was funny."

It probably had a couple of old women on it and some joke about not being able to hear. Loretta took it, said an ungrateful thank-you, and turned her back on him to talk to Nora and her husband, who were seated with Jenna Waters and her husband, Seth.

"Pete called me old," she said, still smarting.

"The Pete Long term of endearment," Jenna said. "Pete never has his foot out of his mouth so don't pay any attention to him. You look great. Happy birthday."

"Where's your man?" Nora asked. "I thought we'd see him here by now."

"He couldn't make it," Loretta said, trying to keep her voice light. It was hard. In addition to flaking out on her, Marlon hadn't sent her so much as a card.

"That's too bad," Nora said. "I'm sure he'll make it up to you."

"He will," Loretta said. But it would have been nice if he'd made it up to her sooner rather than later. Oh, well. *The show must go on.* And it was about to. Bonnie and the girls were strapping on their instruments. "Guess I'd better get over to my drums," she said. "Thanks for coming."

"You done greeting all your fans?" Bonnie teased when Loretta joined them.

"For the moment," Loretta said, and plunked herself down on her drum stool.

Bonnie stepped up to her mike. "Hey, everyone. Good to see so many of you here tonight. As most of you know, it's my mom's birthday. Thirty-nine again, right, Mom?"

A couple of people in the crowd gave appreciative hoots and Loretta nodded and smiled.

"So we're gonna kick the night off with her theme song," Bonnie said. "Okay, Mom, count us off."

Loretta did and Bonnie launched into "Here for the Party," which got the line dancers rushing to the floor.

Yep, it fit. Loretta was going to enjoy the night, even if a certain man with a firm midsection and a winning smile hadn't made it.

After that they went into "Honey I'm Good," followed by the old waltz classic, "Could I Have This Dance?"

They were just finishing up when a woman came into the place carrying a vase with a huge bouquet of roses, baby's breath and greens and a Happy Birthday balloon. Loretta almost lost the beat. Those had to be for her. And they had to be from Marlon.

The song ended and the woman came up to the bandstand. "I'm supposed to deliver these to Loretta Brinks," she said to Bonnie.

"She's there at the drums," Bonnie said, nodding to where Loretta sat.

People were oohing and aahing. So was Loretta.

"This might be a good time for us all to sing 'Happy Birthday,'" said Bonnie, and struck a chord on her guitar.

Everyone joined in as Loretta took the lovely vase of flowers. It was a near perfect birthday moment. The only thing lacking was the presence of the man who'd sent the flowers.

The band took a break and, once at the band table, Loretta opened the little card that had come with the floral arrangement. *I'm sorry I'm missing your big party. Know that I'm there in spirit and will make it up to you when I come down on Tuesday.*

Not until Tuesday? Oh, well. It was still close enough to her birthday to count and she knew he'd make it up to her for not being there right on the day.

"From the mystery man, I take it?" Bonnie said.

"Yes," Loretta said happily.

"He sure knows the right gift to give." Her daughter's tone of voice didn't quite make that sound like a compliment. "Too bad he couldn't make it here for your party."

"He can't help it if things come up," said Loretta.

"I guess not," said Bonnie, and that was the end of the conversation.

It was 1:30 a.m. and Loretta was falling into bed when another text came through. I sure wish I was with you right now. Thinking about holding you in my arms and I can't sleep.

Now neither could she. That champagne was still in the fridge. I can't wait till Tues. Got big plans for you, mister.

That earned her a smiley face. She closed her eyes and could see him, tall and lean with that Sam Elliott moustache and dark hair turning silver at the temples. Let the birthday fun continue.

It took her a long time to get to sleep and when she finally did it was to dream of Marlon, coming up her front walk in a three-piece suit and carrying a little black velvet box. When she finally awoke the next morning she knew, just knew, it was a sign.

Gina's last night was a difficult one. Not for Gina, who was obviously excited to be moving on to the next phase of her life, but for Bonnie, who could feel her daughter's growing discontent. It wouldn't be long before Avril bolted for Nashville.

She knew she had to let go at some point, had to let Avril fly. If only she wanted to fly somewhere else. If only she hadn't been so talented. If only she could be happy with what she had. It was so much more than most people had.

At the end of the night, as they were hugging Gina good-bye, it was all Bonnie could do to keep smiling when Gina said to Avril, "Don't forget. You're coming down to visit as soon as school's out."

When had that been decided?

"For sure," Avril said, dreams of fame and fortune and recording sessions in the studio dancing in her eyes.

Bonnie knew the look. She'd worn it herself once. Ugh.

On top of worrying about Avril, her mother's mysterious friend came down on Tuesday, took Mom to lunch, and then scatted before Bonnie got off work and could join them for dinner and meet him.

"He had a dinner meeting he had to get back for," Loretta explained.

There was always some excuse. Bonnie was beginning to think that Marlon was a figment of her mother's imagination.

Double ugh. The two women who meant more to her than anything in the world were both doing their best to drive her nuts.

"We can't play without Gina," Avril said when the three of them met at Bonnie's place on their usual practice night the week after Gina's departure.

"Sure we can," Bonnie said. "I'll switch to rhythm and you can play bass. It's not ideal but it will do until we can find someone."

"How are you going to do that?" Avril challenged. She was in a mood. Had been since she walked in the door.

"I'll put an ad in the paper," Bonnie began.

"Oh, yeah, that'll work," Avril scoffed.

"And on BandMix," Bonnie continued, pretending she hadn't been interrupted.

Avril scowled. "There are no good musicians here."

"What are we, chopped liver?" Loretta demanded.

Avril made a face. "What does that mean, anyway?"

"I don't know," Loretta said with a shrug. "But don't you worry. Your mama will find someone. The Mermaids aren't beached yet."

"Maybe they should be," Avril muttered. "This band's going nowhere."

"Neither are you until summer, so we may as well keep playing," Bonnie said.

Avril shrugged, and that simple gesture about broke Bonnie's heart.

"She doesn't want to be doing this with us," she said miserably to Loretta after Avril left.

"She's young. She wants to be with her kind," Loretta said.

"If we found a really good bass player, if we made a CD, got play on Spotify…"

"Which you're always telling me is impossible without a label backing you. Look, darling, let's just enjoy our lives and let Avril live hers."

"She's turned Nashville into… Oz."

"Maybe for her it is. Maybe it's the Emerald City. She won't know until she goes there."

Bonnie clawed her fingers through her hair. "I don't want to see her hurt."

"We all get hurt at some point in our lives. And we learn from it. We survive. You did. She will."

"You always want better for your kids," Bonnie said. If

only there was a way to guarantee that. No heartbreak, no disappointment. "Life is good here at the beach."

"And boringly safe. She's at the age where she wants a taste of danger."

"Well, I don't want her to have it." The words came out almost as a wail.

Loretta moved from the chair she'd been lounging in to join Bonnie on the couch and wrap an arm around her shoulder. "I know. It's hard to let our children make their own choices when they're young. Even when they're older," she added with a little smile, giving Bonnie a squeeze.

"Just don't encourage her, Mom. Please."

Loretta zipped an invisible zipper across her lips. "I promise. But at this point nothing either one of us says or doesn't say will make any difference."

Not exactly comforting words. They rattled around in Bonnie's brain long after her mother left. She made herself some chamomile tea and put some smoked clams and crackers on a plate, then settled on the couch and streamed three episodes of *Chicago P.D.* to distract herself.

Then she went to bed where she dreamed that Avril flew away on a small guitar-shaped airplane. "I'll be fine," she called down to Bonnie right before Bonnie woke up.

She probably would be. Bonnie was just projecting her own past hurts onto her daughter. "Wish I was psychic," Bonnie muttered and gave her pillow a punch.

Back to sleep she went, only to see that same guitar-shaped plane. Only this time she was boarding it. "Noooo," she cried, and tried to turn around and run back up the Jetway.

But there was Loretta behind her, pushing her along, saying, "Go, face your demons."

"I don't want to," Bonnie cried. "I like it where I am."

"You don't know what's best for you. I do. Mother always knows best." Loretta shoved her on the plane and a flight attendant who looked like Dolly Parton welcomed her. "About time you came back," she said, then started singing, "Nine to Five."

The plane took off and it seemed they were barely in the air before its engine started choking and sputtering. Next thing Bonnie knew the plane was making a nosedive for the ground.

The captain's voice came over the speaker. "Tighten your guitar strings everyone. It's going to be a bumpy ride."

Then there was her mother, appearing out of nowhere—where the heck had Mom been?—and plopping into the seat next to her. "We have got such fun times ahead of us."

Bonnie's eyes shot open and she sat up in bed, her forehead sweaty and breathing heavily. She hoped that dream wasn't a premonition of things to come. And she decided right then and there that she didn't want to be psychic.

# *Four*

"It seems odd that this man hasn't made more of an effort to meet Bonnie and Avril," Nora had observed to Loretta after Marlon turned into a birthday party no-show. And the more Loretta thought about it the more she had to agree.

"I've got say, I'm starting to find it frustrating that you haven't met my daughter yet," she said to him when he made one of his romantic calls to her on his lunch break. "Maybe I'm reading things wrong. Maybe we're not really serious."

"Loretta, I'm as serious as a heart attack," he insisted.

"Please don't say that," she begged. "That was how my husband died. Remember?"

"Of course. I'm sorry. I would never do anything to hurt you, Loretta. You have to know that. And I am anxious to meet your daughter. She sounds amazing."

"She is. And she knows how to cook a turkey, so how about joining us for Thanksgiving dinner? Pecan pie is one of my specialties."

"You have my mouth watering," he said, giving her hope that it meant yes. "But I've been invited to my brother's for the day. It could be his last Thanksgiving, and you know he's the only family I have left in the world."

Marlon was such a good brother. She could hardly tell him to neglect his suffering sibling to come be at the beach with her. And she wouldn't want him to. But maybe they could all be together.

"I would love to meet your brother." *Hint, hint.* Bonnie and Avril would forgive her if she missed one Thanksgiving celebration. In fact, maybe she could spend Thanksgiving Day with Marlon's family and then he could come to Moonlight Harbor the day after and enjoy a second dinner with her and the girls.

"I'd love to take you, but…"

Loretta frowned. She knew she wasn't going to like what came next.

Sure enough. "I'm afraid my sister-in-law is being very protective of him. His immune system is so weakened. It's only going to be family."

Obviously, Marlon couldn't ignore his sister-in-law's wishes. "Family is important," Loretta said, determined to be understanding.

"Yes, it is. And, Loretta, I hope you know I'm looking forward to getting to know yours. Having never had children, myself it means a lot to be with someone who does."

Those words made up for her disappointment over not getting to spend the holiday with him. "Well, you can always come down on Friday. I'll try to save you some pecan pie."

"I'll sure try to work it out so I can," he said. "But if not, I'll be down the next week," he added, which was a pretty good indicator of the level of effort he was going to put into coming down the day after Thanksgiving.

She adored Marlon, but she wanted more of him than she was getting. She'd been alone long enough. She was ready to make up for lost time. Maybe, much as she wanted it, he wasn't the man she was destined to do that with. Now, there was a depressing thought.

"What is it, my love?" he said.

"I feel like this is going nowhere."

"How can you say that?" he protested.

"I don't see enough of you."

"I don't see enough of you, either," he said.

"Then why aren't we doing something to change that? I could always come to Seattle once in a while, you know."

"I know, but we've talked about that. Look, things will settle down for me eventually and then we'll be able to spend more time together. You are the best thing in my life. I don't want to lose you, my little mermaid. I'm looking forward to snuggling with you in that cozy beach condo of yours and watching the waves roll in. Say I won't lose you."

His little mermaid. How could a woman resist talk like that?

"You won't," she assured him. There would be other Thanksgivings.

Still, it was hard not to feel disappointed.

The disappointment grew like a late-afternoon shadow, spreading over Marlon's charming words and hiding them.

"It's so frustrating," she said to her friend Estella when they met for coffee at Beans and Books.

"That is too bad. But at least you have the girls."

Loretta drummed on her coffee mug, staring at the contents. Normally she adored her coconut lattes. This day not so much. In fact, this day there wasn't much of anything she was happy about, including her friend's ability to minimize her feelings.

She frowned at Estella. "I'm glad it's so easy for you to just shrug off my disappointment."

Estella blinked, surprised by Loretta's tone of voice. "I'm only trying to help you see the glass as half full."

"Easy to do when yours is overflowing," Loretta snapped.

Honestly, sometimes life seemed so unfair. Here was Estella, who wandered all over Moonlight Harbor in her granny jeans and sweatshirts, her face bare of makeup, who had never passed up a second piece of cake since she'd said "I do" and who could have sex anytime she wanted it, condescending to tell Loretta that she should be fine with her present circumstances.

"Loretta," Estella chided, her voice full of hurt.

Loretta could see the hurt in her eyes, too, and instantly regretted her words. A fine way to talk to a friend.

"I'm sorry," she said. "I'm being obnoxious."

Estella didn't contradict her.

"I guess I'm the tiniest bit jealous." She sighed and nudged away her drink. "You and Dale are so happy. He's there every night for dinner."

Estella rolled her eyes. "Yes, and how I wish he'd turn into your Marlon and take me out once in a while."

"But he's there. He's at the table, he's in your bed. He fills your days. I envy that. I wish I still had Eddie. I just… sometimes…" She paused, trying to figure out how to make her friend understand. "I love the girls. They're my life. But Avril won't stay here forever. And Bonnie, well, one of these days she's going to find someone and…" Loretta choked back a sob. Bit down on her lip. "I want so desperately to be with someone, really be with someone, sharing all those little everyday moments that add up to so much."

"Desperation won't make it happen," Estella said softly. She reached across the table and laid her hand on Loretta's.

"Anyway, you are with someone. And if it doesn't work out with him there will be someone else."

"There will never be anyone like Marlon." Loretta sighed. "I was so hoping we could have spent Thanksgiving together."

"I'm sorry that didn't work out," said her friend.

She took a deep breath, managed a shrug. "But it's only one day."

"Christmas has two, Christmas Eve and Christmas Day," Estella pointed out.

Loretta threw off her self-pity cloak. "Thank you for pointing that out. And for being my friend, even when I'm a stinker."

"We're all stinkers once in a while, and I'm happy to be your friend," Estella said.

"And what a wise one you are."

Thanksgiving *was* only one day. She and Marlon would celebrate their own Thanksgiving later. Estella was right. Loretta's glass was half full.

Actually, if she thought about it, it was far more than half. She still had the girls, and they would always love her and include her in their lives. She had Marlon, even if his business and brotherly obligations were keeping him in Seattle. She had enough food to eat and a place to live, not to mention a gorgeous view to enjoy from her living room window. Her cup wasn't half full. It was much closer to the top than she realized. And if her relationship with Marlon kept blooming it would be overflowing in the future. She decided she wanted to finish her latte after all.

Bonnie was working on a new song that she'd titled "Here by the Sea." Kind of stupid, really, but it would be fun to sing at The Drunken Sailor. She was tapping the top of her guitar, trying to think of another word that rhymed with sea besides *me* or *baby* when her cell phone went off.

She didn't recognize the number and said a cautious, "Hello."

"Bonnie, this is Arthur Cork from Beachside Gallery. Your mother gave me your number."

Bonnie frowned. Loretta was determined to find fame and fortune for her daughter, one way or another. But Bonnie didn't want yet another artistic pursuit she enjoyed tainted by ambition and disappointment.

"I know you said you weren't interested in selling any of your paintings, but I'm hoping I can talk you into reconsidering," he said.

"No, I don't think—" she began.

He talked right over her, a verbal lawn mower. "That one you did for Loretta was so unique and whimsical. I know people would go crazy for anything like it. Surely you have a couple more."

"Not for sale."

"Think about it. We could hang them at the gallery, maybe have an art show."

The art business had to be as competitive as the music business. She didn't want to jump back into the fray again.

"Who knows? You could eventually make a lot of money," he said, baiting the hook with something fresh. "Not every artist can make money doing what she loves."

Ha! Didn't she know it.

"I could help you. In fact, how about giving me a chance to tell you what I can do for you. Let me take you to dinner."

Dinner. Bonnie smelled an ulterior motive. Arthur Cork was divorced and looking for a new Mrs. Cork. Nice as he was, he wasn't enough to tempt her out of her manless state. He was in his midfifties, tall and so thin that a strong wind could turn him into a kite. There was no attraction on her part, and it wouldn't be kind to go out with him and raise his hopes.

"I'm sorry Arthur, but my answer is still no."

"I wish you'd at least think about it," he said. "It would be a shame to waste such talent."

Oh, brother. "Spreading it too thick," she said.

"Not thick enough."

Who did he remind her of? Her mother, of course.

"But thanks for the offer."

"I won't give up," he said lightly.

"Knock yourself out," she said. "Thanks for calling," she added, then ended the call and tossed aside her phone.

Painting was something she'd only been doing for a few years. It wasn't her passion. It was simply fun, a pastime, something that relaxed her and provided satisfaction. It was still a pleasure, unmarred by false hope. And now here was someone itching to make her a success.

She frowned at the irony. How hard she'd strived to become a good songwriter, how much of herself she'd poured into creating songs with depth and clever lyrics and strong hooks, that she'd hoped people would dance to, fall in love to, play when they were feeling down. Her music had mattered. And look what had happened. Now something that she had no emotional investment in was saying, "Hey, baby, I'll be good to you." So stupid. So…unfair. And why was she still writing songs anyway? She glared down at her guitar, took it by its skinny neck and locked it in its case.

Mothers were not like guitars. They were never content to be ignored. Loretta called twice and Bonnie, suspecting the reason behind those calls, let them go to voice mail. By the third call she knew it was hopeless and answered.

"I was wondering if you happened to hear from Arthur Cork?" Loretta casually asked.

"Yes, I did. Funny, I don't remember asking you to give him my phone number."

"What can I say? I was in the gallery and he asked."

"You just happened to be in the gallery." Yeah, Bonnie was buying that.

"I was looking for a necklace to match the earrings he gave me," Loretta insisted.

"Did you find one?"

"Don't change the subject."

"I thought that was the subject," Bonnie said.

"I think you should give him a couple of paintings. What would it hurt?"

*My ego.* "I do them for fun."

"It would be fun to make money from them," pointed out Loretta.

"I'm not starving," Bonnie said.

Loretta moved on from art to romance. "I think he's interested in more than your paintings."

"I gathered that."

"He's a nice man."

"He is, but I'm not interested."

"Maybe you should be. He may be divorced, but I hear that's not his fault. His wife left him for an actor in Seattle that she met online. He's still pretty well-off, and he's got a boat."

"Well, there you have it. I guess I'd better call him back."

Loretta was not amused. "Don't be smart."

Bonnie chuckled. "I can't help it. I was born smart." Too bad she hadn't always used those smarts.

"About some things," Loretta said, sounding grumpy. "But when it comes to men."

"I'm even smarter." *Now.*

"No, you're picky," said Loretta, who, so far, had never met a man she didn't like, something that had not worked in her favor.

"I am not," Bonnie insisted. Picky and cautious were two different things.

"You could have had any number of men over the years," Loretta said, warming to the subject.

"And been sorry," Bonnie said.

"Okay, so some weren't so perfect," her mother allowed.

"Yeah, like Larry the drummer," from one of the bands she'd been in when she returned to Seattle. He'd had a drinking problem.

"All right, not him. But there was that doctor."

"Whose daughter hated me."

"Harley Dickerson…"

"Went back to his ex-wife."

"Brody…"

Who Bonnie had dated for about one second when she first moved to Moonlight Harbor. He'd been too much of a player for her. Anyway, once Jenna hit town he couldn't look at anyone else, and after she'd chosen someone else instead of him he'd been broken.

Bonnie had understood, having been broken herself. None of the men she'd met had been able to help her mend.

Brody had lucked out when he found Lucy. Bonnie didn't trust her luck, and she sure didn't trust her emotions.

"I'm happy as I am, Mom," she said, as much to herself as her mother.

"You don't know how happy you could be," Loretta argued.

She knew how happy she'd once been and then how

tragically that happiness had been ripped from her. She knew enough.

"Trust me, Arthur isn't going to be the one to show me," she said.

"I guess you're right. But there will be someone, somewhere down the road, I'm sure of it." Loretta Brinks, the eternal optimist.

Bonnie told her mother she loved her, then ended the call and went to her spare room to paint. Not for Arthur. Not for anyone but herself.

A half-finished mermaid on canvas greeted her. *Let's spend some time together. I won't disappoint you.*

Bonnie smiled and got busy with her paints.

Wednesday night found The Mermaids practicing three-part harmony for the chorus of a new song written by Avril. "Why do I listen to my heart? What does it really know?" they sang. "My head keeps saying I should have left you long ago. I can't let go. I'm such a fool, cause even though it's killing me, I'm bleeding out, still reaching out for you."

How had Avril come up with those lines? Her life had been a skiff on untroubled waters, and yet the lyrics held such angst. The melody was haunting, the kind that would burrow into a listener's mind and stay there. This was a song both women and men would play to feed their hungry misery in the throes of a breakup.

"This song is incredible," Loretta said at last.

Avril beamed like she'd just won the golden ticket in an *American Idol* competition. She turned to Bonnie, the need for praise in her eyes.

It was good. It was worthy of being picked up by an artist and recorded. Avril could become an artist and record it herself.

More likely she would end up singing it in bars to an audience of drunks who wouldn't appreciate the artistry. The gamble was Avril's to take but Bonnie didn't want to lead her to the table.

"It's good," she acknowledged. That was as far as she could bring herself to go.

"Just good?"

Her daughter's disappointment knifed into her. *Oh, baby girl, I'm trying to protect you.* Still, the dying light in Avril's eyes was hard to see.

"Very good," Bonnie amended. Even that didn't seem enough. "The melody is unforgettable."

"Unforgettable," Loretta began to croon as Avril smiled.

"Thanks, Mom," Avril said. "I'm gonna try and get into a writer's showcase and play it when I go to Nashville this summer."

"That will be a fun visit," Bonnie managed.

"I'm not going just to visit, Mom. I want to move there."

*Oh, no. No, no, no.* "Move? What about your job?"

"I'm quitting."

"Quitting!" When had Avril made that decision?

"I want to go for it," she said earnestly. "I think I can make it."

"You can't," Bonnie said, just as earnestly.

Avril scowled. "Thanks for the vote of confidence."

"I've told you how hard it is to make it in the business," Bonnie said, frustrated. Of course, her mother just sat there, silent as the Sphinx, no help at all.

"I gotta try."

"I gotta be me," Loretta began to sing.

It didn't break the tension. In fact, it was completely inappropriate. Bonnie glared at her mother and she shut up.

Bonnie tried a new tack. "What about Kenny?" Ha!

There was a flash of doubt in her daughter's eyes. Bonnie hung on to it like a shipwreck victim clinging to a tiny slice of boat.

"We'll work it out," Avril said.

The anthem of youth. They never looked ahead, never saw around the corner.

"And if it doesn't work in Nashville I can always come back," Avril added.

"To no job," pointed out Bonnie.

"But it is going to work out so that doesn't really matter," Avril said firmly.

Her daughter was about to jump off a cliff—no hang glider, no parachute, no nothing. Bonnie could feel her blood pressure rising. "Avril," she began, her voice stern.

"Let's cool off, you two, and run those harmonies again," Loretta said before Bonnie could go over the mother-daughter cliff.

"Good idea," said Avril in clipped tones.

Discussion closed. Bonnie tried to pretend that all was well as they went through a couple more songs. The tension dissipated. Avril kissed her cheek before leaving and Bonnie told her she loved her.

"But I want to throttle you," she muttered as soon as her front door had closed.

Avril called Gina on her Bluetooth as she drove away. She felt like a balloon that had broken free and was soaring off toward the clouds.

"Guess where I am," Gina said before Avril could get out so much as a word.

"Still in Nashville, I hope."

"At The Bluebird."

It was like saying she was at the Louvre or the White

House. Just as foreign and surreal from Avril's view on the Washington coast.

"That is so dope," Avril said.

"I'm here with a couple of people I met at a Nashville Songwriters Association meeting. We're waiting for the second show to start."

"Don't eat up all the fun before I get down there," Avril said.

Gina giggled. "There's too much to gobble down single-handed. How'd it go with your mom?"

"I just told her."

"I bet her head about blew off."

"I think it would have if Glamma hadn't been there."

"My mom's still texting me every day to make sure I'm all right," Gina said by way of comfort. "Moms never want to let you grow up."

"Oh, they don't mind you growing up as long as you don't go away." But it was too late for that. It was happening.

"She's an adult now, darling," Loretta said, watching from the couch as Bonnie paced in front of her fireplace.

"Barely," Bonnie said irritably. "She's leaving behind a good job and a great man, all to chase a dream that won't come true."

"You don't know that."

"I do," Bonnie insisted.

"Things will work out," said Loretta.

Her mother lived in a bubble of denial. In Loretta Land it was all butterflies and flowers. It was the secret garden with everything all green and glowing. Life was Easter bunnies and Santa and the tooth fairy. Loretta tended to ignore the Bogey Man and gremlins and... Freddie Kruger.

But they were out there. The world was full of thieves

and cheaters and liars and men like the one Avril had dreamed up and put in her song. Bonnie knew they were real. Her old wound had scabbed over, but underneath it still festered.

Rance Jackson had been heartbreak in Levis, all dark and swarthy. He wasn't exceptionally tall but he had a presence that made a girl think he was six-five. He had soulful brown eyes, a jawline Michelangelo could have carved and lips that stopped hearts when he smiled. Bonnie had landed heart deep in love the minute she first met him at The Bluebird Café, The Place to be if you were a musician or songwriter or music lover. It was an intimate venue, crowded with tables and with a long bar at the back of the room, which was always packed. At the front of the room, on a small stage, successful songwriters would play their hits and their works in progress, sometimes three would sit in a circle and share, creating what was called a writers in the round. Studio musicians often formed bands and played there just for the heck of it, bands so good you had to wonder why they weren't rich and famous. Rich and famous, that was what Bonnie had wanted to be. So, it turned out, did Rance.

"You're going to Belmont, huh?" he'd said, as they stood at the bar, waiting for their drinks. It had sounded a little like a put down, although it shouldn't have been since the college was pretty much a feeder for the music industry. "Singer or songwriter?"

"Both," she'd said, raising her chin just a little.

"Yeah? Are you any good, college girl?"

"Yeah, I am. What about you?"

"Both."

"You any good?" she'd shot back at him. "I take it you're not in school."

"Don't need to be, not for music. I been playing in honkytonks in Texas since I was sixteen. And I'm good at a lot of things," he'd added, and pulled out that smile of his like a gunslinger and shot her right in the heart.

She never recovered. She never recovered after he cheated on her, either. But that was just the beginning.

And if, by some horrible chance Avril met him...oh, Lord.

Bonnie didn't sleep at all that night.

# *Five*

Bonnie, Avril and Loretta enjoyed their usual Thanksgiving, which consisted of turkey dinner with all the trimmings to be followed by movie binging. A storm had blown into town, bringing wind and rain, but it wasn't a bad one and Bonnie had a fire going in the fireplace, which made the atmosphere cozy. The power was still on and so was the movie marathon.

"It sucks that Marlon couldn't come down," Avril said. "When are we going to meet him so we can make sure he's not a serial killer?"

"Oh, he's a killer all right," Loretta joked. "He's killing me with kindness."

"Those flowers he sent for your birthday were pretty impressive," Bonnie said grudgingly. But she felt the same as Avril. If her mom was really falling for this man they needed to meet him and give him their thumbs-up.

"You'll meet him soon," said Loretta. "Meanwhile, I guess we'll have to eat all my pecan pie by ourselves."

"I can manage it," Avril said with a grin.

After dinner they settled in the living room to watch a rom-com.

"I do love a good romance," said Loretta as the ending credits began to roll.

"So we've noticed," said Bonnie. Her mother, the dating queen.

"Finding someone to share your life with is the most important quest anyone can go on," Loretta said defensively. "Remember that, Avril," she added. "Love trumps everything. It's what music was made for."

Bonnie noticed her mother didn't include her in that advice. Probably because Loretta knew it was hopeless.

"Glamma, sometimes it seems like you send out mixed messages," Avril said. "I mean, one minute you're talking about going after your dreams and the next you're talking about finding the love of your life."

"Who says you can't have both?" Loretta replied, her fingers drumming on her glass of sparkling cider.

*Me*, thought Bonnie. "Sometimes you have to make choices."

"I know our Avril will make smart ones," Loretta said. She beamed at Avril, and Avril beamed back.

Bonnie went in search of another piece of pie.

They streamed one more movie, then Kenny called Avril and she vanished to go spend time with him, leaving Bonnie and Loretta to indulge in more pie (with whipped cream, of course) and decide what movie they wanted to watch for their Thanksgiving finale.

"*While You Were Sleeping*," Loretta suggested.

"Oh, come on, Mom. We watch that every year."

"We should. It's a good movie," Loretta said.

"How about something a little newer?"

Loretta tapped her chin, thinking. "Okay, how about *Resort to Love?* I watched that when it came out on Netflix.

Loretta had told Bonnie all about that movie. The last

thing she wanted was to watch a movie about a singer in career meltdown singing at her ex's wedding where, of course, they resolved their past and the woman went on to find true love. Yeah, like career meltdowns and lost love ever magically turned into movie happy endings. She knew it would leave her feeling cranky.

"How about something different than what we've been watching? A thriller?"

Loretta frowned.

"Come on, Mom, a change of pace is always good. Anyway, everything can't be about love."

"You're wrong there. In the end, everything is if you've found the right person."

The melancholy expression on Loretta's face was one Bonnie hadn't seen since the first year they lost her dad and it grabbed her by the heart. Both she and her mother had been on their own for years, but the difference in how they'd reached that state was a Grand Canyon–sized chasm. Bonnie's relationship had been toxic and she'd willingly left it. Her mother's had been one of love and respect and she'd been soul bound to Bonnie's dad. Of course, it pained her to have lost it, and of course she'd long to try and replicate it, to recapture what she'd once had.

"Like Dad?"

Loretta sighed. "I miss your father, miss having someone to share a morning coffee with or take a walk with, someone to kiss good morning or even argue with."

"You have me for that," Bonnie said, weakly.

Loretta pressed her lips together and Bonnie could see she was fighting strong emotion. "Sometimes I get so lonely."

"I could die," Bonnie sang, quoting an old Elvis song. Another weak joke.

"Fine," Loretta snapped. "If you don't want to be serious."

"I'm sorry. I do."

Bonnie had thought her mother had shaken off the doldrums years ago. She was always so lively and full of fun, always with a funny quip and a song for every occasion. Her smile never seemed to falter. Until that moment.

"I had no idea you were that unhappy," Bonnie said. They had the band, and when they weren't playing they spent a lot of time together. Her mom had cultivated an active social life even before she started her manhunt. "I mean, I know you've been looking, but I didn't think you were desperate."

"I'm not desperate," Loretta said, offended. "And I'm not miserable. I'm just…lonely sometimes, and I'm tired of living alone. I still have a lot of years left in me, at least ten."

"More than that," Bonnie said, horrified at the short shelf life her mother was predicting for herself.

"I want another chance at love."

"Funny you should use the word *chance*. It is a gamble," Bonnie pointed out.

She'd done a little gambling when she was in her late twenties and then again, for a blink, when she moved to Moonlight Harbor. In the end nothing had come of it. She supposed that was as much her fault as it was the fault of the men she'd dated. Cynicism and suspicion hardly qualified as paving stones for the road to a happy ending.

Her mom, on the other hand, was the eternal optimist, and it made Bonnie sad to think that, so far, all that optimism had failed to pay off. All these years there'd been a hole in her life her daughter had failed to fill.

A big pile of daughter guilt dropped onto her. She'd been so busy with her own life and with Avril…she should have paid more attention to her mom's emotional temperature.

What kind of stinkball daughter didn't realize how un-happy her mother was?

The kind who had a mother who always put on a happy face, no matter what, that kind.

"Oh, listen to me," Loretta said, waving away her earlier despondency. "What a drama queen I'm becoming in my old age. I guess I just wanted you to understand where I'm coming from. I'm not crazy and out of control. I'm simply a woman working to build a better life. I love being with you girls and playing in the band, and I'm glad I moved to Moonlight Harbor to be with you. I just want...more. I want more for both of us," she added softly. "I worry about you."

"You don't need to. I'm fine."

"Easy to say when you're young. When you're old." Lo-retta sighed. "There I go again. I think I'd better have more pie and remind myself how blessed I am to have such a wonderful daughter and granddaughter. While I'm stocking up on calories why don't you get busy and find us a good thriller. A woman's never too old for thrills."

Never too old for thrills. Her mom was full of sayings like that. Bonnie hoped with all her heart that Loretta got those thrills she was longing for with this new man.

"I feel bad for my mom," Avril said as she and Kenny walked along the beach Friday morning, looking for trea-sure under an overcast sky. His dad and brother had given him the day off from the family business and he was happy to be spending it beachcombing with her.

Sometimes, after a storm, what beachcombers called an ocean burp yielded treasures like petrified wood or giant agates. If you were lucky, you might even find a glass float. So far, in all the years she'd lived at the beach she'd only found two. One of those had been after an ocean burp, so she was always hopeful when she went out after a storm.

"How come?" Kenny asked. He stooped to pick up a large rock that was almost an agate, then after examining it, dropped it back on the sand to keep evolving.

"I don't know. I guess because she's all alone."

"She's got your grandma," Kenny pointed out. "And you."

"Yeah, but I'll be leaving."

That made him frown. "Don't remind me."

"It's only Nashville," she said.

"May as well be the end of the world."

"It might not even work out." There was a terrible thought, and it bothered her that he brightened at the mention of it. She, too, frowned.

"Sorry," he said, picking up on her body language. "I'm a selfish pig. But I do want you to go. I want you to make it. You got talent and it wouldn't be right to hold you here."

"Lots of people have talent," she said, suddenly filled with self-doubt. Mom hadn't been blown away by her latest song. Only Glamma had raved about it, and she didn't really count because she raved over everything Avril did.

"Trust me, you'll make it," he said.

"I've gotta try."

"Absolutely."

She gnawed on her lip. "If I did…"

He almost hung his head. "You'd be too successful for the likes of me."

"I would not!"

He shrugged.

She threaded an arm through his. "I hope you don't think I'm gonna stop loving you just because I'm trying to make it big."

"There's love and there's love."

"And then there's our love," she said firmly. "And Moonlight Harbor will always be my home base."

He managed half a smile at that, but it did leave her wondering. Could their love survive a long-distance relationship?

The slate gray sky would soon be giving up the last of its light and the wind was picking up. "May as well pack it in," Kenny said, and her heart stopped. Until he added, "I don't think we're gonna find anything today."

It was Friday morning and J.J. Walker was bored. He knew he shouldn't be. He could go to the gym and work out. He was reading an interesting book about the founder of Uber. He had shows recorded on TV as well as another football game to watch. In spite of that he felt restless.

Spending Thanksgiving weekend alone had been a terrible idea. He should've flown to Florida and hung out with his folks and his younger sister. Sitting alone in his Seattle condo Thanksgiving Day, eating chili and crackers had been so subpar. He'd tried not to think about his ex and his now ex-stepkids all enjoying turkey and ham and candied yams. She'd have bought a big pumpkin cheesecake at Costco. His ex-mother-in-law would have baked rolls and a huckleberry pie and brought along her homemade cranberry relish. He'd frowned at his half-finished bowl of chili and set it on the coffee table, then slouched back on the couch and aimed the remote control at the TV, moving on to the next ballgame.

Friday didn't look like the day was going to be any more exciting than Thursday had been. He should never have sold his two pizza places. If he'd known it was going to be too late and his marriage was in the crapper he'd have kept them. Then at least he'd have a business to get back to.

He should go skiing on Saturday, see if the kids wanted to go. They used to get away and ski once in a while. He texted Stephen, the stepson who he knew would have his phone attached to his hand at all times.

Want to hit the slopes with the old man tomorrow?

The reply came back a few minutes later. Sorry, Dad. Mom hauled Tim and me to Palm Desert for the weekend. Guess she didn't tell you.

Guess she didn't. She didn't have to. She was free to do whatever she wanted. And the twins were in their twenties now. They had lives. They didn't have to report in. It only made sense that they'd spend the holiday with their mom. Still, J.J. felt left out. He'd been the kids' dad since they were four. He'd paid for their ski lessons and sponsored every Little League team they were ever in, footing the bill for uniforms and providing pizza for end of the season parties. He'd been a pretty good dad.

When he'd been around.

"You're never here," Mona used to complain. "All you do is work."

"Not all the time," he'd argued.

"Most of the time," she'd insist.

"Well, I have to work, babe. What do you think pays for the ski lessons, the traveling all-star baseball teams, all those extras the boys want?"

"They'd rather have you," she'd say. "You need to make some changes."

He'd thought it was only a bit of wifely bullying. It turned out to have been more of a warning, like when your doctor tells you to quit smoking. He hadn't heeded it, and by the time he woke up to what he was losing it was gone. She'd found someone else, someone who knew how to step off the fast-spinning world of the workaholic. She'd marched out of his life without so much as a "Let's go to counseling." Maybe she'd thought he was a lost cause.

The boys hadn't exactly fallen into lockstep and followed her, but she'd managed to book them pretty solidly ever since the divorce, moving them into a different sphere, one that included the new man.

"It will always be a tug-of-war from now one," his mother had said when he called her in Arizona with the grim news.

"It shouldn't be," he'd said, pissed.

But it was.

"The boys love you," he told himself. They did. They just didn't need him anymore. It seemed like nobody did. He'd sold his businesses for nothing.

Oh, well. Out with the old, in with the new. Whatever that meant.

He poured himself another cup of coffee and started surfing the net on his phone. What was he going to do with the rest of his weekend? What the heck, maybe he'd go skiing by himself. Get up in mountains, get some fresh air, challenge himself with the Pinball run at Crystal.

His phone rang, interrupting the surfing and the gloomy thoughts. It was his old pal, Lee Stein.

He smiled, powered off the TV and took the call. "You old buffalo, why are you bothering me?"

"What, am I interrupting something? You nursing a TV turkey dinner hangover?"

"I'm not that pathetic," J.J. said. "I had chili."

There'd been no point going to a restaurant on Thanksgiving. Restaurants were zoos on that day. He should have accepted his mom's invitation and gone to be with her and the gang. But being around family as the lone loser was still hard.

"Glad I'm not at your house. It probably smells like skunk," Lee teased.

"You should be used to that. You smell like skunk all the time," J.J. teased back. "Spit it out. Why are you interrupting my solitude?"

"'Cause I figure it needs interrupting. You know, you need to quit enjoying bachelorhood and get hitched again."

Was J.J. enjoying bachelorhood? Not really. He'd met some nice women in the three years since his divorce. And some naughty ones. But none he really clicked with. He was beginning to think that the right woman didn't exist.

Maybe he'd just stay on his own the rest of his life. It wasn't so bad. He could do whatever he wanted whenever he wanted. And if he wanted company he could find it. He wasn't bad looking—not exceptionally tall but broad shouldered and fit, with ruddy skin and reddish hair that announced his Irish ancestry. Following the trend, he'd grown a beard. The beard was a new addition. Mona had preferred him clean-shaven. What Mona preferred no longer mattered. This last thought made him frown.

Every time he thought of her he frowned. She should have given him a chance to fix things. The frown dug deeper into his chin.

"Sick of your own company yet?" asked Lee.

"Heartily."

"Good. Come on down to the coast and save me from having to eat all of Glinda's leftovers by myself. You know what a rotten cook she is."

Glinda was probably sitting right next to Lee, rolling

her eyes. His daughters were probably there as well. Lucky bastard.

"Grab a toothbrush, get in that old beater of yours and get on down here. The girls are abandoning us and the guest room will be empty."

"Yeah?" It was tempting.

"We'll give you a good time."

"I was going to give myself a good time on the slopes tomorrow."

"So I'm saving you from breaking bones. Come on, it'll be fun."

"Okay, why not?" said J.J.

"All right. Department of Fish and Wildlife has approved clam digging for this weekend. We can get us some razor clams and make clam chowder for dinner. Then you can play some pool with me at the old pub. Glinda's got some girl party to go to later and is abandoning me."

"She should have abandoned you years ago," cracked J.J.

"That's what she keeps telling me."

J.J. chuckled. Those two were welded at the hip.

"On my way," he said.

He finished his coffee, then went to the bedroom to grab a change of clothes. He smiled as he got into his Beemer and realized he didn't feel bored anymore.

It was a pleasant ride to the beach. Once he was off I-5 he was on highways that took him through stands of evergreens and logging towns with small houses, many of them forty years old, many of which were being refurbished.

Then he hit Moonlight Harbor with its crazy stone pillars at the entrance, still standing from when the town was first developed in the sixties. The place was a mixture of funky old and upbeat new, the buildings from both eras catering to visitors with restaurants, moped rentals, shops and a fun plex that offered bumper cars and go-carts for entertainment. A family of deer grazed on the grass in the median between the two one-way streets running through the town.

Another ten minutes and he was pulling into the driveway of Lee's beach digs, a three-bedroom rambler with rock in place of a lawn encased in a white picket fence. Lee and his wife were ready for him with a proper Thanksgiving leftover meal of turkey sandwiches, dressing and gravy, and cranberry sauce. Seeing the way they looked at each other about gave him heartburn.

His ex had looked at him like that about a million years ago. Stupid, fool him. He was a walking morality tale, an example of what happened when a man wound up married to his job instead of his woman. If only she'd given him a fair chance to right that ship.

"How's your sandwich?" Glinda asked.

"Great," he said. "Thanks. And thanks for inviting me down."

"Sometimes a man's gotta get some new scenery," said Lee.

After they ate, Glinda made them clean up the kitchen and left to check on things at the pub for Lee and hang out with some girlfriends.

"She's a great woman," J.J. said.

"That she is," agreed Lee. "They're still out there, dude."

J.J. gave a cynical chuckle. "Yeah, I'm holding my breath."

"While you're holding your breath let's play some cribbage. Tomorrow I'll take you out to eat."

They settled down with whiskey and cards and it was a pleasant evening. It sure beat sitting around the condo wondering if he ought to check out an internet dating site.

Saturday found him out on the beach in boots and a thick

jacket with his buddy, working a clam gun to capture the elusive razor clam. A weak sun was out, and the sand was damp and muddy and the air was crisp. A perfect day. They weren't the only ones who thought so. The beach was thick with people, all in search of the same delight.

"You should move down here," Lee said, as he tossed a clam in their bucket. He wasn't much taller than J.J. and was built like a tank. In their college days he'd mowed down his opponents on the football field just like one. He'd gotten his education thanks to a college scholarship. J.J. had waited tables and worked in restaurant kitchens. Glinda had already informed him he would be in charge of making the clam chowder for lunch.

"Yeah? So I can grow moss like you? It's always wet."

"Not in the summer."

"Let me know when you figure out how to make it summer all year long," J.J. said.

"Oh, come on. You know you loved it when we went over to Westhaven and went fishing."

"Just thinking about that halibut we caught makes my mouth water," J.J. said.

"Fishing, clamming, kayaking on the canals, golfing—it's the life."

J.J. brushed the sand off his hands and studied his friend. "Why do I feel like I'm sitting in on a time share pitch?"

Lee shrugged and chuckled. "Just sayin' it's a good life down here."

"For you. You got a great wife and your daughters live nearby."

Lee sobered. "It sucks that things went sideways with Mona."

"It's been three years. I'm over it."

"Yeah? You sure?"

"Sure I'm sure. My life's good. I like my freedom. Got no woman nagging me, no obligations."

"That bad, huh?"

J.J. gave a rueful smile and shook his head. "Okay, so it's not perfect."

"You need a change."

"Okay, what's the hidden agenda?"

"No hidden agenda," Lee said and suddenly got busy checking to see if they'd reached their limit of clams.

Yep, there was a hidden agenda.

Glinda proved it when, after lunch, she said, "Aren't you tired of city living yet, J.J.?"

He set down his glass of beer and looked from one to the other. "Spill, you two. What's up?"

They exchanged guilty looks. "Well," Lee said, "Just thought you might be interested in a new business opportunity."

"Oh, no. You got sucked into a pyramid scheme," J.J. said in horror.

Lee made a face. "No."

"The pub's failing. You need a silent partner. No problem." It would be the least he could do. He'd helped his buddy get into this mess.

J.J. had come down to Moonlight Harbor ten years earlier when his pal had told him about the little beach town pub he wanted to buy, had looked over the books with Lee and the owner, then given it a thumbs-up, although he'd been concerned about Lee getting into the restaurant business.

"It's a tough business," he'd cautioned. "When you buy a restaurant it owns you." He knew that from personal experience.

"I can make a go of it," Lee had said. "We want out of the city and Glinda's up for it."

"Okay, then," J.J. had said.

He'd shared his expertise with his friend and Lee had done okay. But they hadn't talked much in the last couple of years. Between getting divorced and getting his feet back under him J.J. had been a little distracted. Obviously, Lee's investment had gone south.

"The pub's doing great," Lee said.

Well, so much for that conclusion. "Then what's up?"

"What's up is that it's time to sell the business. The girls are grown and one's had the nerve to move out of state. Glinda wants to start traveling."

"You want your life back."

Lee chuckled. "Something like that. I was thinking maybe you might want yours back, too."

So this was where they were going. J.J. held up a hand. "Oh, no. No more restaurants. Too much work."

"Yeah, and you're so busy."

"I'll admit I'm kind of at loose ends, but I don't think I want to work that hard."

"I've already done all the hard work."

"Yeah, right."

"Never mind," said Lee. "Let's go play some pool. You can check out the house band."

"You got a house band? What are they, a bunch of grungy kids in their twenties?"

Lee smiled at that. "Not quite. It's a chick band."

"A chick band. Interesting. So, grungy chicks in their twenties."

"Nope. Mother, daughter and granddaughter. They had another but she's off to Nashville to try and become a star. They're still good though, especially the lead singer. That woman sings like an angel, sometimes like a little devil. And she is something fine to look at. They've really been packing in the crowds on the weekend."

"That's good."

"The place is doing well," said Lee. "I know you shouldn't do business with friends, but since you were in the restaurant business and since you're the man with the business degree, I thought I'd give you first crack at it." He suddenly looked wistful. "I kind of hate to let the place go. It's like losing a part of me."

J.J. nodded. "I know how you feel. I hated to let go of my places. Did it all for nothing," he said bitterly.

His words brought on an awkward silence. He should have kept his shit to himself. He shook off the downer moment. "Let's shoot some pool."

"Good idea," said Lee. "And, J.J., I get you not wanting to get sucked into this business again. I'd have liked you to be the one who takes over The Drunken Sailor, but no worries. The right owner will show up."

Maybe the right owner had shown up, J.J. thought as they drank beer and waited their turn at one of the pool tables. The place was packed. Lots of out-of-towners, but Lee said he had a ton of regulars who came in during the week as well. Line dancing lessons were offered on Sunday afternoons followed by line dancing. A lot of the old guys came in midweek to play darts and Lee had recently started a ladies' night, with half off on drinks on Tuesdays and pool lessons taught by some of the better players, including a guy named Seth Waters, who had been a regular before he got married. According to Lee, he still came in to play pool on Sundays while his wife and her girlfriends line danced.

"You've done a great job of making this the place to

be," J.J. said as they moved to take their turn at a table that had opened up.

"I like to think so," said Lee. "Thank God I got lots of good free advice from a pro when I first started.

"What are friends for?" J. J. responded. He selected a cue stick and chalked it up.

"Go ahead and break," Lee said.

J.J. took aim at the cue ball, sending it clacking into the others. He sank one of the striped ones and then proceeded to clean the table.

"Save some for me," Lee protested.

"Oh, yeah, I can't let you lose. It would hurt your delicate feelings," J.J. taunted.

"And then I'd hurt your delicate nose," Lee shot back.

J.J. did miss the next ball. He stood back and let Lee take his turn.

It was the end of the game for him because he caught sight of a woman with long red hair, a face that would launch a thousand ships, and legs that wouldn't quit entering the place. She wore a short black leather jacket, hanging open to reveal a low-cut green top covering a very nice rack. Those fine legs were encased in tight jeans. She wore black boots that made him think of pirates and was carrying a guitar case. Holy Moly! Was that a member of the band Lee had told him about?

Lee caught him staring. "That's Bonnie Brinks, one of The Mermaids."

"I wouldn't mind hooking her on my line."

"Fat chance. She's a smiling ice maiden. Been single for years."

"Maybe she's tired of being single," J.J. mused.

"Don't hold your breath. But hey, she sure dresses up the place."

J.J. suspected that was about all she did. Lee had a tin ear. He'd probably hired the woman for her looks, despite his claims of her angelic singing.

Behind her came a younger woman, tall like Bonnie but with darker coloring. Also a looker. And next to her walked a woman who'd never gotten the memo that she was a senior citizen, also wearing tight jeans and heels high enough to trip Tina Turner. She sported spiky white hair and the tips of the spikes were colored green. The mother. His mother sure didn't look like that. This woman probably had every old geezer in the place ready to take her out. With all three women being so striking maybe nobody cared what they sounded like.

"Had enough pool?" asked Lee.

"I think I'll go over to the bar and get another drink," J.J. said.

He snagged the last seat at the bar, one near the end next to a scruffy old dude in faded jeans and a peacoat, ordered another beer and watched as the women tuned up. They couldn't sound as good as they looked.

"The band's good," the old guy said. "They sing good, too," he added and chortled over his crack.

"You know them?" J.J. asked.

"Of course. Everybody knows everybody here," the old guy informed him.

"Looks like this is a popular place," J.J. observed.

"Best burgers in town. Plus they have a senior menu."

Lee came up behind J.J., hovering like a salesman in a used car lot. "Hey there, Pete. I see you've met my pal J.J. This is Pete," he said to J.J. "He's one of our regulars. He won our last darts tournament."

"Beat out all the young pups," Pete bragged. "You play darts?" he asked J.J.

"Don't take the bait," said Lee. "He'll just sucker you into a friendly wager and take your shirt."

"Aw, there you go, spoilin' my fun," Pete complained.

A full house and steady patrons. It would be kind of cool to own this pub. A lot of work and time, but it wasn't like he had much going on in his life anyway other than some day trading, hitting the gym and reading. In the last year he'd bought enough books to stock a small library. He needed something more to do. Lately, he felt like he was drifting with no purpose, no adventure on the horizon. What kind of adventures could he have here in Moonlight Harbor?

At nine on the dot the hot redhead stepped up to the mike and said, "Hey everyone, let's get this party started."

J.J. would have loved to start a party with her. His fingers itched to play with that gorgeous red hair of hers.

She looked back at the granny on the drums, who began to bang her drumsticks together, counting off the beat, then the young girl hit the bass and the redhead began to bend those guitar strings all to hell. People rushed to the dance floor as she started to sing. "Get off your chair and get out here and shake your booty. You gotta start this party, so get out there and do your duty."

J.J.'s heart went into overdrive. This place was a gold mine and Bonnie Brinks was the gold. What a voice! The woman was a superstar. He wondered what she was doing buried in the sand of a small beach town.

"So whaddya think? The place is a good investment, right?" Lee said in his ear.

"I'd say so," said J.J. "Looks like the band is bringing in a lot of customers."

"We had a lot of customers even before the band," Lee said. "People want to eat at a casual place with lots of atmosphere when they're at the beach."

"You definitely got the atmosphere," J.J. said. The goofy carved pirate statues were an obvious hit. He'd seen several people taking pictures with them. The pool tables had been in constant use since they'd walked in and the beer was flowing. Lee did have a going concern. The band and dance floor were a bonus. And what a bonus that band was.

The women finally went on break, the older one stopping at a table to say hello to some people. The younger one went to plop down next to a supersized young buck at a table near the bandstand where her drink was already waiting. A boyfriend, of course. The guitar queen headed for the bar, stopping for a quick word here and there, deflecting a fat lounge lizard, nodding and smiling at something another patron said.

She came up to the end of the bar next to J. J. and Lee. "Great job as always, Bonnie," Lee said.

"Thanks," she said. Then to the bartender, "Got my Diet Coke, Madison?"

"On its way," the woman said and got busy getting her drink.

"You've got a great band," J.J. said to Bonnie.

"Thanks," she said. Her smile was a stop sign. *Not interested so don't even try.*

What did he look like? Some middle-aged, desperate horn toad? He was just being friendly. There was no need to give him the ice treatment.

He decided to turn the charm up a notch. "I always wanted to meet a mermaid."

"Now you have," she told him, still with the stop sign smile. The bartender set down her glass and Bonnie thanked her, the ice melting from her smile. But it was back again for J.J. "Try the garlic fries here," she said to him. "They're great." Then she left before he could get in another word.

Mermaids were not so easy to catch.

"Don't put her on the welcoming committee," J.J. muttered.

"Told ya," said Lee.

Slick and charming and no ring on his finger, which, considering his age—around hers—probably meant he'd ditched a wife somewhere along the way, Bonnie decided as she walked to the band table. With those blue eyes and that red hair and matching, neatly trimmed beard, he looked like some kind of troubadour from the Elizabethan era. Add broad shoulders and a well-sculpted chest and he was a regular pheromone factory.

And that stupid line about meeting a mermaid. Oh, yes, he was a charmer.

Who did that remind her of? Rance Jackson, of course.

*Let's get to know him*, urged her sex-starved hormones.

*Not happening*, she informed them even though he was as tempting as sin. She could almost feel the tickle of that beard on her skin. But this was the kind of man who broke hearts—trouble in Levis. There would be no getting to know him.

Put a Mr. Yuck sticker on him and stay far away.

"It ain't over till it's over," J.J. told his pal, quoting the famous Yogi Berra.

"It ain't even started," Lee taunted.

"I'll find a way to start something," J.J. vowed.

He continued to watch Bonnie Brinks throughout the next set. She'd been mellow enough talking with Lee, visiting with patrons, but when she was singing those fast dance songs she caught fire. The fire turned to warm embers when she sang a love song, enough to probably make every man present fantasize about sleeping with her. She sure had that effect on J.J.

What would it take to break the ice?

He wasn't the only one wondering that, if the tool who was trying to corner her by the bandstand was any indication. He was probably early forties, tall with legs like tree trunks and the arms of an overzealous body builder—or a dude on steroids.

She cocked her head and looked up at him as he smiled down at her. He said something that dimmed her smile and moved in closer. She shook her head, tried to move to the side. He mirrored the move, giving her a smarmy smile in the process.

"Uh-oh," said J.J.

Some men didn't read road signs so well, and this guy wasn't seeing the same stop sign she'd given J.J. He was the kind of jerk who gave men a bad a name.

J.J. started to get off his stool. This goon needed a lesson in manners.

Lee caught his arm. "Don't bother."

"She needs help," J.J. said, shaking it off.

"No, she doesn't. Watch."

J.J. watched reluctantly, ready to rush over the second the jerk laid hands on her.

He started to, reaching out to catch a lock of her long auburn hair. "Okay, that's it," J.J. growled.

"Yep, it is," said Lee as Bonnie sweetly smiled at the dude and stomped on his instep.

Sadly for the guy, he was wearing sneakers and her spike heel drove into his foot in a way that had his mouth dropping in pain and him hopping on the one good foot he had left. She gave his arm a there-there pat, and left to join her mother and daughter and the supersized kid at their table.

"Wow," J.J. said. Bonnie Brinks really was something else.

"The woman can take care of herself," said Lee.

No knight in shining armor needed. Darn. So much for impressing her with his chivalry.

But she had to need something. Everyone did. Whatever it was, he hoped he could be the man to give it to her. Maybe he should buy the pub.

# *Six*

"You should see how amazing it looks down here," Gina said as she and Avril talked on the phone. "Everything is lit up for Christmas."

Avril had to squash the jealous bug by reminding herself that Moonlight Harbor was lit up, too. The upcoming weekend would be the Seaside with Santa festival, and that was something Nashville didn't have.

Seaside with Santa was a fairly new celebration on the town's festival roster and people had embraced it in spite of its bumpy beginning, having first taken place during a major storm that left both townspeople and visitors out of power for days. Ever since though, it had been good weather, and the convention center Jenna Waters had been pushing for was about to be built, so soon much of the celebrating would be taking place under cover. Meanwhile, though, every store window twinkled with colored lights, and every restaurant was decked out with wreaths while their lobbies housed trees decorated with shells and painted sand dollars.

"We've got Seaside with Santa this weekend," Avril said.

"I am going to miss that," Gina admitted. "Remember

that awful first parade? Oh, my gosh, all that rain and wind and pieces getting blown right off the floats."

"You got hit in the head with a plastic flower," Avril reminded her and had to laugh.

They'd gone back to Avril's house after the parade and had been partying with friends when the lights went out. They'd wound up stumbling around by the light of their phones and looking for candles. It had been an adventure. They'd roasted marshmallows in her mom's fireplace and made s'mores from the graham crackers and chocolate bars Mom had in the pantry, leftover from their Labor Day party. A lot of people in town had been freaking out but Mom had taken it all in stride, letting everyone sleep on the floor with blankets and sofa pillows and keeping them fed with trail mix and peanut butter and jelly sandwiches and bottled juice. One of many happy memories of Avril's life in Moonlight Harbor.

There were others—Fourth of July celebrations, end of school parties on the deck, graduation parties, flying kites at the beach, the first gig they ever played as a band. Not to mention crabbing with Kenny, going out on his boat, beachcombing and buying saltwater taffy at Cindy's Candies.

She sighed inwardly. She had to get to Nashville. Something inside her akin to a forty-five-knot gale was pushing her south. And yet sometimes it felt like something else deep inside her was begging, *Don't leave.* But there came a time when you had to move on. Her time had come.

She talked more with Gina about all the great things they were going to do together once she hit Nashville until Gina had to go. "Going to The Bluebird tonight," Gina said. It sounded a little like bragging and made Avril frown.

"That's okay. I gotta go, too. I've got my critique group." And one of them lived in Nashville…which was sort of like Six Degrees of Blake Shelton. She was almost there. There in spirit.

Not really there. *Soon*, said that strong driving force, *so get to work.*

When the group met, Sarah, as always, had something to show. Avril envied the confidence with which she sang. "That's a hit," she said when Sarah had finished.

"I hope so," Sarah said. "What have you got?"

"I think I've got the beginnings of something good," Avril said.

"Let's hear it," said Colton.

Avril's heart rate always picked up when she had to share a song she'd written with these two. It was never easy putting her brain baby out there. What if they thought Baby was ugly?

Then they'd help her make Baby pretty. That was what critique groups were for. If she wasn't tough enough to take criticism from these guys she'd never survive the tough world of the music business.

She picked up her guitar and began to sing. "When you run out of love what do you do? That's where we are and I'm stuck here with you. You don't give a damn, I don't give a shit. Looks like we're done. We're at the end of the road. This is it." She stopped singing. "That's what I've got so far."

"Great hook," Colton said. "I like it."

"Me, too," said Sarah.

"Can you say shit in a song?" Avril wondered.

"You can say damn so I don't see why not," said Sarah.

"You got a second verse?" Colton asked.

"Not yet." But she would before the night was over. Their encouragement was great inspiration.

"I can work on it with you," Colton offered.

Colton was always suggesting writing together with them. Avril knew in Nashville everybody wrote songs together, but she wasn't ready for that yet. She liked having total control over her songs, so she never jumped on the offer. Neither did Sarah.

Colton hadn't had much to show lately, and she wondered if he'd hit a dry spot and was hoping to get the creative juices flowing by co-writing. Sometimes it was easier to get a creative spark going when you were bouncing ideas off another person. But that was what they were doing with this group. If this wasn't working for him he was in trouble.

"How about you, Colt?" Sarah asked. "You got anything?"

He frowned and shook his head. "Nothing much. Been too busy."

A songwriter too busy to write songs? Impossible. Yep, definitely a dry period. Or else he was suffering from a case of self-doubt. Songwriters had a way of aborting their own work, deciding before even giving a song idea a chance that it wasn't good enough to develop.

"I got some ideas though," he added.

"Well, let's hear 'em," said Sarah.

"Next week," he said.

"You're in a slump," Sarah pointed out, pretty much saying what Avril had been thinking.

"I'm still looking for a great hook," Colton said. "Avril, save me. Give me an idea."

"Go lookin'," she said.

"Hmm. Maybe I could do something with that."

She laughed. "I didn't mean it as a hook, I meant it as advice."

He gave a snort. "Good either way."

"I have one more, guys. You got time to listen?" Avril asked.

"Sure," he said, speaking for Sarah as well. "Hit me dealer."

She sang what she had, trying to sound confident. "I need to leave, but I can't go. You've nailed me down with guilt. You drove those nails right through my soul…" She stopped. "I can't think of a rhyme for guilt."

"How about still?" Colton suggested. "It's a near rhyme. Look at me, I'm here still."

"I like that," Avril said.

"Any real-life inspiration for this?" Sarah asked. "Is your boyfriend making you feel guilty about moving to Nashville?" Sarah pressed.

"Not really. He's great." Except she knew, even though Kenny was being supportive, he really didn't want her to leave.

"You got a good start," said Colton. "It hits me in the gut."

"Good," she said. Because it had hit her in the gut when she was writing it.

Kenny came over later and they made popcorn and watched an episode of *Wolf Like Me*, then got all clingy and cozy on the couch, Kenny heating her up in all the right places.

"I hate having to leave," he said later. "Wish we lived together."

"I know," she said, and she knew what he meant by that. He'd hinted around several times about getting married, having a family, but she wasn't ready.

"Wish you weren't leaving this summer," he added.

Guilt. There it was, the inspiration for her song.

He held up a hand before she could say anything. "I know, you gotta go. I shouldn't have said that. Sometimes stupid just pops out of my mouth."

She laid a hand on his arm. "It's not stupid to want to be together."

"I can wait," he said. "I really can. It would be wrong to hold you back, like trying to keep the sun from rising. Or trying to catch a mermaid," he added with a sad smile.

"You already caught one," she assured him.

"Yeah, but I need to quit trying to keep her in the boat," he said. He gave Avril a final kiss. "I got an early morning tomorrow. I'd better get home."

She watched as he climbed into his truck and drove off. She did love Kenny. Would Nashville kill that love?

Two weeks after his Thanksgiving visit, Seaside with Santa was in full swing and J.J. was back for it. He wandered about the town on Saturday, observing the swarms of visitors drifting from shop to shop, checked out the heavy traffic, and the good business all the restaurants were doing. Moonlight Harbor had succeeded in turning itself into a tourist destination.

*Tourism, always good for business*, he thought as he sat at a corner table in The Drunken Sailor with Lee and his wife, enjoying burgers and clam chowder. It was certainly good for this particular business and J.J. found himself wishing he'd followed his instincts and bought the place.

The pub was as festive as any other restaurant in town, with a large wreath on the door, wreaths hanging in the windows, and the carved pirates all sporting Santa hats instead of their usual tricorns. The wooden women also wore blinking Christmas light necklaces to accent their wooden cleavage. Patrons showed up sporting red shirts and tops and Santa hats.

J.J. had passed on Lee's offer of a hat. "You're gonna stick out like a Christmas sore thumb," Lee had predicted.

"I'll take my chances," J.J. had replied.

But his friend was right. He looked like the lone party pooper in his white button-down shirt and jeans and loafers.

"People get into the holidays down here," Lee said. "Wait till you see it on the Fourth. It's a madhouse."

"The place has grown like crazy since we first moved down. Investing in real estate is the second smartest thing you can do," said Glinda.

"Yeah? What's the first smartest?" J.J. asked.

"Buying this place," she said with a wink.

One of her friends stopped by to chat with her, and while she was distracted Lee lowered his voice. "Never mind Glinda. She wants out as of yesterday."

"I thought you had a buyer," said J.J.

Lee shook his head, took a swig of his beer. "Pulled out just a couple of days ago. Realized he couldn't swing the financing."

J.J. could. He took a thoughtful draw on his own beer, followed by an onion ring. Lee's cook knew how to make a memorable onion ring, for sure. Good food, some great micro beers, a friendly, *Cheers*-style atmosphere—the place was a great business opportunity knocking. Maybe there was a reason Lee's deal had fallen through. Opportunity was knocking on J.J.'s door. Maybe it wouldn't knock a third time.

The Mermaids entered the pub and several people called out hellos. He watched as the talented redhead waved to several. Her daughter had the same behemoth of a boyfriend with her and Grandma was looking good with some kind of faux fur jacket over her black leather pants and boots. He followed their progress to the bandstand, watched them set down their instruments, then go shed their coats, draping them on their chairs at the same table they'd staked out last time he'd been in the pub. The older woman went to the bar to fetch a drink while the other two started tuning up. An old dude with a beer belly sidled up to the bandstand and started talking to Bonnie. She gave him a tolerant smile, shook her head and nodded to a table near the dance floor that had been staked out by a couple of middle-aged women. The guy said something. Bonnie smiled, said something back to him and he frowned and walked away.

Lee had been watching J.J. watch her. "She gets that a lot."

"What?" J.J. asked, playing innocent.

"Men hitting on her. Old ones, young ones, fat ones, skinny ones. They throw out their best lines, but it never works."

J.J. picked up an onion ring, studied it casually. "You trying to tell me something?"

"I'm telling you you'll never get anywhere with Bonnie Brinks."

"Bonnie's great," said Glinda. "I think she's just waiting for the right man."

J.J. smiled, toasted her wisdom with his glass of beer. There you had it. The right man had arrived. Bonnie the mermaid just didn't know it yet.

The tables around the dance floor filled up quickly and by the time the band was ready to start playing every seat was taken. J.J. mentally kicked himself for not staking out one of those tables earlier. Not that he couldn't hear or see from where he was, but he preferred the idea of watching Bonnie Brinks in action close up. With her red hair and fair coloring she could have been a descendant of Aine, queen of the Irish fairies. The shiny green top she was wearing accented her coloring and allowed a playful hint at her curves. And that voice of hers, he could listen to her sing all night. In fact, he intended to.

The first set's playlist was including many Christmas favorites such as "White Christmas," "Santa's Flying a 747 Tonight" and "Santa Baby." He sat mesmerized as the fascinating redhead went on to the next song and crooned, "You could really make Christmas for me. Put your heart under my tree."

He was willing to bet a lot of men had tried to do just that. What was her story?

Whatever it was, she didn't want to share. Lee had invited her to join them, which she did. She said a brief hello to J.J., then turned her attention to Lee and Glinda. She told Glinda she liked her necklace, asked Lee how he was enjoying the holiday playlist.

"It's great," Lee said.

J.J. listened, looking for an opportunity to join—okay, take over—the conversation.

He jumped in with, "Great job on 'Santa, Baby.' What would you ask Santa for, Mermaid?"

"Nothing. I have everything I need," she said lightly.

"You should still go see the old guy and have a talk," said J.J. "There might be something you need that you don't even know you need." *Like me.*

"Santa's got his lap full just seeing all those kids."

"Yeah, but I'm his pinch hitter," J.J. cracked. "There's plenty of room on my lap for a mermaid."

She frowned. But her cheeks flushed a pretty shade of pink. As far as J.J. was concerned it was a chink in the old mermaid armor. She was into him. She just wasn't ready to admit it.

He decided to switch into serious mode before she could

bring out the stop sign smile and leave. "That one song you played, the one about putting your heart under the tree. It's great. Did you write it?"

"No, a friend of my mom's did years ago. It got a cut on a *Christmas in the Northwest* album, which was a big deal back then. Another friend of Mom's named Pam Cramer sang it."

It was the first real exchange they'd had since he met her. "A nice sentiment," he said, trying to keep the conversation going. "I guess a lot of people are hoping for that this year."

He wasn't sure what kind of response that remark was supposed to generate, but all J.J. got, along with the old stop sign, was an unrevealing, "I suppose so," followed by, "I'd better get back to work."

"Nice try, dude," Lee teased as she threaded her way through the tables. "I guess the old Walker charm doesn't work on everyone."

J.J. gave him the finger and helped himself to another onion ring.

"Don't give up," advised Glinda.

"Don't listen to her," said Lee. "There's plenty of other mermaids in the sea."

Yes, there were, but J.J. would be willing to bet that none of them measured up to this one.

Oh, well. Did he really want to complicate his life with a woman?

Well, yeah. He wasn't cut out to be a monk.

"You'll see a lot more of her if you buy this place," Glinda said, only half teasing.

"Hey, now, we're just here to have a good time," Lee said to her.

So was half the town. J.J. knew the price his pal was

asking was reasonable. *Knock, knock*, whispered Opportunity. *Last call.*

"Let's go over your financials tomorrow," he said to Lee. "I think I want to own a pub."

Glinda let out a squeal. "Free at last!"

"You just saved my marriage, buddy," said Lee. "By spring we'll be in Hawaii, second hornymooning."

J.J. chuckled. "Go for it, you two. If everything looks as solid on paper as it does here we'll have a deal. And don't worry," he said to Glinda. "I won't have any trouble coming up with the money."

"Bless you." She raised her glass to him. "Here's to a new era for all of us," she said, and they all clinked glasses.

A new era. He was ready for that. More than ready.


"Who was that sitting with Lee and Glinda?" Loretta asked Bonnie as she strapped her guitar back on.

"Just some friend of theirs," Bonnie said.

"Pretty good-looking friend," offered Loretta.

"Want me to introduce you?" Bonnie teased.

Loretta frowned and pointed a drumstick at her. "Don't get smart."

Bonnie just chuckled, then started them on their next song, a Christmas one she'd written that was great for dancing the West Coast swing, titled, "Jingle My Bells."

J.J. Walker had jingled her bells. The man practically oozed pheromones. It was unnerving the way simply sitting next to him made her want to plop on his lap and do all kinds of things that would put her on Santa's naughty list. The last man who'd had that strong an effect on her was the first man to break her trust in love. One trip down that jagged road was more than enough. She wasn't going to take another, no matter how many pheromones this man shot at her. She sure hoped he wasn't going to be a regular visitor. He needed to get gone…far away from Moonlight Harbor.

J.J. called his old pal Tony a few days later. "I did it. I bought the place."

"All right! The Tones are ready to be your house band."

Oh, yeah, that. When Lee had first suggested he buy the pub he'd opened his big mouth and told his other old college buddy. Tony had assumed that J.J. would want him and his band to kick things off and J.J. hadn't bothered to disabuse him of the idea. Since he really wasn't going to buy the place. But now he had, and now he was ready to kick himself. The Mermaids were already a going concern. He hadn't even heard Tony's latest band.

But Tony was more like a brother than a friend. Certainly a better one than the brother J.J. had lost to an overdose twenty years ago.

Still, he hedged. "It's a long way to come just to play for a few hours."

"It's only an hour from Olympia," said Tony. "We're in between gigs and the guys will be all over it."

"I don't know if I can afford to pay you." Okay, that was a lie and he was a shit.

"We'll come for free food."

Tony and the Tones vs. The Mermaids—the battle of the bands waged in J.J.'s mind. He hated to lose that all-chick band. They were a draw. Bonnie Brinks was a big draw, and she'd sure drawn him. Which to choose, loyalty or lust?

Loyalty finally won by a narrow margin. "Okay, how about I book you guys for the month of February?" A slow winter month was a fairly safe bet. Anyway, most people had a tin ear. As long as there was booze and a band they wouldn't care. He could always bring The Mermaids back after giving Tony a month. Most venues rotated bands.

"Done," said Tony.

"All right," said J.J. Women came and went. Pals were forever.

Except this woman…

Oh, well. Too late.

Avril and Bonnie came to Loretta's condo for lunch on Sunday, stayed a couple of hours, and then went off to live their lives. Avril was going over to Kenny's family's place for dinner and Bonnie was off to a book club meeting at Lucy's house, which she said was really more about wine and chocolate than books.

Loretta liked to read. She liked wine. And she really liked chocolate. She also knew that her daughter needed a social life of her own, so she'd passed on the offer when Bonnie had invited her to join. The invitation had come a couple of days after her mopey moment at Thanksgiving. She'd shared more than she should have with her daughter and regretted it. Bonnie didn't need to navigate her own social life while having to tug her mama along. Anyway, if Loretta wanted to drink wine she could invite Norah over or Theresia, the owner of the Sunshine Bakery. Or her old friend Pearl, the hairdresser. Or Estella, her newest buddy. She had friends.

The only problem was that those friends all had men in their lives, families, obligations. Yes, they could meet for lunch, but Theresia went to bed with the birds so she could rise with them and begin baking. Norah had her business and her husband and her grown kids and their families. Pearl had that special man in her life now and traveled a lot. Loretta was on her own. She'd been the odd one out socially ever since she lost her husband. She should have gotten used to it but she never had.

Oh, well. She had a man of her own now…when he could make time for her.

She frowned. Was this how she wanted to live her golden years, like some aging mistress, waiting around for her lover to stop by? Marlon was going to have to commit to moving them to a new level soon or she was going to move on.

Except she didn't want to move on, darn it all. She scowled out her window at the gray skies and the ocean, turbulent and frothing with whitecaps. All right. She needed to do something to downgrade the storm building inside her.

Christmas cookies. She'd bake some for Pete. He'd been saying only the night before how much he missed Edie's cookies.

The thought of doing something nice for someone—and getting a sugar buzz in the process as she sampled the treat—was enough to chase away the clouds. She moved to the kitchen and started pulling ingredients out of the cupboard.

She was halfway through making 7 Layer cookies when her cell phone rang—"Let's Hear It for the Boy," Marlon's ring tone. She licked her fingers and grabbed for it. Then, just before saying an eager hello, reminded herself of her earlier frustration.

She cooled down that hello a couple of degrees.

"Loretta, you wonderful woman," he said. "I love hearing your voice."

Simply hearing his was enough to make her melt faster than chocolate in a microwave. *Don't do it*, she cautioned herself.

"Marlon, you're lucky you caught me home," she said, keeping her tone chilly.

"I thought you stayed home on Sundays."

"Not always. I do have a social life, you know." Thank heaven she'd been a little coy about that. No woman liked to appear desperate.

"Well, yes, of course. So, were you busy?"

"Baking cookies for my friend Pete."

"Pete," he said, not sounding too happy.

"One of my admirers from the pub. Of course, you've never met him because you haven't come to hear us sing." If he hadn't already guessed she was in a mood, he knew it then.

"Oh, Loretta, you know how sorry I am I haven't made it down. I hate it when I can't be with you."

"Do you really?" she said as if she couldn't care less.

"I do. You know I do, darling. I don't supposed Pete would share those cookies, now, would he?"

"Why are you asking? Are you coming down?"

"I'm already here. Come to your door."

He was there! Loretta turned, hurried down the hallway and opened the door and there he stood, the wind ruffling his hair, his dark eyes shining.

"Surprise," he said, and held up a huge bouquet of flowers.

"Marlon!" she cried happily, and threw the door open wide. "Come on in out of the cold."

He stepped inside and handed over the flowers—red and white roses with baby's breath and ferns.

"They're lovely," she said. "I'm going to get them in water. You know where to hang your coat."

He hung his coat in the coat closet and joined her in the kitchen, coming up behind her and slipping his arms around her waist and propping his chin on her shoulder, watching as she worked. "That's an interesting concoction you're putting together."

"It's very tasty."

"Just like you," he murmured and took a nibble of her neck, sending a delicious thrill racing through her. Who needed cookies now? Not her.

Oh, no. Hadn't she just vowed to make this man fish or cut bait? Why was she letting him get all chummy and herself all sweet?

"I need to get this in the oven," she said and wriggled free.

He got the message and moved to the other side of the kitchen, settling on a bar stool at the counter.

She pretended to be busy pouring sweetened condensed milk over the top of the ingredients.

"I detected a certain chill in your voice when you answered your phone," he said.

"Did you?" She turned and put the pan in the oven.

"Loretta, have you lost interest in me? Am I going to have to challenge this Pete fellow to a duel?"

Picturing Marlon facing Pete with pistols at dawn brought up such a ludicrous image she couldn't help but smile. But they needed to get some things settled.

"Marlon, I refuse to spend my life waiting on you."

"Oh, now, what kind of thing is that to say when I've brought you something special." He reached into his pants pocket and brought out a small black velvet box. "I wonder what's in this," he said, holding it up and pretending to examine it.

Loretta gasped. "Marlon, you don't mean…"

"What?" He opened the box and showed her the ring with the small diamond glinting in it.

"It's lovely!"

She reached for it and he pulled it away. "You take the ring and you have to take the man," he said, his voice teasing.

"You know I do," she said.

"Then come here," he beckoned.

She came and he gave her a big juicy kiss. "I adore you, Loretta. Let me hear you say you'll be mine."

"I already am. You know it," she said. She watched as he slipped the ring on her finger. It looked old, like an antique.

"It was my grandmother's," he said. "Do you like it?"

"I do."

"I still can't be down here full-time. I have a lot of things to take care of. But I don't want to wait any longer to get married. Let's get hitched. We can sort out the details later."

"Oh, yes!" she said. "I always wanted a Christmas wedding."

"I have an even better idea," he said. "What do you say to getting married on New Year's Eve? We can go to the Moonlight Harbor courthouse. Afterwards I'll take you and your daughter and granddaughter out to dinner. Then I can come hear the band play that night. On New Year's Day we can run off to the Quinault Lodge and spend a couple of glorious days there."

"It sounds lovely," she said. "I've got to call Bonnie." She started for her phone.

He put a staying hand on her arm. "Let's tell her tomorrow. Let's keep tonight just for us."

Marlon was such a romantic. "All right. Just for us."

The next morning, before she could even suggest Bonnie join them for breakfast, he broke the news that he'd gotten a text. Business. He couldn't spend the day with her.

"But it won't be long before we'll have a good, long time

together. Meanwhile, let's get things moving. I need to get you on my life insurance, redo my will, put your name on the checking account."

"I'll have to do all that, too," she said. "I'd better get busy."

He caught her hand and kissed it. "Loretta, I want you to know I'm going to take good care of you. I know that sounds a little old-fashioned but I'm an old-fashioned guy."

What a sweet man. "We're a team. And I have some assets of my own to bring to the team. I have my condo and I have a nice stock portfolio. It's not huge but it's something."

"We'll be fine," he said. "Now, I think I can delay an hour. Why don't you call your daughter and see if she wants to meet us for breakfast. I'll take you girls out."

"That would be wonderful. I know she's been dying to meet you."

"And I've been dying to meet her," he said. "Give her a call and let's get going."

Bonnie was at work when Loretta called, but Lucy, on hearing about the breakfast invitation from the mystery man in her mother's life shooed her out the door. So off she went to Sandy's, the town's go-to restaurant for breakfast.

Her mom and Marlon were already seated when she got there. Loretta was a human Glo-Stick, her cheeks as pink as her sweater. She was beaming at the man seated next to her. He had dark hair shot with silver at the temples and dark eyes and a square jaw under a pretty darned perfect face. He stood as Bonnie approached their table, showing off a fairly trim body.

"Bonnie," he said, holding out a hand, "it is so good to finally get to meet you."

"It's nice to meet you, too," she said as he took her hand. *About time.*

"You're every bit as lovely as your mother says."

"Thank you," Bonnie said. She could see why her mom fell for this man. He was a charmer.

Their waitress appeared bringing some sort of fancy drinks. "Here are your Bellinis."

"I know it's early in the day for drinks," Marlon said, "but today is a special day."

Uh-oh.

Loretta held up her left hand and wriggled it. "Congratulate us, dear."

Bonnie blinked and looked again. She hadn't imagined it. The ring was still there. Her mother was now officially engaged to a man she'd met on the internet and only known a few months, a man Bonnie was meeting for the first time. Warning bells were ringing so loudly in her head she was surprised they weren't being heard all over the restaurant.

Those bells certainly weren't being heard at their table. Both Loretta and Marlon were smiling at her, her mother with elation, him with…smug satisfaction. She didn't like this man.

"Congratulations, Marlon." Bonnie had to force the words out of her mouth. She had other words for her mother. *What are you thinking? You barely know this man. I don't know him at all!*

"I am the luckiest man in all of Washington State," he said. "No, make that the whole USA," he amended. He took Loretta's newly ringed hand and kissed it.

Gag.

"Aww, you're only saying that cause it's true," Loretta quipped.

"So, when are you two planning to get married?" Bonnie hated to ask. She already knew she wasn't going to like the answer.

"New Year's Eve," Loretta said. "We can celebrate at The Drunken Sailor."

"That's awfully soon," Bonnie protested.

"When you find such a wonderful woman, you don't want to wait," said Marlon, smiling at Loretta. "A toast," he said, picking up his glass.

Loretta raised hers, looking at him like a besotted teenager.

Bonnie reluctantly lifted her glass.

"Here's to marrying the most wonderful woman in the world and inheriting a beautiful daughter," he said.

"And to a wonderful man," Loretta said. "And true love."

Bonnie said nothing. She managed a weak smile and let the two lovebirds clink their glasses against hers. She set her glass down, fished around for something to say to stop the runaway train.

"You know, that's not much time to plan a wedding." It was the best she could come up with.

"I had the big, fancy wedding when I married your father," Loretta said. "This time it's a trip to the courthouse and all I have to do is buy Mr. Handsome here a boutonniere. Oh, and a ring."

"I already have something in mind for you," he said.

"Oh?" She gave him a coy smile.

"I'll give you a hint. It has sentimental value, just like your engagement ring."

"Oh, Marlon, that is so sweet. This was his grandmother's," Loretta explained to Bonnie.

"Very nice," Bonnie managed. "Where are you two going to live?"

"I don't mind moving," Loretta said to Marlon, another mermaid ready to swim away.

"I wouldn't dream of making you move. This is your home. You have your band, and your lovely condo."

Which would soon be his as well. Was Marlon a gold digger? If so, surely he could find a more lucrative place to dig.

"I still have the business to deal with," he said to Bonnie. "And, frankly, I think Moonlight Harbor is much more charming than the city. It will make a great home base."

Home base...home run. Bonnie struggled to keep her lips from pulling down at the corners. What was it about this guy? She didn't know. She only knew she didn't like him.

Loretta was already looking at the menu. "Everything looks so good."

Nothing looked good to Bonnie.

Their waitress was back. "You folks ready to order?"

"I am," Loretta said and asked for an omelet and toast.

"How about you, Bonnie?" asked Marlon. "What would you like?"

*For you to go away and stay away.*

# Seven

Bonnie returned to Beach Dream Homes Realty to find the same smooth operator she'd met at The Drunken Sailor coming out the door with Lucy's husband, Brody. Oh, no. What was he doing here? Besides driving up her heart rate.

"Well, hello. We meet again," he said and smiled at her. "Lucky me." Did he ever turn off the charm or was the spigot always on?

"You've met?" Brody asked.

"Briefly," Bonnie said. And then, heaven only knew why, couldn't resist asking, "Are you looking to buy a house down here?"

"I am," he said. "Real estate's a good investment."

"It is here," Brody said.

If Loretta had been present she'd have said something cheeky like, "Look at the treasure that just washed up on our beach."

All Bonnie could think was red tide. This man was too good-looking for her own good, and she didn't like that cocky smile.

"Good luck in your hunt," she said, and continued on inside to her desk.

But first she had to run the gamut—Lucy, her boss, and Missy Warren, the receptionist.

"Now, there's a fine-looking man," said Missy.

"Missy, I didn't know you were looking," Bonnie teased as she hung her coat on the coat rack inside the door.

"If I didn't love the old couch spud I'm married to so much I'd trade him in on a model like that one in a heart-beat," Missy said. "I think you ought to take that handsome thing out for a test run."

Unlike Loretta, who was fighting aging all the way, Missy had embraced the process, accepting her expanding waistline and wrinkles and pulling her gray hair into a bun. She favored comfy slacks and blouses with seashell prints in the summer and bulky sweaters, still paired with comfortable slacks in the winter. Clients coming in felt instantly at home with her and usually wound up showing her pictures of their kids on their phones. Her husband was retired and not interested in much more than watching old John Wayne movies on TV and puttering around the house. Her kids were grown and scattered around the country. She loved the fun of working at a busy real estate office and claimed she would be at her job until she did a face-plant on her desk. The agents and staff of Beach Dream Homes were her extended family. Which, of course, qualified her to offer advice, whether it was requested or not.

Lucy, who was in her coat, purse over her shoulder, was about to go show a house, but she had time to point out to her cynical friend that here was a man moving to Moon-light Harbor who was over thirty to swell the dating pool.

"He's not here yet," Bonnie said.

"Sounded like he's planning to be," said Lucy. "He's a new business owner."

"I didn't know there were any for sale," said Bonnie.

"Me, either. No one's mentioned anything at the chamber meetings."

Both Lucy and Brody were active in the Moonlight Harbor Chamber of Commerce. They'd have heard something.

"Maybe whoever is selling doesn't want it to be common knowledge yet," Missy speculated.

"Or isn't a member of the chamber. Not every business in town is," Lucy said. "Whatever it is, you can bet every single woman in town will be checking it out."

"So you'd better jump the line," Missy said to Bonnie.

"No, thanks. I've got enough man trouble with my mom and her latest. I don't need to add to it with any of my own," Bonnie said as she plunked down at her desk.

"How did it go with your mom's man?" Lucy asked.

"It went," said Bonnie.

"Uh-oh," said Missy. "This doesn't sound good."

"That's because it wasn't good." Even as she brought her computer to life she wondered how she'd ever be able to concentrate on her tasks.

"That's all you've got to say?" Missy demanded.

"There's not much to say. Except that Mom's engaged." Saying it out loud made the whole thing so unnervingly real.

"Engaged!" chorused both Missy and Lucy.

"Good grief, what's her hurry?" Missy asked.

"To be fair, they have been seeing each other for a while," said Lucy, turning Bonnie's gray cloud inside out in a search of the silver lining.

"Not long enough," Bonnie said.

"That's not it though, is it?" said Missy. "It's because you hadn't met him before this. Kind of like being in a fun house and having a Stephen King–style clown jump out at you."

"I guess that's it," Bonnie admitted. "I feel like we haven't had a chance to really get to know him, for him to assimilate. That makes this feel like, I don't know, a gamble."

"I get it," said Lucy, who was aware of Loretta's tendency to rush into love. "You worry."

"I don't want to see Mom get hurt," Bonnie said.

"What makes you think she's going to?" Missy asked. "Did he strike you as selfish?"

"No."

"I saw that giant bouquet he sent for her birthday. It doesn't look like he's stingy," Lucy said.

Missy's interrogation continued. "Did he have dirty fingernails? Bad breath?"

Bonnie half chuckled. "No."

"Were his clothes worn looking? Did he try to get out of picking up the check?"

"No again. He owns his own company, and he had no problem paying for the meal. He ordered Bellini's for all of us to celebrate."

"Sounds like he might be a keeper then," said Lucy.

"Might be," Bonnie said, and that was as far as she could go. Maybe she was being unreasonably suspicious. Maybe she was balking at yet another big change coming in her life so soon after Avril's announcement. Maybe she was a hoggy daughter who didn't want to share her mother.

Or maybe there was something wrong with Marlon.

"And you never know. Sometimes you don't have a good first impression of someone and it turns out to be totally wrong," Lucy said. "Look at Brody and me. We sure didn't get off to a good start."

Missy chortled. "You can say that again."

"When are they getting married?" Lucy asked.

"New Year's Eve."

"That train is sure barreling down the track," said Missy. "You'll probably get to see him at Christmas though, right? That will give you a chance to get to know him better."

"And if he brings you all fabulous gifts you can be sure he's a keeper," Lucy said with a wink.

They were trying to make her feel better. She forced a smile and nodded and told herself to lighten up and give the man a chance.

"I better get going or I'm going to be late," Lucy said. "Don't worry, Bonnie. Things will all work out. They always do eventually."

*But not always the way you want*, Bonnie thought.

She was about to start entering the latest house Brody had listed into the MLS when Loretta called. "What did you think of Marlon?" she asked. "Isn't he wonderful?" she continued before Bonnie could answer.

"He's good-looking," Bonnie admitted.

"And so sweet and considerate," said Loretta. "I'm glad you finally had a chance to meet him."

"Me, too," said Bonnie, glad this was at least something she could be honest about. "Avril's going to be mad she didn't get a chance to."

"Well, she'll meet him come Christmas. Even though his poor brother is so sick, he's still planning on coming down Christmas Day."

"Glad he can fit us in."

Loretta picked up on the sarcasm in her daughter's voice. "Between his business and his brother he has a lot of responsibility."

"And not much time left for you. Is that how it's going to be after you're married?"

"Of course not. Although he will be busy for a while," Loretta amended.

"What does that mean?"

"He can't retire just yet. He needs to grow his company more before selling it. He'll still have to travel."

"He'd better plan on taking you with him," Bonnie said.

"I'm sure he will," Loretta said, proving that this was something they hadn't even talked about. "Well, I'd better let you get back to work. See you later." And then she was gone before Bonnie could ask any more probing questions.

"Don't worry," Missy said from her desk. "Lucy's right. It'll all work out."

Bonnie hoped so.

"What business did you buy down here?" Brody asked as he drove J.J. to the first house on their list of homes to look at.

"I'll let you know once it's a done deal," J.J. said. "I never like to talk too much about something that's not signed, sealed and delivered." Not that there was any problem with this deal, and it was already as good as signed, sealed and delivered. But there'd be plenty of time to share the news after the holidays. Then he'd join the local chamber of commerce, meet with his new employees, all that good stuff. Before any of that the deal needed to close and Lee needed to let his workers know he was leaving. It would be bad business manners for J.J. to go flapping his jaws before that and have an employee somehow find out secondhand that the pub had been sold. That kind of thing made people nervous.

"Understandable," said Brody. "You're going to love living down here. It's a tight-knit, supportive community."

"Seems like it."

"And it looks like you've already met at least one of us," Brody said. "How'd you meet Bonnie?"

"I heard her sing at The Drunken Sailor." *And am mildly obsessed with her.*

As if there was such a thing as a mild obsession. But he hated to admit, even to himself, how much of his thoughts that woman occupied.

"Ah. She sure dresses up that place. She and my wife are good friends. She's a great asset to our business. And she does have the voice. We're lucky to have her here in Moonlight Harbor. She sure could have been a star. Well, here we are," Brody said as they pulled into the driveway of a two-story house overlooking the beach. "I own a place about a quarter of a mile down the beach. This particular house would make a great vacation rental as it has full living quarters down below. Two bedrooms, bathroom, living room and a kitchenette. Good for when family and friends come to visit or a nice extra income stream."

J.J. nodded and followed him inside. The place had been well maintained and the view of the ocean from that second story was a million dollar one, even on a gray, misty day. He could imagine it was a killer on a sunny summer afternoon. The steady *shoosh* of the waves hitting the beach was almost hypnotic.

"These manufactured wood floors are practically indestructible, and look like real wood, and the gray is a good color for the beach," Brody said.

"I like the fireplace," said J.J. It had been tricked out to look modern and masculine, with a gray brick surround.

"Oh, yeah. Nice on a wintry day."

The kitchen had white cabinets and gray quartz countertops accented with a light blue glass backsplash. The two bedrooms on the upper level were all he'd need—one for him and one to use as a home office. They checked out the downstairs with its extra bedrooms. It had a fireplace as well. The kitchenette wasn't as high-end as the upstairs kitchen, but that was okay. He could already envision his stepsons and their friends staying there.

"Come Fourth of July you'll get the best show on earth," Brody said. "You wouldn't believe how many people come down here to shoot off fireworks. It's insane."

Another thing the boys would like.

"I don't think I need to see any more places," J.J. said. "The owners open to an offer?"

"They might be. They put it up late and missed the hot market. What did you have in mind?"

J.J. threw out his number which was fifty thousand less than the asking price. But he'd done some checking on his own before he ever contacted Beach Dream Homes. The place had been on the market for two and a half months, a long time to sit when you wanted out. It put him in a good bargaining position.

Brody nodded. "I think they might take that. Let me make a call."

J.J. crossed the dunes to the beach to check it out while Brody started negotiations. Ah, he remembered that smell of salt air and seaweed. The long sandy beach brought back memories of family vacations when he was a kid— sandcastles, building forts with driftwood, roasting hot dogs. It had been idyllic. Somewhere along the way to adulthood he'd lost sight of the joy of doing simple things like standing in the surf, fishing, listening to foghorns in the distance, taking in that unique smell of seaweed and fresh, salty air that you couldn't find anywhere else. He looked back to where the house stood, waiting for him, and could envision himself entertaining on that deck. He could even picture a certain redheaded mermaid up there, leaning on the railing. Moonlight Harbor was where he was supposed to be, he was sure of it.

He made his way back to the house to find Brody waiting for him. "Countering back," he said. "They'll go for thirty K less."

J.J. nodded. Fair enough. "Done," he said. He was home.

Bonnie tried to be positive when Avril asked her what she thought of Marlon. They'd been about to start band practice when he'd called. Loretta had taken it and was standing in the kitchen with her back to them, talking softly.

"He seems nice," Bonnie managed.

Avril made a face. "Seems nice. What does that mean?"

"It means he seems nice. I was with him for all of an hour, so we didn't exactly exchange our innermost thoughts."

"Well, what did you talk about?"

"Me, you. He wanted to know all about us."

"That's gotta be a good sign," Avril said.

Loretta, still on the phone, giggled like the world's oldest schoolgirl.

Avril grinned. "Think he's talking dirty to her?"

Her mother talking dirty with a man, there was something Bonnie didn't want to think about. "Don't even go there."

"Well, I'm glad Glamma's found someone," Avril said.

Bonnie wanted her mother to find someone, she wanted Loretta to be happy. But she didn't want Loretta to settle for just anyone.

*Listen to yourself*, she thought. *The guy spends money on her, wants to be a part of her life and you're snatching away the welcome mat.* She needed to stop being so suspicious.

"Okay, Glamma, were you two talking dirty?" Avril teased when Loretta ended her call and returned to the living room.

A flush rushed up Loretta's face. "What a thing to say!" she replied, neither confirming nor denying, and Avril giggled. "Now, let's get down to business, shall we?" Loretta said, and picked up her drumsticks.

There wasn't much business to get down to. They'd added all the new holiday songs they were going to, and only a couple needed fine-tuning. They finished up and Avril disappeared, leaving Loretta and Bonnie to relax with mugs of hot cocoa topped with the required mountain of whipped cream.

"I shouldn't be drinking this. I'm never going to fit into my wedding dress," Loretta said.

"You got it already?" It was irrational, but Bonnie felt a little left out. She'd have thought her mother would want to go shopping together.

As if Loretta wanted to drag around a human wet blanket when she went shopping.

"I ordered it online." Loretta brought up the site on her phone and showed Bonnie the picture of an elegant pink sheath with a jewel neckline and matching jacket.

"It's beautiful and you'll look gorgeous in it," Bonne said.

Loretta smiled. "It's going to be a wonderful New Year. You will be my matron of honor, right?"

"Of course," Bonnie said. She might not have been wild about Marlon, but she loved her mother, and she wanted her to be happy.

Still, it was hard attending the impromptu shower Loretta's pals Estella and Nora held for her at Lucy's house. It seemed like all the women in Moonlight Harbor had made time to attend. Cynthia Redmond had provided party favors—small net bags filled with pink saltwater taffy she had left over from the candy store, which she had just sold.

"You're not leaving town are you, Cindy?" Pearl had asked her.

"Oh, no," their favorite candy pusher said. "Why would I ever want to leave Moonlight Harbor? We bought Flying Cats and I'll be busy running that."

"I'll be your best customer," Nora promised. "I love their handmade soaps."

Nora had also contributed to the treats, bringing a red velvet ice cream cake. Lucy had provided the champagne punch and asked Annie Albright to cater the affair, which she did with all manner of yummy little bites, ranging from mini shrimp quiches to crab salad tea sandwiches, and Jenna's sister Celeste had decorated, going crazy with everything from a vintage Kewpie doll in bride clothes as the refreshment table centerpiece to making an archway of balloons over the seat where they settled Loretta as guest of honor.

She was dolled up in red jeggings and a black sweater, accented with a red velvet scarf. She'd completed her outfit with a holiday charm bracelet and a big smile. She was happy, her friends were happy. Bonnie was...wearing her smile over gritted teeth. She needed to quit worrying. She was projecting her own experiences onto her mother.

"Speaking of leaving Moonlight Harbor, you're not, are you?" asked one of Loretta's church buddies.

"Oh, no. In fact, Marlon is looking forward to moving down here. Of course, he'll still have to do a lot of traveling back and forth for his business, but this will be his home base," Loretta said.

Home base, home run. Marlon had snagged himself a good one.

There she went again! Bonnie told herself to cut it out.

Celeste had a game for everyone called wedding Mad Libs, where she would ask guests for various nouns, verbs and adjectives to fill in blanks on wedding vows that would be read once all the blanks were filled in. "But they have to be beach words," Celeste said.

Every imaginable kind of word was thrown out and once Celeste collected all the necessary words she was ready to read. "If the groom was in town we'd make some vows for him, too," she said to Loretta before beginning, "but you'll have to suffer on your own."

Suffer on your own. Bonnie's fretting mind latched onto the phrase like a crab onto a rotting piece of chicken.

Celeste cleared her throat and began to read, "I, Loretta Mermaid, take you Marlon Tidal Wave," she began, and the others all snickered.

"He is a tidal wave," Loretta said. "That man swept me off my feet and knocked me head over teakettle."

"That's how love should be," said Pearl.

Bonnie wasn't so sure. Rance had knocked her head over teakettle, and she'd gotten scalded.

Celeste continued reading, getting snickers and giggles. "And I you with all my worldly clams endow," she finished.

Bonnie tried to ignore the image that popped in her mind of Marlon at the bank, emptying Loretta's account.

"I hope *he's* got plenty of clams," said Nora.

"The man is not lacking for money," Loretta told her. "You should see that fancy car he drives."

Bonnie hadn't. She'd left the restaurant before Marlon and her mom.

"What kind of car is it?" she asked.

"I don't know," Loretta said. "But it's got leather seats. And seat warmers."

"Well, there you go. He must be rich," Bonnie muttered, and her mother gave her The Look.

"I think you should read those vows for real, Glamma," Avril said.

"You silly girl," Loretta said fondly and beamed.

Her mother was so darned happy. How could Bonnie not be happy for her? She needed to quit filtering Loretta's romance through the lens of her bad love experience. It was unfair to both Loretta and Marlon.

"This has been such a wonderful party," Loretta said after she'd opened her last present. "Thank you all, so much."

"It's past time you got your happy ending," Nora said to her.

"Hear, hear," echoed Estella.

*Hear, hear*, thought Bonnie, and hoped Cupid and Santa were listening.

After the shower it was time to begin preparing for Christmas Day. Bonnie bought a ham as well as rolls from the bakery and the makings for the traditional green bean casserole. Avril promised to bring the eggnog and 7-Up for the eggnog punch and Loretta bought a turkey breast and baked a gorgeous layered cake with raspberry filling. Presents got piled under the tree in Loretta's condo where they'd be feasting on Christmas Day and Loretta hung mistletoe in every doorway, anticipating Marlon's arrival on the big day. They were ready.

Christmas Eve they were sitting at her dining table, playing a Christmas trivia game Loretta had found online and eating frosted sugar cookies when the call came. Bonnie could tell by her mother's happy expression that it was

Marlon. She could also tell by the deflated smile that he had bad news.

"Oh, no," Loretta said. "Marlon, I'm so sorry. Of course, I understand," she said, and Bonnie and Avril exchanged concerned looks. "Get back to your brother."

"What happened?" Avril asked.

"His sick brother has taken a turn for the worse," said Loretta.

The same sick brother who had messed up their Thanksgiving.

*Oh, real generous*, Bonnie scolded herself. The man was dealing with hard family issues. She could hardly hold that against him.

"So he's not coming down?" asked Avril.

Loretta shook her head.

"I'm sorry, Glamma," Avril said.

Loretta gave a little shrug. "These things happen."

They seemed to happen a lot where Marlon was concerned. This was the third time he'd promised to come down for something and hadn't. But Bonnie could hardly fault the man for wanting to be with his terminally ill brother. In fact, it showed a genuine nobility of character that Marlon would put his brother's needs over his own desire to spend the day having fun with his future bride and her family. Obviously, Bonnie had misjudged him, and she felt badly about it. She half wondered if some of her animosity came from a deep-seated Freudian resentment over the man who had secured a place in her mother's heart and life, one her father had once occupied.

Good grief, she hoped not. Not at her age, for crying out loud. But, taking an honest look at her attitude toward any of the men her mother dated, it did give her pause. Whatever the cause, she vowed right then to reject any further unwelcoming thoughts and to do her part to make Marlon feel like part of the family once he and Loretta were married.

"The poor man," Loretta said, teary-eyed. "He's close to his brother. This has got to be awful for him."

"Is his brother dying?" Avril asked.

Loretta nodded.

"If he's that bad maybe you two should postpone the wedding," Bonnie suggested. What if they were off honeymooning and his brother died?

Her mother looked ready to cry, but she nodded gamely and said, "Yes, maybe we should."

And suddenly no one was in the mood to play a game. They turned on the TV and streamed a mindless Christmas movie, then Avril left.

"Want me to stay?" Bonnie offered.

Loretta shook her head. "You go on home. I'll see you in the morning."

They walked together to the door and hugged. "I'm sorry, Mom," Bonnie said.

"This is life."

Yes, it was. One disappointment after the other.

"But we're not going to let it ruin our day tomorrow," Loretta said firmly. "We have each other, and we have presents to open and we have green bean casserole."

"And cake, which is even more important," Bonnie added.

"There you have it," Loretta said, and kissed her on the cheek. "Get a good night's sleep and we'll celebrate tomorrow."

"Cause the sun will come out tomorrow?" Bonnie teased.

"Bet your bottom dollar," Loretta replied with a wink.

That was her mom. It didn't matter whether she got

pushed off-kilter or knocked down completely, she always righted herself with a smile. Bonnie had come to realize how hard it was for her to find that smile sometimes, but she never stopped looking. She was the best. And she deserved the best. Bonnie hoped with all her heart that Marlon would give it to her.

Loretta was her usual sunny self on Christmas Day, oohing and aahing over the original design top and agate necklace Bonnie had purchased for her at Beach Babes and raving over the journal Avril had given her to her heart.

"So you can write about all your adventures," Avril said.

"It's such a thoughtful gift. Thank you," Loretta said, and hugged her.

She'd given Bonnie paints so she could keep painting her mermaid pictures, insisting Bonnie was going to be famous, and she'd given Avril a Betsy Johnson carry-on suitcase and purse. Bonnie had appreciated the thought behind the paints. Not so much the luggage.

Avril was thrilled, however. "You are the best, Glamma," she said.

"Anyone for more eggnog?" asked Bonnie.

They were sitting down to dinner when a huge floral arrangement arrived for Loretta. It was a mini tree, made of greens and red carnations and accented with pinecones sitting in a festive red sleigh.

"I bet I know who that's from," said Avril.

Loretta set it on one end of the kitchen bar and removed the card. "From Marlon," she bragged.

"He sure sends you a lot of flowers. He must be really rich," Avril said and joined her.

"It doesn't matter if he is or not," Loretta said. "When

it comes to men, a big heart is a lot more important than a big bank account."

Avril picked up the card and read, "Wish I could be with you." She smiled at Loretta. "Awww."

Marlon sure knew that the way to Loretta's heart was through the flower garden.

Loretta picked up her phone and punched in numbers. Marlon obviously hadn't answered as she started leaving a message. "Marlon, darling, I just wanted to thank you for that lovely Christmas arrangement. You made my day. I do hope you're making wonderful memories with your brother. I'll give you your present when you come down."

"How come you didn't mail it to him?" Avril asked.

Loretta's cheeks turned pink. "It's silly, really, but I don't have his address."

"You could look him up online," Avril said, pulling out her phone. "What's his last name?"

"Smith," said Loretta.

"In Seattle, right?" Avril asked, thumbing away on her phone.

"Yes, Seattle."

"There have to be hundreds of Smiths in Seattle," said Bonnie. Needle in a haystack.

Avril started scrolling, her brows furrowed. "Weird. I don't see a Marlon Smith."

"Well, his number's unlisted. He lives in The Highlands and that's a pretty exclusive neighborhood. I don't think those people list their addresses."

Pretty exclusive! There was an understatement equal to *Houston, we've got a problem.* "Mom, that is filled with ultrarich people," Bonnie said, shocked.

"Well, he does have some money," Loretta said, stymied over her daughter's surprise.

"That much?" Bonnie protested.

The Highlands was home to the out-of-sight rich families such as the Nordstroms and the Boeings. It was the first Bonnie had heard of this. When her mother had told her Marlon lived in Seattle she'd figured Ballard, Queen Anne, Capitol Hill, maybe Magnolia. But The Highlands...

What was someone who lived there doing with little, old Loretta Brinks who lived in a condo in Moonlight Harbor? And what was he doing looking for love on an internet dating site? People like that hired expensive matchmakers. People like that kept to their own kind. Bonnie's earlier suspicions came roaring back.

"Mom, you never told me," she said, trying to keep the panic out of her voice.

"He doesn't like to advertise it."

*Maybe because it isn't true.*

So, who was this man, actually? And how was she going to find out before her mother put on that bridal dress she'd ordered?

"It's been lovely to have you here," J.J.'s mom said as they refreshed their eggnog.

His two younger sisters had cleaned up the wrapping paper clutter and the dinner mess and then gone with their families back to the nearby motel where they were staying so the kids could work off their holiday sugar buzz in the pool. Now it was just him and Mom.

A relief, actually. Not that he didn't love Mary Catherine and Elizabeth, but they were always pestering him about his love life. Had he met anyone new? Had he tried a dating service? Elizabeth's husband had a new secretary who was single. California wasn't that far away. He could come stay with them. The nephews would love it.

He wouldn't. Her boys were spoiled brats who shot off their mouths to their mom with no consequences. "They're high-spirited," she liked to say. Was that what you called it these days? He'd never allowed his boys to talk to their mother like that.

The boys. He may have screwed up his marriage, but at least he hadn't screwed up his relationship with them.

They'd sent down presents for him: a whoopee cushion to use on their cousins, a package of Gummi Bears, some personalized golf tees, and a leather bracelet with silver beads bearing their names that would be his most valued possession. They'd all FaceTimed that morning, but it wasn't the same as being together.

"We'll get down to the beach come summer," Stephen promised.

J.J. had his doubts. Even though he'd bought his place with them in mind it would take something big to get his stepsons there.

"They'd come down for a wedding," said Mary Catherine with a wink. "Online dating..."

"Andrew's secretary," put in Elizabeth.

"Isn't it time for you to leave?" he'd grumped, and they'd laughed.

"Your life won't always be this way," Mom said now as they relaxed while Christmas carols played softly in the background.

"Yeah, I know," he said. He hoped she was right because he didn't want it to be.

"The New Year's right around the corner and who knows what that will bring."

The image of a certain gorgeous redhead sprang to mind. Yeah. Who knew?

\* \* \*

Marlon called Loretta the day after Christmas. "How was your day, my love?" he asked.

"It was lovely. The only thing keeping it from being perfect was not having you with us. But I do love that pretty floral arrangement."

"I'm glad. There's more coming. It should arrive today."

"Marlon, you are too good to me."

"Can't be good enough," he said.

"And now, how was your day with your brother?"

"It was hard to see him wasting away."

"We should postpone getting married."

"Oh, no, Loretta. I need you now more than ever."

"But what if he…dies?"

"He did rally yesterday, so we may have him for a while longer. Anyway, he and I talked. He doesn't want me to put my life on hold."

Loretta understood that. Those trips around the sun went by too quickly.

"Well, if you're sure," she said.

"I'm sure."

"Marlon, I was wondering." How to ask this? Bonnie and her suspicious mind—honestly!

"Wondering what?" he prompted.

"Bonnie was a little surprised to learn where you live."

"I don't brag about it," he said.

"She also wondered why you didn't hire some high-end service to help you find a wife."

"I tried that. The kind of women those services provide just want to be trophy wives. Or they're looking to expand their empires. I wanted someone who'd love me for myself, not my money."

Of course. That made perfect sense, and Loretta was sorry she'd even allowed so much as the tiniest dab of doubt to try and worm its way into her happiness.

"You needn't worry about me. I learned years ago that money isn't everything. And I'm too old to be a trophy wife."

"Never say that. You are a trophy I will proudly show off."

Loretta's doorbell rang. "There's someone at the door."

"It might be my gift. I'll hold."

She went to the door and, sure enough, there was an Amazon package propped next to it. "Ooh, I think it is," she said. She picked up the package, kicked the door shut and hurried for scissors to open it. Then, with the phone on speaker, she dug into the package. Out came a black lace chemise.

"Oh, Marlon, this is lovely."

"Thought you should have something special for our wedding night," he said. "I can hardly wait to see you in it."

"And I can hardly wait to show you." Thank heaven she'd stayed in shape all these years. Well, as in shape as possible. Nothing was as perky as it was when she was young, but Marlon was no young stud, either. A stud, but not young.

"I've got to go," he said suddenly. "Be down in plenty of time."

"All right. I love you, too," she said, but he was already gone. Oh, well. He knew how much she loved him.

She called her daughter and relayed their conversation about his choice of dating platform. Bonnie didn't have much to say after that. What could she say?

The big day of the wedding arrived. Loretta was all smiles and looked elegant in her pink lace sheath. And

Marlon looked ready for a *GQ* shoot. Bonnie could understand why her mother fell for him. She hoped desperately that she was wrong and that an even bigger and painful fall wasn't waiting in Loretta's future.

"You haven't found any proof that he's anything other than what he says he is," Lucy had told her after Bonnie's internet search had proved fruitless. "I think you're going to have to suck it up and smile through the day."

And so, at four in the afternoon, there she was, sucking and smiling.

Avril was smiling, too, as trusting as Loretta. Marlon had been all charm as they waited their turn before the judge. "Three generations of beauty," he'd said. "And all so talented. And Avril, I hear you're Nashville bound."

"I am," she said.

"From what your grandma tells me I'm sure you're going to make it big."

Of course, this was what both Avril and Loretta wanted to hear. Marlon could do no wrong.

Bonnie hoped he didn't do too much wrong with her mother's savings account before the real him emerged. If only she'd been able to solve the mystery of Marlon before this day.

The ceremony was short and efficient and afterward the bridal party went to Lucy and Brody's house for a buffet dinner. Lucy had invited some of Moonlight Harbor's favorite people to share in the festivities. Nora Singleton and her husband were present, along with Pearl Edwards and her special man and Jenna and Seth Waters, Estella and her husband, and Patricia Whiteside, who owned the Oyster Inn. She and Loretta often went out for coffee after their sessions at Waves Salon. The bigger celebration would take place later at The Drunken Sailor.

Of course, there were presents, the kind that came in envelopes and offered dinners out at local Moonlight Harbor restaurants.

"This is so kind of you all," Loretta said as the bunch filled their glasses and prepared to toast them.

"Live long and prosper," cracked Nora's husband.

"We intend to," Loretta said.

"I am one lucky man," Marlon said, and slipped an arm around her waist.

"Yes, you are," Bonnie said.

The party lasted until eight. Then it was time for the bride to change into her favorite green top and black leather pants and become a mermaid.

"Wow!" Marlon said, taking in her drummer chick look. "You could be on the cover of *Rolling Stone*."

"I could, but they haven't called yet," Loretta quipped.

"I can hardly wait to watch you ladies in action," he said as he followed her out the door.

Bonnie said nothing. She'd been watching Marlon in action all day, dishing out flattery, slapping backs, smiling a smile that struck her as cocky. The chorus of the old song "Smooth Operator" kept spooling over and over in her mind. There was something—she couldn't put her finger on it—that didn't ring true about the man and she was not looking forward to spending the whole evening with him, not to mention having him in their lives from then on.

They arrived at The Drunken Sailor to find a big CONGRATUATIONS LORETTA AND MARLON sign hanging over the door. All the regular patrons wanted to shake Marlon's hand and kiss the bride.

"You better be good to her," Pete said to the groom.

"I intend to," Marlon said, smiling at Loretta.

Maybe he really did. Maybe that smile was genuine. Maybe Santa really could fit down a chimney.

The band played their first set and when it was time for their break, Bonnie forced herself to smile and announced the happy news that her mother was now an old married lady.

"Forever young," Loretta called from her drum seat, correcting her.

"Yes, forever young," Bonnie said, and smiled at her. *Oh, Mom, I do want you to be happy.* "And now, it's time for the bride and groom to have their first dance. How about you two come out on the dance floor?"

Marlon came to the bandstand, took Loretta's hand and led her onto the dance floor to whistles and applause and Bonnie started strumming her guitar and serenading them with the old country classic, "May I Have This Dance?"

There were sighs from the ladies as he looked lovingly at Loretta and waltzed her around the dance floor.

Then there were gasps as a pudgy, middle-aged woman with dirty blond hair wearing jeans, Uggs, and a winter jacket stormed onto the dance floor. "Harvey Bickerstaff, take your hands off that woman!"

# Eight

Bonnie's stomach was suddenly filled with rocks. *Oh no. No, no, no!* This wasn't happening to her mother. This was worse than anything she'd imagined.

Marlon, Harvey, whatever his name was, froze, staring at the woman like she was the Grim Reaper coming after him, and Loretta stared at him, her eyes big as two blue softballs. Then, as if poked with a cattle prod, he gave a little leap and went hurrying over to the newcomer. Loretta followed him and Bonnie unstrapped her guitar and hurried after them. Avril was on her way, too, turning them into their own little parade.

He caught up to the woman at the edge of the dance floor, near a table where a couple were enjoying burgers and mini buckets of garlic fries. "Mitzi," he began.

"You…you…double dealing, rotten bag of shit," she ground out. Then, just as the rest of the parade arrived, she grabbed a glass of beer from the table.

"Hey!" protested the diner as she did so.

Too late. His beer was already running down Marlon's face.

"What are you doing to my husband?" Loretta cried.

Ignoring her, the invader picked up the woman's bucket of French fries and threw them at Marlon like a pitcher going for the third strike-out.

"My fries!" the woman protested and grabbed her plate before Mitzi the party crasher could throw her burger.

Marlon ducked and the fries went skittering across the dance floor.

"He's not *your* husband, he's *my* husband!" Mitzi snarled at Loretta. Her eyes were narrowed to slits and she looked like an angry computer-generated dragon, ready to breathe fire.

"What?" Loretta said weakly.

"We're married!" Mitzi informed her.

"That can't be," Avril protested. "They just got married today."

"What! You're a damned bigamist?" his wife screeched for all the patrons to hear.

That was when Loretta's eyelids fluttered and shuttered. She fell backward in a faint, right into the arms of Pete, who'd arrived barely in time to catch her.

Bonnie was ready to grab something and bean Marlon, too. "You're married?"

"Somebody call 9-1-1," hollered Pete.

"This is all a misunderstanding," Marlon began. He tried to reach for Mitzi's arm, probably to get her out of the pub and himself out of the spotlight.

"Oh, yeah?" She jerked it away and gave him an angry shove, making him stumble back a step. "I understood pretty damned good when we said "I do" in a church full of people and signed a wedding license. You, you…all those sales trips you had to take. All those times you offered to walk the dog. You were with her or calling her! On your business phone," she spat. The woman only had a small purse slung over her shoulder, but she freed it and whacked him with it anyway, calling him a fresh name with each new hit.

"Mitzi, please, I can explain," he said, holding up his hands to ward off attack.

"You mean he doesn't own his own company?" Avril asked in shock. "He doesn't live in The Highlands?"

The woman stopped whacking long enough to turn her angry glare on Avril. "What? We live in Bremerton and he's a bloody salesman." She whirled back on Marlon.

He'd sure done a good job of selling himself to Loretta. "What had you planned to do, milk my mother dry?" Bonnie demanded. He'd have probably drained Loretta's savings, sold her small amount of stocks and moved on. But not before he'd enjoyed many a mini vacation (free sex included) at the beach.

"I finally got smart and borrowed money from Mama and hired someone to follow you. And now I find you doing—" whack, whack "—this, you rat bastard, you!" Whack, whack, whack. "I'm going to kill you!" That was the end of the speech. The purse wasn't doing its job well enough so Mitzi reached out for his throat.

"Baby, wait," Marlon said, stumbling over Loretta as he backed away. "It didn't mean a thing."

Loretta had revived in time to hear this and, with a groan, she passed out again.

"I'll help you kill him," Bonnie growled, advancing on Marlon along with Mitzi.

Moonlight Harbor's finest arrived just in time to stop them—handsome Victor King and his middle-aged partner, stubby Frank Stubbs, their leather gun holsters creaking.

Then came the medics to make sure Loretta hadn't had a heart attack.

Meanwhile, out-of-towners were happily aiming their phones and recording the whole mess.

Lee, the pub's owner, led "Marlon" and Mitzi and the police back to his office where they could sort out their mess in private. Too late for that.

Bonnie stayed with her mother, hovering as the medics checked her vital signs. She'd revived again and now was crying, her eyeliner running down her cheeks. She suddenly looked old. And broken.

Bonnie couldn't reach her with the medics working on her but, in between questions, managed to get in an, "It'll be okay, Mom."

Loretta shook her head and kept crying.

"I should'a decked him," muttered Pete, who was also hovering.

"I'm okay now, really," Loretta said between tears.

"She just had a shock," Bonnie explained. More than that. She'd just endured an emotional earthquake. Marlon the tidal wave had struck.

Loretta gave a giant sniff and Pete raced to the same table with the diners Mitzi had robbed of their food and grabbed a napkin, muttering, "Sorry," to the goggle-eyed pair, then returned and handed it to Loretta.

"Thank you," she managed and blew her nose. Then started to get up.

"Just lie still," cautioned the paramedic.

"I don't have time to lie still," Loretta informed him. "I have to find my husband, the bigamist." Then she was off and running while the shocked medics gaped at each other.

Bonnie and Avril fell in step with her, Pete shadowing them. "I'm so sorry, Glamma," Avril said.

"Not half as sorry as he's going to be," Loretta said, the light of battle in her eyes.

"So, are you guys even married?" Avril asked, and Bonnie shot her a warning look. This was hardly the time to bring that up.

"Of course not," said Loretta. "If we were, after what I'm about to do to him, I'd be a widow. Again."

"Mom, calm down," Bonnie cautioned.

"Calm down? Calm down? I just got married! To Harvey Bickerstaff!"

"Dirty rotter," said Pete.

The regulars called out as they passed, "Sue him, Loretta!"... "Get him locked up!"... "We love you, Loretta!"

"I'll marry you, Loretta!" called out a geezer who looked even older and scruffier than Pete.

Bonnie knocked on the office door and they were admitted...all except Pete, who Frank told to stick around to give his statement as a witness. As if they were lacking for witnesses. Everyone in The Drunken Sailor had seen what happened.

They were barely in before Loretta marched up to Marlon and pulled back her hand, winding up to slap him in the face. Right in front of Victor and Frank. Assault. Great.

"Whoa, now," said Victor, catching her hand before she made contact. "Let's not do anything we'll regret."

"I already did!" Loretta cried.

"Me, too," said Mitzi. "I want him in jail!"

So, it appeared, did the police, informing him that he was under arrest.

"Arrest!" he protested.

"Fraud is a felony, sir," Victor informed him.

"Oh, Marlon, did you mean anything you said to me?" Loretta asked as they led him toward the door.

"Of course I did," he said. Slimy creep.

"What *did* you say to her?" Mitzi demanded.

Marlon exercised his right to remain silent.

"And your brother," Loretta began.

Mitzi's eyes got big then narrowed back to dragon slits. "Brother? He doesn't have a brother. All he has is a dead-beat sister."

Loretta shook her head, fresh tears trickling down her cheeks. "I must have looked like such easy pickings."

"Who else have you married?" his wife demanded, following them out.

"There's more of us?" squeaked Loretta.

Marlon still said nothing, leaving the answer to his first wife's question a mystery. Bonnie was willing to bet there were others somewhere. In the Highlands. Not.

The slime. She wished Victor and Frank had allowed her mother to slap him. She put an arm around Loretta and hugged her.

"Happy New Year," Loretta said and managed half a smile before the tears took over.

Of course, it was anything but happy. Loretta was champagne that had lost its bubbles.

She wanted to be left alone the next day. "I need to begin the new year thinking about my life," she said.

It was something Bonnie could understand and identify with.

Avril and Kenny had plans for the day. So did everyone in Moonlight Harbor, naturally. Bonnie ate a late breakfast of toast and coffee, then tried to paint. That only worked for so long before she found herself feeling restless.

It was impossible to get what had happened to her mother out of her mind. Did the poor woman have a cosmic Kick Me sign on her back? Being widowed had been a huge blow. Being betrayed seemed almost worse to Bonnie and she worried that, this time, Loretta wouldn't be able to get her mojo back.

She stood in front of the sliding glass door and watched the wind beat up on the water of the canal. Troubled waters, so symbolic of what their New Year's weekend had turned into.

One of her mother's favorite songs was the old Simon and Garfunkel classic, "Bridge Over Troubled Water." Bonnie wished there was a way she could be that bridge for her.

It seemed that her guitar, which was sitting in the corner, was calling to her.

She picked it up and started to strum. Then she got inspired and grabbed her iPad and began to note down some lyrics.

> I know you got your heart broke, I know right now it's bad.
> But don't you let him win by shedding tears, don't let him see you sad.
> There's more to you than he ever saw, than a man like him deserves,
> So keep on walkin' down the road, something good's around the curve.

She stopped strumming. Where was she going with this? She strummed some more and let her mind wander back through her own life. And then she had the chorus.

> Not every princess needs a prince, a prince can be a pain.
> You still got your crown, and the sun will shine again.
> Keep on glowin', keep on goin', don't let him steal your song.
> Save it for the day some lucky king will come along.

She smiled. She'd finish the song and play it for her mom at The Drunken Sailor. And make everyone join in on the chorus.

She worked on finishing it in between helping Loretta fill out paperwork and make phone calls that week. She accompanied her mother to the courthouse to get her fake marriage annulled, and, most important, spent hours helping Loretta mentally sift through the detritus of the disastrous relationship.

"I was such fool," Loretta said as they sat in her living room, watching the unrelenting waves crash against the shore. "How could I have been so gullible?"

*Easily*, thought Bonnie. She'd been as trusting, herself, once upon a heartbreak.

"What were the odds?" she said in an effort to make Loretta feel better. She hadn't liked Marlon, but she'd never imaged he'd turn out to be a bigamist.

"Whatever they were, they weren't in my favor," Loretta said and sighed. "Ah, well, maybe I'm supposed to learn to be content just as I am." Her lower lip wobbled a bit, but she pressed it into submission.

Bonnie wished she knew what to say to that. She wanted her mother to be happy, felt badly that Loretta, who was such a romantic, wasn't getting her storybook ending. "I'm sorry, Mom," was all she could manage.

She finished the song and played it on Saturday night. The regulars were happy to sing along and give Loretta hugs and encouragement.

"That was so sweet of you," Loretta said to her after she'd announced the band was taking a quick break.

"Except Mom got it wrong," said Avril. "You're not a princess, Glamma, you're a queen."

"Thank you, darling," Loretta said, and hugged her. "I

sure feel like the queen of the losers," she said to Bonnie as Avril went to join her boyfriend, who was already waiting with her drink at the band table.

"You're not. The loser is Harvey Bickerstaff."

Loretta chewed on her bottom lip. "Do you think I'm becoming a naive old woman?"

"What? No. This could happen to anyone," Bonnie said, and added, "At any age."

"Well, I'm done being so foolish. No more online dating for me," Loretta said. "In fact, no more men."

Bonnie was sure Loretta would change her mind about finding a man, but she hoped that her mom meant what she said about the online dating. Too risky.

Still, lots of people found their soul mates online. It was all wrong that Loretta hadn't. She'd gone fishing for a nice man to spend the rest of her life with and instead she'd reeled in a troll. She deserved to find a man who would love and appreciate her.

Pete stopped by the band table to tell Loretta she looked darn good for a woman who'd just had the shit kicked out of her.

"Thank you," she said, her voice wooden.

He sat down next to her. "Loretta you are one fine woman, and you didn't deserve that."

She sure didn't. For the hundredth time Bonnie kicked herself for not meddling more, being a bigger wet blanket.

After her mother had mentioned Marlon-Harvey's supposed neighborhood Bonnie had done her own online search for Marlon Smith but had come up with nothing other than a link to an obituary for a Marlon Smith, a farmer in Idaho. Who knew? Maybe that was where the fake Marlon had found his name. She should have done what the weasley imposter's wife had done and hired a private detective.

Should have, would have, could have. She wanted to cry. She'd let her mother down.

"She's lucky he was found out when he was," Brody had said to Bonnie. "I'm sure he had every intention of draining your mom's assets. God only knows how many other women that con artist has taken for a ride."

Sadly, Harvey had taken something from Loretta that was far more valuable than her money. He'd taken her joy. If only one of the local men, like Pete, had what was needed to restore that joy, Bonnie thought, watching him doing his best to console her mom. Sadly, they didn't.

Pete rubbed his scruffy chin, cleared his throat. "How about you let me take you to the Fish Shack for lunch tomorrow? That popcorn shrimp will cheer you right up."

Good, old Pete. He wasn't much, but he wasn't a fake.

"Pete, I'm not interested in doing anything with any man ever again," Loretta said sourly. "Right now I hate the whole lot of you."

His head snapped back as if she'd slapped him. "Whoa, now, we're not all bad."

"No, only the ones I pick," Loretta grumbled.

"She needs some time," Bonnie said to him, and he nodded and vacated his seat.

Another one of Bonnie's fans was approaching. Pete shook his head and said, "Don't bother. She's a man-hater now."

"Maybe you should get together with Pete. He likes you, Glamma," said Avril.

Loretta shook her head. "I'm done, darling." She looked at Kenny, who'd been watching her exchange with Pete goggle-eyed. "A good man is a rare find. Remember that."

"Like me," Kenny said and gave one of Avril's long dark curls a playful tug.

"At least I still have you girls," Loretta continued. "And I'm still a Mermaid," she added.

"And a pretty hot one you are," Bonnie said. Thank God they had the band.

Loretta's only response to her daughter's compliment was a bitter snort.

"It's true, Glamma," said Avril. "You could be on the cover of *Rolling Stone*."

"Or featured on one of those true crime shows," Loretta grumbled.

"The people on those are usually dead and you're not," pointed out Bonnie. "Come on, Mermaids. Break time's over."

Okay, so she was cutting their break a few minutes short, but her mom needed a distraction.

During their second set Loretta about banged the skin off her drums, and when Pete came up to make his usual request that the band play "Crazy" she answered for Bonnie with an emphatic, "No."

"Okay, okay," he said. "Don't hit me with one of those drumsticks."

"Then you'd better move away," Loretta snarled.

"Uh, Mom," Bonnie said.

Loretta waved away the coming scold. "I know, I know. Give 'em what they want. But not tonight. They'll take what they get and like it."

Happily for The Mermaids, their fans did take what they gave them and loved it. Several women gave Loretta a thumbs-up when the band sang the Carrie Underwood classic, "Before He Cheats." Bonnie suspected if anyone had discovered Marlon-Harvey's car there would have been some serious anonymous damage done.

They'd just gotten their drinks and settled down for their last fifteen-minute break of the night when Lee, the owner of The Drunken Sailor, joined them. "Good crowd tonight, ladies."

"Yes, everyone wanted to be here to see what new drama might unfold," Loretta said sourly and took a draw on her tonic water.

"Loretta, I'm sure sorry that happened to you," he said. "You didn't deserve it."

She shrugged and took another drink.

"Good thing for him the cops took him away," Lee said. "I think if they hadn't he'd have been hauled out back and had the crap beaten out of him. We all love you, Loretta."

"Thank you," she said.

Lee cleared his throat and continued. "On another note, I wanted to give you ladies a heads-up. I've sold the place."

Loretta choked on her drink and Bonnie stared at him.

"So we're done playing here?" Avril asked, sounding shocked.

"No, no. Don't worry," he said. "It should be a smooth transition. You're the house band. I doubt it will affect you at all. J.J. knows a good deal when he sees one."

"J.J.," Bonnie repeated.

"You met him. He's a good friend of mine. He's been here a couple times."

Bonnie remembered. The image of a sexy, well-built man with hair almost as red as hers in jeans and a shirt as white as his teeth sprang to mind. The same man she'd met coming out of Beach Dream Homes Realty. The new business was…oh, no. Mr. Yuck had bought The Drunken Sailor. Of all the gin joints in all the world…

She nodded, not saying anything, trying to ignore the sudden buzzing of her hormones.

"Lee, I didn't know you were planning to sell," Loretta said.

"Well, the wife wants to see more of me, wants to travel. She's got family in Montana and our son in California just had his second kid."

"Family is important," Loretta said diplomatically.

"Anyway, like I said, it should be a smooth transition," Lee assured them.

"Thanks for letting us know," Bonnie said.

"Didn't want you to hear it through the grapevine," he told her.

Normally that would have prompted Loretta to start singing the chorus of the old Motown song, "Heard It Through the Grapevine."

"A song for every occasion," she used to quip. There was no quipping this night. Harvey the heart wrecker had drained the zest from Loretta's cup, right down to the last drop.

She did manage a polite response, however. "I'm glad you're going on to a new adventure, Lee. Life's short and you don't want miss out on anything."

Like Loretta just had. Bonnie sighed inwardly. Men like Harvey Bickerstaff should be fed to the sharks.

So should men like J.J. Walker, the new owner of The Drunken Sailor, Bonnie decided come the end of the month when the man sat down with her on Saturday night after the place had shut down for the night. He'd left her unsettled from their very first encounter, and having him around so much since he became the pub's proud owner, left her feeling unsettled and…stirred up. This night was no different.

He'd just handed over the band's pay for the weekend and she was about to leave and divvy it up with her mother and daughter when he dropped the bombshell. Slowly. He started out by saying, "Nice job tonight."

"Thanks," she'd said. "We work hard." Why had she felt the need to tell him that?

"It shows." His smile faltered. "And I hope I can use you in the future."

Use them in the future? What was that supposed to mean? "As in?" she prompted.

"I should have told you earlier. I have another band lined up for February."

"Lee led me to believe we'd still be the house band."

"I wish he hadn't."

She nodded slowly. "I see."

"It's not like that," he began.

She held up a hand, cutting him off. "No need to explain."

"No, I want to."

She stood. "It stands to reason. New management."

"It's not really like that. I have a friend who has a band."

A likely story. "Of course," she murmured.

Her cynicism must have bled through because he tried a half smile and an, "Are you always so suspicious?"

Yes, and it seemed every time she turned around someone was proving her right to be that way. She bobbed her head. "Only of people I don't know."

"Hey, it's not my fault you don't know me. I tried to get to know you the first couple of times I came down here."

Aww, hurt feelings. Wasn't he the sensitive little soul?

"I guess you did. Too bad I wasn't in the market for new friends."

"Yeah, too bad." He sounded more offended than regretful.

"So good luck with the new band. The Mermaids will swim off to better waters," she said. It could have been a cute parting remark, but it came out sounding snippy. She was tired and now she was frustrated and worried that losing their gig would be yet another disappointment for Loretta. So let there be snip.

He gave a snort of disgust. "Don't let the door hit you in the tail on your way out."

What a jerk. She wouldn't come back and play at his place for all the money in Moonlight Harbor.

"No, wait, I'm sorry," he said.

"You might just be," she told him, and walked away, anger putting an extra briskness in her step.

"What's wrong?" Loretta asked when Bonnie returned to give them their money.

"We're done here," Bonnie said. "New owner, new band coming in to play next month."

Avril gaped in surprise. So did Loretta. Then the happy expression she'd only recently found got lost again and Bonnie wished she could feed J.J. Walker to the sharks right along with Harvey Bickerstaff.

For a woman with such soft curves Bonnie Brinks sure had some hard edges. She hadn't even let him explain.

He frowned as he watched her storm out of the pub, her mother and daughter trailing after her. It was a wonder she didn't walk with a limp considering the size of that chip she was carrying on her shoulder. He wondered what had happened to make such a sweet-looking angel-voiced woman so sour.

He'd probably never know. Maybe he didn't want to

know. Maybe he'd go find himself a woman who was more mellow, who'd give a guy a chance to explain, dig himself out of the hole he'd dug and fallen into.

Except he didn't want another woman. He wanted Bonnie, wanted to get to know her, wanted to find the secret to turning that stop sign smile to a green light. He wanted to be able to make her laugh like he'd seen her do with some of the regulars. She'd gotten under his skin and he itched to get her out of there and into his arms.

"Let her go," he advised himself. That woman would be more trouble than she was worth.

Except, deep down he didn't think she was.

"Guess you pissed her off good," called Madison, as she stepped behind the bar, purse in hand and her coat over her arm.

"It's a gift," he called back.

He finished the last chores of shutting down for the night, flipped on the closed sign, locked the door and walked to his car. Went home, went to bed and wondered if and how he was going to be able to see that mermaid again.

# *Nine*

"I guess The Mermaids are done," Avril said.

"They're done here, that's for sure," said her mom. She looked ready to garrote the new owner with a guitar string.

"I don't get it. We pack the place every weekend," said Glamma.

"The new manager has a friend who has a band," Mom explained.

"It pays to have friends," Glamma said. She was trying to sound up, but Avril could see the disappointment on her face. Poor Glamma. She loved playing her drums.

"We had a good run here," Mom said.

Now the run ended. The Mermaids getting tossed was a sign. Avril was doing the right thing. It was time to move on. And move away.

Gina confirmed it when Avril called to tell her the news the next morning. "It's just as well. You've got a new life waiting here."

"Truth."

"And at least with the band gig over your mom won't be able to guilt you about leaving."

"She'll probably find some way," Avril said.

"Once you're here you won't look back."

The thought that had been haunting Avril for weeks popped out of her mouth. "Except what about Kenny?"

"I don't know. How's that gonna work with you here and him back there?"

Avril wasn't sure. "I can be there part-time and here part-time."

"Good luck with that," said Gina. "If you're gonna be involved in the music scene people expect you to live here."

"Then he'll move to Nashville." And leave his boat, his business, his family, everything he loved to chase her dream. He'd do it. He loved her. But it was asking a lot.

"How's he going to fit in down here?"

"He loves music."

"Yeah, but he doesn't make it. And what about his boat? His family business?"

"He'd give it up for me. And there is fishing down there. I saw a website offering charters for fishing on Percy Priest Lake."

"You think that's gonna cut it?"

She was about to answer yes when Gina continued. "I could be wrong, but I think he'll end up feeling pushed out here. It's either tech or music and neither one of those is really him. All of us who came here for the music live it and breathe it—writing sessions that go late into the night and showcases. Making connections. And if you do start to make it there's traveling and playing county fairs. It's all-consuming."

Avril enjoyed performing, but her real love was songwriting. You didn't have to travel to do that.

"I'm glad I'm not with anyone right now. I don't have time," Gina continued. "You're not gonna either and if Kenny doesn't become dead weight he'll feel like it."

"Gee, thanks for the encouragement." This was not what Avril wanted to hear.

"Just keepin' it real. I get that Kenny's a great guy and you two are crazy about each other."

"We are."

"Hey, I could be wrong. Maybe you guys can make it work."

"We can," Avril insisted.

Except was it fair to Kenny? Was she being selfish to ask him to give up so much of himself, to toss aside his life to follow her dream?

What did they most have in common? The beach.

There was no beach in Nashville.

She sighed. Kenny would be over later. Suddenly she wasn't looking forward to seeing him because she knew what she had to do.

He arrived at his usual time with take-out pizza and a six-pack of Coke. She'd made peanut butter cookies, his favorite. The plan had been to eat pizza and stream movies. It was their own little tradition, and Avril was going to end it. To end them.

On seeing his round smiling face and that scruffy brown beard he was growing her heart gave a squeeze. Kenny was the best beach treasure she'd ever found, and she was going to break up with him. What was she thinking?

That it was the right thing to do, of course. It was time.

"Hey there, Mermaid," he said, like he always did.

Mermaid, his nickname for her. Except The Mermaids had lost their gig and soon she wouldn't be one at all.

He stooped and gave her a smacking kiss on the lips, then moved to her little living room and set the eats on the coffee table. She followed him, trying to find a way to ease into the conversation.

He was already flipping open the box. He grabbed a piece and took a bite, smiled at her, said around a mouthful, "It's getting cold. Grab the plates."

She pulled a couple of plates from the cupboard, brought them over and set them on the coffee table. Picked up a can and popped the tab. Set the can down.

"What's wrong?" he asked.

"The Mermaids got fired," she said and dropped onto the couch.

He sat down next to her, his weight making the cushions bounce like choppy seas. He took another giant bite of pizza and plopped the last third on a plate. "That's nuts. Why?"

"The new manager wants to bring in a different band."

"He's nuts. You guys are what half of the town goes there for."

Avril shrugged. "It's always done good. But this is a sign."

His eyebrows pulled together, carving worry lines on his forehead. He set the plate back on the coffee table. "A sign of what?"

*Now or never.* "That it's time to move on."

His face relaxed. "Oh, yeah. Nashville."

"Not just Nashville." This was so hard to come right out and say.

He looked at her, puzzled, shook his head. "What are you getting at?"

"Us. We need to break up." She was doing the smart thing. But she felt sick.

He looked like she'd just told him his fishing boat had sunk. "What?"

"I'm sorry, Kenny. I don't know what the future holds."

"I thought we talked about that, had it all settled."

"Not in a way that makes any sense. You're a sea dude and I'm about to be landlocked. Kenny, we're going different directions. This isn't gonna work." The words were out but they left behind a trail of something slimy. The sick feeling worsened.

He shook his head, his brows so close together it was as if he had a unibrow. "You're breaking up with me," he said in disbelief.

"It's for the best," she said. "Please, try to understand."

"I understand all right," he said bitterly. "I don't cut it. Now that you're gonna be a big star you're too good for me."

"What? No! I didn't say that."

"You don't need to." He stood so suddenly he banged into the coffee table, spilling his can of pop and creating a brown pool on the wood. "Shit," he muttered. He righted the can and started for the kitchen.

"I'll clean it up," she said.

He ignored her, grabbed the towel hanging from the oven handle and returned and silently started mopping it up.

"Kenny, please, don't," she begged. There he was, cleaning up her mess.

He finished in silence, went to the closet that housed her washer and dryer and put the dirty dish towel in the washer. Then he came back down the hall, took his keys from the mermaid key holder hanging by the door—the one he'd bought her for her birthday—and left without so much as a good-bye, kiss my ass or I hate you.

Of course he hated her. He had to because she sure hated herself. She flopped down, buried her head in a sofa pillow and sobbed. She couldn't keep him waiting forever. This was the right thing to do. But it felt wrong. All wrong.

*A good man is a rare find*, her grandmother had said. She'd just put her rare find on a boat and cut the moorings.

She had to. She'd done the right thing.

Still, when her phone dinged with a text an hour later she jumped for it.

You had to do what you had to do but I'll always love you.

"Oh, my gosh, he just made a rhyme. Did he even know it?" she said to the empty room.

He'd probably been thinking all the way home how to respond to her. Kenny was a man who considered his words. He knew the power of them.

Another text came in. You mean more to me than any pearl in the sea. If you change your mind I'll be waiting. Always.

Another little rhyme coupled with a big, noble sentiment. She was the shit princess. She tossed aside her phone and grabbed for the drenched sofa pillow again.

"What's wrong with me?" she asked Gina later that night when she called her friend for a girlfriend shrink session.

"Nothing Nashville can't cure," Gina said. "You need to be free. Anyway, there's lots of cute guys down here."

Colton Gray's face sprang to mind. One of those sexy blue eyes winked at her. She blinked.

"I don't need to be looking for a replacement for Kenny," she said to both Gina and herself.

"You'll be looking to replace everything. It's gonna be a whole new life."

A whole new life. The words were seductive. They pulled her away from her guilt and her unhappiness and the emptiness she'd felt after Kenny left, lulling her into a dreamless sleep. She awoke the next morning, her very real dreams waiting to greet her. She'd done the right thing.

Loretta felt like someone had shined a spotlight on her as she walked into Waves Salon. She wasn't friends with any of the women in there, getting their nails done and their hair cut, but some of the faces looked familiar—it was, after all, a small town—and she knew that they knew who she was. She could tell by the way one middle-aged woman in Moira's chair stared at her, by the way the new hire, Stephanie, looked at her as pityingly as did the old woman whose hair she was cutting. She suddenly knew how celebrities felt when every bad thing in their lives became fodder for the tabloids and the internet.

Except she wasn't a celebrity, and she wasn't suffering just so someone else could be entertained. If she didn't need a cut and color so badly she'd have turned tail and run.

"Be with you momentarily," called Moira, who always loved using the biggest word she could find to fit the moment.

"I'm in no hurry," Loretta called back. Except she suddenly was. She wanted to get out of there, go back to her condo and binge-watch the old TV series *Nashville*.

Moira finished painting purples and pinks on the woman's hair, moved her to a different chair for the color to take and summoned Loretta over.

"Same color and cut?" Moira checked and Loretta nodded. "Okay, I'll get your color ready and be right back."

Another woman had come into the salon, and she settled in to wait her turn and tuned in to the Loretta channel. Loretta tried not to squirm.

Moira returned and got to work. "I heard what happened to you. I'm sorry."

"Everyone's heard," Loretta said. "Guess I won't be getting any chocolates for Valentine's Day." She sounded like a bitter, old woman. How disgusting.

"I didn't hear it from Victor," Moira was quick to say, referring to her husband, Victor King, one of the officers who had showed up at The Drunken Sailor on that fateful night.

"Of course not," Loretta said. "I know Victor's too noble to gossip."

In the mirror she caught sight of Moira's other client, whose face was suddenly looking as pink as the color Moira had applied to it. The woman had been watching them, listening to their conversation, but suddenly became very busy with her phone. She was probably passing the news to all her friends. *You'll never guess who's in here. That dumb woman who married the bigamist.*

Loretta wanted to stand up and shriek, "Stop staring at me!" But that would do no good. She was the current roadside wreck. People couldn't help but look.

"I'm glad you got out before he could hurt you anymore," Moira said simply.

Before meeting her husband, Moira had come out of a relationship that had been both verbally and physically abusive. Even though she'd worked hard to build a good life in Moonlight Harbor and had wound up with a very good man she hadn't forgotten the pain of love mistreated.

'You're right, of course. At least I escaped with my bank account intact." If not her heart or her pride. "I should have known better. There were enough clues that something was off with him." If only she'd been willing to look at them.

"Hey, you're not a detective."

"Even Inspector Clouseau could have seen these."

"Who?" asked Moira.

"Never mind," Loretta said. "Good Lord, I feel old." *You are old. An old fool.*

"Well, you're not. You're young on the inside and that's what counts," Moira said firmly. "I'm glad you escaped that tool. Now you'll be ready for when someone better comes along."

"I'm not holding my breath," Loretta said. She sounded as cynical as her daughter.

A new thought occurred. Watching her tumble over the cliff had probably cemented Bonnie's cynicism about love. She'd be more determined than ever to keep her heart closed off to any possibilities.

Loretta sighed inwardly. It was shocking how much a woman's decisions rippled out to affect others. "I could have my own reality TV show: *Loretta by the Sea.*"

"It could happen to anyone," Moira said.

Loretta doubted it.

"Anyway, it's not about what shit gets thrown at us. It's about what we do with it," Moira continued. "You never let the bad stuff get to you and that's inspiring."

Inspiring. She hadn't been very inspiring lately. She'd been nothing but a Debbie Downer, the kind of cranky, sad old woman nobody wanted to be around. Heck, she hadn't even wanted to be around herself.

But Moira's words gave her pause. She could either be an inspiration or a pathetic loser. Losing was a temporary experience, not a chronic condition. Maybe it was time she picked herself up, dusted off her bottom and got back into life.

She called her daughter later.

The first words out of Bonnie's mouth were, "How are you doing?"

"I'm doing fine. I may have been down, but I wasn't down for the count. Let's go out Friday."

"Okay. Where?"

"To The Drunken Sailor. The new band starts this week-end, doesn't it?"

Bonnie let out a disgusted grunt. "What are we, mas-ochists?"

"Maybe. I'm curious to see what band could possibly be better than us."

"A lot of bands, Mom. But okay, fine. It's not like I've got anywhere else to go."

Or anyone to go with. Her daughter was a beautiful, in-telligent woman. She didn't deserve to be alone.

*Neither do I*, thought Loretta. Sometimes it didn't seem fair that she'd lost her husband when he was only middle-aged. It certainly didn't seem fair that she'd fallen prey to an imposter pretending to be a decent human being. But then, as she'd said to both her daughter and granddaughter many times, life wasn't fair.

A woman could still rise above that though and find a way to make it good if she chose. Loretta was going to prove it—to her daughter, her friends, to those gawkers in the salon and, most of all, to herself.

"We should have gone to a movie," Bonnie said to her mother as they settled in at a table at 8:30. Why were they torturing themselves like this?

"I think the show here will be much better," Loretta said.

It seemed to Bonnie that they were the show. Heads had turned when they walked in. Loretta's true crime experi-ence was the hottest thing to hit Moonlight Harbor since the epic Seaside with Santa storm and power outage. At least Harvey had only been a bigamist and not a serial killer.

Her mother was still with her and not on posters all over town with the heading HAVE YOU SEEN THIS WOMAN?

The place smelled the same, like grilling beef and frying potatoes. Voices were loud at a couple tables where the patrons were on their third beers.

Their server, a girl named Cara, arrived to take their orders. Bonnie noticed she was having a hard time looking them in the eye. "What would you like?" she asked.

"Mud pie," said Loretta. "And coffee."

"Same for me," Bonnie said, and the girl bobbed her head and hurried away.

"Funny how I used to love walking in here," Bonnie mused.

"I know. Now it feels more like walking the plank," Loretta said. "But I don't care I'll take plank walking over sitting home and moping. I'm done doing that and I want all of Moonlight Harbor to know it."

Bonnie studied her mother. Loretta was wearing a scoop neck black top over her jeans. Her hair was freshly cut and dyed, the green tips more intensely green than usual. She'd put on her reddest lipstick and rhinestone drop earrings dangled from her ears. She looked like a movie star, no longer young but still attractive enough to inspire admiration. And Bonnie had to admire her. Loretta was stepping over a pile of shattered dreams and moving forward with courage and determination. With her spangles and foxy hair she was a warrior suited up for battle with life.

"I think they will. You look amazing," Bonnie said.

Loretta stopped tapping her fingers on her water glass. "I do?"

"You do. Have I told you recently how proud I am of you?"

Loretta smiled at that. "Daughter dear, you just made my night."

"Glad to be of service. I'm not just saying that though. I mean it. What you've gone through would have about killed most women."

"I doubt it. Bad things happen," Loretta said. "But so do good things."

"I'll drink to that," said Bonnie, and they both picked up their water glasses and saluted each other.

Loretta took a sip, then put hers down and looked around. Someone must have waved at her because she smiled and wiggled her fingers.

"One of your admirers?" Bonnie teased.

"They are legion," Loretta said with a grin. She moved her gaze a different direction and her lips flattened to a straight line. "Here comes the band," she said.

Bonnie turned and watched as four men slouched in, wearing jeans and tennis shoes or army boots, their jackets sparkling with raindrops that had hitched a ride inside. One was tall and skinny with a long basset hound face and dark thinning hair. He walked ahead of the others, carrying a guitar case. The next man after him was bearing part of a drum kit. Obviously, the drummer. It looked like he was hiding a beer belly under his jacket. The third band member also had a guitar case and a shaved head meant to hide a runaway hairline. He was nice looking in a Vin Diesel sort of way. The last carried a long skinny case and was obviously the bass player. He was short and thick and wore glasses. All of them looked to be edging toward their fifties. Weekend warriors as the saying went. Probably a bunch of guys who'd all been in bands when they were in high school and wanted to relive the dream.

Bonnie couldn't blame them. Making music was a high no musician ever wanted to give up.

"They don't look half as good as we do," Loretta observed.

"For a crowd like this looks don't matter as long as they can give people what they want."

Loretta harrumphed.

Cara arrived with their pies and drinks. "It's on the house," she said.

Bonnie caught sight of J.J. Walker over by the bandstand, shaking hands with the tall musician who she'd suspected was the band leader. They talked for a moment, standing with their hands propped on their pockets. J.J. said something and the guy smiled and gave his shoulder a friendly bump with his fist. It paid to have friends. Look what it got you. A gig…and a free slice of pie.

"Thanks but bring us the check," Bonnie said to Cara and gave her piece a vicious stab with her fork.

"Now, why'd you do that?" Loretta protested after the girl left.

"I'm not taking anything from that man," Bonnie informed her.

"Suit yourself, but you're picking up the tab then," Loretta said.

They watched as the band came in and out with the rest of their equipment and started setting up. Other people were watching, too. Okay, this felt weird.

"Hurry up and finish your pie and let's go," Bonnie urged.

"What's your hurry? Have you got a hot date?" Loretta retorted.

"This is awkward."

"I want to hear what they sound like. Just a couple of songs and then we'll leave."

"Unless they're really good. Then I'm gone on the first verse," Bonnie said. "Because I'm not a masochist."

"Enjoy your pie," Loretta suggested.

Enjoy it? She was probably going to choke on it.

J.J. started walking their way. Looking at him brought an uninvited sizzle to her chest. "Oh, great, look who's coming," she said cynically.

Loretta knew without even looking. "Put on your big girl panties and smile."

Bonnie didn't want to, but she knew her mother was right. She needed to make up for her less than businesslike behavior when she and the new owner had parted. His not offering them a contract to play at his establishment had been no reflection on them. But her behavior had been, even if he had been a jerk to dump the band at the last minute.

She forced a smile as he got near the table. He wore jeans and loafers and a blue shirt that he'd probably picked to match his blue eyes. And there was that toothpaste ad smile. The sizzle got hotter.

No sizzling allowed. She told her hormones to turn down the heat.

"Ladies, it's nice to see you," he said.

"Thanks," Bonnie managed.

"Can't get enough of your mud pie," added Loretta.

J.J. pointed to Bonnie's piece, which was only missing one small bite. "Or not."

"I decided I wasn't in the mood," she said. Now she sounded surly, but big girl panties be damned. Surly was all he deserved.

"Join us, please," Loretta invited him and kicked Bonnie under the table.

He slid in next to Bonnie. "If you don't like the pie, how about a drink?" he asked. "On the house."

"Thanks, but we've got drinks," she said, holding up her coffee mug to prove it."

"For later then."

"Thanks, but we're not going to stay that long."

"Just long enough to check out the competition," Loretta said, bestowing the same flirty smile she'd always given the older patrons who needed buttering up on J.J.

"Ah." He nodded. "Did you daughter tell you that the leader is a friend?"

Loretta nodded. "It's admirable to help out your friends."

*And give the house band no notice.* Bonnie shoved away her plate.

The band had been tuning up. Now they began to play an old Doobie Brothers classic, "Listen to the Music." Except it wasn't very listenable. In fact, it was downright painful. The drummer was off the beat and the harmonies weren't on pitch. Bonnie found herself scrunching up her face and half lifting in her chair in an attempt to psychically bring them up to the right pitch. Across the table, she could see her mother was doing the same thing. She stole a glance at J.J. Either he had gas or his ears hurt.

A couple of people got up and danced. Several regulars kept looking around as if trying to see who'd punked them.

Bonnie could sense J.J. squirming next to her.

The song ended and the tall man stepped forward. "All right, that was an oldie but a goody. Just like a lot of you out there," he added, pointing to the bar where Pete and a couple of his cronies were seated.

Pete glared at him.

"Yikes," murmured Loretta.

"I'm Tony and these guys here are the Tones."

"The Monotones," murmured Loretta.

"We're gonna be bringing it to you all month, playing the songs you love to hear," Tony continued.

"How about 'Sounds of Silence'?" called Pete.

"Hey, that's a good one," said Tony, pointing at him. "Here's one to make your mama get up and dance," he said, and they went into "All About That Bass"

Some of the line dancers got up and made a half attempt to dance, but soon sat back down. For Tony and the Tones it wasn't quite all about anything.

"You are a good friend," Loretta said to J.J.

He suddenly had something in his throat he needed to clear. "Uh, if you ladies will excuse me."

He was about to stand up, but suddenly there was Pete, right next to the table. "Loretta, who are those morons?" Pete demanded.

Bonnie refrained from an evil chuckle, but she couldn't help getting in a dig. "They're Tony and the Tones, Pete," she said sweetly.

"They stink," said Pete. "Why aren't you girls playing instead of sitting around eating?"

"You'd have to ask the new owner," Bonnie said, and looked to J.J.

Pete turned his frown on J.J. "You the new owner?"

"Yes, I'm J.J. Walker."

Pete didn't bother with the niceties. He got right to the point. "Why ain't The Mermaids up there?"

"We're just trying out a new band," J.J. said, making it sound like he had some invisible partner somewhere to share the blame.

"Oh, you have a partner?" Bonnie asked.

"No, I meant we as in the restaurant, as in me."

"Well, un-try 'em. They stink," Pete growled.

Male feathers were getting ruffled. J.J.'s easy smile ran away. "The band will be playing all this month."

"Then don't be surprised if you ain't got many people here next weekend," Pete said. "There's other places to get food."

"We should be going," Loretta said, unhooking her purse from the back of her chair. "Night, Pete. Thanks for the pie," she said to J.J.

"Good luck with your band," Bonnie taunted before getting her purse and following her mother out.

"That was quite the band," Loretta said as they crossed the parking lot. "I think they need a new name."

"Yeah? What would you name them?" Bonnie asked.

"Tony and the No Tones," Loretta said.

Bonnie had to laugh. "Perfect for them."

"That poor man," Loretta said.

"What poor man?"

"The new owner of The Drunken Sailor."

"Don't feel too sorry for him. He cut us loose."

"Yes, but we can always find other places to play. All he has is the pub. If he loses business he's in trouble."

Bonnie shrugged. "Oh, well. I'm sure he'll manage to stay in business. They do have great food."

"And we have a loyal following. I'd be surprised if he didn't feel the pinch."

Feel the pinch—that welcomed an image into Bonnie's mind that had nothing to do with business.

J.J. watched as patrons headed for the door instead of the dance floor. The crusty old dude named Pete had taken his pals and vamoosed, and line dancers were packing up their boots and leaving. At this rate the bar tab was going to be pitiful.

He looked over to where his old pal was stretching to reach the high notes on a Roy Orbison song. *Come on, Ton, you can do it.*

He couldn't. Had Tony been this bad when they were young? How could J.J. not have noticed when Tony and his buddies played at their frat parties. He must have had different players. Or else J.J. had always been too drunk or too busy hitting on girls to hear.

Even more painful than listening to Tony's band was remembering how good Bonnie Brinks's band had been and how they'd pulled in the weekend crowd. He also remembered how good she'd smelled when he'd been sitting next to her. This sailor needed to catch that mermaid and bring her back before his ship sank.

# *Ten*

Bonnie rounded the aisle at the grocery store late Saturday afternoon and there was Arthur Cork from Beachside Gallery, looking over the chips section. His face lit up at the sight of her.

"Bonnie, nice to see you."

"Nice to see you, too Arthur," she said.

"I hear you're not playing at The Drunken Sailor anymore. Your mom told me," he added. "She was in the gallery this morning."

Who needed a local newspaper when Moonlight Harbor had Loretta Brinks?

"So I got to thinking, you might have some extra time on your hands."

Bonnie knew what was coming next and she wasn't sure she wanted to hear it.

Sure enough. "For painting."

She half smiled. "You never give up, do you?"

"Not when I see talent waiting to be discovered. Come on, Bonnie, why not give it a try? Let's put a couple of your paintings in the gallery and see if they sell. A nice little bit of extra income for you. Minus my commission, of course."

"Of course," she said.

"So, what do you say?"

It was nice to have her creativity appreciated by someone, even if it had nothing to do with music. Maybe she should give it a shot.

"Okay, I'll give you a couple," she said.

"Nothing to lose, right?"

Only a little more of her self-esteem. But what the heck? Painting was a fun creative outlet, and with The Mermaid beached she had time on her hands. If she sold a couple of hers and brought in some money so much the better.

She said good-bye to Arthur, then returned to her mission, which was to buy microwave popcorn along with some pop for the movie night she was hosting for Lucy, Jenna Waters, Nora Singleton and Loretta. Movies were a fun escape, and friends were good medicine—both of which Loretta needed.

Brody was in Palm Springs for a tennis tournament and Seth had a darts competition at The Drunken Sailor. Nora's husband was around, but she never let a little thing like that stop her from hanging out with the girls, especially when it was going to be a double feature of Jane Austen movies.

Loretta arrived ten minutes early, bringing a box of cupcakes from the bakery. She threw off her poncho to reveal a black sweater over cuffed jeans and shooties. She'd accented her outfit with a necklace featuring wire-wrapped red sea glass. It looked new.

Bonnie took the cupcakes and hugged her. "You look great."

"Yes, I do," Loretta said with a kind of determination, as if someone, might have been thinking otherwise.

"I like that necklace. Is it new?"

"Yes. Retail therapy," said Loretta. "Open that box. I need a cupcake. Carb therapy," she added.

"How about plain old counseling therapy?" Bonnie suggested.

Loretta sneered. "I already had a session."

"You did?" Bonnie asked in surprise.

"At Waves. Moira makes a great shrink."

She followed Bonnie into the kitchen and as soon as Bonnie had set the box on the counter she dug into it and started peeling the wrapper off a red-frosted one. Bonnie gaped as half the cupcake disappeared into Loretta's mouth.

She took another. "One for the road."

"You're not leaving. You just got here."

"Then one for..." Loretta waved the cupcake around as she searched for a clever saying. "One for my other hip," she said, and snickered at her own cleverness. She took in Bonnie's horrified expression. "Now, don't look at me like that. I'm working my way back to happy, so let me embrace a few extra calories along the way."

"If that's what it takes, go for it," Bonnie said.

"What it really takes is determination and I just stocked up on that."

Bonnie's heart swelled with admiration. "Mom, have I told you recently how amazing you are?"

"Oh, I'm sure you must have," Loretta joked.

"No, I mean it. I'm serious."

Loretta turned serious, too. "Thank you, darling. But really, what other choice does a sensible woman have but to move forward? In real life there is no rewind."

There sure wasn't. If there was Bonnie would have hit that button long ago.

The friends arrived promptly at seven, bearing chocolate and cookies, as well as a veggie tray with hummus dip. Nora was dieting.

"It's weird to see you at home on a Saturday night instead of at the pub," Lucy said as they settled in with their drinks and bowls of popcorn.

"It's a nice change," Bonnie lied. "Anyway, I have something new on the horizon."

"You got another gig already?" Jenna asked.

"A painting gig," said Bonnie, and proceeded to share about her deal with Arthur.

"Does that mean I'm going to have to pay for my birthday painting?" Lucy asked with a fake pout.

"No. But it does mean I'm going to actually have to paint more."

"You've got time now that the band isn't playing," Loretta said.

"That may change," said Nora. "Guess who I talked to today."

"A rep from William Morris Talent Agency," Loretta cracked, and stuffed the last of her third cupcake in her mouth.

"Not quite. It was Sam Carruthers."

The owner of Sandy's. Bonnie could feel the hope springing up in her mother.

"I told him The Mermaids weren't playing at The Drunken Sailor anymore. Don't be surprised if you get a call from him," Nora said.

"Working again," Loretta said, her eyes bright with enthusiasm.

"We don't know that yet," Bonnie cautioned her, not wanting her mother to get her hopes up.

"You will be. I gave him your number," said Nora. "He's practically salivating."

It would appear he was. The next day Bonnie found a voice mail on her phone. "Hi, it's Sam from Sandy's. I hear The Mermaids might be free. How about coming over and playing at our place for the rest of the month. We don't have as big a dance floor as The Drunken Sailor, but I can meet whatever Lee was paying you."

Before she could reply, Bonnie needed a mother-daughter conference. She called Avril and told her the news.

"I was kind of thinking The Mermaids were done," Avril said. "I'm leaving come summer, you know."

"I know." And she didn't like to think about it. "But how about sticking it out with us until the end of school? It would mean a lot to Glamma."

Playing the grandmother card worked. "Okay," Avril said.

"Good. I'll tell Mr. Carruthers we're a go."

She did and he was delighted.

Loretta was even more delighted when Bonnie called her and told her they were once more employed. "I need new earrings!"

While Loretta set off to buy new earrings, Bonnie packed up two mermaid paintings and drove to the art gallery.

"These are so commercial," Arthur said, looking at them. He smiled like a man in a restaurant seeing a surf and turf meal set before him. "You'll be the next Thomas Kinkade," he predicted.

"Right." Arthur was so full of it.

Still, she liked the idea of getting recognition for...talent? She wasn't sure she could apply the word to her paintings. She'd never considered herself talented when it came to the visual arts. Music had been her passion.

"It's just so weird," she said when she called her mother

to tell her that her paintings were now hanging in Moonlight Harbor's art gallery.

"I think it's fabulous. I'm glad you're doing this. You should walk through every door that opens because you never know where it will lead."

Bonnie knew where the songwriting door had led. No place good. But this was different. Her paintings were hers and hers alone. No one could steal them or claim credit for them.

Unlike a song that played over and over on the radio or internet for the songwriter to hear, paintings went away, never to be seen again, but they went into homes where families and their friends could enjoy them. In that sense a painting was like a song, resonating with people and weaving itself into a corner of their lives. Maybe her mermaids would find homes and bring a smile to whoever met them.

The thought made her happy and she drove away singing Rayelle's "Gonna Be a Good Day."

It was, and so was the rest of the week, filled with easy hours at work, painting and band practice.

"We are going to have a crowd," Loretta predicted. "I've told everyone where we're going to be playing."

"Can we do my new song?" Avril asked.

"Of course," Bonnie said.

Anything for her daughter. If only singing Avril's songs was enough to keep her safe in Moonlight Harbor. It wouldn't. If Kenny couldn't keep her home nothing would.

"What a shame," Loretta had said when Bonnie told her later that Avril had broken up with him. "He's such a nice kid."

"He was so good to her. I thought they were joined at the heart and I couldn't believe it when she told me," said Bonnie. Her daughter was cutting ties right and left.

She pushed aside the upsetting thought. At least they had a little more time together before she had to let go.

A crowd was waiting for The Mermaids when they walked into Sandy's lounge to set up. "Half of Moonlight Harbor's here," Avril said in surprise as she set down the bass guitar she was carrying.

"Of course they are. They love us," said Loretta, who waved at a table where Jenna and Seth Waters were seated with Jenna's friend Courtney Greer and her fireman husband. Nora Singleton and her husband and Tyrella Lamb and her man were at another table. Pete and two of his cronies were nursing beers at the table next to them.

So many friends, Bonnie thought, seeing that Lucy and Brody and their kids were present also, along with all the line dancers who normally went to The Drunken Sailor. How were they all going to fit on that small dance floor?

The Mermaids set up, tuned up and then started up. "It's good to see so many of you here," Bonnie said into her mike.

"We love you!" called an overly happy drinker.

"And we love all of you," she said. "So, let's get this party started." She moved into her song she always kicked the night off with and the line dancers rushed the floor. Oh, yeah. It was going to be a good night.

It wasn't a good night over at The Drunken Sailor. The restaurant did okay from about five to seven but then the place turned into the restaurant version of a ghost ship. Alcohol sales would be through the basement.

Tony and his crew arrived and set up and the sight of them didn't do J.J. any good. "Give me a Jack on the rocks," he said to his bartender Madison.

She did and leaned her elbows on the bar and regarded him. "You know why nobody's here, right?"

He nodded, took a sip.

"Everyone's loyal to The Mermaids. We stick together."

Small town–itis. Except it was more than that and he knew it. Why hang out to hear an inferior band when the best band in town was playing somewhere else? He frowned and downed the rest of his drink.

Tony joined him at the bar. "Hey, where is everybody?"

"At Sandy's," said Madison. "They went to hear The Mermaids."

"The Mermaids?"

"They were the house band before I bought this place," J.J. explained.

Before seeing The Mermaids in action he'd thought of local lounge bands as musical wallpaper—background for the drinkers and a beat for the dancers. Bonnie Brinks and her crew had showed him how wrong he'd been. They provided a party atmosphere and were almost like celebrities with their good looks and casually flashy outfits. They had a following and now that following had moved away, leaving the pub feeling hollow. J.J. was feeling pretty hollow, himself.

Tony leaned back against the bar and scanned the non-crowd. "Don't worry, dude. Once word gets out that Tony and the Tones are here we'll pack 'em in."

"More like unpack 'em," Madison said as Tony sauntered off to the bandstand. "Hashtag: clueless."

Just what J.J. had been. He was going to have to do something fast if he wanted to keep his place a popular watering hole.

The band started playing again. It was an old song by the

Beatles that his parents had played when they were young. "Nowhere Man."

Another couple paid their tab and left, leaving behind a total of three women in the lounge, and one of them was reaching for her coat. Meanwhile, there stood Tony and the Tones, living out the lyrics, playing their songs for nobody.

J.J. tossed back the last of his second drink. It didn't help him feel any better.

Valentine's Day. Avril had no romantic plans, but she had plans, staring with making it a celebration in her music classes. She'd brought in a karaoke machine and was letting the kids ham it up, performing their favorite songs. Some of them even arrived with Valentine cards for her.

Shane Hawkins gave her one, along with a confident smirk. She thanked him—politely but not warmly—and opened it later to see that he'd added a note under the sappy poem inside. *You and Me, Miz B, by the sea after I turn 18. I'll bring the champagne.*

"Yeah, and who's gonna buy it for you," she muttered, and threw the card in the trash.

The other cards were all respectful and appreciative, telling her she was the best and wishing her a great day. *Hope you go someplace awesome with someone awesome*, wrote one of the girls.

The words gave her heart a sharp prick. That was what she would have been doing if she hadn't broken up with someone awesome.

But just because he was awesome it didn't mean he was the right awesome for her. She hoped Kenny had found someone and was planning a big night. She hadn't seen him since the breakup. She thought of her own upcoming big night. Not exactly flowers and dinner out and hot sex, but it would still be good. And come next Valentine's Day she'd be in Nashville with someone new. There would be more Valentine's Days in her future. Great ones. She wished the same for Kenny.

"Happy Valentine's Day," Loretta said to her empty condo. Here was another emotional hurdle to jump.

If she was still with Marlon, *no, Harvey*, she'd have been receiving a floral delivery. Or maybe getting chocolates. Or both. She'd have been making him a special meal. They'd have had a fire in the fireplace and cuddled on the couch and watched the waves come in.

The waves had come in all right, sneaker waves, drowning her hopes and stealing her happiness.

But what about that poor Mitzi? How awful to find your husband had been not only cheating on you but marrying the other woman to boot. What was she feeling this day? Burning anger, sorrow, loneliness? All of the above, probably.

Loretta grabbed her phone and a cup of coffee and curled up in an armchair, went on Facebook and did some searching. It didn't take long to find Harvey's first wife. Mitzi Whipple Bickerstaff's status said divorced. She hadn't lost any time in losing the loser. Good for her.

Loretta read her latest post. I'm not divorced yet, but I soon will be. Losing the last name and the loser who gave it to me. Friend me on my new page...unless you are anyone connected with him. I want nothing to do with you. I hate my life I hate him. I will be single but never again looking. I hate men. That is all.

It was a sad summary of where the woman's life was. Loretta sure got it. She hit the message button and typed, I'm sorry your soon-to-be ex did this to you. I'm not real fond of him myself. Neither of us deserved what he did to us. We both deserve better. I wish you all the best. Living well is the best revenge.

Maybe the last thing this woman wanted was to hear from her, but Loretta wanted her to know that her pain was felt and understood. She took a sip of her coffee, then headed for the shower. She'd wasted enough of the day. She'd get dressed and put on her makeup. Then she'd take herself to the store and buy some chocolates. Just because she wasn't with someone didn't mean she couldn't celebrate love. If you didn't do that then the Harveys of the world won.

So celebrate she did. She bought her chocolates, then she took Patricia Whiteside, owner of the Oyster Bay Inn, to lunch. Patricia had been widowed for almost two years and special days like Valentine's Day were still hard for her. They reminisced, shed a few tears and wound up counting their blessings and toasting each other with chocolate martinis.

Afterward she went to the florist and bought herself a bouquet of red and white roses complete with greens and baby's breath, all in a red mercury glass vase. It wasn't cheap but so what? She was worth it.

"Happy Valentine's Day from me to me," she quipped to the florist as she pulled out her charge card.

She left the florist's and went home to make meatloaf, Bonnie's favorite comfort food, and a chocolate silk pie, which was Avril's favorite. It wouldn't be the romantic evening she should have had, but it would be good to be with the two people she loved most in the world and who loved her back.

Avril arrived first, bringing a card game called Exploding Kittens. The very name sounded gross to Loretta, who, even though she wasn't a cat lover, still thought doing bad things to animals shouldn't be a joke.

"Okay, then, we can play Uno," Avril conceded, and handed over a gift bag.

"What's this?" asked Loretta opening it. "Oh, Godiva chocolates. How sweet!"

"I figured somebody should give you chocolates for Valentine's Day," Avril said as they hugged each other.

"You are such a sweet girl," Loretta said. "Pretty on the outside and the inside."

"Yes, I am," Avril agreed like the cheeky little thing she was. Her gaze fell to the coffee table where Loretta's box sat. "Looks like somebody beat me out."

"Yes, me." Loretta pointed to the flowers on the dining table. "And flowers. I decided I wasn't going to wait for a man to make my day."

"Good idea," Avril approved.

Bonnie was the next to arrive, brushing rain from her winter jacket. She pulled off her knit cap, and those lovely auburn locks tumbled out. Her daughter was such a beautiful woman. Loretta was determined to resign herself to being alone, but she sure hated to see Bonnie in that state. She still had many years ahead of her and more adventures. Adventures were always better when shared with someone who loved you.

Shared adventures. The memory of the fake relationship she'd had with Harvey the romance illusionist sprang to mind. She kicked it out.

Bonnie carried a plastic grocery bag. From it she, too, produced a box of chocolates.

"Looks like I wasn't the only one who thought you needed Valentine's candy," Avril said to Loretta.

"There's more." Bonnie produced a small heart-shaped

box of off-brand chocolates. "From Pete. He didn't want you to be depressed."

"That was sweet of him. I am going to be on chocolate overload."

"Don't worry, Glamma, we'll help you eat 'em," said Avril.

They did, eating their way through a game of Uno and a movie. It was a lovely evening. *Take that Harvey Bickerstaff!*

Before she headed to bed, she checked her phone. There was a message in the Facebook message app from Mitzi.

That was nice of you. I got to admit, at first I hated you. I thought you were some kind of home-wrecker. But that was before I learned that rat bastard had married you. The only home-wrecker was Harvey. He may have wrecked my home, but I won't let him wreck my life. Don't let him wreck yours either. Yeah, living well is the best revenge. Let's both get some.

We will, Loretta typed back. You couldn't keep a good woman down.

It had been a good day and a nice evening with Bonnie's mother and daughter. Although they really needed to start watching something on Valentine's Day besides romcoms. All those over-the-top declarations of love, all those sappy, happy endings—they left Loretta and Avril smiling and hopeful and Bonnie feeling grumpy.

"Love works things out in the end," Loretta had said to Avril...under the influence of chocolate.

Right. Look how well love had worked things out for Loretta. Look how well love had worked things out for Bonnie.

She remembered her first Valentine's Day with Rance. They'd both been broke so she'd bought him his favorite candy bar—a Three Musketeers—and a packaged Moon Pie. He'd taken her out for hamburgers.

"It won't always be burgers," he'd said. "Someday it'll be steak and champagne. I'll have a fancy house and a private plane. Stick with me, Bonnie. I'm goin' places."

Yes, he was. But he wound up going without her.

Back home, she picked up her guitar and began noodling. Then, as she often did, started writing down a song.

Feels like forever since you left, since I felt your fingers on my skin.
You've been gone so long, but the memories keep comin' back again.
What can I say about what I'm feelin', about what goes through my mind?
Just keepin' it real, I want you to know how I really feel.

Ha! Now for the fun surprise in the chorus.

I miss you…like I miss a toothache or a pain in my ass.
I need you…like I need an earthquake or a heart attack.
And I want you, yeah, tonight, you know I want you.
I want you to never, never, never ever come back.

"Oh, yeah, I'm good," she told herself after she'd polished her melody. A second verse and this song would be ready to go…nowhere.

She sighed. Maybe she shouldn't have given up and

run away from a fight. Maybe she should have stayed in Nashville. Her mother was right. She could have made it, but she'd let her confidence get shaken. She kept blaming Rance—and there was plenty to blame him for—but in the end she was the one who'd turned her back on her dreams and allowed her world to get small.

At least small was safe. Like a cocoon. And other than the niggling discontent she felt on days like this, she was happy in her cocoon. Rance Jackson did a great job of trying to ruin her life. She was never going to let another man in to finish what he'd started.

But when she saw J.J. Walker slip into a table in a dimly lit corner of Sandy's lounge the next Saturday night her stupid heart gave a happy skip. She almost lost her place in her song, an old Dolly Parton number Loretta was partial to, "Why'd You Come in Here Lookin' Like That."

The song said it all. He was in jeans and a crisp white shirt worn under a leather jacket. Coupled with that well-trimmed beard and well-maintained body it made for one sexy look. Yep, Temptation in Levis.

*Let's fall into temptation*, begged her hormones.

Nope, nope, nope. He'd have to go tempt some other woman. She was not taking a bite of the love apple.

But why was he there?

# *Eleven*

Bonnie could feel J.J. Walker's gaze on her as she sang, and it continued to disconcert her. Darn it all, this needed to stop. People watched her all the time when she sang, especially men.

But none of them goosed up her heart rate, made her fingers fumble on her guitar or left her forgetting lyrics and having to quickly improvise.

"You okay, Mom?" Avril whispered in between songs.

"I'm fine," Bonnie whispered back. *For someone whose panties are on fire.*

Darn the man. He wasn't *that* good-looking. She'd dated hotter bodies.

But his…it was as if he was carrying an invisible rope, lassoing her and drawing her to him.

Her mother would define that as soul mates. Bonnie knew better. There was no such thing.

*Come on*, urged Team Estrogen, *you can't win if you don't get in the game.*

She was done with games, and she didn't want anything to do with him in spite of the fact that everything about him said, "Take a chance on me." No way. She was not going to walk the tightrope over Heartbreak Gorge. She'd tried enough times to get on it after Rance and had never made it across. She wouldn't this time, either.

It was obvious J.J. wanted something to do with her. Again, she could feel him watching her as the band went on break and she stopped at a couple of tables to talk to people. Next thing she knew he was following her when she went to the bar to get her tonic water. *Go away!*

He didn't. She turned around and practically bumped into him. He was so close she could smell his woodsy cologne, feel those male vibes radiating off that sculpted chest hiding under his white shirt. He probably worked out.

*We'd like to work out with him*, shouted the team.

She told them to shut up, then to him, said, "Did you want something?"

"Yes, you."

*You.* Her heart got in the act and started tap dancing.

"The Mermaids," he quickly corrected himself. "I want you back at The Drunken Sailor."

"You have a band," she reminded him.

"No, I have a mistake, and I'm paying for it."

"We all have to pay for our mistakes," she said her, tone of voice far from empathetic.

Maybe she should have been more empathetic. Heaven knew she'd paid for her mistakes, and it wasn't fun.

"Carruthers only has you for this month. What would it take to lure you back to my place?" he asked.

*To my place.* That simple phrase got her hormones going again.

"How about meeting me for lunch tomorrow. Let's talk," he said.

Lunch with J.J. Walker. Her heart danced faster.

It was only lunch. Except she didn't want to go to lunch with J.J. That would feel too much like a date.

"I'll stop by the pub but not to eat," she said.

He looked like his mommy had just told him he couldn't have a skateboard for his birthday. "I'm happy to bribe you with food."

"Mermaids can't be bribed," she said.

"I guess not. Well, stop by then. And save me. I'm drowning."

The man was the king of hyperbole. "I'm sure that's an exaggeration."

"Yeah? The number of people we have over there right now couldn't fill one table here. Look, I'm not above begging. Come in and talk at least. Please."

"All right," she said, and he smiled. That smile, it was electric.

She shouldn't meet with J.J. Walker. She should stay at Sandy's where it was safe.

Loretta was smirking when Bonnie joined her and Avril at the band table. "Already crawling to you?"

"He's pretty desperate," Bonnie said.

"He's pretty good-looking," said Loretta, and from the glint in her eyes Bonnie could tell she was slipping into matchmaking mama mode.

"That has nothing to do with anything," Bonnie said.

"Make him offer a lot more money," said Avril.

"Make him take you out for dinner," said Loretta.

"Not happening, Mom. We don't need any more romantic disasters in this family." Loretta's smile withered and Bonnie wanted to slap herself. *Way to go, mouth.* She reached across the table and caught Loretta's hand. "I'm sorry, I didn't mean that the way it sounded."

"I know," Loretta said with a wan smile. "I sure wouldn't

want either of you to go through what I went through. But I still believe in love. Without love we wouldn't have any songs to sing."

"Speaking of, we'd better get back to singing," Bonnie said.

Her mother was right though. Love and all its highs and lows dominated the songs they sang. Love kept the wheel of life turning. Without people in your life to love you didn't have a life. But Bonnie had people in her life—her mother and daughter. They were enough.

*Don't lie to us*, said Team Estrogen. *We know better.*

*No, you don't*, she told them. The saying that love is blind was no joke. With your eyes shut it was a lovely dream. But walking around with your eyes shut you bumped into trouble and got hurt. It wasn't worth it.

Still, knowing that, it was hard to fight the attraction she felt for J.J. Walker when she sat down with him at an empty table in The Drunken Sailor. Like many of the restaurants in town, the place was open to catch any straggling weekend visitors who might want to grab a bite before they started back home. There weren't many diners present though and, imagining that kind of turnout on a busy weekend night, she could only guess the air of depressed quiet that would have hung over the place.

"This is what it looked like on Saturday," said J.J. "I hope you feel a little sorry for me."

"After you gave us heave-ho with no notice? You're kidding, right?"

"You can't blame me for being a good friend."

He did have a point, and she had to admire his loyalty. "A good friend with a tin ear," she couldn't help observing.

"I knew I'd made a mistake the minute I heard them. Still, we go way back, and when I bought the place he assumed I'd want his band to play. I'd have been a rotten friend if I didn't at least give him a chance."

"That's pretty noble of you."

"Oh, yeah. Noble. But bad business. Look, I'm sorry I didn't give you more warning, I really am. I handled that all wrong."

Yes, he had.

"I like it here. I want to stay, and I want to keep this place going. From what I understand it's been around for a long time. I don't want to be the one to run it into the ground. So name your price. I'll give you a contract for the next six months."

That was music to any musician's ear. But, "Better make it three," Bonnie said.

"Why's that?" he asked.

"My daughter's headed for Nashville come June."

"That still leaves two mermaids," he said. "A duo."

They probably could make it work. Loretta played bass as well as drums. Bonnie could program drums and keyboard for a fuller sound. More money that way, which would be nice. Her mom would probably go for it, but she wasn't sure she wanted to commit. It would be more work. Maybe all she'd want to do after Avril left would be to paint.

"The Mermaids will give you three months, then we can take it from there. How's that sound?"

"Better than not getting you at all. Come on into the office and I'll give you a contract."

He printed off two copies of a contract for them to sign and she tried to keep her eyes from turning in the direction of his jean-encased butt. It wasn't easy to do because he was a beautifully built specimen. He laid the contract on his desk. Even his hands were beautiful. Long, tapered fingers, perfect for playing the piano.

She couldn't help asking. "Do you play the piano?"

"Wish I did," he said. "I played sports growing up—baseball, soccer—my dad coached my Little League team. I was on a lot of winning teams, went to a lot of playoffs. Played in high school, too. It didn't leave a lot of time for music. Although I always thought it would be cool to be in a band. Seems to me that women love musicians."

"They do," Bonnie said. "But God knows why. Musicians are a flaky bunch."

"Are you?" He moved the contract over for her to sign.

"No. And I don't do flakes."

"Who do you do?"

*You, you, you!* chanted the team.

"Nobody," she said firmly.

"Yeah? So, there's no one in your life right now?"

"I have people in my life."

"I mean, are you with someone?"

"No."

"Then how about lunch this week? Or dinner?" His smile was a lady slayer.

Bonnie could feel it starting, that crazy heart upheaval that accompanied falling for a man. She was determined not to go there.

"Sorry," she said. It was no lie. She was sorry. J.J. Walker's smile, his charm, his very masculinity drew her like the proverbial moth to flame. "I appreciate the offer, but I'm not interested in getting involved with anyone."

"Okay, we can just have lunch and not get involved. Come on, give me a break. I'm new here. I need friends."

*Don't say yes*, she told herself. It would like hugging an octopus. Before she knew it she'd be entangled.

"Just lunch," he pressed. "I'm not asking to sleep with you."

*Well, that's disappointing*, groaned the team.

"Okay, lunch. My mom would enjoy it."

He blinked, then smiled. "Two Mermaids instead of one. Fine with me," he said, proving he was a good sport.

Another thing in his favor. Darn.

"How does The Porthole at noon tomorrow sound?" he asked.

*Risky*, she thought, but she said yes. Lunch with a man who had a killer smile. She was a fool.

"I think that sounds great," Loretta said when Bonnie told her about her conversation with J.J. "He obviously wants to make up for his error in judgment. And a woman should never turn down a free meal."

The meal was delicious. J.J. insisted they start with crab cocktails, and after that they enjoyed scallops and salmon along with the restaurant's freshly baked French bread.

"The food here's as good as any I've ever had in Seattle," he said.

"You're surprised?" Bonnie asked.

"We may be small, but we've got class," Loretta added.

"Yes, you do," he agreed. "I already told your daughter, I like this town. It's got a good vibe."

"That's because it's full of good people," Bonnie said. "I moved here from Seattle, years ago when my daughter was little. I've never regretted it."

"The place has grown since then," put in Loretta. "Word's gotten out and we have a lot of new people moving here. I hope it doesn't change us."

"Hopefully, those new people can make it even better," he said.

"You think J.J. will make it better?" Loretta asked when they finally drove away.

Bonnie wasn't sure if her mother was talking about the

town or her life. "I guess that remains to be seen," she said
cautiously.

"I would love to see you find someone," Loretta said.
"As long as he's not a bigamist," she added.

Bonnie was happy to see her mother could smile a little
now over the mess she'd stepped into. "I'm glad you found
out about Harvey when you did. He probably would have
robbed you blind."

"It wouldn't have been hard to do since I was already
blind. I feel for his wife, who's divorcing him by the way.
What a horrible thing to discover about the man you thought
you could trust."

"I think we're too quick to spend our trust sometimes,"
Bonnie said, thinking of her own past.

Loretta sighed. "Yes, we are. But some people are worth
investing it in."

Was J.J.?

She found herself almost wanting to be able to spend
some of her hoarded trust when he dropped by the office as
she was getting off work. He held up a bottle of wine from
St. Michelle winery. "Have wine, will travel."

"Are you inviting yourself to my house?" she asked.

"I am. You got time for a drink?"

Missy was still manning the reception desk and answered for her. "Of course she does." Missy loved stepping over boundaries.

J.J. smiled his toothpaste ad smile. It showed off that
perfectly squared jaw. Why was this man not with someone? There had to be a reason. He was too good to be true.

"I've never had drinks with a mermaid before," he said,
bringing out the charm again.

That charm had put her on the defensive when she first

met him. Now, after having had lunch with him, she was finding it…charming. And it would be churlish to object.

"I guess you're coming over. This isn't a date though," she informed him.

"Of course not."

"You can follow me."

"Love to," he said and crooned, "I will follow you," a line from a song only Loretta would know. He didn't have a bad voice, but it was pitchy. He really did have a tin ear.

"Where'd you learn that song?" she asked as they walked out the door.

"My mom and dad used to sing it to each other all the time."

"That's sweet," she said.

"They're a great pair. Wish I could have followed in their footsteps."

What did that mean? They were to their cars so it wasn't the time to ask.

But once they were back at her house, sitting in the living room and enjoying the fire he'd built for her in her fireplace, she circled back to it. "What did you mean when you said you wish you could have followed in your parents' footsteps?"

He took a sip of his wine. "Stayed married. It didn't work for us. Nobody's fault, really, just different ideas of what we wanted out of life. I wanted to be a workaholic. My wife got tired of it."

"Do you have kids?"

"Two stepsons, twins I helped raise from the time they were four. Good guys, but they're both in college and have jobs now. It's getting harder and harder to see them."

"I won't be seeing much of my daughter come summer."

Bonnie could hear the resentment bleeding into her voice and silently cursed Nashville for luring Avril away.

"They gotta live their own lives, don't they?" he said. "I guess we do, too." He took another drink of his wine. "So, you don't have anybody in your life, Mermaid? How is that possible?"

"I stay away from sailors," she joked.

"No desire to lure them to their deaths, huh?" he joked. "Not that kind of mermaid?"

"Not that kind. I'm really not looking for anyone."

"Sometimes that's when you find someone."

"Too risky."

"Sounds like you got burned."

"That's ancient history."

"Okay by me. I like current events better."

That darned smile of his. She took a sip of her wine and it caressed her tongue. It was a good one. Expensive. J.J. was trying to make an impression.

Little did he know he didn't have to try at all. She should have never agreed to let him come over. She could tell by the way he was looking at her that he wanted to kiss her. That wasn't happening. Not then. Not ever.

She hurried through the rest of her wine, then said, "Well, thanks for stopping by."

"I guess we're done here," he said.

"We are."

He downed his last swallow and stood. "For tonight. I don't give up."

"And I don't give in."

He said nothing to that. He didn't need to. His cocky smile spoke volumes.

At the door she handed him his coat and thanked him for sharing his wine.

"I enjoyed talking with you," he said. "You're a fascinating woman."

"Not really."

"You fascinate me."

His words pushed up her heart rate. She opened the door before she could do something stupid, like suggest he stay for dinner. "Good-bye."

"Good night," he corrected, and sauntered off down her walk.

Next door, Lucy's Ranger was parked in the driveway. She hoped Lucy hadn't seen that she had company. If she had, there would be an interrogation. Lucy was a hopeless romantic.

There was no hope that this...whatever...with J.J. Walker would go anywhere. Bonnie wasn't going to let it. She had a crippled heart to protect.

She grabbed her sketch pad and began to pencil out an idea for a mermaid painting. A boat, a sailor. With reddish hair and a beard. He was reaching out, trying to catch a mermaid who was diving off his boat. But she was out of reach, nothing left of their magical moment but a splash and a tail.

"Be that mermaid," she told herself. "Don't get lured into the boat."

Out of the blue, Loretta got another message from her old friend Lawrence. Was just thinking about you, it said. How are you doing?

I went through some rough waters recently, she typed. She drummed on her phone with two fingers, trying to decide if she should share all the gory details of her failed romance. The idea of looking like a foolish old failure stopped her. Besides, she and Lawrence were just chatting. He wouldn't want to hear all her soap opera drama. But I'm doing fine now, she finished. And she was.

Glad to hear it, he typed back. You always had so much spunk.

Still do, she said to both him and herself.

The next morning she smiled as she discovered she had another message from him. Got to remembering how you were going to make it big in Nashville.

That was what she'd told him. That was what she'd told everyone, including herself. I never did. True love took me away. But I have a lovely, talented daughter and granddaughter, and my granddaughter is off to Nashville this summer.

So you passed on your talent. Good for you.

How about you? Any kids?

He sent her a smiley face emoticon. Got a daughter and a son and two grandsons. They visit when they can. Son loves to come here to Arizona and golf with his old man.

You like to golf? We have a nice golf course here. She shouldn't have said that. It looked like she was trying to lure him up to Washington.

"I guess I am," she muttered. Even after the disaster with Harvey, she still wished she could find someone to spend this last part of her life with.

Yeah? I may have to come check it out. Got a pretty nice motor home.

She couldn't help but envision her old friend coming to visit and staying for a long time. Walks on the beach, eating ice cream cones at Good Times Ice Cream Parlor, sitting on her balcony and watching the sun set over the water.

We've got a nice campground here in Moonlight Harbor and you know how gorgeous our summers can be in the Pacific Northwest.

Sure do. You might just see me.

I might just like that, she replied. Then hoped it was really Lawrence she was talking to and not some fake Lawrence. But, of course, it had to be the real Lawrence. What faker would talk about losing his wife? What faker would know the name of Loretta's husband?

Her daughter obviously had the same concern. "How do you know it's not someone pretending to be him?" Bonnie asked when the three women met for band practice.

"Did he post, 'Tell me more about yourself'?" Avril asked.

"No. And I know it's really Lawrence."

"Just be careful, Mom," said Bonnie.

"Yeah, we don't want you to get hurt," added Avril.

"I don't want me to get hurt, either," Loretta said. Once was enough.

But the more she chatted with Lawrence the more she knew it was him. They had too many old friends and memories in common.

Always meant to get back for our fiftieth high school reunion, he typed during one of their online visits. But after losing Carol I didn't feel like socializing.

Understandable, she typed back.

Did you go?

Yes. Gary Grimes is still as obnoxious as ever and Norm Hardy has remarried. A lovely woman. Mary, Karen, Kathy and Earlene haven't changed a bit. And I loved catching up with Sue and Donna.

Wish I'd gone. Did you take pictures?

No, she lied. She hadn't liked how she looked in any of the selfies she'd taken during her blast into the past. She and her girlfriends had all looked so...old. She'd deleted them from her phone.

Suddenly she wanted a great picture of herself to share with Lawrence. There wasn't a single decent one on her page. They were all photos of the girls or the beach or her latest culinary creation.

Saturday night she decided she needed a picture of the band. On break she got Pete to take one of her and Bonnie and Avril and she made sure to give her sexiest band chick pose.

"There you go," he said, handing the phone back to her. "Who's this for, anyway?"

"A high school buddy. He wants a recent picture."

Pete frowned. "I thought you were through with men."

"I am. This is a friend."

"You got lots of men here who want to be friends," Pete informed her.

She ignored him, looking at the picture he'd taken.

"That's really good of you, Glamma," Avril said, peering over her shoulder.

Loretta made a face. "I look old."

"You are old," pointed out Pete.

"There you go using that word, again," Loretta said with

a scowl. "Am I going to have to beat you with my drumstick?"

"There's nothin' wrong with being old. Happens to the best of us," he said.

It happened much sooner than you ever dreamed it would when you were young, and it seemed the less sand left in the top of the hourglass the faster it fell to the bottom. She could feel herself in the middle of that sand slide, reaching out, trying to hang on to every moment left to her.

This renewed friendship with Lawrence probably wouldn't go beyond the connection on their phone screens, but it was still one worth developing. She messaged the picture to him and captioned it Beach Nightlife.

Maybe, at some point, he'd come to Moonlight Harbor and check it out.

He messaged back. Looks like a good summer destination. Will you show me around?

I think I could be persuaded, she replied coyly. It would be fun to see him. And, unlike her daughter, maybe, if the opportunity arose, she could be persuaded to take one more chance on love.

It was the last night for Tony and the Tones, thank God. Although J.J. hated having to be the bad guy he also hated to see his business running in the red. "So, whaddya think?" Tony said when J.J. paid him.

"I think it was great seeing you, but this is it. I've got another band coming in next month."

The resigned expression on his friend's face told J.J. that Tony had been expecting this. He nodded.

"Sorry, nothing personal, but you're just not bringing 'em in."

"I know. I let you down. I'm sorry, man."

"No worries," J.J. said. None now that he had The Mermaids coming back. He clapped his friend on the back and they did the bro hug. "Anytime you and Ginny want to come down and hang out I got a guest room in my new place."

Tony gave a half smile. "I might take you up on that." He looked to where his musicians were sitting, enjoying the last of their free drinks. "Maybe I'll put together a different band."

"Might not be a bad idea," said J.J.

"I'll let you know when I do."

"They'll have to be really good to beat the band I'm bringing in," J.J. cautioned.

Tony shrugged, accepting his fate. "You never know."

"You never know," J.J. agreed and left it at that.

The Mermaids were back at The Drunken Sailor and the place was packed with out-of-towners as well as the regulars, who had rewarded J.J. Walker for coming to his senses and bringing them back by returning in full force. The owner of Sandy's had been sorry to learn that he'd been scooped but had been a good sport.

"Frankly, I don't have the room in my lounge to pack 'em in without getting a visit from the fire marshal. I wouldn't be surprised if, at some point The Sailor doesn't, either," he'd said. "You all are something else. You could really go places."

It was too late for Bonnie to go anyplace. The same held true for Loretta. And Bonnie wished Avril wasn't going to try. If only she had some magic shield she could send along with her daughter to protect her from disappointment. Sadly, there was no such thing. She'd tried her best to keep Avril home, but she wanted to fly. All Bonnie could do was hope that she didn't fly too close to the sun like Icarus and get burned.

If only being a big fish in a small pond was enough, she wished as the line dancers and couples vied for space on the dance floor. It was like a honkytonk scene from a movie—the band playing and the crowd rocking out. Everyone was in a party mood.

"That was great," Loretta said after they finished their last set. "It's nice to be loved."

"Everyone loves you, Glamma," Avril said to her. "You're dope."

"Only half as dopey as my fabulous granddaughter," Loretta said, giving her a one-armed hug. "Wait, that doesn't quite sound right," she said.

Avril laughed. "I know what you mean."

J.J. came over just in time to hear their conversation. "You're all fabulous. It's good to have you back."

"It's good to be back," Loretta said, speaking for all of them.

He turned his killer smile on Bonnie. "I was wondering what you're doing for breakfast tomorrow."

Loretta instantly inserted herself into the conversation. "Take her to The Porthole. They have those amazing Belgian waffles."

"I have work to do tomorrow morning," Bonnie said. "I have to paint."

"Gotta keep up your strength for that," said J.J. "A quick breakfast?"

"All right," she said, "but it's not a date."

"All we're doing is eating."

Yeah, she believed that. Next he'd be trying to sell her oceanfront property in Arizona.

"You should give up," she told him as they sat in the restaurant waiting for their order the next day. Their window table provided a view of a gray, drizzly sky brooding over the beach. "I'm not interested in a relationship."

"Who said anything about a relationship? I just didn't want to eat breakfast alone."

"My mother would have been happy to go with you."

He smiled at that. "I bet she would. I like how friendly your mom is."

"She's too old for you."

He chuckled. "Maybe. She's sure young at heart though."

"That she is," Bonnie had to agree.

"How's she doing?" Of course, he'd know about what had happened to Loretta. Everyone knew.

"She's already moving on. My mother is a very resilient woman."

"A good quality to have, considering how much life knocks most of us down. You can't stay on the mat for the count. You gotta get up."

"Maybe it's safer to stay down," Bonnie argued. "You get up again and you'll get hit again."

"If you don't get up you'll never win," he countered.

"You are the eternal optimist, aren't you?" she said.

"Why not?"

"Because that's not real life," she said, irritated.

"Life isn't all bad, either, Bonnie," he said. "I don't know what happened in yours, but it looks to me that you've got some good stuff going on now."

"I do," she agreed. Even if she wasn't setting the world on fire, she had her friends, her mom in her corner, a job she enjoyed and a chance to play her music.

"So, maybe it will keep going on."

"Maybe."

"You're having a good time right now, right?"

She had to smile and admit that she was.

"Well, there you have it. I'm good luck," he said.

When it came to men there was no such thing. She had to stop seeing this man. This was the last time she was going to do anything with him.

So, of course, when he offered to teach her how to play golf on Saturday—not a date—she said yes. Good grief, what was she thinking?

That maybe it was time to get up off the mat.

# *Twelve*

March is not a balmy month on the Washington Coast, but the morning J.J. took Bonnie out on the golf links some leprechaun had gotten busy and brought out the sun and blown away the wind. (No small feat considering how windy it could get.) The air still had a nip in it, but it was nothing a Pacific Northwest girl couldn't handle.

They weren't the only ones out. As they drove up she saw several groups of men and women, either teeing off or zipping along the course in their golf carts.

"I've driven by this course a million times but never once been on it," Bonnie confessed.

"Never felt the call of the ball?" J.J. asked.

"Never had the time and the money at the same time."

"So, did you do anything sporty?"

"In high school I was too busy with music and then, later with single parenting. I always thought it would be fun to learn to ski," she said wistfully, "but that really wasn't in the budget."

"That's even better than golf," he said.

"As long as you don't break your leg." It would be hard to rock out on a stage when you were in a cast.

"Done that."

"Was that the end of your skiing?"

"Of course not. Gotta feed the addiction."

"I don't know if I would. I hate pain."

"Yes, but when you love something enough you risk the pain."

Memories of nights at The Bluebird and the thrill of the few times she's been in small studios, recording demos for songs she'd written, sprang to mind. At one time she had loved her life in Nashville, but in the end she'd let the pain outweigh it and she'd left. What kind of coward did that make her?

"Anyway, you only live once," he said.

"Living pretty high. Those are pricey sports," she observed. Golfing, skiing, buying restaurants. Obviously, J.J. wasn't hurting for money.

But neither was she now, really. She wasn't rich but she was okay.

"I had the money, and after the divorce I sure had the time. Now there's something I wish I'd been smarter about."

"Time?"

"Yep. I was a grade A workaholic. It took me too long to learn there's more to life than success."

"That's easy for people who've been successful to say."

Was there a little bitterness creeping into her voice? It needed to creep right back out. She had a beautiful daughter and a good life in Moonlight Harbor.

"Actually, it's harder than you think. That lesson cost me my marriage."

"You seem pretty determined to make The Drunken Sailor a success," Bonnie couldn't help saying.

"I don't want it to fail, for sure, but I'm not going to let it consume my whole life. There are too many other interesting things to do in this world, not to mention interesting people to do them with."

*Like us!* cheered Team Estrogen.

Bonnie neglected to tell her hormones to shut up.

"Come on, let's grab a bucket of balls and find you a club to rent."

"I don't think I'm very athletic," Bonnie warned him.

"You won't know until you try. Come on, no stalling."

*Yeah*, said the team, *no stalling.*

"I figured we'd stick to the driving range today," he said as they walked into the clubhouse. "That way you can get a feel for what it's like to hit."

The golf club was small, a dining area with a smattering of tables and chairs, a retail section offering golf balls, shirts and gloves. Some clubs for rent, buckets of balls in two different sizes.

J.J. bought a glove for her, ignoring her protests that she could afford to pay for one. "The person who does the inviting does the paying," he said.

"You're probably wasting your money."

"Spending money on a beautiful woman is never a waste."

They found a club he thought would work for Bonnie, then went out to the driving range and set up at one of the stalls. "Let me show you how to hold it," he said, and demonstrated.

She mirrored it and he adjusted her hands a little. His hand on hers was enough to start Team Estrogen doing cartwheels. She told the girls to settle down and let her concentrate.

*We are concentrating.*

*On golf*, she clarified.

He moved behind her and put his hands on her arms,

positioning her. "Now you want to stand about this far from the tee."

*Yippee!* squealed the team.

"A couple of things to remember," J.J. said as he moved away and set a ball on the tee. "You want to keep your eye on the ball. You're going to want to straighten up and watch where it goes, but don't do that. Keep your head down until you've followed through with your swing."

Sports were never Bonnie's thing, and now here she was about to hit that little ball with this little club. This was a fail waiting to happen.

"Follow through with my swing," she repeated and wondered if she sounded as twitchy as she felt.

"You can do it," J.J. assured her.

She gritted her teeth, stared at the ball and swung with all her might. And missed it completely. How was that possible?

"Don't try to kill it," said J.J. "Just swing nice and easy. "Here, let me help you."

He stood behind her again, all that hard male muscle up against her back, his arms alongside hers, his hands covering hers.

*Go, go, go,* cheered the team.

Go, go, go was right. The air might have been brisk but Bonnie was sure feeling the heat.

"Okay, here we go," he said. Together they swung and the ball lifted and sailed off past the hundred-yard marker.

"Wow," she breathed, watching it.

"Yeah, wow," he said behind her, his breath tickling her ear.

She looked over her shoulder and smiled at him. He smiled back.

"I bet you think I'm going to kiss you," he said, his

voice teasing. "But I seem to remember you telling me you weren't interested in a relationship."

*Well, we are!* screamed the team.

"I'm not," Bonnie said as much to herself as him.

"I think I read somewhere once that it's a woman's prerogative to change her mind."

"When I do I'll let you know."

He stepped away and put another ball on the tee. "That was a telling response."

"What?"

"You didn't say you'd let me know *if* you were ready. You said you'd let me know *when* you are." He grinned at her. "I can wait."

She had said that, hadn't she? Freudian slip? Was she moving toward wanting to take a chance on love?

*When you love something enough you risk the pain.* J.J.'s words flashed across her mind. Did she love being with him enough to risk getting hurt? Maybe she did.

"Okay, try it on your own now and let's see what you got. Keep your head down. Take it nice and easy."

Nice and easy, that was good advice, for both her golf swing and whatever was going on with J.J.

She kept her club angled the way he'd shown her and bent her knees a little as she'd been instructed. Looked at the ball. Checked her stance. Looked at the ball again.

"You're ready," he said. "Don't forget to swing all the way through up past your left shoulder. Nice and easy."

She pulled back the club and swung. Nice and easy. Watched it scoop up the little white ball, swung her club all the way to the sky, and, as J.J. let out a whoop, looked to see her ball sailing in a beautiful long arc. Wow! Had she just done that? Instant high!

"Nice job," he said. "I think you could get good at this."

"That was luck." It had to be.

"Let's see how you do with a few more," he said, setting down another ball.

That one went well, too. Then she hit a couple of grounders.

"Remember to keep your head down," he said. "Don't lift up."

Head down, knees bent, follow through. Don't lift up. Try and get coordinated.

She had several more misses, but she also hit some balls that made her feel like the queen of the links.

"Not bad for a first day," he said, as they went to return the empty bucket and her club.

"I could get into this," she said.

"Want to go again?"

"I do," she told him. And not just for the fun of hitting golf balls.

*Touchdown*, whooped Team Estrogen.

*This isn't football*, she told the girls.

*We don't care what it is as long as you score.*

"I don't know about you, but I'm hungry," J.J. said once they were back in his car. "How about lunch at the Lighthouse? We can get some chowder and go watch the waves."

"That sounds good," she said.

And it was good, sitting in his car at the edge of the beach, watching the sun tickle the sea.

He looked out at the waves, contentment on his face. "If I had a journal, know what I'd write in it?"

"What?"

"Had lunch at the beach with a mermaid. Life is good."

"You're full of it," she scoffed. But she couldn't help smiling. Life was, indeed, good. Maybe it could it get even better…if she had the nerve to find out.

* * *

Sarah didn't show up for the critique group online meeting so it was only Avril and Colton. He had an idea for a song, but the lyrics were pretty subpar. She spent the next hour helping him rewrite them and shape them into something that had plenty of spark.

"Man, you are good," he said after they'd finished.

Yes, she was.

"You really belong down here."

Yes, she did. "I'll be there come summer," she said.

"You're gonna love it. I'll have to take you to The Bluebird when you get here. And the Commodore Lounge at the Holiday Inn in the West End has always got some good writers playing. I got a chance to play there last week."

"How did it go?"

"I killed it," he bragged, but his self-deprecating smile seasoned the bragging with a dose of humility. "So, what have you got? Need help with anything?"

"I just started something. I think it's pretty good."

"Let's hear what you got?"

She sang through her first verse and chorus, ending with the line, "It feels all wrong, but you know I'm right."

"That's good shit," he said when she'd finished. "Feels real."

It was real. She knew she was doing the right thing breaking up with Kenny, but she felt like in the process she'd punctured a hole in her heart.

"You writing this from personal experience?"

"I broke up with my boyfriend. It felt all wrong to stay together when I'm leaving."

"The right thing to do," Colton approved. "It's a whole 'nother world down here. People who aren't musicians or songwriters don't get it. You need to be with people who do."

Like him? She hoped Colton wasn't part of the reason she'd broken up with Kenny. That would have made her feel like a cheater. And she would never cheat on Kenny.

Probably what attracted her to Colton was the new life he symbolized. He was Nashville. He shared the same dream as she did. He breathed that same ambitious air, had that same need to be making music. Kenny was supportive, but he stood outside the tribe. He didn't speak the language.

"Nashville's gonna be a whole new beginning for you," Colton said.

It was, and that new beginning was taking her into a new world, one with a very different atmosphere. Kenny wouldn't be able to breathe for long in it, she was sure. She did love him, and she loved Moonlight Harbor, but she loved her dream of building a music career more, of breathing songs and harmonies, of hearing other singers singing her songs. Nashville was her Mecca, not Kenny's. She'd move away and he'd move on, and someday she'd look back fondly on the time they'd had together. But she wouldn't regret the choice she was making now, she was sure.

J.J. Walker was becoming a habit. Not an addiction, Bonnie told herself. Only a habit, like biting her fingernails or having a morning latte at Beans and Books. She could end this growing…whatever…anytime she wanted.

She just didn't happen to want to. Being with him was easy and fun. She liked golfing on Saturdays and trying to hit that stupid little ball. She loved the high she got when it sailed up into the air and far away. It was almost therapeutic.

And being with J.J. was good therapy. He felt like someone she could trust. She hadn't experienced that with a man in…ever.

"You two are good together," Loretta kept telling her.

"We're only friends," she kept insisting. Friends who golfed together, had lunch together, went to the movies together. Companionship was a good thing. They didn't have to mix in love and sex. If they got that involved it was bound to ruin everything.

"Friends with bennies?" Missy once probed. "Otherwise, I don't know why you're wasting your time."

Maybe it was a waste of time. Probably not fair to J.J. if she wasn't going to let what they had go anywhere serious. She should bag the golf lessons, the lunches. Stay home and watch Netflix. Cut the man loose. But still, she wasn't ready to break the habit.

On this Saturday night in early May, as she looked to where he always sat at the bar and saw him watching her, she could feel the heat all the way up on the bandstand. Who knew sparks could fly so far?

*How about those bennies?* her hormones nagged.

*No*, she told them firmly. *We are not going to go all crazy and jump in with our whole heart and mess this up. I have to live here and so does he.*

After the band quit for the night, he was on hand to pay them and tell them how good they sounded.

"As always," Loretta joked.

"As always," J.J. said. To Bonnie he said, "That green top looks incredible on you. Is it new?"

"It is," she said. "And since when do men notice things like a new top?"

"Since they see one on a mermaid," he replied with a grin.

"Say dear, I'm going to catch a ride home with Avril tonight," Loretta said. "Don't go walking out to the parking lot on your own?" As if there was any danger of anything happening to Bonnie in The Drunken Sailor parking lot or anywhere in Moonlight Harbor.

"I'll see she gets to her car okay," J.J. said.

"Thank you," Loretta said to him. "You enjoy the rest of your night," she said airily, as if the evening was just beginning.

"Stay and have a drink," J.J. said to Bonnie.

"The bar's closed," she reminded him.

"I know the guy who owns the place," he said with a wink.

Maybe the evening *was* just beginning.

Soon they were the only people left in the pub. It felt cozy and intimate. And natural. And when he lifted his glass of whiskey and softly said, "Here's looking at you, kid, and I never get tired of it," that felt natural, too.

When he finally walked her to her car, and asked, "When are you going to let me kiss you?" her brain went on vacation and her hormones assured her it was perfectly natural to say, "How about now?"

The sparks became a fire, and he pressed her against the car and lit her up completely. Team Estrogen went berserk, and before she knew it she was kissing him back like a starving woman, letting him lift her onto the hood and...

*What are you doing?* scolded her brain, charging in and putting an end to the foolishness.

"Okay, this is more than a kiss," she said, pulling away and disappointing the team.

He smiled down at her. "This is more than a friendship, don't you think?" She didn't answer, so he continued. "Look, I don't know what might have happened in your past."

"Nothing good. I've been down that road and it ended in a lot of hurt."

"Not every road leads to hurt," he said.

Enough had. She could still remember the bitter words, and in one breakup getting a beer bottle thrown at her, barely missing her head. Still, the worst had been the one with Rance.

"Hmm, that sounds like a great hook for a song," she quipped. Except it wasn't one she could write and have it come off with any authenticity.

"Take a chance with me, Bonnie."

She shivered, wrapped her arms around her. Even with her jacket on, the night was cold.

"It's hard to take a chance when you've been betrayed," she said, her voice barely above a whisper.

"He cheated on you?" guessed J.J.

There'd been others, but only one He. "Oh, yeah. And then some. Nothing's ever worked out since."

"I'm no cheater," J.J. said. "And talking about roads, when you take the one that involves stepping on other people it never ends anywhere good."

"It did for him." The bastard.

"He hasn't gotten to the bad part yet, but he will. We all do eventually."

"Sometimes I think I'd like nothing better," she admitted. "But life's too short to spend it dreaming about somebody's downfall."

"Life's too short to spend any of it living halfway," J.J. said.

"I'm not living halfway," Bonnie insisted.

"You're not? I am. Living solo cuts out half the good stuff."

"You are quite the philosopher," she said.

"I am. In fact, I'm a lot of things."

Yes, he was. Smart, sexy, generous.

"I'm not a user. I'll take your heart though. When you're ready to give it to me," he hurried to add.

"I don't know if I'll ever be ready," she warned.

"I'm going to gamble that you will. I'll wait. You're worth it."

"You could be waiting a long time. Life is short, remember?"

He grinned. "Then I better work harder at convincing you to take a chance on me." He began to channel ABBA, singing their famous song about taking chances.

"Stop already," she said with a laugh. "You're hurting my ears."

He stopped singing and smiled that cocky smile. Then he turned serious. "I'm not giving up. I'd be crazy to. We've got something good and I think it can only get better."

She pondered those words all the way home and continued to once she was in bed. Handsome men were the devil's own sirens, luring unsuspecting women to crash on the rocky shores of heartbreak. J.J. couldn't be one of them. She was sure he wasn't.

She wanted to believe that. But then she remembered what had happened with Rance.

That first songwriting session with Rance was music magic. "You have got it, lady," he said, as he looked at the lyrics she'd written. "I can do something with this. There's women out there looking for hit songs."

"Yeah?" she asked eagerly. "Think this could be a hit?"

"Once I give it a melody. Lemme see, here," he said, and began strumming. Then he started singing the first line of the first verse. "You think you know it all, but you ain't so smart. You need to learn a thing or two about a woman's heart."

The melody coupled with her words gave her goose bumps, and they multiplied as he sang on. Of course, some of the excitement she was feeling could have had a lot to do with the fact that they were sitting so close she could feel the sexual current between them. He was the hottest thing she'd ever seen, and she wanted to kiss him and feel those big, gorgeous hands of his on her.

"What do you think?" he asked after he'd put a melody to the verse.

"I think it's a hit," she said. "Someone's gonna want this."

Someone did. "Love Lessons" got picked up by a small publisher and Bonnie and Rance were on their way. Not only to success but to love. Sitting side by side on a Sunday evening on his old sofa, their guitars in their laps, trying out lyrics and melodies, her sometimes singing harmony— it felt like heaven.

The first time he kissed her she knew she'd found heaven. "I could get used to this," he said.

"Let's work on that," she said, giving him a cheeky grin.

So of course, they did. Soon they were sleeping together and she was spending more time in his place than in her dorm room. She had to force herself to concentrate on her classes and spent every minute of every weekend with him, usually neglecting her homework. Who needed school when you could get a real-life education hanging out with Rance and other songwriters and singers, all determined to make it in the music business?

She walked around in a happy fog, barely seeing the ornamental cherry trees in bloom. And, once school was out, the sizzle of Nashville summer was nothing compared to the fire he built in her.

"I think I'm in love," she said to her friend Carolina James.

"I think you're in heat," Carolina teased.

"You can't have love without heat," Bonnie said.

It turned out you could have heat without love though.

What a fool she'd been, a regular heartbreak rodeo queen, thinking she could hang on to Rance. Of course, she hadn't been able to.

J.J.'s talk of stealing hearts… Did he have any idea what a cruel thing that could be? Rance Jackson stole hers, then stole her song. Worst of all, he stole her ability to trust.

But did she want to keep giving him that power? Was she going to let him steal her future, too?

# *Thirteen*

"I think you like more than golf and movies," Loretta observed as she and Bonnie enjoyed a quick lunch of popcorn shrimp at the Seafood Shack. "About time you found someone."

"This is nothing serious. We're just hanging out."

"A lot," said Loretta.

"That doesn't mean anything."

"In your case it does. I've never seen you with someone this long."

"It hasn't been that long," Bonnie pointed out.

"It is for you, and I'm glad to see it. He's such a nice man. I think he's good for you."

"He is," Bonnie admitted. "I feel comfortable around him."

"There's a good sign," Loretta said.

"It is, but there's no need to rush. I'm in no hurry to get hurt."

"We all get hurt at some point in our lives, but you have to move beyond those hurts. You can't move into the future if you never really bury the past."

"I have," Bonnie insisted. "How's your shrimp Louie?" she asked hoping to divert Loretta's attention.

It didn't work. "No, you haven't, darling. If you had, you wouldn't be so afraid to take a chance on your future."

Bonnie sighed. "Sometimes I wish I could be more like you."

"Gullible?" Loretta said, shaking her head.

"No. Brave. Willing to try again."

"You have that opportunity now. I hope you'll take it. Remember, every person who comes into your life isn't going to bring along something bad."

"You're right, of course," Bonnie said. J.J. was not Rance. She needed to stop hoarding her trust as if he were. He'd been nothing but kind to her and honest in his dealings. Maybe it was time to let go of the tight rein she'd been keeping on her feelings and allow herself to fall completely into love.

Loretta wanted a lot of things for her girls, but tops was finding a soul mate. She'd had that with her husband, and she knew how satisfying it could be.

"I so want to see them happy," she said to Lawrence as they FaceTimed.

They'd fallen into the habit of chatting twice a week and she looked forward to those times. Lawrence wasn't nearly as good-looking as Harvey had been and didn't have the same repertoire of charming endearments. What he did have was honesty and an authentic interest in her life. Talking with him made her happy.

"Of course you do," he said. "We all want that for our kids. I remember when my Lori was going through her divorce. I was ready to murder the bum."

"But look how well she's doing now," Loretta pointed out.

"Oh, yeah. I'm proud of that girl. She went back to school

and got her master's degree in counseling. Now she's helping other people who are struggling with hard things. And
she's happily married. Your Bonnie will find her way, too.
I'm sure of it. This new man sounds like an okay guy."

"He is, and with Avril leaving soon she's going to need
someone to help her adjust."

"She's got you," pointed out Lawrence.

"She won't always have me." Parents couldn't stick
around forever.

"She'll be fine. And remember how you're always saying she needs to let Avril go?"

"Yes." Loretta already knew where he was going with
this.

"Maybe you need to let go a little, too. Your girl will
find her way, don't worry."

"Don't worry, be happy," Loretta sang, quoting an old
Bob Marley song.

"That's right," he said with a grin.

"Thank you. Talking to you always makes me feel good,"
Loretta said.

"I'm cheaper than a shrink," he joked.

"I swear, with me dumping on you, you might as well
be," she said.

"Anytime. I'm happy to be a sounding board."

He was more than that. Lawrence was balm for her
wounded heart. If the relationship they had never grew
beyond friendship, never turned into hearts and flowers
and thrills and chills she'd be okay with it. His friendship
was something she could count on, solid and secure. After
what she'd gone through, that was worth more than gold.

As soon as school was out Bonnie had a new challenge,
seeing Avril off at the airport without looking like Mama

Stick-in-the-Mud. How hard it was to watch her girl disappear into the airport, letting her fly off into an uncertain future.

"Looks like The Mermaids are a duo now," Loretta said once they were back in the car and ready to head home to Moonlight Harbor.

Bonnie didn't say anything. She couldn't. Her throat was crammed too tight with tears for any words to sneak past.

Loretta reached over and laid a hand on her arm. "I know it's hard, but there comes a point when you have to let your baby go."

Bonnie nodded, still unable to speak.

"I cried all the way back to the airport after dropping you off at Belmont," Loretta continued. "I prayed every night that you'd be okay."

"You should have prayed harder," Bonnie said, finding her voice.

"I'm sorry things didn't go the way you wanted."

"You have no idea," Bonnie said.

"Because you never told me much about what happened."

"It's all water under the bridge now so it doesn't matter."

It really didn't except for those times when Bonnie thought about what she'd lost and what she'd given up and got mad at herself. But enough of that. Spending time with J.J. she was finding her own version of that yellow brick road, and even though she was barely inching her way down it, she was experiencing a new kind of happiness. Lately, she hardly noticed the scars on her heart.

But they were still there and the hurt had been horrible. She didn't want Avril to get hurt the way she had.

She'd tried one last time to talk her out of going. "The music business has changed since I was there. I hear you'll get paid for any song you write but you won't get royalties. It's a new system now and it doesn't do songwriters any good."

"There are ways to get your music out there, ways you didn't have when you were in Nashville," Avril had insisted.

Yes, things were always changing, maybe for the better. Maybe Bonnie was wrong. Maybe she was misinformed. It was a brave new world for musicians now, thanks to technology. But… "If you need money let me know."

"Don't worry. I'll be fine."

The confidence of youth yet to be tested. Bonnie could only hope her concern for her daughter was unfounded and that she was seeing trouble through the dirty lens of her own past experiences. Everyone who went to Nashville didn't get used. Some of the lucky ones actually were able to carve out a career. She could only hope Avril would be one of them. Either way, whatever happened next to her daughter was out of her control.

Avril was already in love. Nashville was party city.

Gina's band gig hadn't worked out, but she'd already sung in one writer's showcase and was sure that any day she'd be on stage at the Ryman. The stars in her eyes were contagious.

"More people come here now than to Las Vegas," she said to Avril as they climbed onto a party trolley being towed by a tractor.

"Wow," was all Avril could think to say.

She'd dumped her suitcase in the small living room of Gina's apartment as soon as she'd arrived and they'd headed out immediately to enjoy the city, starting with chicken at Hattie B's and then walking to the giant food court next door to get ice cream. The rolling party was the next adventure, and they were sharing it with a tipsy, happy bunch of women all out enjoying a bachelorette party. They all wore matching white sleeveless tops trimmed with pink ruffles and denim shorts, along with cowgirl hats and white boots.

"Not a cowgirl among 'em," said Gina.

"Wooo," the girls called, waving their drinks at the crowd of pedestrians clogging Broadway, taking pictures and ducking into tourist shops. Every bar on both sides of the street had a band playing and the music came out at them in a roar loud enough to make their ears ring.

Gina hoisted her drink, too, and waved at the people they were passing, and Avril joined right in. This city was so smokin' hot. She was going to love it here.

"My head is spinning," she said late that night after they'd hit several bars. She fell on the couch and announced, "I'm gonna be so hungover in the morning."

She had definitely drunk more than she'd intended. But Nashville was a furnace, hot and humid—a very different weather system than the one she was used to on the Washington Coast.

"We need water," Gina said, and went to the kitchen and poured them both a glass. She came to where Avril was sprawled and handed her one. "Here, this will help."

Avril took a big drink, then laid her head back against the couch. She knew she was smiling like a fool. "I can't believe I'm here."

"Believe it," said Gina. "And sleep in as long as you want tomorrow. I gotta go to work, but I'll be back in the afternoon and then we can go out and I'll take you over to the Country Music Songwriters Association so you can join."

"Thanks. And thanks for letting me crash here," Avril said.

"Hey, what are friends for? Anyway, it's nice to have the company."

"Like you need it. You've already met people," Avril pointed out.

"Yeah, the waitresses at Waffle House are super nice, and I've met a couple of songwriters by going to some showcases, but it's not the same as being with your bestie-best."

Avril's phone dinged with an incoming text. You here?

"That can't be your mom. You already texted her," said Gina.

"It's Colton." Avril thumbed back her reply. Yep. Just got back from doing downtown with Gina.

He sent a thumbs-up emoji followed by, You two want to go out tomorrow? Songwriter showcase.

"Want to go to a songwriter showcase?" Avril asked Gina.

"Sure. Where?"

Where? Avril texted.

Commodore Lounge at The Holiday Inn. West End. I'm playing some of my stuff.

We'll be there, Avril texted back.

KK, came the reply.

"So I finally get to meet the amazing Colton," said Gina.

"He is pretty dope."

"And now that you're not with anybody…"

"I don't want to rush into anything," Avril said. "I still have the feels for Kenny."

"You were right to break up though. You guys are going in different directions. Well, you're going. He's staying."

"I know. It was the right thing to do, but I still feel like I broke off a piece of myself and left it in Washington."

"I guess you did. But lizards can regrow their tails," Gina said.

"What? That is so rando."

"No it's not. I'm just sayin' you can regrow that part of you that you left behind, and I bet Colton's just the one to help you."

*He very well could be*, Avril thought.

Still, that night on Gina's pull-out bed, snuggled under a blanket to fight off the cold nip from the air conditioning, it wasn't Colton Avril dreamed of. It was Kenny. He was on his fishing boat and it was sinking. She woke up with a start. What the heck was that about? Her guilty subconscious, she decided.

The morning called for more water and aspirin and lying around waiting to feel human again. She finally did though. Rather than sit around an empty apartment she grabbed her phone and went out to explore more of the city.

On foot. Yuck. She was going to have to get a car.

Fortunately, she'd sold hers before she left, and she had enough money to buy something used. She also had enough saved up to get a place of her own, but was glad Gina had insisted she stay with her for a few weeks so she could take her time deciding where she wanted to live. She'd be kicking in money toward the rent, so it was a win-win. And if being temporary roommates worked they could always get a place together once Gina's lease was up.

It was midmorning and the heat hit her like a wave when she stepped outside. Yow! This was going to take some getting used to. She was sweating by the time she found a coffee shop, so abandoned the idea of a latte and got herself an iced coffee instead. Ah, better.

Cooled off, she ventured back out into the heat and wandered around town. She stopped at a couple of souvenir shops where she found a T-shirt with Nashville emblazoned on it for Glamma and a key ring shaped like a guitar for Mom. Then she walked to the Ryman Theater where so many famous country singers had performed. She took a selfie with the statue of Loretta Lynn and texted it to Glamma and Mom.

Very cool, Mom texted back.

Glamma's response was better. Two stars together. Glamma was the best.

Another text came in from Mom. Glad you're having fun.

Avril hoped that meant she was starting to understand. She should, for crying out loud.

After all her walking, Avril was sweating again. She decided that someone should invent wearable AC. This was gross.

But every city had its faults. This was nothing another iced coffee couldn't fix. At the rate she was going she'd have to drink gallons of it.

When she got back to the apartment she was a sweaty mess all over again and ready for a second shower. It's hot here, she texted her grandmother. I feel like I'm living in a furnace.

You'll get used to it, Glamma texted back. How are you liking Nashville?

It's great. Going to a songwriter showcase tonight.

Lucky you. Wish I was there. Be sure and send me a picture of you on Music Row.

Will do, Avril said, and followed that with several hearts. At least Glamma was excited that she was here.

She wished her mom was, too. Mom had finally stopped

with all the doom and gloom crap, even though she wasn't happy that Avril was in Music City. She'd have to deal with it. This was Avril's life, and, unlike her mother, she wasn't going to quit on her dream.

She filled in the time waiting for Gina to come back by working on a song, writing about coming to Nashville. It poured out of her. *All my life I been searchin'*, she wrote, *searchin' for this.*

It seemed like she had, indeed, been waiting all her life to get to Music City and now here she was. She'd been circling the city for years and she'd finally landed. The words poured out of her like a lyric waterfall. She read the last line of her chorus and smiled with satisfaction.

*I never knew what home was till now.* Yep, that said it all.

Gina came back, bringing a pizza she'd picked up after work for their dinner that night. "Sorry, I can't afford to go out to eat every night."

"Hey, me, either," Avril assured her. "Pizza is great, and I'll pay for half."

"What did you do while I was gone?" Gina asked.

"Went out, got some gifts for Mom and Glamma, and got coffee. Iced. Halfway home I was ready to dump the last of it on my head."

Gina snickered. "It gets a little hot here."

"A little? Now I know what a pancake feels like. Only at least the pancake gets to leave the stove eventually."

"That's what air conditioning is for," said Gina.

"If yours ever breaks we'll broil to death."

"What else did you do besides broil and bitch?"

"I wrote a song. Wanna hear it?"

"Of course," Gina said, and plopped into an armchair, the only other piece of furniture in the room besides the couch and a coffee table.

Avril got her guitar and played her newest brain baby.

"That is solid platinum," Gina said. "I want to make it my next single. Can I?"

Avril had thought she'd make it her launch song, but friendship won out over ambition. And besides, she was flattered that her friend loved it enough to record it. "Sure," she said. Gina had linked up with a guy who had his own home studio and was already putting songs up on iTunes and TikTok. Maybe they'd make some money. Ha! That'd show Mom.

Energized by pizza and pop and excitement over getting out and into the music scene, she co-piloted Gina to the motel's lounge, an intimate venue with a small stage. As they walked in she saw two men wearing jeans and T-shirts standing with hands propped on their guitars, talking to a woman with a clipboard.

The blond-haired, blue-eyed heart-heater was Colton. He glanced her way, saw her and smiled and waved her over. The guy with him was lean and redheaded, taller than Colton, but Colton, with his good looks completely overshadowed him.

"Hey, you made it," he said and gave her a hug.

"We had to come hear you," Avril said, returning it. He felt nice to hug.

"You must be Gina," Colton said, holding out a hand.

"Yep," she said.

"This is Jimmy Wills and Pam Whiting. Pam runs the show here."

"Nice to meet you," said Pam. "Are you songwriters?"

"You bet we are," Gina answered for both of them. "And singers."

"Well, send me a demo and maybe we can work you into

a show in the future," Pam said and handed them each a business card.

Wow! Only her second day in Nashville and she was already making connections. "That would be great," said Avril. "Thanks."

"Looks like we're going to have a good crowd tonight," Pam observed.

The place was starting to fill up and Gina suggested she and Avril get a table before they were all gone.

"Save us a seat," said Colton. "We'll join you after our set."

"You got it," said Avril.

"Wow," Gina said as they walked away. "Just. Wow."

"I know. It will be so cool to start performing here."

"That, too, but I was talking about Colton. Chihuahua, he is hot."

"He's got a good voice, too."

"You've never exactly raved about his songs," said Gina as they settled at a table.

"Well, they're okay."

Gina let out a snort. "You can't make it here on just okay."

"Sometimes it's about connections."

"True, and it looks like we made a good one tonight. We need to do a show together."

"That would be fun," said Avril. It would be a good place to start.

Their waitress appeared and they both ordered beer. By the time their server returned with their drinks the place was packed.

Jimmy kicked off the performance. "Hey, y'all, thanks for coming out," he said, and was greeted by applause and whoops from the audience. "I'm Jimmy Wills and this is my pal Colton Gray. We've got some songs for you tonight that I hope you're gonna like." This inspired more applause. When it had stopped he got right down to business. "I wrote this song for Ashley Cooke. It's called 'On a Bad Day.'"

"On a Bad Day" was crazy good. Gina leaned over after and whispered to Avril, "We need to write with him."

Colton took his turn next, and his song was…okay, but even Jimmy singing harmony with him couldn't elevate it to the same level as the one Jimmy had sung.

The evening went on, with both men singing their songs. Jimmy's all sparkled with that hard to describe specialness that screamed *hit*. Colton's couldn't compare with what his friend was doing.

"Hard to compete with Jimmy," Gina observed, opting for kindness.

Yes, it was, but the business was all about competition. Even Avril knew you couldn't rise to the top unless you were the cream in the bucket. Still, Colton was gorgeous and he had the pipes. And the fire in the belly. You never knew.

The set ended and the guys joined Avril and Gina at the table. "So, what'd ya think?" Colton asked.

"I think you're gonna look great on TikTok," Avril said. That was true.

"I'm shook," Gina said to Jimmy. "Your songs are great and you sure know how to come up with a hook."

He smiled and blushed. Actually blushed. Jimmy was that rare breed of man, both talented and modest. In some ways he reminded Avril of Kenny.

Kenny. He would have loved hanging out in this lounge, listening to music. The thought made her feel wistful. She'd done the right thing in breaking up, but she missed the guy.

"I worked up a thirst," Colton said. "You girls want another beer?"

"One's enough for me," said Avril.

"I'm driving," Gina said. "I better quit while I'm behind."

"Hmm, I wonder if there's a song in that," Jimmy said thoughtfully.

"I'll write it with you," said Colton, and gave him a slap on the back. "Whaddya want, bro? I'm buying."

"Anything wet with alcohol," said Jimmy. He shook his head and smiled as Colton walked to the bar. "That guy never misses a chance. He's gonna make it big-time someday."

"Because he never misses a chance?" Gina asked.

"That's what it's about down here. You grab every opportunity by the throat."

"That's why we're here," Gina said and smiled. "And to make friends, too. I haven't been here that long and Avril just hit town."

"Friends is what it's all about as far as I'm concerned," Jimmy said, and the smile he gave Gina showed he really wanted to be friends with her.

Colton returned with two beers. "What'd I miss?"

"Nothing," Avril said. "We were just talking about how important friends are."

"You got that right," Colton said. He raised his glass. "Here's to friendship."

"To friendship," they all echoed, and clinked glasses.

Another songwriter had taken the stage, this one a woman who looked about Avril's mom's age.

"She's starting too late," Colton said as the woman began to sing.

Too late. Avril thought of her mom, who had so much

talent and was still so pretty. The thought of what she could
have done and been and missed out on made Avril sad. Too
late came too fast. She sure didn't want to end up like her
mom, missing out on living the life she was meant to live.

The rest of the week went by faster than a tornado.
Colton went with her when she bought a car from one of
the car rental agencies—"Not because you can't do it on
your own," he'd said. "But some of these guys can be sex-
ist dinos and take advantage of a woman."

They hadn't. She'd impressed him with her negotiating
skills and had purchased a used Chevrolet Spark LT hatch-
back with wireless phone connectivity. With wheels she was
set to go, and the first thing she did was take a drive around
the city, familiarizing herself with the various streets and
freeway entrances and exits.

She also drove to Music Square. Which was nothing
like her grandmother had described. With the exception
of a couple places, almost all those adorable little houses
that Glamma said had once housed recording studios and
publishers were gone, replaced by giant buildings and what
looked like either condos or apartments. The few that re-
mained were home to hair salons or lawyers' offices or
holistic health places.

Glamma was horrified when Avril reported it to her. "I
can't believe it," she said mournfully. "What is Nashville
without Music Row and Music Square?"

"A party town," said Avril.

"Soulless," said Glamma, refusing to look on the bright
side.

"I saw Curb Records and RCA though," Avril offered.

All she got in response was a sigh. But then Glamma
moved on. "But you're liking it there?"

"Oh, yeah. I've already gone to two songwriters showcases and I've written three songs. And on Friday I'm going to The Bluebird Café to hear Tony Arata." Glamma's supposed admirer who she claimed wrote "The Dance" for her.

"How great! You say hi to him for me, okay?"

"I'll try," Avril said, not wanting to make any promises. She wasn't sure she'd be able to get up the nerve to talk to such a songwriting superstar.

"And I want to hear all about it afterward," Glamma said.

"You will," Avril promised.

She ended the call with a sigh. If only Mom would get so excited about her new beginning in Music City. She hadn't actually talked to her mother since she arrived, only texted her a few times—once to let her know she'd gotten there in one piece, another text with a picture of Gina's apartment and one of her new car as well as a picture of the Country Music Hall of Fame with its cement keyboard. When she'd sent Glamma the picture of it she'd received a reply that she'd be in there someday. Mom had merely replied, Glad you're settling in. As underwhelming as her response to the one Avril had taken with the statue of Loretta Lynn, and adding a heart didn't make it any less so.

But what had she expected? Her mother couldn't get past the fear that Avril was going to fail. The more fun she was having and the more people she was meeting who could help her get somewhere the more pissed she was getting over her mother's attitude. Maybe Mom was a little jealous that Avril was actually doing what she'd tried to and couldn't. If that was the case it was her problem, not Avril's, and she'd have to deal with it.

Meanwhile, Avril had another music adventure waiting. Going to The Bluebird! Ever since the TV show *Nashville* the place had become a huge tourist destination and it was probably easier finding diamonds on the sidewalk than it was getting tickets to get in. But Colton had managed to score two. "Doors open at 8:30. I'll pick you up at quarter after."

He was picking her up. Did that make it a date? So far his vibe had been friendly, but she wondered if come Friday it would get…friendlier.

She had mixed feelings about that possibility. Interest, yes, but also guilt. It hadn't been that long since she'd broken up with Kenny and she still missed him. But she was also getting the feels for Colton. She cautioned herself not to jump into any new relationship. She had time.

"You are lookin' fine," Colton said, when she met him at the apartment door wearing tight jeans, boots and a scoop-necked sleeveless top.

She'd also worn the turquoise necklace that Glamma had given her for her last birthday. Her hair was down, falling in waves to her shoulders and she'd updated her eyelash extensions earlier that day. She had to agree. She did look good.

So did he. Good enough to make her heart rate skitter. Maybe she was ready for a new relationship.

"You look pretty tasty yourself," she said. Not that he'd dressed up. He wore jeans, flip-flops and a black T-shirt that said *Music is Life. That's Why Our Hearts Have Beats.* In between those two statements was an electrocardiogram readout with treble and bass clef symbols cleverly inserted in it. The T-shirt was dope. The way he filled it out was even better. If he led her to the love cliff she could probably fall.

"It's the shirt," he said.

"I like it," she said. *And I like you.*

Colton was easy to be around and encouraging. What was not to like about that?

The café was in an unimposing strip mall building. It

had a scalloped awning over its entrance with its name written in script. Nothing to take pictures of, really. But she did—a selfie of Colton and herself, which she'd post on Instagram later.

But then she walked inside. It was small, with all of ninety seats, which would explain why tickets for shows there sold out so fast, but it reeked of music history, and looking at the wall of signed pictures of various artists who'd played there and seeing the neon bluebird flying in front of a yellow rainbow gave her goose bumps.

"Wow," she breathed.

"Yeah, that was my reaction the first time I came here. It's magic."

It sure was. The place filled almost instantly, and the sound level rose with excited chatter as people ordered drinks and settled in for the evening. But a hush came over the crowd when Tony Arata and his friends went on to play. Seated on a stool in the front of the house, wearing a polo shirt and jeans and sandals, he looked like the man next-door who'd be out mowing his lawn on a Saturday, unprepossessing, with a round face behind glasses, graying hair cut short, and a smile that was enough to make everyone there feel like they were his new best friend. Humble and entertaining, he had the audience in the palm of his hand from the minute he joked about leaving his home in Thunderbolt, Georgia, for Nashville and what he referred to as the poignant moment he had with his father right before he left where Daddy hugged him and said, "Son, I think you've lost your damn mind." Everyone chuckled.

Except Avril. She could identify. It was what her own mother thought. Listening to the man sing she felt like she was rising on wings, ready to fly. He made it. So could she.

The people with him were great also, including songwriter Carolina James, who had written hits for everyone from Martina McBride to Faith Hill. She looked forty-something, had long, blond hair and wore jeans and a red shirt with Tomato written on it in white. If Mom had stayed in Nashville would she have been up there singing with those people?

After the concert Avril screwed up her courage, and she and Colton stood in line to talk to Mr. Arata. Once she got to him her throat felt suddenly parched and her tongue was tied up like a pretzel.

Colton stepped into the gap, shook the man's hand and said, "It's an honor to meet you, sir."

"That's kind of you to say. You a songwriter?"

"I am," Colton said proudly.

"And this young lady with you?"

*Now or never. Say something!* "I am, too," Avril said. "I think you knew my grandmother. Loretta Brinks?"

He smiled politely but it was obvious the name wasn't registering. "Brinks?"

Maybe Avril should have added, "The Cougar." He looked younger than Glamma. Avril could feel her face heating and it was probably as red as the T-shirt Carolina was wearing.

"You meet so many people," she said, giving him a pass.

"There are a lot of good people here," he said kindly.

Carolina, who'd been standing next to him, chatting with someone, turned and stared at Avril. "Did you say Brinks?"

Avril nodded.

"You by any chance related to Bonnie Brinks?"

"That's my mom," Avril said. What the heck?

Someone else had claimed Mr. Arata's attention. Avril barely noticed. She was too busy trying to take in what Carolina had just said.

"How do you know my mom?" she asked.

"I knew her when we were young and trying to make it as songwriters. It was almost the end of an era." Carolina shook her head. "Things have sure changed since then. It's a whole different world now." She pulled herself out of her reverie. "Are you a songwriter?"

"I am," Avril said.

"Me, too," said Colton, and introduced himself.

"Well, good luck, you two. You got a tough row to hoe."

Good Lord, she sounded like Avril's mom. But Carolina had made it.

"That's not to say you can't succeed. You young ones are finding new ways of getting your music out there all the time."

"But we can learn a lot from the superstars like you," Colton said to her, sucking up.

She gave him a flirty smile. "Yeah?"

"I'm teachable," he said, and smiled, showing off dimples.

Colton never let an opportunity to advance his agenda get past. It seemed kind of pushy to Avril, and she felt embarrassed by association.

"You are an ambitious one, aren't you?" Carolina teased.

"Reach for the moon and maybe you catch a star," he said.

She chuckled. "I bet you're gonna catch your star. How about you?" she asked Avril. "Are you reaching for the moon, too?"

"I want to get my music out there," Avril said simply.

"I bet your mama's proud of you," Carolina said.

"I'd love to hear more about what it was like when you were first starting out," Avril said. "Mom doesn't talk about it."

"I can imagine not." The woman seemed to consider

for a moment. "I tell you what. Meet me at 8th and Roast Tuesday at ten. I'll buy you a latte."

"Thank you," Avril said.

"Holy shit," said Colton as they moved away. "Talk about an uberconnection. That woman's written songs for everyone on the planet, including Rance Jackson. She's a legend."

"Funny, my mom never said anything about knowing her." Why hadn't Mom given her the name of someone who could help her find her feet in Nashville? It was strange. She was tempted to text her mom right then and there and tell her who she'd just met, then decided to wait. Maybe she'd see if Carolina would let her take a selfie together. She could send it to Mom. Maybe even gloat a little. *See, there are people here who want to help me.* The thought made her smile.

Back at her apartment after Colton pressed her against the door and gave her a kiss that melted her from her chest down to her toes, she was really smiling.

"There's more where that came from," he said and gave her neck a nip.

"I might have to come back for seconds," she said, but then, when he was ready to oblige, laid a hand on his chest. "Next time." Sexy as he was, she wasn't going to rush into anything. She not only had to find her footing in Music City, she also needed to find it romantically.

"I'm ready whenever you are. I'm into you. Been into you ever since you joined our critique group," he said.

"Yeah?"

"Oh, yeah. I think we've got something here. Let's keep it going."

"Good idea," she said, then gave him a quick kiss before slipping inside and shutting the door.

She smiled and her heart skipped as she heard him on the other side, calling, "I'm hooked."

Gina had been stretched out on the couch, streaming a show on her computer. "You are such a man-eater," she teased as she sat up. "How was the show?"

Avril plopped down next to her. "Stellar."

"Tell me every deet."

She'd barely settled in to tell Gina about her adventure when she got a text from Glamma, wanting to know how she'd enjoyed being at The Bluebird.

It was great, she texted back.

Did you get to meet Tony?

She didn't have the heart to tell her grandmother that he didn't remember her. Didn't get a chance, she lied.

Oh, well. He might not remember me anyway. It was a long time ago. Just a chance meeting with a bunch of other musicians.

And he'd just happened to get inspired by Glamma to write a song. Yep, Glamma was a legend in her own mind.

Tell Mom I'm doing great, she texted. Met an old friend of hers. Going out for coffee next week.

Work those connections, Glamma texted back.

She intended to. Maybe, in the process, she'd actually learn more of what had happened in Nashville to turn her mother so against the place.

# *Fourteen*

"I'm tired of hiding inside with the AC going. It's time to get out of Arizona," Lawrence said as he and Loretta were enjoying a Friday afternoon chat. "I'm thinking it's time to hit your beach town."

"You come on up and I'll have the best halibut dinner waiting for you that you've ever had," she said.

"It's a deal. I'll get working on that right now. I think you said there's a campground in town, right?"

"Yes, not far from the pier."

"I'll give 'em a call tomorrow and see how soon I can book a spot. That halibut dinner sounds real good. I'm looking forward to it. And to hearing you and your daughter sing, too."

"We are worth the trip," she said.

"*You* are worth the trip," he corrected her. She could feel the happiness from that remark deep in her chest. This was what the term *heartwarming* meant.

Loretta was in high spirits that night when The Mermaids sang, and she went to bed wearing the biggest smile she'd donned in a long time. *Don't get your hopes up*, she cautioned herself. The last thing she needed was to rush into a relationship.

Still, the idea of seeing her old friend was enough to give her pleasant dreams all night long. The best one was of her and Lawrence walking on Moonlight Beach, hand in hand. Harvey popped up out of nowhere and fell on his knees in the sand to beg her forgiveness.

"I didn't deserve you," he said.

"You're right, you didn't," she replied, and then she and Lawrence strolled off into the sunset with "(I've Had) the Time of My Life" playing in the background.

She woke up sure it was a sign. Lawrence messaged her that he'd gotten a spot and was on his way. Those camper spots were hard to come by in the summer. It was another sign! She immediately called Waves Salon and made an appointment for a hair tune-up and a manicure.

"It's good to see you smiling," Moira said when Loretta came into the salon.

"There's always something to smile about," Loretta told her. "I'm moving on. Better days ahead." Whether it turned out to be lasting friendship or budding romance—either way she'd be happy.

Bonnie finished packing up two new paintings to deliver to the art gallery. Two stayed in her painting room—one she wanted to touch up more and the other she was saving for Lucy's birthday and would deliver it at the party Brody was planning for her the next weekend. She was happy with how it had turned out and hoped Lucy would like it. It featured a sea cave with a weathered board propped in front of it. Home, Sweet, Home was carved into the board. The fish-tailed resident sitting on a boulder in front of it looked exactly like Lucy. Next to her sat her husband and favorite

Realtor, wearing board shorts, a T-shirt emblazoned with their company name, and a sailor hat. She was kissing his cheek and winking.

Bonnie smiled as she settled the paintings in the back of her car. This was turning out to be a fun way to earn a little extra money. If she painted faster she could earn quite a little. The first ones she'd delivered to Arthur had sold in two days.

He was glad to see her. "Paint faster or clone yourself," he teased.

"No problem. I'll get right on that," she said.

"You really do have a gift."

"I'd always thought it was for music," she said.

"Creativity usually branches out into other areas," he said as he hung the first picture. "And lucky for us that yours is this. You need to do a show. Maybe Labor Day weekend? What do you think?"

"I don't know," she said. The idea of having to come up with enough paintings for an art show felt overwhelming. "I don't think I could paint enough mermaids for you by then."

"We could do a show featuring you and two of our other local artists," he suggested as he took the other painting to hang.

"I'll think about it," she said.

"Do. People are loving your mermaids. I know you'd have a successful show."

"I appreciate your confidence in me."

His back to her, he casually asked, "Any chance you could appreciate more than my confidence?"

Arthur was a nice man, but there was no chemistry between them. She hated it when men put their self-esteem on the line like this and she had to trample it.

"Arthur, you're a sweet man, but I'm not looking to get

into a relationship," she said, hoping that he wouldn't take it personally.

*Liar, liar, panties on fire.* What the heck did she think she was developing with J.J.?

"Well, you can't blame a guy for trying," he said.

"You don't get anywhere in life if you don't try," she said consolingly.

She'd never said that to her daughter. She would have if Avril had wanted to run marathons, take up painting, become a famous writer. Anything but the music business. So far Avril hadn't shared a lot about how she was faring with making connections. Or whether she'd gotten a job. She was living off her savings but how long would that last? Maybe if she ran out of money she'd come home before she got her heart broken.

"She's going to be fine," J.J. assured her as they sat on a blanket on the beach Sunday night, drinking bottled margaritas and enjoying the bonfire he'd made.

"I know I have to let her go and do her thing," Bonnie said with a sigh, "but it's hard."

"You've raised her well. Quit worrying and enjoy the sunset. And move a little closer. With the sun going down, it's getting cold. We need body heat so we don't freeze."

She lifted an eyebrow. "Freezing at the beach in summer, right in front of a fire?"

"It could happen. You'd hate to see me freeze to death, wouldn't you?"

"That would be terrible," she said and scooted up against him.

There was sure no chance of her freezing around J.J. He turned up her thermostat in a way no man had since... memories started rolling in like a fog.

*No,* she told herself firmly, *don't even.* She was not going to allow Rance to come sneaking into the present and ruin a lovely moment. Maybe even a lovely future if she could shake the ice off her feet and really commit to moving into it.

Even sea snails knew when it was time to leave their confining shell and move to someplace bigger and better. She sighed again. Good grief, surely she was smarter than a sea snail.

"Still thinking about Avril?" he asked.

"No, snails."

One corner of his mouth lifted. "Now, there's a jump."

Jump. At some point that was what she was going to have to do, step off the ledge she kept clinging to, step out and believe that, this time love would provide the net to catch her.

"Lawrence should be here later today," Loretta announced when Bonnie took her to lunch at Sandy's.

"Good. I want to meet him," Bonnie said.

"My little love guardian," Loretta said fondly.

"I want to make sure you don't get hurt again," Bonnie said. "You don't have to be in a hurry."

"I know," Loretta said.

Bonnie was about to say, "Do you? Really?" when her mother changed the subject.

"It sounds like our girl is having a great time in Nashville," Loretta said.

"I guess," Bonnie said, choosing not to share how little she'd heard from Avril.

"Did she tell you she met someone who knew you?"

Bonnie's heart tumbled down into her stomach, taking away her appetite. She pushed around the shrimp salad on her plate. Who had Avril met? What was she learning?

"Did she say who?" Bonnie asked, trying to keep her voice casual.

"No. Any ideas what old friends of yours might still be down there?"

She did, but she shook her head.

"Hopefully, whoever it is will open some doors for her."

*And then slam them in her face.* Oh, Lord, who exactly had Avril met?

That evening Loretta hosted both Lawrence and Bonnie for dinner. Unlike Harvey the fake, Lawrence appeared to be the real thing, with a wallet stuffed full of pictures of his kids and grandkids. Talking about his deceased wife made him tear up, talking about his kids and their accomplishments made his face light up. He wasn't handsome like Marlon, just an average-looking older man with thinning hair and a thickening waist. But his smile was genuine and his connection to her mother real, and if something developed between the two of them Bonnie would enthusiastically give them her daughterly blessing. After so many years alone, Loretta deserved to find someone to share the rest of her life with.

It was great to see her mother in such good spirits. Now, if only she didn't have to worry about Avril. The fretting had left her unable to concentrate at work earlier and had stolen her appetite for the lovely piece of halibut on her plate.

Who had Avril met and what was she learning? All these years later, Bonnie could only hope her past didn't come back to burn her. To burn both of them.

"Thanks for inviting me," Avril said as she and Carolina settled down at a table with their coffee in front of them. Carolina had paid, which Avril thought was really nice.

"Everyone needs someone to show them the ropes," Carolina said. "This is the least I can do for your mom."

"It's weird. She never said she knew you."

Carolina took a sip of her coffee. "Well, darlin', we didn't part on the best of terms. It can get complicated down here."

"Complicated?"

"Relationships, insecurity, misunderstandings…living here is like living in a country song." She moved on before Avril could press her for more details. "But don't you worry. I'm gonna do what I can to help you. I'm back at The Bluebird again tomorrow, singing along with a couple other up-and-coming writers I think you should meet. We're doing a six o'clock show. I'll get you in if you like."

"That's kind of you. Thank you," Avril said.

"We can be kind here. Next time you talk to your mom, be sure and tell her that."

Carolina's words were cryptic to say the least. Something had happened with her and Mom when Mom was in Nashville. That much Avril was sure of. But what? Obviously, Carolina wasn't going to be the one to tell her.

Carolina left and Avril stayed behind and called her mom.

Mom answered with a cautious-sounding, "Hi sweetie."

"Mom, I just had coffee with Carolina James."

Her announcement was met with resounding silence.

"Mom?" she prompted.

"How'd that go?" Mom asked.

"It went great. She's offered to help me. She said to tell you they can be kind here in Nashville."

"I suppose so."

"She also said you were friends, but you didn't part on good terms. What was she talking about?"

Mom sighed. "We had a falling out."

"I figured that. But why?"

"It doesn't matter. It's water under the bridge. But darling, be careful. Don't share too much of yourself or your work too quickly. Yeah, there are good people down there just as there are anywhere, but there are also people who only care about themselves and getting to the top. They'll walk over you and smash you into the dirt to do it."

"Is that what happened to you?" Avril persisted. "Did Carolina walk all over you?"

"It's in the past and it has nothing to do with you. Just remember what I said, okay?" Avril wanted to push for more, but Mom was already claiming she had to get back to work. "I love you," she said. "Have fun and be careful." And that ended the call.

Avril stared at her phone as if all her mother's secrets would come spilling out. They didn't. She drank the last of her latte and left to walk at Lake Radnor State Park.

There, ambling on the unpaved path that wended along the lake, sheltered from an already hot morning by ash trees as well as pine and cedar, she tried to clear her head of all the questions bouncing around in it. Her mother was as placid on the surface as the lake, sparkling blue in the sunlight, but there were things lurking beneath that calm surface, things that had turned her bitter against the city beloved by every country music fan in the country. What were they? Would Avril ever find out?

"My mom is a mystery," she confessed to Gina as they got ready to go line dancing at The Wild Horse Saloon with Jimmy and Colton. "She's got some kind of past from down here that she's been hiding from me all these years."

"Maybe cause it's none of your business," Gina suggested.

"But maybe it is. Whatever happened sure affected her attitude about me moving here."

"Everybody's got their issues," Gina said with a shrug. "But your mom's aren't yours."

"Good point," said Avril.

She had enough to do working on living her own best life. She didn't need to be wasting time poking around in her mom's past. Anyway, if Mom had wanted to share she would have. So Avril stopped trying to solve the mystery of what happened between Mom and Carolina and put on her boots.

The Wild Horse Saloon, located in a tall redbrick building, was in the heart of historic Nashville, with the Cumberland River right behind it. It was a three-story space offering everything from Southern cooking to live-music acts and free line dancing lessons. Not that Avril needed any. Although she was never able to get on the floor when The Mermaids played the Drunken Sailor Friday and Saturday nights, she'd been there plenty of times on Sundays and taken advantage of the free lessons.

The guys were waiting for them outside the club, next to the large figure of a horse standing upright and wearing cowboy boots and a vest.

"You girls look great," said Jimmy, who was leaning against the horse.

"I second that," said Colton.

"You ready to dance your boots off?" Jimmy asked, smiling at Gina.

"Hey, that's not a bad hook," Colton said.

Jimmy gave him a slap on the shoulder. "He never stops."

"I like a man who never stops," Avril said.

"Then I'm your man. Come on, ladies, let's go shake it."

"Is there construction or something going on here?"

Avril asked as they went in, pointing to the chain-link fence and brick rubble.

"More like reconstruction," Jimmy said. "Some shithead exploded an RV down here on Christmas morning. Hit over forty businesses, including The Wild Horse. They're still working on putting the buildings back together."

"Why would somebody do that?" Avril said, shocked.

"Why do kids shoot up schools? Why do countries go to war?" Colton replied. "Sometimes it's a shit-suckin' world."

"But not all the time," said Jimmy. "There's still good people in this world, and I remind myself of that on a regular basis."

"We sure met up with two of the good ones," Gina said, giving Jimmy a smile. Oh, yeah, good feels were blooming there.

They were blooming for Avril, too, as she and Gina walked down Broadway later with the guys. Gina and Jimmy were talking up a storm. Colton and Avril were holding hands and stopping frequently to look in store windows and share a kiss.

"Next time we go out it's gonna be just the two of us," he said as he pulled her up against him.

That was okay with her. This all felt so right. She was ready to start a new relationship, one that fit with her new life.

"I'm in love," Gina announced once the two of them were back in the apartment. "Jimmy is so sweet. And guess what, he wants to get together and try and write something."

"Go for it," Avril said,

"Are you and Colton gonna write something together?" Gina asked.

"Probably, but I'm not ready yet."

"That's what it's all about down here," Gina pointed out.

"I know."

And if she and Colton got serious he would expect her to want to write with him. But so far every lyric she'd come up with was a gem. She wasn't sure he could give her a melody worthy of any of them.

*Talk about conceited*, she thought as she snuggled up on the pull-out. Who did she think she was, Justin Wilson? Carolina James? But as her eyes drifted shut she couldn't help wondering if one of the ways Carolina would help her would be to write a song with her. Maybe she could work up her nerve and show a couple things to Carolina. Like Colton said, you had to reach for the moon.

She felt like she'd landed on the moon when she found herself seated in a table up front at The Bluebird Wednesday night, Carolina introducing her to a friend, a thin woman with red hair who looked about Carolina's age. "This is Dixie Dunn," she said to Avril.

"Like in Brooks and Dunn," said Dixie.

"But no relation," Carolina said, and her friend stuck out her tongue at her.

"She's done okay," Carolina said. "Gotten some hits."

"No song of the year award though," Dixie said sadly, and tossed back the last of the amber liquid in her shot glass. "Y'all made me sad, Caro. Now I need another drink. What'll you have, darlin'?" she asked Avril.

Avril wasn't a huge drinker. "A Coke would be great."

"With some rum in it?" asked Dixie.

"No, just the pop."

"All righty then," Dixie said, and wandered off through the growing crowd to the bar at the back of the room.

"Is she singing tonight?" Avril asked.

"Eight o'clock. If she doesn't drink herself off her ass first," Carolina said and shook her head. "That woman."

That woman did, indeed, like to drink. Avril hadn't even finished her Coke before Dixie was on to her third shot of whiskey. Avril hoped she wasn't driving that night.

The women were about to go on when Dixie waggled a finger at her and said, "You know, you look like someone. Can't be though, but damn you got his face for sure. Well, except for the green eyes. But same chin, same nose, same hair color. You are practically the spittin' image of old Rance."

Avril had to have misheard. "Rance?"

"Rance Jackson, girl."

"That's not possible," Avril said.

It was ridiculous. Mom would have said something if Avril had such a famous father. Anyway, her father was only a one-night stand. "Nothing but a sperm donor," Mom had said.

"Was your mama Bonnie Brinks?" Dixie asked.

Unease began to creep up Avril's spine. "Yes."

The woman clapped her hands together. "I knew it. That explains the green eyes. Him and your mother were once an item. Who knew Bonnie had a baby with him? Rance hasn't never said a thing about having a kid."

"That's not possible," Avril said.

"You never know in this town," Dixie said with a hiccup and a giggle. "Your mama never said anything?"

Avril shook her head. She was starting to feel sick. This woman was wrong. Delirious.

"Maybe she just wanted to forget. He was a wild one, just couldn't help himself when it came to women and whiskey. Bonnie thought she could tame him, but in the end she couldn't. He cheated on her with Carolina and then they wound up together. Yep, just like a soap opera. Or a country song. 'Your Cheatin' Heart,'" she added with another giggle and hiccup.

Was this possible? Was Rance Jackson her father? And this woman who was being so nice to her, she who stole her mom's man?

"Yep, you sure look a lot like Rance. Bonnie, too, now that I'm really lookin' at you," Dixie said with a nod.

Carolina James and Rance Jackson had driven her mother out of Nashville and Carolina was pretending it was nothing.

White-hot fury swept through Avril. She was sure she was going to explode. Up on stage, Carolina stood with two other women around Avril's age and was strapping on her guitar. Avril had no desire to hear the woman or see her. Ever again. She pushed away from the table, nearly knocking over her chair.

"Where you going?" Dixie asked as Avril grabbed her purse. "Things are just starting to get good."

No they weren't. They were getting horrible.

# *Fifteen*

Gina was gone when Avril got back to the apartment, out with Jimmy and Colton, working on coming up with a hit song. She needed to talk out what was going on in her head to someone. Not Glamma, who was obviously clueless. Anyway, she was busy with her new boyfriend. For sure not her mother, not until she could get to the truth, and she had no idea how she was going to do that. Frantic to talk to someone she called Kenny.

"Hey, there," he said, delighted surprise in his voice. "How's Nashville?"

"I don't know," she said.

"You're not having fun?"

"I have been. Up until tonight."

When her world had tilted on its axis. She started pacing the living room. "Were you busy?" *With someone?* He should have been.

"No, just sittin' around, watching TV. What up?"

"I need someone to talk to before my head explodes."

"What's going on?" he asked, concern in his voice.

"I might have found my dad." Saying the words kicked up the storm inside her to a hurricane level.

"No shit? Who is he?"

"If the drunk woman who told me is right it's Rance Jackson."

"Rance Jackson," Kenny repeated. "*The* Rance Jackson?"

"That's what she said."

"Why wouldn't your mom have told you?" Kenny wondered.

"Maybe cause she's bitter. He cheated on her with another woman."

"What an ass hat."

"Yes, but I had a right to know he was my ass hat," she said, angry tears filling her eyes. "And it gets worse. I met this woman who's had a buttload of song hits, Carolina James, and she's kind of offered to help me."

"That's good, right?"

"Wrong. She's the one Rance cheated on my mother with." Thinking of how nice Carolina had been to her and how she'd lapped up that kindness like a thirsty kitten made her swear.

"Kind of a soap you got going down there."

And nobody had bothered to tell her she was a member of the cast. "Now I know why Mom is so anti-Nashville. But if this is true she should have told me. Why didn't she tell me?" she demanded, her voice rising.

"You don't know for sure that it's true," Kenny said, the voice of reason.

She took a deep breath. "No, I don't. Gossip isn't proof."

"What are you going to do?"

"What should I do?"

"Find out the truth and go from there. The guy might not even know he's got a kid. He'll want to know."

"You think so?"

"I would."

A text came in as they were talking. From Carolina. We Should Talk.

"Great," said Avril. "Now the man-stealer wants to talk to me."

"So suck it up and talk to her. You need answers. She's got 'em."

"This is such a mess," Avril said tearfully.

"You'll sort it out. Don't' let it distract you from what you went there to do."

Kenny was the best. She'd cut him out of her life, made him feel he wasn't good enough for her, and yet here he was listening to her troubles and offering advice.

"I'm sorry I called you," she said. "It's not fair to call and dump on you after…"

"Dumping me?" he supplied with a painful play on words.

"I'm sorry."

"Don't be. What are friends for?"

"You're still my friend." It was half statement, half question.

"You know I am."

It was a relief to hear.

"I'm always here for you. You know that."

"You shouldn't be."

"Avril, I still love you. That didn't stop just because we broke up," he said, which made her feel like a poop queen. "Talk to the woman and figure this out. Then you can get back to living your best life."

"I guess," she said, although she didn't want to. "Thanks for being there."

"Anytime you want to talk I'm here," he said.

"Kenny, you're the best."

He chuckled. "I know. Hang in there. Things'll work out."

One way or the other.

They said their good-byes and she almost fell into the old habit of ending with, "I love you."

She supposed in a way she still did, in spite of what was happening with Colton. Even though Colton was her future, Kenny owned an important part of her past. They had a history together that she had yet to write with Colton. You didn't erase history with a snap of the fingers. Or a move to a new place.

With the call ended, she sat thinking, discovered a ragged spot on one fingernail and picked at it. She could have called Colton. Should have called Colton.

But he was working on a song. It would have been rude to interrupt the creative process.

She peeled off more of her fingernail. She shouldn't have called Kenny. He'd been busy, too, working on getting on with his life.

"Selfish," she scolded herself, and vowed never to call him again. Reaching into the past was no way to fix the present.

Good grief, when did her life get so messy? Oh, yeah, since she landed in Nashville.

Another text came in from Carolina. I'll tell you what happened.

She had to know. Okay, she texted back.

Meet me at The Pancake Pantry tomorrow. I'll buy you breakfast.

I'll buy my own, Avril texted. No way was she going to take anything from this woman.

The next morning she sat at a table, ignoring a plate of buttermilk pancakes and glaring at Carolina James.

"Dixie is a fool," Carolina said. "She should have kept her mouth shut."

"Yeah, it would be a shame to learn the truth," Avril said, and shoved away her plate.

"If your mom had wanted you to know she'd have told you."

"I think if there's a chance Rance Jackson is my father I have a right to know."

"Only your mom can confirm that," Carolina said. "But I can tell you what happened between us."

"Your friend already spilled the tea."

"I wouldn't necessarily call her a friend. She's someone I know, have known for years—Nashville may be a city but the music business is a small town."

"So, what happened?"

Carolina took a deep breath. "I did get together with Rance. But I thought he'd broken up with your mama. He told me they were through, insisted they were only writing songs together. I believed him. Hell, I wanted to. I was in love with him. Half the women in Nashville were. He was sexy and talented, and we all flew to him like moths to a porch light. When your mama accused me of stealing him I realized that he'd lied to both of us, but she never believed I wasn't cheating with him, no matter how hard I tried to explain my side."

"But you didn't give him up. So much for the girlfriend code."

"I did until they broke up for good. Then, like a fool, I came back for more. I eventually married him, which was a big mistake. He really was a lyin' dog. But back then he was an addiction I couldn't kick. Anyway, when I learned

Bonnie was your mama I thought the least I could do to make up for what happened between us was to help you."

Avril took a deep breath. What to say to all this? She had no idea.

"Dixie's right. You do look a lot like your daddy."

Avril found her voice. "If he is my father why didn't my mom tell him about me? Or me about him?"

"I don't know. There was something else going on, I'm sure. More than just what happened with Rance and me. Whatever it was, it was enough to make her leave and cut all ties."

"She should have told me. I had a right to know. And he had a right to know he had a kid."

Carolina pushed away her plate, too, her eggs and toast ignored. "He probably still does. Although whether he'll believe it or not, who knows?"

"Why wouldn't he?"

"A lot of people try to prove they're related to stars who are rich."

Avril scowled. "He'd think I'm some kind of fake? A leech?"

"He won't if he believes his eyes. Or sees a DNA test."

"I'm not gonna beg someone to accept me," Avril said.

Carolina smiled. "Good for you. You don't have to grovel to anyone. And if you want me to, I'll still help you. If you believe what I just told you."

"I do," Avril said. "I know how easy it is to get taken in by a man," she added, thinking of Glamma.

"Love makes fools of us all," said Carolina. She nudged Avril's plate back at her. "Eat up, girl. One thing you learn when you're starting out in this town and that's never turn down a free meal."

Avril managed to eat some of what was on her plate

although she was too wound up to even taste it let alone enjoy it. She insisted on paying for her breakfast, determined not to be a leech.

Back at the apartment, she brought up pictures of Rance Jackson on her phone, trying to imagine his face with her long dark hair. She went into the bathroom and looked at herself in the mirror, comparing what she saw to what was on her phone screen. Same coloring, same nose. She did look a lot like Rance. Crap.

Instead of calling her mom, she opted to reach out to her grandmother. Glamma had to know something, and she had a better chance of worming information out of her than she did her mom.

Her response proved how wrong that theory was. "Rance Jackson?" Glamma repeated. "Whatever makes you think that?"

"Glamma, what did Mom tell you about why she left Nashville?" Avril asked, dodging the question.

"Other than that she hated it there, nothing. She'd, uh, gotten pregnant and…"

"By who?"

"Darling, she didn't say, and it wasn't my place to push for details she didn't want to share. My job was to be there for her and give her the emotional support she needed."

"It wasn't a one-night stand, Glamma. She was with someone. She was with Rance."

"What? No. She would have told me. I don't know where you're getting your information," Glamma said.

"From a reliable source," said Avril. "I can't believe Mom never told me."

Her grandmother sighed. "I guess you two are going to have to have a serious conversation."

"I guess we are," Avril said. "She lied to me, Glamma, and she'd better have a good reason for doing it."

"Now, dear, don't go off all half-cocked."

"Half-cocked? I'm not half-cocked, I'm pissed. Look, I've gotta go," she said before Glamma could start defending Mom. There was nothing to defend. What her mother had done was inexcusable.

She called her mother and barely gave her time to say hello. "Rance Jackson is my father, isn't he?"

There was a moment of stunned silence before Mom asked, "Who told you that?"

"Never mind who told me. Is it true?"

More silence.

That confirmed it. "It is. All this time I had a father and you never told me. You kept me from him. I can't believe you did that."

"You don't know everything," Mom began.

"You got that right, because you told me nothing. Now who knows if he'll even believe I'm his kid. All those years I could have had a dad like all my other friends, and you kept me from that."

"I kept you from a lot of things that would have been bad for you," Mom insisted.

"Yeah, right. Thanks a lot," Avril said and pushed End. End of conversation. End of…everything.

Bonnie felt ill. She could feel the blood draining from her face as if some invisible vampire was sucking her dry. She shut down her computer. She had to get out of the office, try to find someplace where she could think. Breathe.

"I need to go home," she said to Lucy.

"You don't look good," Lucy said. "Are you okay?"

Bonnie shook her head. "Avril."

"Is she hurt?" Lucy asked in concern.

"No, but we've got a problem. I... I have to fix this." She sounded almost hysterical. Probably because she was.

"If there's anything I can do," Lucy offered.

"Thanks," Bonnie managed and bolted from the office.

There was nothing anyone could do, not unless they could send her back in time to start her whole adult life over. Her phone started ringing as she got in the car. It was Loretta. Oh, Lord, had Avril called her, too?

Bonnie ignored it and raced toward home, to her little house on Sand Dollar Lane where she'd always felt so secure, where she'd finished raising Avril, made happy memories. Would she and her daughter ever make any more memories in that house? Was this fixable? Would Avril ever want to speak to her again? Sobs surged out of her.

If only she'd never caught Rance with Carolina. It was a horrible vision, remembering seeing them naked on his couch, their clothes strewn all over the floor.

"I don't believe this," she said.

"Bonnie?" Carolina squeaked, trying to hide behind him.

"You traitor," Bonnie spat, then added, "Both of you!"

"Bonnie, wait!" Rance said, reaching for his pants.

She didn't.

They'd been in love, together, planning to have a future. Rance's betrayal had felt cataclysmic. But that had only been the beginning. There'd been worse to come. And now, more fallout.

She was barely in the house before her mother arrived. "Darling," Loretta said, and held out her arms and Bonnie fell into them, weeping.

"Come on. Sit down," Loretta finally urged, and led

her to the couch. She fell on it, grabbed a sofa pillow and kept crying.

Loretta went to the sink and got her a glass of water. Why did people give you water when you were having a breakdown? What was the purpose of that? Was she supposed to drown herself with it? Bonnie shook her head.

Loretta set it on the coffee table. "Avril called me."

This started Bonnie crying all over again. "She called me, too. She hates me, Mom."

"She doesn't hate you. She's just mad."

There was a supersized understatement.

"I think it's time you told me what happened in Nashville," Loretta said.

"He broke my heart, Mom. The bastard broke my heart."

"Why didn't you tell me?" Loretta asked gently.

"What would have been the point? What was the point of telling anyone?"

"There's a point now. Spit it out."

It was still so humiliating. "He cheated on me with my best friend. She claimed he told her we'd broken up. Who knows?"

Loretta let out a deep breath. "Even cheaters have a right to know their kids."

"Yes, but not thieves."

"What are you talking about?"

"He stole my song, Mom. He stole 'Drunken Dreams.'"

Loretta's head snapped back. "What?"

"He stole it and got a hit out of it and denied I had any part in it. I wrote the whole damn thing and he took it."

She remembered Rance shrugging after she'd played him what she'd come up with. Inspiration had hit hard and she'd dashed the song off on a piece of steno pad paper. She'd had two verses and the chorus, both lyrics and music, and had been sure it would be a great hit. All it needed was some fine-tuning, maybe a bridge. His ho-hum reaction had left her feeling a little hurt and a lot discouraged.

"I think it's good," Bonnie argued.

"It needs a lot of work," he said.

"Well, then, let's work on it. You can sing it when you get a contract with a label."

He grinned. "That's right around the corner."

She grinned back. "I know. You're gonna be the next Garth Brooks."

"And you can be my Trisha Yearwood," he said. "Come here, Trisha."

When Rance made love to her Bonnie forgot everything else. She forgot about that piece of paper and left it behind at his apartment when they went off to Tootsie's Orchid Lounge. She remembered two days later, but when she looked for it on the coffee table where he'd carelessly tossed it, it was gone.

"Where's my lyric?" she asked.

He shrugged. "Sorry. I tossed it. It wasn't that good, babe. We can do better. Come on, let's do some writing."

They wrote a song, but Bonnie didn't think it had the potential hit power "Drunken Dreams" had. In fact, nothing they wrote together was all that good, but life went on.

She sold a couple of songs to small publishing houses. She and Rance kept seeing each other, writing together—nothing that exciting, but she knew at some point they'd strike gold. It was a winding road to success, but she was on it with Rance and life was beautiful.

Then she caught him with Carolina. That had been the end…until he convinced her that Carolina had been a mistake and "It didn't mean nothin'." Fool her, she believed him. And she was excited when he finally got that deal with a label. All was good until she learned that he wasn't really through with Carolina. They'd been spotted at some hole in the wall at the edge of town, cozied up in a dark corner and practically glued together.

She tracked him down at the studio, waited until he was done with his recording session, then slapped his cheating face. "I never want to see you again, you rotten piece of shit!"

"Hey! What the…" he started to protest.

"You and Carolina deserve each other," she said.

He made no reply to that. What could he say?

Six weeks later she found out she was pregnant. She'd been debating whether or not to tell him when she got hit with the next lightning bolt. At a writers in the round at The Bluebird he had played the song that was going to be the first release on his CD. "Drunken Dreams."

She hadn't been there. She'd kept away from Rance like the heartbreak plague that he was, trying to decide when and where to tell him about the baby. She learned about it from a friend who'd heard him.

"Looks like his star is on the rise," the guy said. "Man, wish I'd written that new song with him. It's gonna be a monster hit."

She had to ask, "What song?"

The shock when he told her almost knocked her on her butt. "That's not his song," she growled. "I wrote that."

The guy had looked at her, his expression half surprise and half doubt. "He didn't say anything about writing it with anyone."

"That bastard. He stole my song!"

"You got any way to prove it?"

She would have had. If Rance hadn't conveniently "thrown out" the piece of paper with her lyrics.

She called him. "What the hell, Rance?"

"Bonnie." He said her name as if she were the last person he ever expected or wanted to hear from.

"Tell me I'm wrong and you didn't perform a song I wrote and claim it was yours? Tell me that it's not coming out on a CD with me getting no writing credit."

"What are you talking about?" he demanded.

"You know what I'm talking about, you thief. 'Drunken Dreams'?"

"You're crazy, you know that?"

"You're not going to admit it, are you? You stole my song. Did you even bother to add a bridge?"

"I don't know what you've been smokin', Bonnie, but this conversation is as over as we are."

"Do you even have a conscience?"

He said nothing to that. In fact, he said nothing at all. He was gone.


"That was when I decided I wasn't going to tell him about the baby," Bonnie finished dully. She took the tissue her mother had brought her and blew her nose. "No way did I need a cheater and a thief in the life of my child."

"Oh, sweetheart, I'm so sorry," Loretta said sadly.

"It was awful, Mom. It's still hard to see him so successful and know that part of how he built that success was by stealing from me. I've tried not to think about it, but every once in a while it gets to me."

"Like around the time of the Country Music Awards?"

"Then, and when I've written a really good song and think I should be doing more with it than playing in a pub in a small town."

"You do have talent," Loretta said.

"Well, I learned the hard way that you need more than talent. Anyway, I love it here. Moonlight Harbor's been good to me."

"I wish you'd told me."

"What would be the point?"

"Maybe I could have helped you cope, helped you work out a strategy for telling Avril. She needs to hear the truth, you know. The whole truth."

Bonnie rubbed her aching head and groaned. "She won't even talk to me."

"You're going to have to go talk to her."

"Nashville?" No, there had to be another way.

"Hair of the dog that bit you," Loretta said. "It's well past time you faced down your past. It's the only way you're going to get the future you want."

Her mother was right, she knew it. She swallowed hard.

"I'll go with you," Loretta offered.

Bonnie shook her head. Much as she wanted her mother's comforting presence, she didn't think she could stand having Loretta around to watch whatever fresh humiliation lay in store for her as she tried to unravel the tangled mess she'd made.

"Are you sure?"

"I'm sure. You stay here and enjoy your visit with Lawrence. I'm a big girl. I'll be fine."

What a joke. She'd probably never be fine again.

"I'll call J.J. and tell him The Mermaids aren't playing this weekend," Loretta said.

"No, I'll call him," Bonnie said. "I wish I'd never gone to Nashville," she added miserably.

"I wish you'd never left. You could have made it, probably outshone Rance Jackson and gotten your sweet revenge in the process. He's not that good."

Bonnie gave a bitter smile and shook her head. "Right."

"It's true. You're twice the singer he is. And obviously, he can't write or he wouldn't have had to steal your work. It's time to go back and battle your demons, dear. Long past time."

Bonnie didn't know about the demons, but it was time to go fight for her relationship with her daughter.

She called J.J. after her mother left. "I'm afraid The Mermaids can't play this weekend. Something's come up."

"Got a better offer?" he teased.

"Not really. I have to go to Nashville."

"Where you daughter is? Is she okay?"

"Not really," Bonnie said. Fresh tears rushed to her eyes. The pain started streaming up her throat again, making it hard to talk. "I've gotta go. Sorry," she managed and ended the call.

J.J. sat a moment, tapping his phone on his leg. What was that about? Something not good, for sure. He and Bonnie had become close, close enough for her to confide her worries to him. So what was this about? Whatever was going on it had to be big for her to clam up on him and cancel an appearance. And if it was something big, she shouldn't have to face it alone.

He didn't have Loretta's phone number, but he'd been to her place several times with Bonnie. He grabbed his car keys and headed out the door.

# *Sixteen*

Bonnie dropped off Lucy's birthday present before heading to the airport. "I'm sorry I can't make your birthday party," she said. "I've got to get to Nashville and see my daughter. I know I'm leaving you in the lurch at the office, too. I...don't know when I'll be back."

Maybe on the next flight if Avril wouldn't speak to her. The thought made her stomach turn over.

"Don't worry about it," Lucy said and gave her a hug. "Whatever is going on, it'll be all right. Mothers and daughters fight but they always make up."

What if she and Avril were the exception to the rule? All Bonnie could do was nod again.

"Meanwhile, let's look at this painting," Lucy said, unwrapping it.

Her look of glee on seeing herself as a mermaid would have delighted Bonnie under normal circumstances. Sadly, she was a long way from normal.

"I love it!" Lucy declared and gave her another hug. "You are so talented."

She obviously had a talent for screwing up her life. "I

have to get going," she said, not wanting to delay so much as another minute, and headed for the door.

Lucy walked with her. "Hang in there. And safe travels."

Safe travels. Maybe the plane would crash and she wouldn't have to face her daughter.

There was a sick, selfish thought. "I didn't mean it," she said as she got in her car, just in case God was listening. "Please get me there in one piece and help me get my daughter back."

Fixing things with Avril was a big order. What if she couldn't? What if Avril wouldn't forgive her? The horrifying worry rode with her all the way to the airport, went through security with her and settled in next to her at her gate. It would have been wrong to drag Loretta away from her visitor, but Bonnie still found herself wishing she had her mother with her. She was tired of carrying her disappointment and hurt alone, tired of having one foot so cemented in the past it prevented her embracing what she had with J.J., kept her from taking that leap into a truly committed relationship. All that had happened was so far in the past. What did it matter now?

It mattered a lot because the past had seeped into the present and stained her relationship with Avril.

*Stop obsessing*, she told herself as she settled into her window seat. *You'll find your way through this*.

An older woman claimed the aisle seat and gave her a friendly hello. She looked ready to chat so Bonnie took out her phone and tried to pretend an interest in the latest gossip on the Moonlight Harbor Facebook group page.

The door was about to shut when she heard a familiar male voice say to the woman, "Excuse me."

She looked up to see J.J. moving to the middle seat.

"I got the last seat on the plane," he said, settling in next to her.

"What are you doing here?" She had to be hallucinating.

"Thought it was time I saw Nashville," he said, sitting down next to her.

"Right. Mom told you."

"Not all the gory details, but she did make it sound like a dangerous mission."

Bonnie gave a bitter snort. "You could say that."

"When you're in danger you need backup."

"You didn't have to do this," Bonnie said.

"I know. I wanted to. There's no need to walk a rough road by yourself when you have people who care." He took her hand and threaded his fingers through hers.

Looking at their linked hands, she felt comforted. "Thank you."

"Glad to be of service," he said, and gave her hand a squeeze.

"You may regret this. It's going to be one gigantic mess."

He looked to where the older woman sat. She'd pulled out a paperback novel and was diving into it.

"Want to talk about it?" he asked, lowering his voice.

No. She wanted to pretend none of it was happening. She wanted to keep her whole pathetic past hidden. Instead, she nodded. Then she poured out the whole ugly story.

"You're right. That is pretty…complex," he said when she'd finished. "But you've got this. And I've got you."

He gave her hand another squeeze when the plane finally descended to Berry Field Nashville International Airport. She squeezed back and braced herself.

It hadn't been hard to let J.J. convince her to drop her reservation at a Best Western when she learned he'd booked rooms for them at the historic Union Station Hotel, and as he drove their rental car through the city to it, a little excitement bled through her dread, whispering, *Nashville, I'm back*. The hopes and dreams that lived in the city, the energy of the place, it was a drug she'd been without for too long. If only she was returning under different circumstances.

She'd gotten the address of Gina's apartment from Gina's mother and, rather than call ahead, decided a surprise visit was the best way to go, so after they'd checked into their room, she made her way to the apartment.

"Want me to go with you?" J.J. had offered.

"No, but thanks."

"It'll be okay," he'd said, and kissed her.

It didn't start out okay. Her daughter opened the door, smiling, obviously expecting someone else. At the sight of Bonnie her smile collapsed. "Mom."

"Let me in. We need to talk," Bonnie said.

"I don't want to talk to you."

The words fell like a pickaxe on her heart, but she steeled herself. "Okay, then I'll talk and you listen. I need to tell you everything that happened here and why I never told you about your father. Then you can decide if you still want to hate me."

Avril's lips were a thin line in a face of granite, but she stepped aside and let Bonnie enter.

Gina was sitting on the couch, her bass in her lap. A guitar was propped against a chair. Obviously, the girls had been writing.

"I'll, uh, catch up with you later," Gina said. Then with an awkward hello to Bonnie, she grabbed her purse and scrammed. Avril must have shared with her best friend what a rat her mother was.

She didn't offer Bonnie anything to drink. Instead, she

sat down in the chair, picked up her guitar and began noodling.

How to scale this wall? Nothing short of a catapult would
do. "Rance did more than cheat on me. He stole my song."

Avril's fingers stilled. She looked up at Bonnie in shock.

"'Drunken Dreams.' It was his first hit and I wrote it.
All of it, and he stole it."

Avril gaped at her. "What? Seriously?"

"Seriously. I played it for him when we were together.
He said it wasn't that good and even though I didn't agree
with him I let it go. Left the paper with the lyrics on it behind at his apartment and never saw it again. I learned I
was pregnant after we broke up and was trying to decide
what to do when I learned from a friend that he'd played it
at The Bluebird and took credit for writing it. He put it on
his first album and it became a monster hit. Other artists
recorded it, too. He could have shared the credit, shared
the money, but when I confronted him about it, he told me
I was crazy. He broke my heart in so many ways. Maybe
I could have gotten over the cheating, but the stealing, the
gaslighting..." Bonnie shook her head. "I didn't want a
thief in my life, and I didn't want you to know that about
the man who was..."

"A sperm donor," Avril supplied.

"It was how I thought of him after that. He was the biggest mistake I ever made and the reason I left Nashville. I
realize now though, I should have told you. Maybe I didn't
because, deep down, I didn't want you to think of me as a
loser and I didn't want to pass on the hate."

Avril's eyes filled with tears. "Mom, I'm sorry."

"Can you forgive me?" Bonnie asked, then held her
breath.

The guitar was instantly abandoned and Avril fell on her

knees, putting her head in Bonnie's lap and crying. "I'm sorry, Mama. I'm so sorry."

And then Bonnie was crying, too, and they were hugging each other.

"You should have told me," Avril said at last. "It would have explained so much about why you didn't want me to move here."

Bonnie nodded. "I guess now you know why. I was afraid you'd get hurt, used, broken."

"I don't break," Avril said.

"Maybe you're stronger than me."

"I don't know. You had to be pretty strong to keep going with your life."

Bonnie shook her head. "I didn't stay and fight for my dreams. I turned tail and ran. Maybe I've been running ever since," she mused, then quickly moved on. "But I want to see you succeed and live your best life. I really do."

"Then want to come hear me play tomorrow night? Gina and I are singing at the Commodore Lounge in the West End."

"Of course I do," Bonnie said.

Avril bit her lip.

"What?" Bonnie prompted.

"Carolina will be there."

Carolina. Bonnie froze.

"She's bringing someone she wants me to meet."

Maybe Carolina really was trying to make up for the past. Still, Bonnie hesitated.

"She says she really thought you and Rance had broken up when she hooked up with him."

Bonnie took a deep breath. "It's water under the bridge."

"Then you'll come?"

She'd already messed up badly once. She wasn't going to do it again. "I wouldn't miss it for the world."

Avril beamed. "Awesome! Hey, some of us are going to Hattie B's for dinner. Come with us."

"Sure," Bonnie said, then remembered J.J. "J.J. Walker came down with me. Is it okay if he comes along?"

"Yeah," Avril said, but it was a hesitant yeah.

"Glamma told him I was coming down and he showed up at the airport. Moral support."

"Shit, does he know everything?"

"Afraid so. I told him on the plane," Bonnie said, hoping her daughter wouldn't get angry all over again.

Avril considered a moment, then shrugged. "I guess he may as well know what he's getting into hooking up with you."

"He's just here as a friend."

"Right."

"No, really," Bonnie insisted.

"Mom, he's a nice man and he's perfect for you. You deserve to be happy."

Maybe she did.

"And at least you won't ever have to worry about him stealing your songs. Only your heart."

Bonnie smiled at that. "You're a smart girl. You know that?"

"Not really. If I was smart I'd have given you a chance to explain."

"You have. Thank you," Bonnie said, and hugged her again.

It felt so good. No matter what life brought to her from then on she didn't care. She had her girl back.

That night as she and J.J. walked up Broadway, the thrill

that was Nashville once more came over her, this time full on. "I still love this city," she said to him.

"I bet it's changed a lot since you were here the first time."

"A ton," she admitted. "I could never make it here as a songwriter now."

"Never say never," he said, and took her hand.

"There's more to life than songs."

"Yeah, but songs are all about life. What would it be like without them? Or the people who write them? You've written some good ones."

"I think you might be prejudiced," she said.

"Nope. I know good stuff when I hear it."

"Tony and the Tones?" she teased, and he frowned. "It's one of the things I love about you," she said. "You're loyal."

"Something you love about me, huh? Maybe someday there'll be a whole lot you love about me."

Maybe someday had arrived already. If she could bring herself to admit it.

The restaurant didn't take reservations and the line to get in was a long one in spite of it being early in the evening. But the aroma of fried chicken and spices that floated out onto the street explained why so many people wanted to eat there. They jumped the line and joined Avril, who was with Gina and two men she introduced as Colton and Jimmy.

"Nice to meet you," Colton said. "Avril tells me you're a songwriter, too."

"Sometimes," Bonnie said, and left it at that. "Now, tell me about you?"

He proceeded to, and between him and Avril, Gina and Jimmy, Bonnie didn't have to contribute much to the conversation.

After dinner, the kids were ready to move on to a bar, but

Bonnie begged off, claiming she was tired from the flight. She was tired, but not from flying. Nashville was two hours ahead of Moonlight Harbor, so it wasn't late for her, but the emotional day had taken its toll and she was wiped out.

"Are you really tired?" J.J. asked as he drove them back to the hotel.

"I could use a nightcap," she said. Something to relax her and help her sleep wouldn't be a bad idea.

Although, enjoying a nightcap in the hotel's bar wasn't so much calming her down as stirring her up. "You know, my daughter thinks you're perfect for me."

He grinned, took a sip of his whiskey. "What do you think?"

"I think she might be right, and I think it's about time I stopped letting my past screw up my future."

He grinned at her over his glass. "Know what I think? I think you have a very smart daughter."

Yes, she did, she thought after he'd walked her to her room, snugged her up against him and given her a kiss that melted her. Maybe she wasn't so tired after all.

"You're beat," he said softly. "Get some rest."

Rest after a kiss like that? Who was he kidding?

But she did sleep, soundly, beautifully, and somewhere in that hour where darkness is about to give in to light, where hopes and dreams take over the subconscious, she dreamed that she was no longer alone in bed, but that a strong arm was wrapped around her.

"We're gonna be happy," J.J. whispered.

Dreams were only dreams. But sometimes they did come true.

"How'd you sleep?" he asked her when they met for breakfast.

"Great," she said.

"Not me. It took me forever to get to sleep."

"Time difference?" she guessed.

"Life difference," he said, and she didn't have to ask what he meant. Things were changing and she was feeling it, too.

The venue where Avril and Gina were singing was a small one, a good place for her daughter to start out, Bonnie decided as she and J.J. joined Colton and Jimmy at a table. Bonnie was pleased to see that an up-and-coming young songwriter like Jimmy was offering moral support to her daughter. He seemed genuine, not a BS spinner like Rance had been. Colton she wasn't so sure about. She hoped, after hearing what had happened to her, that Avril would be careful about whom she trusted.

They'd just ordered drinks when two more people entered the lounge. Bonnie felt their presence even before she turned and saw them. Her heart gave a stutter and she set her jaw. *You can do this.*

"Glad we're not late," Carolina said as she sat down at the table next to theirs. She was still blond, still slender, dressed in ripped jeans, the red "tomato" shirt, a fashion trend that Martina McBride had started in protest over a radio consultant's warning not to play too many songs by women. According to him, men in the business were the salad and women only the tomatoes.

Rance Jackson settled into the chair across from Carolina. He was no longer the callow youth she'd first known. He'd matured, hitting his prime with broad shoulders and a fuller body, a tiny hint of gray sparkling in his hair. The smile on his face died at the sight of Bonnie.

Her heart was going like a jackhammer. *Tough it out,*

she told herself. *The past doesn't matter.* She saluted him with her drink. "Nice of you to come out tonight."

He cleared his throat. "Good to see you, Bonnie."

Carolina turned to her. "It is." Her words were actually sincere. "I'm sorry we lost touch. I'm sorry about a lot of things."

"Me, too," Bonnie managed.

That was all there was time for. The girls were on stage and their host was introducing them.

Bonnie had always sung with her daughter. Watching her perform was another experience entirely. Her voice was as beautiful as ever and her stage presence excellent.

After singing a couple of songs she smiled a smile that looked just like her father's and shared a bit about herself with the audience. "I'm from Washington State, a little beach town on the coast, and before I came down here I was a mermaid. Yeah, I know. You're wonderin' what I did with my tail. Well, it's stuck in my britches," she said and the audience laughed. "I really was a mermaid. It was the name of my band. I was in it with Gina here, and my mom. Mom's here tonight, and I'd like her to come up and sing a song with me that she wrote. We played it all the time at The Drunken Sailor."

Now Bonnie's heart dropped into her boots. Oh, no. Singing a song she wrote in front of Rance? She couldn't.

"A lot of people have heard this song and really liked it. We even got it up on YouTube," Avril continued, a subtle message that she considered the song theft proof. "Come on, Mom. Get up here and sing with us."

Get up and sing in front of Rance, pretend that she was still part of this world, let him sneer at her and gloat—she couldn't. She sat glued to her seat in spite of the fact that people were already clapping.

"Get up there and show 'em what you got," J.J. said.

Carolina was suddenly out of her seat, leaning over her. "You're back. You belong here. Get up there and prove it."

Bonnie shot a look to where Rance sat. He appeared far from comfortable. Hard to be comfortable with a guilty conscience.

She, on the other hand, had nothing to feel guilty about. She was a songwriter. This had been her town. It still was, and the only way to prove that was to own her power, get up, and sing.

She walked to the stage, her heart hammering. Avril offered Bonnie her guitar and she took it, told herself this was no different than playing at The Drunken Sailor. People were here for the music. She was going to give it to them.

Or have a heart attack.

She started playing her opening riff. It was greeted with applause and whistles. That was all it took to rev her up. "Get off your chair, get on the floor and shake your booty. You gotta start this party, so get out there and do your duty," she began, and somebody let out a "Yow!"

She roared on into the song, the girls jumping in to sing harmony. People stood and started waving their arms and stamping their feet and clapping. It was healing balm to her heart. She'd reclaimed something she'd lost: herself.

The song ended to whoops and applause, and a giant whistle from J.J. As she settled in her seat, Carolina leaned over and said, "Welcome back."

Welcome back. To a repeat of the soap opera she'd once lived? Probably not. It was cathartic to perform, but now she was done.

"Not here to stay," she said.

"You should be. Nashville owes you. We all owe you," said Carolina.

Rance said nothing.

But that was okay. Bonnie didn't need to hear a thing from him.

Although her daughter did.

After the performance, Carolina made introductions. Colton was ready to glom onto Rance, telling him he had a song he was sure would be a hit for him, but Carolina verbally moved him away, saying, "Maybe another time. Right now I think Rance and Avril have some catching up to do."

Colton looked at Avril in surprise. "Catching up?"

"You interested in grabbing a bite after this set?" Carolina asked Avril as the next group of songwriters set up to go on. "Rance is buyin'."

Rance's smile looked forced.

Avril had to have seen it, too. "I don't know," she said.

So far Rance had said nothing.

Bonnie could feel the curious gazes of Colton and Jimmy and wondered how it would affect the relationship Avril was developing with them. Maybe not for the better. Would one of them use her to get to Rance? If so, it wasn't hard to figure out which one that would be.

Avril was looking at Bonnie as if asking permission. She had to give it. "People change," she said. Maybe Rance had. A little. If he hadn't her daughter had been warned.

"Come with us," Avril said to Bonnie.

This had to be a father-daughter meet. "I'm feeling pretty tired, but you go ahead."

"Okay," Avril said, her reluctance plain in her voice.

Resolution, healing—it was for the best. Bonnie still felt on the verge of hyperventilating. She bolted for the bathroom.

She was in there, splashing cold water on her face, when Carolina walked in and stopped next to her at the sink.

They stood for a moment, looking at their faces reflected in the mirror, two women who had once been friends and now were strangers.

"Why is he here?" Bonnie demanded, reaching for a paper towel.

"He needed to know," Carolina said. "Anyway, the cat's already out of the bag and down the alley."

Bonnie was sure she was going to be sick. She splashed more water on her face, grabbed another paper towel.

"People change, Bonnie."

She'd said the same thing to Avril in an effort to mend fences, but even though for her daughter's sake she wanted to believe it, she didn't.

"If he hurts her I'll kill him," she said.

"He won't. He's not a monster."

"You sure about that?"

"He broke my heart, too," Carolina said softly.

"You shouldn't have given it to him. Neither should I."

"Love makes fools of us all."

"He stole 'Drunken Dreams' from me. I bet he never told you that."

Carolina's gentle smile vanished. "What? No way. He's a cheater but he wouldn't sink that low."

"People will do a lot of things when they're trying to make it in this business," Bonnie said. "You know that."

Carolina was silent a moment, studying her. "That's why you left, isn't it?"

"I'd had enough."

"What a waste. You had what it takes. Still do," Carolina added. "I can think of several people who'd like to do that song you sang."

"Yeah, yeah," Bonnie said.

"No, seriously. I'm not just shinin' you on."

Bonnie gave a disgusted snort and tossed the paper towels in the garbage, started for the door.

"I really thought you guys were over," Carolina said, stopping her in her tracks. "I know you never believed me, but you should have."

"And you should have asked me if we were. You knew how it was with us."

"I knew how it was with Rance and a lot of women," Carolina said. "I wanted to believe I was the one he'd stay with."

"Yeah? And how'd that work for you?"

"I bet you know. Our split was in all the tabloids."

"And yet you're here with him tonight."

"I'm here for your kid. Anyway, he and I worked through it, made a peace accord. Life's short. Why waste time thinkin' about what was bad when there's still good to be had."

Bonnie nodded. Then said thoughtfully, "You know, there might be a song in there somewhere."

Carolina cocked her head, grinned. "There might. Want to write it together? I could hear Miranda Lambert singing it."

"Would we have witnesses?"

Carolina laughed. "What? You afraid I'll steal your song?"

"It's been known to happen."

Her old friend sobered. "That was beyond shitty of him and that's not me. With the wrinkles sneaking on it's already hard enough to look at myself in the mirror. Let's at least have breakfast tomorrow."

"Can I bring someone?"

"That good-lookin' someone you're here with tonight?" Bonnie nodded.

"Sure. Is it serious?"

"Maybe," Bonnie said. Then corrected herself, "Actually, it is."

"Well, good for you. When you find a keeper you gotta hold on tight."

"Have you found one?"

"Nope. That damned Rance, he's an itch I can't stop scratchin'."

"Poor you," Bonnie said.

"What can I say? I'm a masochist."

Pining for a narcissist.

The narcissist cornered Bonnie as everyone was getting ready to leave. "I'm not taking a paternity test," he said under his breath. "I'm just here cause Carolina threatened to leak this to the press."

So he hadn't changed. "Still a shit, aren't you?" Bonnie said in disgust. She moved farther away so Avril couldn't hear this ugly conversation. "But that's fine with me. I don't want you in her life. I was right not to tell her about you."

"If she's my kid why didn't you tell me?"

"*If* she's your kid? Seriously?" she hissed and he had the grace to blush. Anyone with eyes could tell they were related. "And you have to ask? After what you did to me?"

She didn't need to spell it out. He knew. "That again? Come on, Bonnie."

She could feel her anger rising. "Come on, Bonnie? That's all you've got to say? And then you wonder why I never wanted my daughter to know you were her father. Carolina almost had me thinking you'd changed, but you haven't. Do us all a favor and leave Avril alone."

"Hey, if she's mine," he began.

"Of course she's yours, you slime. Unlike you, I never slept around."

He held up a hand. "Okay, okay. Let's bury that bone. Look, I'm sorry things went south with us."

"It was you who took them there."

"I know. Too much booze, too many wild oats."

He would always have excuses for his bad behavior.

"But this isn't just about us," he said.

"I know. This is a whole new person you could hurt. Rance, if you have any decency in you, don't put yourself in her life if you're going to break her heart."

"She's the only kid I've got," he said, doing an about face from his earlier denial. "You shouldn't have kept her from me."

"We've just been over that. And only a minute ago you were balking at the idea of even having a daughter."

"So, I guess I do, and I want to be in her life. Don't poison her against me."

"If by that you mean tell her what you did to me, it's too late. She knows."

"You are a vindictive bitch," he snarled.

"She had to know. It was the only way I could explain not wanting you in our lives."

The hard shell fell away and she saw hurt in his eyes. He looked down, studied his boots. "Okay, I admit it. I did stuff I shouldn't have." It was probably as close as he'd ever come to admitting he'd stolen her song. "But I can make it up to you."

"What? You gonna finally tell people who wrote 'Drunken Dreams'?"

"You've still got talent. I bet you got a lot of songs sittin' in the drawer. We could record something together."

"Oh, yeah. I'd love to do something with you. Not ever. You broke my heart, Rance. Worse, you stole my hope, my faith in…people. What kind of person does that?"

He ran a hand through his hair. "I admit, I wanted to make it so bad back then I hurt a lot of people."

"You're a hurtaholic."

"So maybe I'm in H.A. I can make it up to you. I'll help you."

"The best way you can help me is to help my daughter." *Our daughter.* She couldn't bring herself to say it.

He looked to where Avril stood, talking with her friends. "She looks like my little sister," he said softly, and Bonnie heard the hurt in his voice. His little sister had died from a drug overdose when she was seventeen.

"She's a good kid," Bonnie said.

"I bet she is."

"She's my whole world."

He got the message. "I'll be good to her—I swear it."

"If you want to keep your hide you'd better be," she said.

He nodded, then called to Avril, "Come on, Avril, let's go get us some grub."

J.J. came alongside Bonnie and put an arm around her shoulders. "She'll be okay," he said as Rance and Avril walked off.

"I'm watchin' over her. Don't worry," Carolina said and followed them out.

*Don't worry.* Easier said than done. But her daughter was a grown woman and Bonnie was going to have to let go and let her find her way, wherever that way led.

# *Seventeen*

Lawrence's timing couldn't have been better. He'd rolled
into town like a sturdy rock, just in time for Loretta to lean
on. When he'd first announced he was coming she'd envi-
sioned fun and laughter, him coming to The Drunken Sailor
to hear her sing with her daughter, a happy family FaceTime
gathering with Avril. The fun had evaporated with Avril's
angry call from Nashville, and after that, instead of being
the perfect hostess, Loretta had been a wreck.

Lawrence had taken it all in stride, listening sympatheti-
cally as she told him of her daughter's troubles. He'd taken
her out to eat, walked the beach with her, kept her supplied
in chocolate and assured her on a regular basis that everything would work out.

"Your daughter is a lovely a woman and I'm sure your
granddaughter is, too," he'd said more than once. "They'll
find their way through this. You'll see."

She'd tried to believe him, tried to have a little faith that
everything would be okay, but it had been hard. Her girls'
troubles had occupied space in her mind and heart, leaving
little room for joy. The relief she'd felt on hearing they'd
made up had been followed by fresh concern over how they

were going to deal with Rance Jackson. Avril wanted to know her father. Bonnie wished him at the bottom of the Cumberland River. Loretta could understand how they both felt. Happily, Lawrence could understand how concerned she felt, and she found his presence to be a great comfort.

"At least some things are going well," he pointed out as they set up the Scrabble board. "I bet your granddaughter is going to be a great hit at that place she's performing."

That was one thing Loretta didn't have to be concerned about. Avril would, indeed, be wonderful.

They were halfway through their game when the call came from Bonnie. Loretta connected after one ring.

"How was Avril's showcase?" she asked.

"Your granddaughter was a huge hit," Bonnie said.

"She was a hit," Loretta reported to Lawrence, who gave a thumbs-up. Then, to Bonnie, "I knew she would be."

"Rance was there."

"Oh?" Loretta said cautiously.

"They're off to get something to eat."

"Well, that's a good sign," Loretta ventured.

"I hope so," Bonnie said. "I hate the idea of having him in her life."

"There's not much you can do to change things now, I'm afraid."

"I know." Bonnie sounded sadly resigned.

"Things will work out," Loretta assured her. "You know the saying, the truth will set you free."

"I guess, in a way, it has. I don't have to keep waiting for the other shoe to fall."

"She knows who he is and she knows who you are. She'll use that knowledge wisely, I'm sure," Loretta said and hoped she was right.

"Thanks, Mom. You always know what to say."

"That's me, I'm a real smarty," Loretta said.

"Are you with Lawrence?" Bonnie asked.

"Yes, he's beating me at Scrabble."

"You're not letting him win, I hope," Bonnie teased.

"Of course not," said Loretta. "Now, I'm about to make a very big word, so I can't talk any longer. And I suspect you have better things to do, like go celebrate your daughter's successful performance."

"I do," Bonnie said. "Say hi to Lawrence."

"I will. You go enjoy the rest of your evening."

"I'll try," Bonnie said.

"What will be will be," Loretta sang in parting.

"I love you, Mom," Bonnie said. "Thanks for always being there."

"I love you, too, darling. Good night."

"Everything going okay?" Lawrence asked.

"Time will tell," Loretta said, her earlier positivity leaking from her voice.

"What will be will be," Lawrence said.

*Please let it be good*, she silently prayed.

Carolina suddenly decided she was too tired to go out. "You two go on. You've got a lot to talk about," she said once the three of them were in the parking lot.

Avril wasn't sure she wanted to spend time with this stranger without a buffer. She hesitated.

"Dino's has the best burgers in town," Rance said. "You can follow me."

"I'll put it in my maps app," Avril said. Why she'd said that she wasn't sure. Maybe to prove that she could take care of herself and didn't need this man to get her to a restaurant or get her anywhere.

He nodded. "Okay."

"I guess we do have a lot to talk about," he said when she met him at the entrance to Dino's, a Nashville staple for late night dining.

"Maybe we do," Avril said.

She should have been excited to be getting something to eat with Rance Jackson, actually thrilled to learn he was her father. But with what she'd learned about him she wished she hadn't agreed to meet him or at least that she had her mom with her.

He didn't react to her response, instead asked her how she was liking Nashville.

"I've made some friends here," she said.

"You need friends if you're gonna make it here." He led the way to a table and they settled in. "Try a burger. They're the best in town."

Anything hitting her stomach would be taking a roller coaster ride. "I'll just have a Coke," she said.

"Not hungry? I'd'a thought you'd worked up an appetite after your show. You got talent."

"So does my mom," said Avril.

His easy smile turned sour. "She tells me I'm your daddy. She should'a told me about you."

"I know why she didn't."

He rubbed his forehead. "Look, your mama and me, we had issues."

"Sounds like it. She told me about 'Drunken Dreams.'"

He scowled. "Not that again."

"I believe her."

A shadow of guilt skittered across his face. "Look, she might have given me some ideas." He waved the past away. "It was a long a time ago and people's memories get hazy."

"Hers is crystal clear."

"I'm sorry your mama had a problem with that."

*Mom* had a problem?

He hurried on before she could demand what the heck that remark was supposed to mean. "But what's past is past. Let's talk about now. I can be a big help to you, get your songs to the right people."

"Or just steal 'em."

His eyes narrowed and he pointed a finger at her. "Hey, enough of that."

"This isn't gonna work," she said, and started out of her chair.

He reached out and caught her arm. "Look. Let's start over. I really do want to make things up to you."

Avril raised an eyebrow. "Just me?"

"To both of you," he amended. "Like I said, you got talent. Let me help you find your feet here."

"It would be nice if you helped my mom, too, since you screwed her over so bad you about ruined her life."

He gave a cynical snort. "She was with someone tonight. Her life doesn't look too ruined."

"You have no idea," Avril said in disgust.

"I can't undo the past. Let me see what I can do now, in the present. I got time day after tomorrow. Come to my place and play me some of your songs."

"Only if there's a witness. I want Carolina with me."

He made a face. "Oh, come on, now."

"And Mom."

"I don't think either one will come. Carolina's pretty busy these days," he said. There was no need to say why he didn't think Mom would come.

"I bet they will. But, hey, if you're not interested that's okay. I'm going to make it with or without you."

He held up a hand. "I'm not a total shit. Bring 'em."

"My mom's boyfriend, too?"

"What the hell. The more the merrier."

Avril smiled. She could imagine how merry it would be for him.

She stayed long enough to drink her Coke and get his address and phone number, then left.

Gina was still out when she got back to the apartment. She texted her mom and Carolina. Then Colton, who immediately asked if she wanted someone to ride shotgun.

She was impressed by his supportiveness until he added, I got a new song idea. Maybe we could all work on it.

She was trying to figure out her relationship with her dad, figure out who she was, and here was Colton horning in again. It didn't sit well.

No thanks, she texted. Gotta go.

"You can't blame him for trying," Gina said when Avril showed her the text later.

"I know, but I thought we were in a relationship, thought I was turning into a girlfriend. Now I feel more like a rung on a ladder."

"It's all about connections. You know that."

"I don't see you asking to come along."

Gina shrugged. "I don't need to. I've got Jimmy. He's my rung on the ladder."

Avril blinked. "You're using him?"

"Of course not," Gina said, rolling her eyes. "I'm crazy about him and we're working together. That's not using, that's helping. Colton would probably do the same for you."

Of course he would. She was being supersensitive, probably because of what had happened to her mother. Still, Colton's constant jockeying for opportunity bothered her. Now that she had connections to famous people she couldn't help wondering if people were going to want to be around her for what she could do for them instead of for who she was. Including Colton.

But no, he'd been into her before this all happened. They were a good match. He was fun to be with and he could light her up like a firecracker. They shared the same passion and goals. And so what if he could be pushy? You had to be. And if they ever wrote anything great together she knew he'd do whatever it took to get it out there. She was getting the life she wanted here, the life she'd dreamed of. She didn't need to be jinxing it with goofy, insecure thoughts.

"How long are you staying in town?" Carolina asked as she and Bonnie and J.J. started on their second cups of coffee.

"Just long enough to make sure Avril is going to be okay," Bonnie replied.

"So at least a few days?"

"I could stand to hang around longer," J.J. said, and ate the last bite of his toast.

"You both should. I know it looks all glitz and party on the surface, but we've still got heart," Carolina said. "I really think we should try and do some writing together, Bonnie."

Bonnie was aware of J.J. smiling next to her. "I'll see how things play out," she said, determined not to make a commitment.

After that, there was nothing to say.

J.J. insisted on paying for breakfast.

"You, sir, are a true gentleman," Carolina drawled, smiling at him. "And a keeper," she said to Bonnie. "Can you clone him?"

"One of me is probably enough," J.J. said.

"Enough for me." Bonnie smiled at him and threaded her arms through one of his.

"This place makes you smile," he said as they walked back to the rental car.

"Moonlight Harbor makes me smile," she corrected him.

"This is a different kind of smile. It goes...deeper. It's like you've found your roots."

"Those roots were sitting in very unhealthful soil," she said.

"You think it still is? Things change."

"Only on the surface."

"I don't know. Carolina said Nashville has heart."

She was right, it did. It was full of good people doing good things and, even though the industry had changed, people were still making great music.

"You should stay awhile, write some songs with your friend."

"Former friend," Bonnie corrected. "I'm not sure we could ever go back to what we once had."

"You never know. Why don't you hang around, see what happens?"

She shook her head. "No. Moonlight Harbor is home now."

"Home is where the heart is," he said, smiling at her.

"Are you trying to get rid of me?" she teased.

"What do you think?" he said softly.

"I think I know where my heart is," she said. "And I'm fine in Moonlight Harbor."

Nashville was an itch that was begging to be scratched, but like with chicken pox, scratching wasn't a good idea.

Seeing Rance again probably wasn't a good idea, either, but Bonnie still went with Avril to his place in Brentwood.

Fire-breathing dragons couldn't have kept her from going along to watch over her daughter's interests.

His home was an enormous modern colonial-style mansion with a separate apartment over the garage. It came complete with an expansive front lawn and a long driveway.

"Wow," Avril breathed as they stepped inside, taking in the huge hallway and high ceilings and shining hardwood floor. She set down her guitar and looked around like Cinderella seeing the prince's castle for the first time.

"This is what the success gods bring you," Rance said to her, putting an arm around her shoulders.

This was what thievery brought you. Bonnie tried not to grind her teeth at the sight of him with that arm around her daughter. Their daughter. The truth was out now, and she was going to have to share. Ugh. She could already feel a headache creeping across her forehead.

Seeing Avril wriggle out from under him helped stop the creeping.

"Come on into the living room," he said, pretending to be unaware of the rebuff. "Mira's got sweet tea and a bunch of snacks for us. Mira," he hollered. "Company's here."

A moment later a trim woman who couldn't have been more than thirty came down the hall. She wore a white blouse, ripped jeans and sandals. Like Bonnie, her hair was red, and she looked like an overdressed Victoria's Secret model. Her hair was pulled up in a ponytail to show off diamond earrings glinting in her ears, and the engagement ring with the huge stone in it had to have cost a lot of pretty pennies.

"This is try number three," Rance introduced her. "We're gettin' married in August."

"But you don't have to call me Mama," the girl said to Avril, smiling at her.

"Good to know," Avril said, looking uncertainly at Bonnie. *What the heck?*

Bonnie gave her head a small shake. *Your daddy in action.*

"Congratulations," J.J. said politely.

"Good luck," said Bonnie. Not the politest thing to say but certainly the most honest.

"Its gonna work," Rance insisted. "Mira isn't in the biz."

*She only has to survive you giving her the business*, Bonnie thought.

The living room was cavernous and tastefully decorated with simple but expensive furniture and some very fine original art pieces. Bonnie wondered which of Rance's many women had helped with that. They settled in a grouping of leather furniture around a glass coffee table laden with glasses and a pitcher of tea, an overflowing charcuterie board, as well as a bowl of chips and a plate piled with Moon Pies.

Rance picked up one and bit into it. "You can't come to the South and not eat a Moon Pie," he said to Avril. "Right Bonnie?"

"I ate a few when I was here," she admitted. She took a small plate and put some grapes and cheese on it.

"So, I never got your name," Rance said to J.J.

"J.J. Walker," J.J. said, and leaned across the coffee table to shake hands.

A line from an old Beatles song popped unbidden into Bonnie's mind, "Hands across the water..." Or across the coffee table.

"What do you do?" Rance asked him.

"I own a pub down at the beach."

"The one Avril mentioned, where the girls played?"

J.J. nodded.

"Always wanted to own me some little dive," Rance said. Oh, let the pissing contest begin.

J.J. smiled and leaned back against the sofa cushions crossed an ankle over one leg, spread his arms across the back of the sofa, one arm hovering over Bonnie's shoulders. "I like the laid-back pace."

"So you're a beach bum," Rance joked.

"Yep," J.J. said, unruffled.

The doorbell rang. "That's probably Carolina," Rance said. "The woman will be late to her own funeral."

"I'll get it." Mira the model popped up from her seat and went to answer the door.

A moment later female voices drifted in to where they sat. Then Mira appeared with Carolina in tow. Carolina was still a good-looking woman, but standing next to fresh, dewy Mira didn't do her any favors. It was a good thing she'd already secured her connections and made her reputation when she was young. Age shouldn't matter and neither should looks, but, alas, it was a fact of life that youth and beauty opened doors in a place where both were considered as marketable as talent.

"Sorry, I'm late," Carolina said. "Oh, Moon Pies!" She grabbed one along with a plate. "Mira, you can't cook worth shit but you sure know what to buy."

"She don't need to cook," Rance said.

Probably not. They probably never ate at home and catered any parties they had. For a poor boy who had grown up on the wrong side of the tracks he's done all right for himself.

"Anyway, she's got other talents," Rance said, winking at Mira.

Ugh. Had she thought comments like that were cool

when she was young? "Were you always this slimy?" she couldn't help asking.

He looked at her, both hands out in a typical, I-don't-get-it gesture. "What?"

She shook her head in disgust.

"Everyone got enough to eat?" he continued. "Then let's go on into the music room and play some songs."

The music room was almost as large as the living room, with home recording equipment and a small sound booth on one side of the room and a sofa and several overstuffed armchairs on another. A vintage jukebox stood in one corner and the walls were decorated with all manner of song awards. Bonnie kept her eyes averted.

Rance plopped onto an oversized chair and Mira perched on the arm of it. "So Avril, what else you got besides what we heard the other night?" he asked as the others found places to sit.

Avril took her guitar out of its case, did a quick tuning and then began to play. It was a song about a breakup with a fresh take, comparing the falling apart relationship to running out of gas on a deserted road. Her voice was beautiful with just a touch of the grit and growl that was currently so popular. So much talent being laid on the altar of success. Would Avril be okay if her songwriting dream didn't come true?"

"I love it," Carolina said when she finished.

Rance nodded. "It's a strong song. What do you want to do with it?"

Avril's brows pulled together. "What do you mean?"

"You want to sell it or record it?"

"You want to be an artist who writes her own songs or do you want to be a songwriter?" Carolina clarified.

Avril had enjoyed being part of The Mermaids, had

loved being on the small stage, but in spite of that ham bone she was a little shy. Bonnie had a hard time picturing her touring and playing to massive crowds. It was the creative process she most enjoyed.

"I want to write songs," Avril said.

If Loretta was present she'd have started crooning Barry Manilow's song about writing the songs that make the whole world sing. Avril could do that. She had a gift for pulling people into her musical stories.

"You got the pipes, you know," Rance said. "I could sign you to my label."

*And screw you over.* "I think she wants to be a free agent," Bonnie said, and he frowned at her.

"I'd like to write songs, maybe play at cool small venues like The Bluebird," Avril said. "I just want to do music."

Rance nodded. "Fair enough."

"My publisher will eat that song up," Carolina said. "How about I take you over and have you play it for my A&R man?"

"You can use my publisher," Rance said.

Two people fighting over her daughter—it was a dream come true for Avril. Bonnie wasn't sure she completely trusted Carolina and she sure didn't trust Rance at all. "I think you need to take a little time and think about what you want to do," she said to Avril. "There are plenty of publishers out there."

"Yeah, but not ones that have my kind of clout," Rance said.

"I don't know," said Bonnie. "I've still got a couple of songs with BMG. I bet someone there would like to meet Avril."

Rance almost pouted and Carolina laughed. "You're

gonna make us sweat for what we want, aren't you?" she said to Bonnie.

"I'm going to make sure Avril's interests are protected," said Bonnie, and her daughter looked gratefully at her.

"Looks like you've got people fighting over you," J.J. said to Avril once they were back in the car.

"It's kind of overwhelming," Avril said.

Bonnie turned around in the seat to face her. "You don't have to be in a hurry to make a decision."

"I bet you don't want me to go with my...with my dad." Avril made a face. "It's so weird calling him that. It's so weird to realize I have a dad."

"I should have told you," Bonnie said with a sigh. "It was wrong."

No matter how hurt she'd been, no matter how bitter, she should have, at some point, told Avril.

"I get why you didn't. And I don't know if I'll ever be able to really think of him as a dad."

"He might want to make up for lost time though," said J.J., ringing in as the voice of reason. "I know I would if I were in his shoes."

"One big difference. You have character," Bonnie said.

"Maybe he does now, too," said J.J. "He sure can afford to."

Bonnie faced forward, said nothing. But J.J. had given her something to think about. Rance had wanted his success so badly. How many deals with the devil had he made to get it? And did it eat at his conscience? What did he have to show for all that success he'd fought so hard for? Two ex-wives and a fiancée who could very well be more in love with his money than with him. Yes, he had the big house and the money but how many people did he have in his life who truly cared for him? Really loved him?

Avril's phone began to play "Here for the Party," Loretta's ring tone. "Hi, Glamma," she said. Then, "Yes, you wouldn't believe how well everything went. He loved my song. So did Carolina."

Bonnie couldn't hear what her mother was saying, but judging from Avril's giggle she was sure it was something encouraging.

"Mom's going to get me in to see someone at BMG, too." A moment's pause. "Yeah, she's the best."

Her daughter's words warmed her through and through. She sure tried to be. Maybe she didn't always make the best decisions, but she had the best intentions.

They dropped Avril off at her apartment, promised to meet her and her friends later at the Commodore Lounge. "Where to now?" J.J. asked as Avril walked away.

"Is there something you'd like to do?" So far he'd been caught up in her soap and following her agenda. It was time they did something for him.

"I'm here for you," he said.

She smiled. "That would make a nice song hook."

"Why don't we go back to the hotel and you see if you can use it somehow," he suggested.

"Oh, I don't know."

"Hey, when inspiration hits you have to be ready to catch it. Right?"

She smiled at him. "You are really something else. You know that?"

"I know that. Glad you're finally figuring it out," he said with a grin.

"But what would you like to do before we go home?" she asked.

He shrugged. "How about the Country Music Hall of Fame?"

Where she'd always hoped she'd be someday. She sighed inwardly, but said, "Sure. I think you have to have reservations to get in. Why don't you see if you can find us a time tomorrow."

"Will do," he said.

"And while you're doing that I'll see if I can get my daughter an appointment with someone at BMG."

"You gonna go with her?"

Bonnie shook her head. "No, she has to do this on her own. Although I'd like to. I wish I could…"

"Protect her," he finished.

Bonnie sighed and nodded. "I love her more than life. I can't stand the thought of her getting hurt."

"We all get hurt at some point," J.J. said.

"I don't want her to get hurt the way I did."

"She's a smart woman. She'll be fine."

He parked the car and walked with her to her room. "Make your call, then get going on that song. But first…" He slipped his arms around her and gave her a kiss that melted her bones.

"Was that for inspiration?" she joked.

"No, that was for me," he said with a wink.

"Well, I still found it inspiring."

"And I find you inspiring. You are a most amazing woman, Bonnie Brinks."

"Right," she said, unimpressed by his flattery.

"You are," he insisted. "All that talent wrapped in a such a beautiful package. And you're a smart negotiator, too. Avril's lucky to have you in her corner."

Negotiating. An interesting term for trying to keep her daughter safe from predators.

"J.J., sometimes I wish I'd never come here in the first place," she said.

"If you hadn't you wouldn't have your daughter."

He was right. "Thanks for reminding me."

She hugged him fiercely, pressing her cheek against his chest. She could feel his heart beating—steady, reliable. His arms around her, offering strength and comfort. She didn't want the moment to end.

"I can write anytime," she said.

"Like now," he said before she could get any further.

She tried to pull him into the room with her. "Come in and keep me company then."

He shook his head. "Quit stalling. You have a song to write. Get in there and spin gold and I'll take you out to eat when you're done."

He gave her another kiss, then walked down the hall to his room. She watched him go, watched him open his door. He waved at her, called, "Text me when you're done." Then he shut the door.

She went inside her room, sat on the bed and tried to settle her thoughts.

She was still trying when her mother called. "I know Avril is excited, but how are you doing?"

"Okay. Rance is ready to take over."

"And take advantage?" guessed Loretta. "Is that what you're thinking?"

"Afraid so."

"He is her father. He's not going to hurt her, at least not intentionally."

How did her mother ever get so naive? "My gosh, Mom. Father's hurt their kids all the time."

"That is a small slice of society," Loretta insisted. "And before you say anything about him hurting you, let me tell you what adults feel for their children is very different than what they feel for each other. They may fall out of love, they may stomp on each other's hearts, and yes, they may even use and abuse each other, but they hang on to their kids. He's only just found her. He's not going to want to lose her."

"He wasn't that excited to hear he had her in the first place," Bonnie said.

"It had to come as a shock."

Yeah, just like finding out she was pregnant all those years ago had come as a shock to her.

"But I bet he's adjusting. I also bet he won't want to give up his status as a beloved country star. If he does his daughter dirty it will get out."

"Good point," Bonnie said. "Still, it's so hard to trust him."

"Broken trust never mends well. Things will work out though."

Hopefully. After talking to her mother, Bonnie made the call to BMG. Then she sat on her bed, trying to gather her thoughts.

She hadn't written a song in this city in years. She hadn't even brought her guitar. Living in Nashville, writing songs, this was Avril's dream, not hers.

But it had been hers once. Now she was here, and even though it was for a short time, how could she not do what she'd done all her life, at both her highest moments and her lowest? How could she not write a song?

She got thinking of her daughter and the words began to pour out of her.

It's hard to let you go, to let you choose your own road.
The future's so unsure and I don't want to see you hurt.
But whatever path you choose, I'll be there for you.
Your life is waiting. Go with God, and take my blessing, too.

Tears began to form as Bonnie moved on to her chorus.

Walk proud my daughter. It's time to leave.
I want to see you live your best life, so run toward
your dreams.
Climb up that rainbow, chase that silver cloud.
Keep bein' the best you can and you'll make your
mama proud.
And remember, no matter what you do,
I'm with you in spirit. I'm here for you.

She cried, then wrote some more and cried again. She
was done by late afternoon, and she used her garage band
app and recorded her song a cappella. Then she smiled. It
was good. She could see someone like Martina McBride
singing it.

She texted J.J. I got something.

That brought him right over to her room. "You sure do,"
he said after she'd sung it for him. He was stretched out on
her bed, looking up at her as if she was Dolly Parton the
Second. "Now, what are you going to do with it?"

She shrugged. "Probably nothing. Just writing it was
cathartic."

"I bet it would resonate with a lot of parents," he said.
"Don't you think there's some woman singer who'd like
to sing it?"

"Maybe."

"For sure. You've written several good songs," he said.

"So have a lot of people in this town, and they haven't
written good songs, they've written great songs. Anyway,
I had my chance and I blew it. If I wanted that success I
should have stayed here and fought for it."

"There's no reason you can't armor up and get back in the battle."

She wasn't sure she had the gumption. Plus, "I like my life in Moonlight Harbor. I've met a lot of great people there," she added and smiled at him.

"You could always keep your place in Moonlight Harbor and come back for summers. In fact, who in their right mind would want to live here in the summer? I feel like a clam in a steamer."

She chuckled. "But the rest of the year it's lovely."

"Well, then? Why not give it a try?"

Just like that? Put aside the bad memories and come back like some starry-eyed fool. "You make it sound so easy."

"It should be. You already have a head start over people who move here not knowing anyone. You have established contacts in the business. Who, I might add, owe you."

"I don't want to build a stairway to success on guilt."

J.J. shrugged. "Why not? Some people built it on betrayal."

He was sure doing a good job of arguing for her to pack up and leave Moonlight Harbor. All this nobility with no mention of how much he'd hate to see her go?

"So you'd let me go, just like that?"

"Who said anything about letting you go?" he said, running a hand up her arm. "I like this place. I wouldn't mind finding a restaurant to invest in down here."

"But what about The Drunken Sailor?" she protested.

"What about it?"

"You own it. You'd sell it?"

"No, it's a moneymaker. I'd find someone to manage it. I'm thinking Seth Waters might be open to that. He's grown his own business to the point that he doesn't have to be on site doing everything himself anymore, and I think he's looking for something new."

"Sounds like you've got things all figured out," she said. "How long have you been thinking about this?"

"Ever since our first night here."

"Really?"

"Really. If you're supposed to be here it will become clear and you'll know," he said, "and if you decide to take a second chance on yourself, you'll have someone in your corner. I'll be here with you."

"I appreciate the support," she said. "Still, that's a big sacrifice."

"There's no such thing when you love someone."

"Love someone." She repeated it like a parrot learning a new word. It was a very big word to master, one she'd never dared try to master.

He gave her a funny look. "Let me clarify what that means. It means I want to take what we've got to the next level."

"Next level," she parroted again. "As in commitment?"

"In case you haven't noticed, I already am committed. I think it's time we really became a couple, don't you?"

As in seriously committed, offering her heart up on a platter and trusting him not to carve it into pieces. If it were any other man she'd be running for the door. But this was J.J., the man who had become her biggest fan, her confidante, the man who had dropped everything to come with her to Nashville and offer emotional support, the man who would willingly uproot his life for her.

"Have I been deluding myself?" he asked. "It seemed like you felt the same way about me, that we were really becoming close."

"We were. We are," she corrected herself. "They'd been

moving toward this all along, and she realized she wanted to keep what they had growing. She wanted to truly commit.

"We can be closer," he said, playing with her hair. He threaded his fingers through it, running them up the back of her head.

It felt so wonderful, she didn't want him to stop. She didn't want what they had to stop. She wasn't quite sure how he'd done it, but this man had slipped past her defenses.

"Bonnie," he said softly.

"Oh, shut up and kiss me," she said. She leaned over him and hit his lips straight on. Bull's-eye.

It was a long, lovely kiss, with his hands delightfully full of her hair and then circling around to caress her chin, her neck, her shoulders. J.J. Walker knew how to kiss a woman.

"I take it that's a yes," he murmured.

*Yes!* Screamed Team Estrogen.

"Yes," said Bonnie, and kissed him again.

They were on the verge of R rated when Avril called.

J.J. groaned as she reached for her phone.

"Hey, just wanted to see where you wanted to meet for dinner," Avril said.

Oh, yeah, they were supposed to be going out together that night. "Can we catch up with you tomorrow?" Bonnie asked. "Something's come up."

J. J. snickered and kissed her collarbone.

"Oh, uh, sure. No problem."

"I got you an appointment in the afternoon. I'm sure we'll have something to celebrate later. I'll call you in the morning," Bonnie promised."

"Late morning," J.J. said.

"Is J.J. with you?" Avril asked.

"Yes."

"Huh. I guess you *are* busy. Have fun, Mom," Avril said, and ended the call.

"Oh, my, I think she knows what we're doing," Bonnie said. Awkward.

"What we're going to be doing all night long," he said, running a hand down her thigh.

*All night long.* The old Lionel Richie song sprang to mind. Partying all night long with J.J.—there was no one she'd rather be with. In fact, much as she'd thought she loved Rance, she was realizing what she'd had with him was a shallow puddle. This was a deep well, one she could drink from for a long time to come, maybe for a lifetime.

"That was lovely," Lawrence said to Loretta when she finished singing for him. They were at her condo, sitting out on the balcony and enjoying a balmy summer evening in Moonlight Harbor.

She set aside her guitar. "It's a song my daughter wrote years ago."

"She was very talented," he said.

"Still is."

"Like her mother," Lawrence said.

The admiration in his eyes and the warmth in his voice wrapped around her, warming her heart and she couldn't help comparing him to Marlon... Harvey... Creep. That man had always known what to say, but the words had never come from his heart. Lawrence meant every word he said.

And he was for real. So far on his visit they had Face-Timed with his daughter and her family twice and his son once. Real family, nothing hidden...like a wife. How she'd love it if he'd stay in Moonlight Harbor indefinitely, but she supposed he'd want to be off soon in his motor home, ready to see more of the country.

"You're too kind," she said.

"I'm only speaking the truth," he assured her.

"Which is more than I can say for the last man I was..." she almost said "with." But, honestly, she wasn't sure she and Lawrence qualified as a with. Granted, they'd spent plenty of time on Facebook and on the phone before he ever came out to visit. And they'd been together every single day since he'd arrived, but he'd made no move to kiss her. "Spending time with," she amended.

"Someone was foolish enough to let you go? I can't believe it."

"Oh, he wanted me," Loretta said bitterly. "He wanted me in addition to the wife he already had."

"The rotter!"

That sad episode was still such an embarrassment. How could she have been so foolish! But, really, how often did a woman encounter a bigamist and a con artist all rolled into one.

"I'm glad you got smart and told him where to go, and if he chose his wife over you that was his loss."

She realized that Lawrence might have thought she'd been sucked into having an affair, making herself the proverbial Other Woman. "He didn't have much choice. She showed up at our wedding. It was the first I'd heard of her and she of me."

Lawrence's eyes did the frog eye bulge. "No."

"Yes," she said, and sighed. "Honestly, Lawrence, it was enough to make me give up on love."

His brows drew downward. "Not forever, I hope. I mean..." He cleared his throat. "I rather thought we had something good going."

"Oh, Lawrence, we do. And you're nothing like him."

He smiled, hesitated a moment, then said, "Loretta, if

the right man came along would you take another chance on love?"

She smiled back. "I might."

"You know, I always thought you were something else. Not in my league, of course, but if I'd been braver I'd have asked you out."

"You were always a good friend," she said. "I'd have gone."

"You would?"

"Of course."

He shook his head. "Well, then, more the fool me. You went out with the jocks and the rich boys. I figured I didn't stand a chance."

"You got me through enough breakups with those jocks and rich boys," she reminded him, and he chuckled.

"That I did," he said.

"And I'm sure you were very happy with the girl you ended up with."

"That I was. But I've been so darned lonely since she passed. It's no fun eating breakfast alone, having no one to watch a sunset with." Again, he hesitated. "Loretta, I don't suppose…"

This sweet man was trying to get something important out, and she wanted him to. "What?" she prompted.

"Do I have any chance of making you fall in love with me? I know I'm no Kevin Costner," he began.

"I don't need a Kevin Costner," she said. "And I don't need a slick dresser with a slick line. I need someone with a beautiful heart who loves music."

He raised a hand. "I volunteer. I love music. I also love the way you look, the way you laugh and that kind heart of yours."

His words were honey for her soul. "And how about my meatloaf?" she teased.

"That, too."

"You dear, sweet man," she said. She moved to his chair and bent over and bestowed a kiss on him. Their first kiss.

He reached up and took her face in his hands and kissed her back. Quite expertly. Marlon/Harvey/Creep had been an expert kisser also, but Lawrence's kiss had something his never did. Heart.

They pulled apart far enough to look into each other's eyes and she could see such sincerity in his. "That was like getting kissed by a fairy right out of Narnia," he said.

"I thought Prince Charming," she said, making him grin.

"Do you think I could take another visit to Narnia?" he asked softly.

"I certainly do," she said, and kissed her balding, sweet Prince Charming again.

Harvey had put her through hell, but God had been kind and brought along someone even better. A song from her younger days, "Almost Paradise," began playing in her mind. She'd gotten close to a dream of finding love again and that dream had fallen apart, but look what she'd found this time—no dream but possibly, at last, the real thing.

Later that night, as they held hands and watched the moon send its beams dancing over the water, she sent up a prayer of thanks. It was never too late for dreams to come true.

And if they were coming true for her, maybe they would for her girls as well.

# *Eighteen*

"About time," Bonnie muttered as she and J.J. stood in front of the tribute to The Judds, who had finally made it into the Country Music Hall of Fame in 2022. "They were long past due," she said to J.J.

"Agreed," he said. "But they did finally make it. Maybe you will someday, too."

"A little late for me," she said.

He shook his head at her. "Never say never. You don't know what the future holds."

"You're right. But right now I'm happy enough in the present, and that's not a bad thing."

"Good to appreciate what's already on your plate," he conceded.

She chuckled. "Spoken like a true restaurant owner."

"I never thought I'd be doing that again," he said. "Which proves you should never say never. Just see what happens and go with your gut." He put an arm around her. "I'm glad I went with my gut. It brought me to Moonlight Harbor where I found a drunken sailor and a mermaid. Now, how many men get a chance to meet a mermaid?"

"You lucky man, you," she said, blowing off his flattery.

He sobered. "I am. After my marriage blew up I figured that was it. I never thought I'd find what I've found with you."

"I feel the same way," she said. "And I don't need to have my picture or some outfit I wore sitting behind glass in here. Oh, I wanted it once. It was my own little idol I bowed down to every day. I was wrapped up in becoming, I don't know, the next Shania Twain or Dolly Parton, so busy trying to make it that I lost sight of what this city is all about. It's not about walls of gold records or fancy cars or big houses. It's about music and all the connections and joy that music brings to our lives. Yes, Nashville does tribute to the greats in the business, but all along what they were doing was giving tribute to the music."

J.J. nodded thoughtfully. "You know what? That was profound."

"I don't know about that."

"I do. Don't always be so quick to sell yourself short. You are so much more than you realize."

"I don't know about being more. I just want to be me. To the fullest."

And that she could be anywhere…if she had J.J by her side.


Avril had to pinch herself as she drove away from BMG Publishing. She'd just gotten a publisher for her song. She'd considered long and hard before that appointment, knowing she had a sure thing waiting with either Rance or Carolina, but both of those options felt fraught with sticky complications. This felt right. And she felt great.

More than great. It was all so…amazing. She had to be dreaming.

"I still can't believe it," she said when she called her mom to tell her the news.

"I'm glad for you, darling," said Bonnie. "And I'm proud of you."

Her mom happy for her success. She pinched herself again. She was really making it happen and her mom was finally on her side. She was the music version of Pinocchio—no longer a wannabe but a real songwriter.

"Next step is to join ASCAP," Mom said. "That's what I belong to."

Following in her mother's footsteps...except she wasn't going to make the same mistake her mother had and get messed over.

Her mother offered to pay her one-time membership fee as a present. Also, Avril figured, as a sort of blessing.

"Thanks, Mom," she said. "It means a lot."

"You got the golden ticket," Gina said when she returned to the apartment late that afternoon and Avril told her. "I am so shook. We need to celebrate!"

"We are. Mom's taking us out to Monell's."

"Southern fried chicken. Yum!"

They had a full table since her mother generously offered to take out not only Gina, but Colton and Jimmy as well.

"This is really nice of you," Colton said to Mom. "Thanks for including me."

"I knew Avril's friends would want to celebrate with her," Mom said to him.

"Majorly," said Colton.

"We're all going up together," said Jimmy, and raised his glass of beer to Avril. "Here's to a monster success."

"I'll second that," said Colton. "Way to go."

She'd done what she set out to do. It was such a high she could barely eat.

The high deflated just a bit when Jimmy proposed going

to the Orchid Lounge and Mom backed out. "We've got an early flight in the morning."

"Flight?" Avril repeated. "You're leaving already? I thought you'd stay longer. Didn't Carolina want to write with you?"

Mom hedged. "I came here to straighten some things out and that's been done. You're launched now and in good hands. I don't have to worry about you anymore."

"You didn't have to worry about me at all," Avril informed her.

Mom smiled at that. "It goes with the territory when you've got kids. You go have fun with your friends. And promise to keep me posted on how things are going."

"I will," Avril said, and hugged her. "Thanks, Mom. I love you."

"I love you more," Bonnie replied, and hugged her back.

Mom and J.J. got in their rental car and drove off and Gina and Avril hopped in her car to follow the guys to the lounge. Music and tequila shots—the perfect way to end the day. She was still excited and so, so very happy.

But the next morning, after texting a final good-bye to her mom, she felt like something was off. It was as if Mom was leaving with a piece of her, the piece that belonged to Moonlight Harbor.

That probably shouldn't be so surprising. Having her mom with her had been like a homecoming in reverse. Mom had brought a taste of home to her.

But Moonlight Harbor wasn't her home anymore. Her home was Nashville.

What was Kenny doing? Was he thinking about her? She hoped not. He needed to move on just as she was doing.

Still, he'd want to know about this latest development. She fired off a text. I did it! I got a publisher.

Knew you could do it, came the reply.

Sweet Kenny, her biggest fan. Even though things hadn't worked out for them maybe they could still be friends.

"Men never want to be friends," Gina said. "It's all or nothing with them."

"Kenny will always be my friend," Avril insisted.

"Let me get this straight. You dumped him but you want him to still be there for you." Gina raised an eyebrow.

Yeah, it was pretty selfish.

"I guess having Mom here got me all nostalgic," Avril said.

But then, eating ribs at Losers Bar and Grill and listening to a great band, followed by an equally great steamy grope session at Colton's apartment later, she told herself nostalgia was all well and good, but that saying was true. You couldn't go back.

That night she dreamed she was a mermaid. She was on a boat. In the far distance she could hear Tim McGraw singing "Live Like You Were Dying." She managed to get herself overboard and back into the water. It was night and a thick fog surrounded the boat.

A male figure, barely discernable, leaned over the rail and called, "Where are you going?"

"To land," she called back.

"You don't belong on land," the man called.

"I sure do," she replied and swam for all she was worth. Once on the beach, she found herself flopping, trying to stand upright. "I need legs!" she cried. "Somebody, give me legs."

Lo and behold, under a sprinkling of glitter, she was transformed, and she popped out of the cloud in a fringed cowgirl dress, her tail gone and her new legs in cowgirl boots.

She turned toward the water and hollered, "See! I told you I belonged on land."

"You don't," the voice came back.

"I do!" she cried. "I do!"

She awoke with the words still on her lips.

Bonnie called Loretta as soon as she was back home to check in. "I'm glad everything went well," Loretta said.

"It did. I'm glad I at least got Avril lined up with a publisher, and into ASCAP. That way she can't get taken."

*By Rance.* Bonnie didn't need to say his name. It went without saying who she was thinking of.

"And how did things go with J.J.?"

Bonnie smiled. "He is an amazing man."

"I'm glad you're finally realizing that," said Loretta. "Please tell me something…anything happened in Nashville."

"Come on, Mom. You know what happens in Nashville stays in Nashville," Bonnie joked.

"Ha! I knew it. You two have fallen into the love pond."

"I think maybe we have."

"He's a good man. I think you can safely entrust your heart to him. The way he dropped everything to be with you, that was knight in shining armor stuff."

Bonnie had to agree.

"I think you need to write a song for him."

"Maybe I will."

She spent the next couple of weeks doing just that—when she wasn't holding down the fort at the office for Lucy and Brody or getting ready for the art show Arthur had talked her into doing in August—polishing the lyrics, fine-tuning the melody. J.J. was over often and she felt downright bubbly inside when she looked at him and thought of how very long she could make that song if she started listing all the things she loved about him and about how he made her feel.

She played the finished product for her mom and Lawrence the following day as they sat on the back deck of Bonnie's house, enjoying garlic bread and Mermaid Stew, a chowder concoction Loretta had dreamed up.

"What do you think?" Bonnie asked as she set aside her guitar.

"I love it. I especially love the line about him being the sun that chased away the gray skies," Loretta said.

"It's kind of trite." But it was so true. He had. Bonnie watched as a family of ducks swam by. It was so peaceful in Moonlight Harbor. "Maybe I need to admit that in the song," she said, inspired. "It's trite, but it's so true..."

"I got the last good man when I got you," Loretta sang, smiling at Lawrence, who actually blushed.

"Too bad we don't have Avril to sing third part harmony," said Loretta. "I suppose we won't see her this summer now that she's so busy."

The paddle board Avril had used so often sat propped up against the deck, ignored. Hopefully, she would still make summer visits and use it, but Loretta was right. Avril would be too busy launching her songwriting career to come home for a visit so soon. Songwriting dates, playing writers showcases, making song demos—yes, her life would be full.

Something stirred in Bonnie, something that felt a lot like yearning. It made her antsy and she pushed it away. Never mind that stupid buzz she'd gotten when the plane had landed, never mind that Carolina had texted her about writing together. Nashville was history. Her future lay in Moonlight Harbor with her mom and J.J. and all her friends. This was home. This was safe.

This wasn't Nashville.

And that was a good thing. No past to wade through, no issues.

"Oh, well," Loretta said. "She's doing what she wants to do. And we have you back, just in time for The Mermaids to play this weekend. We should play your new song."

"Good idea," said Bonnie. Who cared where she played her songs as long as she got to play them? She missed having her daughter in the band, but at least she still got to sing with her mother.

Seeing the way Lawrence looked at her mom and the way Loretta looked back, Bonnie found herself wondering how long The Mermaids would even be a duo. Lawrence had that motor home and wanted to see the country. If he invited Loretta along on the adventure she'd probably accept.

"It looks like your mom and her old friend are getting pretty close," Jenna Waters observed when Bonnie joined her and Seth at their table in The Drunken Sailor for a chat on Friday night.

Bonnie looked across the dance floor to where Lawrence sat, keeping her mother company at what was traditionally the band table. "Yes, they are."

"Think it's serious?" Jenna asked.

"I hope so," Bonnie said. "She sure deserves to find some happiness."

"We all do," said Jenna. She smiled at J.J., who was approaching their table.

"Everyone having a good time?" he asked, and pulled up a chair next to Bonnie.

"Of course," said Jenna. "Seth got his onion ring fix tonight so all is good."

"Best onion rings in town," said her husband. "Best place to hang out, too."

"You can't beat the entertainment," J.J. said and slipped an arm over the back of Bonnie's chair.

It wasn't a gushy PDA, but it said something all the same.

It was classy and cool, like the man himself. She smiled at him. "We're singing a new song next set."

"Yeah? One you wrote?" he asked, and she nodded.

"I love your songs," Jenna said. "It seems to me Avril isn't the only one who should be going to Nashville."

Bonnie waved away her comment. "I'm good here."

"You're good wherever you are," J.J. said.

She began the set with the song she'd written, merely introducing it by saying, "I wrote this for someone special." Anyone watching the way she and J.J. looked at each other as she sang it would know exactly who that someone was. He was the first to applaud when she finished with, "What else can I say? You are the sun that makes my day." It left her feeling warm all over. Yes, he was the sun in her life.

And her inspiration. She finished the painting he'd inspired just in time for the art show Arthur had asked her to be part of. Two other artists, a photographer and a glass blower, were displaying their work, which took the pressure off Bonnie.

"Hey, is that me?" J.J. asked, standing next to her in the gallery as they waited for the doors to open.

"How'd you guess?" she teased.

"It looks like me."

"You're much better looking," she assured him. Still, she had tried her best to portray that kissable chin of his and his Irish red hair and well-trimmed beard, had tried to capture the easygoing smile she'd come to appreciate so much.

"I like the fact that the mermaid is serenading me. I assume that's you."

"It is." Hard not to know it was her since the mermaid had her red hair and green eyes.

J.J. summoned Arthur over to where they were standing. "Take this down. It's sold."

His gesture zapped her with delight. "Really?"

"Really. No one else is getting this. Or my mermaid," J.J. added.

Arthur grinned at Bonnie. "How much you want to bet your paintings will all be gone before the show is over?"

"I wouldn't be surprised," said J.J.

"If they are it won't be that impressive since I don't have many," Bonnie pointed out.

"I know. Wish there were more. You need to get busy."

"Believe me, I'm busy," Bonnie said. What was left of summer would be brief and she much preferred to spend her free time golfing with J.J. or hanging out on a secluded area of beach down by the jetty that they'd claimed and he'd dubbed Mermaid Beach.

The first patron walked in the door. It was Tyrella Lamb, who owned the hardware store. She had her fiancé in tow. "We're looking for art for the new house," she said to Arthur.

"You've come to the right place," he assured her.

She led her fiancé over to where Bonnie stood with J.J. "Lucy told me I absolutely need original art for the house," Tyrella said to her. "After seeing the painting you did for her I have to agree."

She looked at the four paintings still on the wall. One of the mermaids was young and looked a lot like Avril. She wore a cowgirl hat and a big smile. Another sat on a rock, flying a kite. The third was older and plump, perched on the prow of a kayak, holding an ice cream cone. The kayaker, a hefty man, was trying to grab the cone, which she was keeping out of reach while laughing. The mermaid that caught Tyrella's eye was Black and slender with green dreads. She was leaping out of the sea, sending sea spray in all directions. Her face wore an expression of bliss, with her eyes closed and a big smile.

"That's me!" Tyrella exclaimed.

Bonnie hadn't painted it with Tyrella in mind, but the mermaid was perfect for her.

"I'll take it," said her man. "My wedding present to you, babe," he told her.

Bonnie smiled as they kissed. It warmed her heart to see something she'd started as a mere pastime being enjoyed by others. And appreciated.

"These are so original," raved another woman who came in shortly after.

Original. Yes, they were. They were all hers and no one could take credit for them.

"Let's get the mermaid flying the kite," Jenna Waters said to her husband, Seth. "He and my girl flew a lot of kites together when she was young," Jenna explained to Bonnie. "She just got engaged and this will make a lovely wedding present."

"Oh, my gosh," raved Nora Singleton when she came in. "I have to have the mermaid with the ice cream cone. "I'll hang her up in Good Times. Mermaids and ice cream parlors at the beach just go together," she said to Bonnie with a wink.

"That they do," said Bonnie.

Ten minutes later a woman from Los Angeles who was at the beach visiting family bought the last mermaid.

"I could have sold twice as many," Arthur told her. "I knew you'd be a huge success."

A huge success. In a creative arena where she'd never thought of trying for success. It felt good. But it wasn't the same as that studio high she used to get when making a song demo, it couldn't match what she felt when Avril left BMG with a song contract. She was an addict and she should never have opened that giant, glitzy bottle that was Nashville. Standing there, surrounded by friends and collectors, all she could think about was getting in a room with a guitar and another writer.

How was she going to kick this addiction for good?

"We need to go celebrate," said J.J. "Catch you later," he told Loretta and Lawrence and led Bonnie out of the gallery.

He had a small cooler in the trunk of his red Miata convertible, and once they were parked at the beach, he opened it and produced two bottled margaritas, well chilled, along with crab salad sandwiches.

"And chocolate," he said, showing her two gourmet chocolate bars.

"Okay, this is seriously impressive," she said as he handed her a bottle.

"Not as impressive as you. Here's to your success," he said, clinking bottles.

They leaned against the car and watched the waves dance over the sand. Success, she mused. It was such a strange thing, never showing up where you wanted it.

"It's not enough, is it?" J.J. said quietly.

"Oh, so now you're a mind reader?"

"I saw how you looked when you saw Nashville from the plane," he said.

She took another drink, shook her head. "Nashville is so in the past."

"It doesn't have to stay there."

"Yes, it does."

He studied her. "You can do anything you set your mind to. Don't ever think you can't."

"Now you sound like my mother," Bonnie joked.

"I don't want to be your mother," he said.

She let him take the bottle from her hands and set it on the hood. Then she let him draw her to him. The feel of his hard chest up against her was more than a turn-on. It was a comfort. This was the kind of man a woman could count on. Could trust. He was no dream killer. He was part of the dream—the most important part.

"Your wife was a fool to let you go," she said, slipping her arms around his neck.

"And for that I will always be grateful," he said, and kissed her, his lips gentle on hers.

Her cell phone rang. "Girls Just Want to Have Fun."

He groaned. "Your mom."

She nodded.

He shook his head and gave her a half smile. "Tell her she has lousy timing."

"Hi, Mom," Bonnie answered.

"Lawrence and I are at the gallery. All your paintings are gone and so are you. Where are you?" Loretta demanded.

"I'm at the beach with J.J. Celebrating."

"Oh," Loretta said. This was followed by, "I guess you're busy."

"I guess so," Bonnie said, smiling at J.J.

"Give him a kiss for me," Loretta teased. "Bye." And then she was gone.

"That was quick," J.J. observed.

"She knows I'm busy. And I intend to get a lot busier," Bonnie said and kissed him again.

Kissing. Colton was amazingly good at it. And he sure had the magic hands.

So Avril wasn't sure what was keeping her from falling into bed with him.

"You guys are such a great pair," Gina said as Avril got

ready to meet him for dinner. "I don't know what's stopping you."

"Me, either," said Avril. "I guess I'm just not ready."

"Well, when the time is right you'll know. It sure was right for me and Jimmy. I do so love that man."

"He's easy to love," said Avril.

So was Colton with his superstar good looks and his charm. What the heck was her problem?

Dinner was pick your fav at Assembly Food Hall, which had to be the world's largest food court. Colton opted for a Philly steak sandwich and Avril got fish tacos. They were almost as good as what she'd have found in Moonlight Harbor.

They were halfway through their meal when Sarah called Colton. He put it on speaker.

"Hey, you two," Sarah said. "How's it going down there?"

"You won't believe what's going on with Avril," Colton said. "Turns out she's country royalty."

"Yeah? You Kenny Chesney's love child?" Sarah teased.

"Try Rance Jackson's," Colton said.

Avril could feel her cheeks heating. It was embarrassing hearing people talk about her like she was tabloid fodder.

"He and my mom were a couple when she was young," she explained. "It's a long story," she added, not wanting to spill any more tea than they already had.

"Wow! And here I was about to brag on my online pitch."

"How'd it go?" Avril asked.

"Great. And guess what."

"You're Kenny Chesney's love child?" Colton teased.

Avril didn't think he was funny.

"I'm coming down," Sarah squealed.

"Awesome," said Avril.

"Not until September. Colton, can I crash at your place?"

"Sure," he said.

Avril felt the corner of her lips pulling down. Sarah hadn't even asked if she could stay with Avril and Gina.

Of course not. There was no room at Gina's place. Colton had a spare room, the same one he'd offered her when she first talked about coming down. There was no reason to feel jealous.

Except she was.

"Yay!" Sarah said.

"Yay!" said Avril. But as soon as they ended the call she lost some of her enthusiasm. "You were sure quick to invite her to stay with you," she said to Colton.

"You jealous?" he teased.

"No," she lied.

"You are," he crowed. "Good."

After they'd finished eating, they went to the Commodore Lounge, which was becoming a weekly habit.

The women playing that night were good, and Avril enjoyed their songs, especially one that the woman named Honoria had written about chocolate. She smiled when Honoria sang the line, "Put a chocolate kiss on my lips."

Avril turned to share the smile with Colton, knowing he'd appreciate the cleverness of the lyric. But he didn't turn her way. In fact, he wasn't even watching the singers. Instead, he was typing something into his phone.

She looked over his shoulder and saw what he'd written. A chocolate kiss on my lips. He'd found it clever, too. He was probably making notes so they could talk about the song later.

Honoria's friend sang a couple of songs next, and once again Avril saw Colton making notes on his phone. What the heck?

"You sure took a lot of notes," she said later when he was driving her back to the apartment.

"Just getting down some ideas," he said.

"Yeah, but those ideas are taken," she pointed out.

"Doesn't mean you can't springboard from them," he said.

"True," she said, but wasn't sure she was convinced.

Back at the apartment he came in for a final drink. They had the place to themselves as Gina was over at Jimmy's. "You getting tired of sleeping on the couch yet?" Colton asked as she snuggled up next to him.

"Yeah, I have to admit, I am. We're gonna go looking for a bigger apartment."

"Instead of doing that, why don't you move in with me?" he suggested, running a finger along her collarbone.

"You've got Sarah coming down."

"I'm not inviting you to stay in my spare room," he said, and took a taste of her neck.

It was tempting. He was tempting. What was she waiting for?

"I'll think about it," she said.

"Let me give you something else to think about," he said, and kissed her.

Gina wouldn't be back for ages so there was plenty of time for "thinking." But in Colton's arms, with her eyes closed, all she could see was him writing down lines from another person's song.

He was only writing down ideas. Nothing wrong with that, right?

Was that how the problems started with her mom and Rance?

# *Nineteen*

Love was in the air, as the saying went, and it was so thick at the table where Bonnie sat in Sandy's restaurant with her mom and Lawrence she felt as if she were in a pink cloud. For all she knew, there were invisible Cupids and bluebirds circling their table. The two were like a pair of teenagers, giggly and silly, and her mother's face glowed. Good for Mom. It was past time she found her prince. And this one was genuine. Bonnie had no reservations about him.

"Your mother is one wonderful woman," Lawrence said as they chatted about their previous day's adventure going fishing in West Haven.

"Some kind of wonderful," sang Loretta and he grinned.

"If you'll excuse me, I must find the little girls' room," Loretta said. "Feel free to talk about me while I'm gone as long as it's all good," she added with a wink.

She was barely gone when Lawrence said, "Actually, I did have something I wanted to talk to you about without your mother hearing." He cleared his throat. "I know you two are close."

"We are."

"Which is why I wanted to let you know how I feel

about her. I'd like to marry Loretta, but I don't want to break you two up."

"Nothing would ever break us up," Bonnie assured him.

"I'd sure appreciate your blessing," he said.

Lawrence was a sweet man and a huge contrast to some of the losers Loretta had fallen for (especially a certain recent one).

"I'd be happy to see you and my mom get married. Although, well, um." How to say this? "You haven't been together all that long."

"True," he admitted. "But I love her like crazy. Loved her in high school even, but I always thought she was too good for me. Then we connected on Facebook, and I took a chance and came out here and, well, after losing my wife I never thought I could be this happy again. I think I can make her happy, too."

Lawrence wasn't a fake and, like he said, he and Loretta were hardly strangers. "Mom's just as happy as you, and I think she's found a super great man."

"Then, you wouldn't mind if I asked her to marry me? You'd be okay with that?"

It was a sweet gesture, and endearing. "You're grown-ups. You don't need to ask my permission," Bonnie said.

"Oh, but I do. I want our kids to be supportive, not angry or resentful."

"I take it you've talked to yours?" Bonnie said.

He nodded. "They all know how much I loved their mother. They also know how lonely I've been. My daughter actually tried to match me up with her neighbor. That was a scary experience."

Bonnie snickered. "That was brave of her."

She'd never tried to match Loretta up with anyone. Loretta had preferred to do her own manhunting. And she hadn't been very good at it. Until Lawrence. Lawrence was someone Bonnie's dad would have approved of. She almost felt as if he was watching from heaven and heaving a sigh of relief.

"I know it looks like I'm rushing things, but at my age you don't know how many years you have left. I think Loretta feels the same way. But she'll want your blessing."

"Of course, she has it. So do you," Bonnie said. She reached across the table and covered his hand with hers.

He blushed, nodded, patted her hand with his other. Then he cleared his throat again. "I know Moonlight Harbor is her home, but I thought she might be open to traveling with me a little."

Bonnie knew what he was implying. Of course, it was the same thing she'd thought. If Loretta rumbled off into the sunset in Lawrence's motor home it would be the end of The Mermaids. The end of an era.

But a new beginning for her mother, one she deserved. She'd been a loving mother and doting grandmother, always there for Bonnie and Avril. It was past time for her to start living for herself.

"You go and have as many adventures as you can. I hope you two will make Moonlight Harbor your home base though."

"I think we can do that."

"And your kids will have to share you with us on holidays," Bonnie added with a grin. "We'll alternate Thanksgiving and Christmas. How's that?"

He beamed at her. "That sounds fine to me. And now, since I have your permission, I'd like to propose to Loretta on Friday night. I was thinking I'd get brave and do it right there at The Drunken Sailor, maybe on your first break."

Loretta had been publicly humiliated at The Drunken

Sailor. What a great turn-around for her to receive a proposal of marriage there.

"She'd love it," Bonnie said. She waved at her mother, who was approaching—a signal to Lawrence. He nodded and smiled and dropped the subject.

"Have you two been saying wonderful things about me?" Loretta joked as she slipped back into her seat.

"Of course," Lawrence said, and winked at Bonnie.

She winked back. Exciting times ahead for her mother. *And what about you?* came the thought. *You just going to hang around the beach and paint and write songs that go nowhere?*

Maybe she would. So what? Anyway, Moonlight Harbor wasn't nowhere. It was home. It was where she was finding her own prince. Why would she want to leave that to go gamble her heart and happiness in Nashville?

Still, she couldn't help feeling a little sad as she and her mom sang "Islands in the Stream," a request from one of their older patrons, on Friday night. They'd been singing together for so long it had become one of the underpinnings of Bonnie's life. Loretta's departure would leave a big hole.

The song ended their first set. "We'll be back in a few," Bonnie said to the crowd. "So don't go anywhere."

"You two sound good," Pete Long called to them as they started past him on their way to the band table. "But you need to get your kid back."

Good old, Pete, the master of the backhanded compliment.

"Afraid that won't be happening, Pete," Bonnie informed him.

"She's got a publisher in Nashville now," Loretta bragged. "Our girl is busy making her mark on the world."

"She gonna be the next Reba?" Pete asked. "She needs to come home and do a free concert."

"I'll have to suggest that next time I see her," Bonnie said, and steered her mom to the band table where Lawrence and J.J. sat waiting with drinks for them.

"You were wonderful," Lawrence said to Loretta.

She sat down next to him and gave him a kiss on the cheek. "Oh, you're only saying that because it's true."

He chuckled and smiled at her like the besotted man he was. Then he cleared his throat. "Uh, Loretta, I have something important to ask you."

"Oh? Well, go ahead," she said.

"I'm hoping I'm not making a fool out of myself for nothing, but here goes."

He got up, walked around to the other side of her seat where the dance floor was and where he'd be in plain sight of everyone. Then, he gingerly lowered himself to one knee, nearly fell over pulling a ring box from his pocket, but in the end, managed to stay upright, and opened it.

"Oh, Lawrence," Loretta gasped, looking at the diamond ring inside.

"Will you marry me?" he asked.

"Of course I will!" she cried.

"Yes!" His hands shot up in victory, and anyone who hadn't seen what was going on certainly did in that moment. Patrons and friends all started applauding, then let out a collective gasp as Lawrence lost his balance and tipped sideways, falling to the floor with a yelp.

Loretta, Bonnie and J.J. all jumped up and helped him get to his feet.

"I bungled that," he muttered.

"No, you didn't," Loretta said, throwing her arms around his neck. "You got the girl."

Once more, everyone applauded as she kissed him.

People rushed over to congratulate the couple and admire Loretta's engagement ring, and amid the hubbub Bonnie said to J.J. "I don't think you'll have The Mermaids for much longer."

"Ah, the motor home," he said, and she nodded.

"I suspect Mom's going to be singing 'On the Road Again,' once she's married."

"Good for her," J.J. said. "Maybe you need to start looking for some more Mermaids."

She shrugged. "Maybe."

She knew her heart wouldn't be in it though. It wouldn't be the same. Still, life was about change. One thing she knew for sure, she was happy to see her mother's changing for the better.

Hers had changed for the better, too, she realized, as she and J.J. teed off at the golf course the next morning. After their game they planned to take a picnic lunch to the beach. Then, that evening, they were going over to Jenna and Seth's house for a dinner party to celebrate Loretta and Lawrence's engagement before the band went on. Yes, life was good at the beach. She really couldn't ask for more.

"When are you guys getting married?" Avril asked Loretta when she and Loretta and Bonnie FaceTimed on Sunday.

"First weekend in October," Loretta said. "We want to hit the road right afterward. But if you can't make it back then we can always change the date," she hurried to add.

"Don't worry. I'll be there," Avril promised. Glamma finally finding true love—oh, yes, she wouldn't miss that celebration.

"Want some company?" Colton asked when she told him

as they jogged the path in Radner Park. "I've never been to Washington. I hear it's pretty cool."

Somehow, it didn't feel right bringing a stranger to Glamma's wedding. "It's probably going to be just family," she said. There was a lie. Most likely, all of Moonlight Harbor would be invited.

He shrugged. "Okay. No problem. Just thought it would be fun."

"It would be," she said. Colton *was* fun. And he was the kind of charmer who showed off well. Still, something at the back of her mind said, *Don't do it. The timing's off.*

Maybe more than the timing was off. They were off. She hadn't felt quite the same toward him since the night she'd caught him writing down lines from another songwriter's song.

"So, you want to do some writing tonight?" he asked when they were done jogging and stretching out by their cars.

They'd done some writing together over the last few weeks, but so far hadn't come up with anything she felt comfortable taking to her new publisher, and that bugged him. And it kind of bugged her that it bugged him.

"Let's wait till we have something really great to show," she kept saying.

"We do," he kept insisting.

He was looking at her, waiting for an answer. "I don't know," she said.

"I've got a great lyric."

"Yeah?"

"Oh, yeah."

Who could resist a great lyric?

"All I need is a bridge," he said.

"I want to see it," she said, because you never knew when you would strike creative gold.

He pulled up the lyric on his phone and handed it to her. She stared at the opening words to the chorus. *Everything about tonight is right.* She'd heard that line, heard the woman sing those same words at the Commodore. She read further. He'd changed a word here and there, but that didn't make the song his.

She looked up at him. "This is the same song we heard Camille sing."

"No, it's not. The words are different."

"How?" Avril demanded.

"I took out *you*," he said, pointing to the first line. He pointed to the second line. "And there's no *me*."

She raised an eyebrow. "You changed two words and that makes it yours?"

He shrugged. "Okay, so it's pretty close. We can make some changes."

She handed back the phone. "Yeah, like the whole lyric."

"Hey, you can't own a title."

"But you can own a lyric. Come on, Colton. We can do better than that."

"Yeah?" He scowled at her. "Seems to me you're getting pretty picky. I give you something that could be a hit and you dust me."

"Dust you! If you're going to steal from another songwriter you deserve to be dusted."

"This isn't stealing," he insisted.

Once again, she thought of what had happened to her mom. One of Glamma's favorite sayings came to mind. *If he'll do it with you he'll do it to you.* She'd been referring to her lucky escape and talking about men who cheated on their wives but it sure applied to writers who would cheat other writers. Sometimes that desire for success made it hard for people to find the straight and narrow. It appeared that Colton was losing his way, and Avril didn't want to get lost with him.

"You come up with something on your own and I'll work with you, but not on this," she said.

His scowl deepened. "Aren't you little Miss High and Mighty ever since you got a song deal," he sneered.

"What, because I've got ethics?"

"Yeah, well, it's easy to have ethics when you're riding on the gravy train."

His bitterness was a huge buzzkill. All she could think of was her mom and Rance Jackson—Rance Jackson who lived in a mansion in Brentwood while her mom had a little house in Moonlight Harbor.

And yet, who was better off, really? Her mom had a clear conscience and a really nice man. Rance had success and a love life that sucked. Anyone with eyeballs could see his fiancée was using him. Another Glamma saying popped into her mind. *What goes around comes around.* Avril wanted good things to come around to her, and helping Colton steal someone else's song sure wouldn't set that in motion.

"Sorry," she said. "That's how I feel."

He heaved a long-suffering sigh. "Okay. I still don't think I did anything wrong, but fine if you don't want to work on that. We can do something else."

"Not tonight," she said. Maybe not ever.

Monday morning Bonnie got a call from Rance. "Rance?" What was he doing with her phone number? She sure hadn't given it to him.

"I got your number from Avril," he said as if reading her mind.

Why on earth would her daughter be sharing her phone number with Rance? Avril knew how Bonnie felt about him.

"Listen, you remember 'I'm What You Need'?"

It was one of the songs they'd written together, before everything fell apart.

"Yeah," she said cautiously. What was he up to?

"Well, Ashland Craft wants to sing it."

Ashland Craft was one of many young, up-and-coming country music artists. But this was an older song, done years ago.

"How'd she hear the song?" Bonnie asked.

"I played it for her. Oh, and by the way, Miranda Lambert really likes 'Open Range.'"

It was a song she'd written with Carolina. "Who showed her that?"

"Carolina."

This was just weird. "What is with you two?"

"Just extending the old olive branch. You gonna take it or what?" he added, almost defensively.

Only a fool would say no. "Yeah, I guess I am. Not that I want anything to do with you."

"Like it or not, we're stuck with each other," he said, "'cause I am gonna be part of Avril's life."

Alligators were part of life in the Everglades, tornadoes were a part of life in Kansas and snakes were a part of life in Eastern Washington. It looked like this Nashville snake was going to be part of her life now, like it or not.

"Come on, Bonnie, let's let bygones be bygones."

Easy for him to say. He wasn't the one who got cheated on and cheated out of a dream.

But maybe a new dream was forming. She sighed, mentally prying her fingers off the past.

"So, what do you say?"

"I say it's about time," she said, and had to smile and shake her head. Life was strange.

Later, over lunch at the pub, she told J.J. what had happened.

"I think this is a sign," he said. "You need to go back, back to where it all started. It's time to finish writing your story."

"I like the story I'm writing here with you," she insisted.

"Who says I won't be part of the story there?" He reached across the table and took her hand. "Bonnie...oh, hell, this isn't the place. Let's get out of here."

"Where are we going?" she asked as they got in his car.

"To Mermaid Beach," he said.

They didn't talk as they drove, didn't talk as he took her hand and led her across the dunes to their favorite log where they sat and looked at the sparkling blue water. He kept his eyes focused on that water as he said, "I want you to marry me."

"What?"

He turned and smiled at her, and she could feel a heat rushing up into her chest that had nothing to do with the sun shining on them. "How does that song go? Take my name and make it yours. What do you say? Would you please make me yours? I love you, Bonnie and I want to be with you wherever life takes you."

"But," she began.

"No buts. You either want me like I want you or you don't."

"You know I do," she said softly.

"Then let's make it official. Marry me. You're the sun in my life. If you leave without me the whole world will turn gray."

"I don't have to leave."

"Yes, you do, and we both know it." He wrapped his arms around her. "It's time for you to go claim the success you're due. And I want to be there to help you claim it. I'll be good to you, I promise."

"You already are," she said, and could feel the tears rising. "I never thought I'd find anyone I could trust."

"Well, you have," he said simply. "I'll never betray you, never hurt you. You have my word on it. So come on. Give me an answer and let it be yes."

She would never find another man like this. Her future was calling and she didn't want to walk into it alone. Didn't want to walk into it with anyone but J.J.

"Okay, yes," she said. Then, seeing how his eyes lit up, she repeated herself. "Yes, yes, forever yes!"

The words were barely out of her mouth before his lips were on hers and he was kissing her like a starving man. That kiss said it all. This was love. Not the naive love she'd felt for Rance, not the starry-eyed love that saw only what it wanted, the love that couldn't tell the difference between charisma and character. This was the kind of love that would carry her over any choppy seas and always guide her to a safe harbor. This was what she'd needed all her life. She wrapped her arms around him and kissed him back for all she was worth, grateful to have found him, hoping she could make him as happy as he was making her.

Who knew what the future really held? It didn't matter because of the man who was holding her. Nashville was calling. It was time she answered the call.

# *Twenty*

"That's a big leap," Lucy said when Bonnie told her of her decision to relocate.

"I know, but it's time." It was past time.

"Does this mean we're never going to see you again?" Missy wanted to know.

"Of course not. I'll be back for visits."

"So, you're keeping your house?" Lucy asked.

"Were you hoping I'd want to sell it?" Bonnie teased.

"Not really. You shouldn't. Real estate here is only going to go up in value. You should keep J.J.'s, too, for a vacation rental. Anyway, once you're a huge success you'll be able to afford to own houses down there and here."

A huge success—funny how the definition of that could so quickly change.

"I think I already am a success," Bonnie said.

She'd been hiding her left hand behind her back. She brought it out and showed off the new diamond ring on her ring finger.

"Oh, my gosh!" cried Missy, putting a hand to her heart.

"I'm so happy for you," Lucy said, and hugged her. "And

to think you once said there weren't any men here in Moonlight Harbor worth getting together with."

"To think," Bonnie said with a smile.

"I'm happy for you," Arthur said when she stopped by the art gallery to turn in one final mermaid painting. "Does this mean you're not going to paint anymore?"

"I don't know," she said honestly.

"If it does, will you do me a favor?"

"What?" she asked, not willing to commit without knowing what he was asking.

"Will you paint one last one...for me?"

She smiled. "I will."

She did. She painted a mermaid in an artist's smock, sitting on a boulder at the edge of a beach, busy with a painting. Her subject sat on a blanket on the sand, legs outstretched, enjoying the sunshine. He looked a lot like Arthur.

He came close to tearing up when she presented it to him. "This will be worth a lot someday," he predicted, then corrected himself. "Actually, it's worth a lot right now to me. I'm never going to part with it. And if you paint any more mermaids..."

"You'll be the first to know," she promised.

Maybe she would. Or maybe she'd simply enjoy writing songs and singing at intimate venues. Whatever lay ahead, she was ready for it.

Fall had arrived which called for morning coffee. Avril was at 8th and Roast, getting a latte when Colton and Sarah came in. At the sight of Avril Sarah looked almost wistful and as if she wanted to say something, but Colton turned her around and out they went. Sad to think of what good friends they'd once all been when they were meeting on-line, sharing song ideas and dreams.

Avril and Colton had broken up before Sarah got to town. She'd gone to listen to him while he sang in a writer's show-case at a new bar he'd discovered. He'd made some changes in the lyrics of one of the songs he'd claimed was his, but not enough to keep her from recognizing them from another song they'd both heard performed by another songwriter at the Commodore Lounge. No wonder he wasn't singing it there. Someone would have recognized it.

She stared at him as he rode his happy high afterward while they waited for the next performers to go on, talk-ing about getting Gina to record it. "Then we can put it on TikTok," he'd said. "Make some noise."

All those plans for something that really wasn't his. That was when she'd known she couldn't be with him. She wasn't about to repeat her mother's history.

His reaction when she'd told him had gone no deeper than a frown, proof that she'd hurt his pride but not his heart.

"We can still write together," he'd said.

"No, we can't. You can't be trusted."

He'd given a disgusted snort. "Fine. I'll write with Sarah. She's a better songwriter than you are anyway."

And that had been that. She'd come to the bar with him, but she'd called an Uber and left alone. No, not completely alone. She'd left with her self-esteem and her future songs in safekeeping.

"I'm proud of you," Mom had said. "You're going to be fine."

She was fine. She still had Gina to hang out with, and Jimmy, who had cooled his friendship with Colton. She had Carolina watching over her like a surrogate mom. Carolina had been kind enough to write with her and they'd come up with a really cute song titled "Girls Kick Butt" which several up-and-coming female artists were interested in. She'd also written a song with Jimmy and Gina that his publisher liked as well. She had dancing at The Wild Horse, and nights at the Commodore. She was already meeting some supernice men, ones who shared her passion for music but also had plenty of confidence in their own ability and would never stoop to stealing so much as a rhyme from someone else.

Still, she felt a moment of sadness as she watched Sarah and Colton leave. She hoped Sarah would be okay. Colton had made Sarah choose between them and she'd obviously chosen him. Maybe she already was regretting it. It was easy to lose your way in an exciting city where hope pulsed on every corner and it seemed every street was sprinkled with stardust.

Avril came home the week before the big event and got pulled into a whirlwind of happy activities. Every day had something planned—a bridal shower for Mom, picking up guests at the airport and delivering them either to Mom or Loretta's place or the Driftwood Inn, lunch with all Glamma's friends, and a big party at the beach with the out-of-town guests and local friends of both Glamma and Mom's, complete with a roaring beach fire to combat the nip of fall in the air. Lawrence's family fawned all over Glamma, and they were awestruck when they learned Avril was a songwriter living in Nashville.

"They are a talented bunch," Lawrence bragged and smiled at Loretta.

The highlight of the beach party came when Bonnie sang

a song to Avril that she'd written for her. The men clapped and the women cried. Avril cried the hardest.

"That was amazing," she said later as the fire died down and people began roasting marshmallows.

"I meant every word of it," Mom said. "I want you to be happy wherever life takes you."

So far life had taken her to some pretty interesting places, but in spite of that her future felt nebulous. She didn't tell her mom though. It would make her sound flakey.

Come Sunday Loretta hauled her to church, showing Avril off as if she were a conquering hero. Maybe, in a way, she was. She'd gone to Nashville and made a dream come true.

As for Rance Jackson, her newly found daddy, she was taking that relationship slower than a sleepy slug. In some ways she felt sorry that she hadn't learned about him when she was a child, but in other ways she felt relieved. Children didn't always see clearly and the idea of having a daddy would have definitely given her tunnel vision in regard to his character. While he wasn't the devil incarnate, he wasn't exactly a man of honor, and she was determined not to let him too far into her life.

"Yeah, but he's Rance Jackson," Gina had argued. "And he's your dad. How many people can say they have Rance Jackson for their father?"

"There are dads and there are dads," Avril had said.

"He might have been more of a dad if your mom had told him about you."

"I get why she didn't. He screwed her over real good. Some people just can't help being selfish."

"He's not being so selfish now."

Avril had shrugged. She wanted to believe that the man who was her father had changed, that he wasn't the selfish jerk he once was, but it was hard not to question his motivation. It was in his best interests to try and help her. It made him look noble. She wasn't sure yet how noble he was.

Certainly nothing like J.J., who was completely there for her mom. She'd never seen her mother happier. The fact that J.J. was so supportive of Mom coming to Nashville and finally finding songwriting success made him a superhero. He was so there for her.

Avril was happy for both her mom and grandmother, but she also couldn't help asking herself who was there for her. Mom and Glamma, of course, but they had men in their lives and were going to be busy. Avril had...no one serious, no one she wanted to get serious with. Maybe that was why her future felt nebulous.

"I guess you're going to be in Nashville full-time, right along with your mom," said Cindy Redmond when Avril came into Flying Cats, looking for a fun wedding present.

Cindy, like everyone else in town, was fascinated with Avril's new life, but what they all didn't get was how special life was in this friendly beach town, filled with good people and good times, sunny summer days and beautiful sunsets over the ocean.

"I don't know yet," Avril said. "My mom's keeping her house here. It would be nice to be able to come back in the summers. It gets pretty hot down there."

"This is always a good place to come back to. I hope you will. And your mom and Loretta." Cindy smiled. "A double wedding, what a fun idea. It's going to be the event of the season."

That it was. The Moonlight Harbor Evangelical Church would be packed to overflowing, and the reception later at The Drunken Sailor would be both a wedding celebration and a going away party for The Mermaids. Gina and

Jimmy were flying up specially to help with the send-off, and Gina would be playing bass once more.

"We'll miss hearing all of you play," Cindy said. "Maybe once in a while you can come home and play for special events like the Fourth of July."

"Maybe," said Avril.

Practicing the song that the three of them were going to sing a cappella at the wedding was bittersweet. "Bless the Broken Road" pretty much summed up both her mother's and grandmother's lives. They'd each traveled their own broken road to find true love and she was glad they had. But it was going to be hard to see Glamma drive off in her motor home with her new husband.

Avril hadn't thought about parting when she was the one doing it, sure that Glamma and Mom would always be in Moonlight Harbor, always there and waiting for her if she returned. Now it was like standing on a pier and feeling the pilings crumbling beneath her. Of course, Mom would be in Nashville. But...

They finished the final chorus, their harmonies perfect, the ending spot-on. "We are good," Glamma said, beaming.

"Kind of sad it's going to be our last song together," Avril said. Mom and Glamma were both nice enough not to point out that she'd had no qualms about leaving their band only a few months ago.

"It's time for the Mermaids to swim in new directions," Glamma said. She beamed at Avril and Mom. "I am so proud of you two. You've both accomplished so much. You are amazing women."

"We should be. Look who raised us," Avril said, earning herself a teary hug from her grandmother.

"We need to reward ourselves," Glamma said. "Let's go get ice cream."

The three of them drove to Good Times Ice Cream Parlor where they all ordered double scoops—one of sand pebble (butter brickle with peanuts) and one of deer poop (chocolate ice cream with chocolate-covered raisins).

"It's not going to be the same without all of you," Nora Singleton said as she handed over the last cone. Mom held out her charge card and Nora waved it away. "On the house. It's the least I can do for our mermaids. You are coming back to visit once in a while, aren't you?"

"Of course," Mom assured her. "I'm keeping my house on Sand Dollar Lane."

"Good. You know you can take the girl out of the beach but you can't take the beach out of the girl," Nora said.

The bell over the door jingled and three teenage girls entered, all with long hair and braces.

"Oh, my gosh, it's Miss Brinks," said one, and the trio hurried over to where Avril and her mom and grandmother stood. "We heard you were back from Nashville," gushed the group spokesman, a girl named Lila, who had been in Avril's jazz choir. "You're going to be a star now, right?"

Avril smiled and shook her head. "No, but I hope some stars are going to sing my songs."

"Wow," breathed another girl. Her name was Celina, and Avril had had her in class also. The poor kid couldn't lift a tune let alone carry one.

"I'm glad," said Lila. "Except I hate that you won't be teaching this year."

"Me, too," said Celina. "I got a guitar for my birthday, but with you gone there's nobody to teach me how to play it."

"I'm sure there's somebody," Avril said. "Musicians are like dandelions. We're everywhere."

"Nobody like you," said Celina.

"I bet whoever the new teacher is will know how to play the guitar."

Celina wrinkled her nose. "We met him on student orientation day. He's old, and he has bad breath."

Avril wasn't sure what to say to that.

Fortunately, she didn't have to say anything.

One of the boys from school had entered the parlor with a friend, immediately taking the girls' attention.

"I can hardly wait to hear your songs," said Lila before joining the others.

"Neither can we," Glamma said as the girls and boys drifted over to the counter to make their selections.

"Ah, young love," Glamma said, watching them flirt.

"Ah, old love," Bonnie said, winking at Avril.

"Seasoned love," Loretta corrected. "I'm not old."

"Of course not," Bonnie said.

"I didn't say anything," Avril said, holding up both hands.

"Speaking of young love, I thought maybe you'd have brought along your young Nashville man to come to the wedding," Glamma said.

Avril shrugged. "That's over."

"You can bring a date, someone from around here," Glamma said.

"I'm sure everyone here already has someone."

"Maybe you'll want to invite an old friend," Glamma continued.

An old friend. "Was Kenny invited?"

Mom shook her head. "We didn't think it would be a good idea since you two aren't together."

Probably not.

"But he is an old friend," Glamma added.

And he had been a friend of the family. Hmm.

That night both her mother and grandmother were busy with their future husbands and Avril found herself at loose ends, hanging around Mom's house and wondering what Kenny was doing.

Not that she had any right to know. She hadn't talked to him in weeks because, of course, she'd moved on. But now she was wondering if she'd moved on as far as she'd intended. What *had* he been doing? Had he started seeing someone? She wanted to see how tan he was from his days on the water. She wanted to see…him.

He probably didn't want to see her. She pulled out her phone, bit her lip, stared at it. There was nothing wrong with calling and inviting him to the wedding. She brought up his name and pressed Call.

"Avril?" He sounded so surprised to hear from her. Of course, he would be. She'd hardly called him since she dumped him, and once had been to barf her troubles all over him. "Where are you?"

"Mom's house."

There was a moment's silence, followed by, "You with someone?"

"Nope. It's just me. By myself. There is no one."

"I'll be right over," he said, and ended the call.

Right over. Suddenly she had the tremors. Right over.

She rushed to the bathroom, brushed her teeth, checked her makeup, fussed with her hair. By the time the doorbell rang her heart was in overdrive. *Kenny!*

She ran to the door and opened it and there he stood, big and broad shouldered with that same smile she'd taken so much for granted. Foolish her.

"Oh, Kenny!" she cried, and threw her arms around him.

His arms tightened around her. "Oh, man, I've missed you," he said, his breath tickling her hair.

"I've missed you, too." And then she couldn't help herself. She kissed him. And he kissed her back. And they stood in the doorway for a long time, going at it.

At last she said, "Come on in," and led him to the living room couch.

"Are you back for a visit?"

"Glamma's getting married. So's my mom. They're having a double wedding and I wanted to invite you to it."

"Wow," he said. "Awesome." Then he ventured, "What about you?"

"I'm not getting married."

"I hope not, not with the way you just kissed me. But I don't get it. You were moving on. We broke up."

"I know," she said, and suddenly found it hard to look him in the eye. "I..." She was great with lyrics. Why couldn't she put what she was feeling into words?

He didn't help her, just sat there waiting.

"I was wrong," she finally said. "My life doesn't feel right without you in it. I tried to move on, but it was a wrong move. I know it's selfish to even ask for a second chance, but I need one."

There was that wonderful Kenny smile again. "Oh, man, I can't believe what I'm hearing. I am awake, right? I'm not dreaming, 'cause I could be. I've dreamed about you so many times since you left."

"You're not dreaming," she said, and took his face in her hands. Then she kissed him again, and his arms wrapped around her and pulled her so tightly against him it left her almost breathless.

"I've missed you so much," he said when they finally broke apart.

"I missed you, too," she said. "I didn't even realize how much." Colton had seemed so amazing, but she'd never felt the deep contentment around him that she did with Kenny. Colton had been all flash and no substance. Kenny was... "You're my anchor."

"Except anchors keep you in one place," he said, his smile falling off.

There was that. It was part of why she'd broken up with him to begin with.

"I don't want to be an anchor. I wanna be the wind in your sails."

Her heart did one of those painful yet happy squeezes. "Kenny, that was so poetic. And sweet."

"No, I mean it. I can find something else to do. I don't have to fish."

"Yes, you do. You were born for the sea."

"No, I was born for you," he said earnestly. "I may be a fisherman, but I'm also a man in love with an amazing woman. I'll do whatever you need me to do. And if that means moving to Nashville I'm there. You're more important than some fishing boat."

His sacrificial attitude put tears in her eyes. "You are something else," she said.

"So are you," he told her, and kissed her again.

They spent the evening out on the deck, drinking beer and talking about their lives. He was fascinated by her many adventures and shocked to learn about the lack of scruples she'd seen in some of her struggling songwriter friends. She decided she didn't need to go into specifics about one songwriter in particular. It didn't matter. He didn't matter.

"It happens," she said.

"Sounds like a shark tank down there," he said.

"In a way, it is. There are good people though, and I've met some of them."

"Things are really taking off for you."

"They are."

"You need to be there," he said.

That was what everyone said. If you weren't part of the songwriting community you weren't considered worthy of a place at the success table. But what was success? Really?

That night she dreamed that she and Kenny were on a paddle boat going down the Cumberland River. People stood along the bank, waving at her and calling, "Good-bye! See you later." Then the scenery shifted. She was on Kenny's fishing boat, surrounded by a bunch of mermaids dancing in the water, waving and calling, "Welcome home." Then they began to sing. It was a lovely song, and it was still echoing in her head when she woke up.

She sat up, grabbed her phone and dictated the lyrics. "You're my heart and you're my home. I'm where I need to be."

She was. Right there in Moonlight Harbor.

"It's a sign. You should stay," Gina said when Avril called her to tell her about her dreams.

"I should be there if I'm going to get anywhere," said Avril.

"You already got somewhere. And your mom's gonna be here."

"I don't know if I can keep the momentum going if I move back home," Avril said.

Then she realized what had just come out of her mouth. Back home. She felt like the rope in a tug-of-war.

She'd finished showering when Kenny called. "I'm putting the boat up for sale."

Crap.

The afternoon of the double wedding of Bonnie and Loretta Brinks was, indeed, the social event of the season. The wedding party was made up of the children of both brides and grooms and their families. They spread out across the front of the church like a choir, ready to sing. Not that anyone needed to. The three pros had that covered.

Pastor Paul's wife did the flowers, turning the sanctuary into a burst of autumn glory. The brides both wore dresses in shades of turquoise, their hair crowned with seashell headbands accented with green pearls. Every woman present dabbed at teary eyes when The Mermaids sang together for the last time.

Then it was on to The Drunken Sailor for appetizers and drinks and a three-tiered cake covered in blue frosting waves and dotted with frosting seashells. There was dancing with music provided by The Mermaids for the first set and then, for the rest of the evening, a DJ. Even Mermaids deserved a break and a chance to be on the dance floor.

It was crowded with line dancers and couples doing the two-step, including Gina and her man Jimmy, who was already talking about coming back for a longer visit. There was only one slight mishap when Nora Singleton got a little carried away doing the Tush Push and lost her balance and pushed herself onto her tush. Fortunately, her husband and Tyrella got her back up with no harm done.

The brides and grooms cut the cake and then joined Avril and Kenny and other family members at what had been turned into a very long band table. Both Lawrence and J.J. looked like men who had won the lottery, and Kenny said as much.

"We have," said Lawrence, and kissed Glamma.

"Me, too," Kenny said. "We should be seeing you soon." He turned to smile at Avril. "I think I got a buyer for the boat."

"Don't sell it," she said.

His eyebrows pulled together. "What?"

"Don't." She looked at her mom. "I'm not coming back to Nashville. At least not to live."

She never thought she'd hear herself say those words, but they were exactly the words she needed to say. It was the right decision. She knew it. Deep down she'd known it the minute she drove back into town.

Her mother looked at her in surprise. "But we've found the perfect house. There's plenty of room for both of you."

"To come visit," Avril said. She took Kenny's hand. "We both will. But I belong here."

Kenny gaped at her. "But Nashville."

"Will be my second home." She turned to her mother. "I went. I made a dream come true. Just like you're doing, Mom. But there's more to my dream. I know that now. I'm a mermaid," she added with a grin. "I need to be near the sea."

Glamma reached across the table and took her hand. "It's a wise woman who knows where she needs to be to build her best life."

Mom put her hand over both of theirs and simply smiled at her, teary-eyed.

"Anyway, somebody needs to keep the house here in good shape and watch over J.J.'s vacation rental," Avril said with a grin.

"It's a good place to raise a family," Bonnie said, smiling at Kenny, who was suddenly wearing a Cheshire cat grin.

"I think so, too," he said and draped an arm over Avril's shoulders.

It was time for champagne and speeches, and several of the locals stepped up to the mike to make one.

Pete Long, wearing a white shirt and red bow tie with his jeans, pointed a finger at Lawrence and said, "You better be good to that old girl or you'll hear from me."

"I'm not old," Loretta shouted, and everyone laughed.

Evening approached, signaling the end of the festivities. It was time for both couples to depart for their new lives. The brides threw their bridal bouquets, making sure that both Gina and Avril caught them. Jimmy grinned and Kenny gave Avril a thumbs-up.

Then everyone went out to the parking lot where Lawrence's motor home sat, decorated with ribbons and signs to let the whole world know it was going to be inhabited by a bride and groom.

"I love you, dear," Glamma said, hugging Avril. "The next wedding I attend will be yours."

"Drive safely," Mom said to Lawrence and kissed his cheek.

Then she hugged Glamma tightly. For a minute Avril wasn't sure she was going to let go. When she finally did her cheeks were damp with tears. "I love you, Mom," she said. "Thank you for always being there."

Glamma put a hand to her cheek. "I love you, too, daughter."

She hugged Mom again, and then, after giving Avril a final hug, climbed into the motor home to cheers from all her well-wishers.

Then it was time to drive Mom and J.J. to the airport. They would be visiting another beach for their honeymoon, one in Hawaii.

"Take care of The Sailor," J.J. said, shaking hands with Seth Waters.

"You know I will," he said.

"And take care of my girl," Mom said to Lucy.

Lucy smiled at Avril. "I have a feeling she's going to do just fine taking care of herself."

As Avril and Kenny drove the newlyweds to the airport

there was much excited banter and talk of future fun, including Thanksgiving and Christmas in Nashville. And, of course, an earlier visit to see the new house and maybe do some mother-daughter songwriting.

It all sounded exciting and fun, but Avril still found herself tearing up as she watched her mom and J.J. disappear into the airport terminal. Moonlight Harbor without her mother, it was going to take some getting used to.

"We could still move there," Kenny offered as they drove away.

Avril shook her head. "Nope." Like a certain famous woman with those ruby slippers once said, there was no place like home.

Kenny took her to the beach the next night and brought out two pieces of leftover cake he'd had the server put in a container. "Take the piece on the right," he said, "and don't choke on it."

"Like I'm gonna choke on a piece of cake, you goof," she said.

"It's not the cake I'm worried about you choking on." He turned on the dome light in his truck. "Look."

She did and saw the ring stuck in the frosting. "Oh, my gosh," she breathed. She looked at him, tears swimming to her eyes.

"Start thinking about what kind of cake you want," he said.

Avril loved cake, but her piece went forgotten. She loved kissing Kenny much more.

After they came up for air, he reached across her and pulled a piece of folded paper out of the glove compartment. "I wrote something. For if you said yes."

Her heart skittered. "You did?"

"Don't laugh. It's a song."

"You wrote a song?"

"For you."

"Aww, Kenny," she said, her heart turning over.

"It's not very good, but it's how I feel."

"Sing it to me."

He cleared his throat and began to sing, "'I found myself a mermaid on the beach one day. She was the sweetest thing I'd ever seen and she stole my heart away.'" He sneaked a look at her, checking to make sure she wasn't laughing at him.

"This is so cute," she gushed. And it was. He was.

"'I never thought I could keep her but it's looking like I can. I'm in love with my mermaid and I'm a happy man.'" Seeing her smile, he really got into it, his head bobbing as he sang his chorus. "'A happy man, happy as a clam. That's what I am, a happy, happy man.'"

And she was a happy woman. She applauded enthusiastically, and he beamed.

"I know it's kinda goofy, but I hoped it would make you happy."

"It does. You do!"

He handed over the paper and she pressed it to her heart.

"So you like it?" He looked almost bashful.

"I adore it. And I adore you. You are the best beach treasure I've ever found," she said.

"Thanks for coming home," he said simply, and gave her cheek a gentle brush with his finger.

Yep, Dorothy was right. No place like it.

They celebrated by feeding each other the cake, but it wasn't nearly as sweet as the kiss that followed.

Late that night, still too excited to sleep, she slipped out of bed and went out to the kitchen in her mom's house, her home. Moonlight was dancing on the water of the canal. The sky was dotted with stars. And she was so happy it ought to be illegal.

Everything was falling into place. Now she had one more thing to do. She fetched her laptop and typed up an ad for the local paper, offering her services as a guitar teacher.

Then she had one more ad to write. She smiled as she typed the heading: MERMAIDS WANTED.

\* \* \* \* \*

# *Mermaid Stew*

*The Mermaids want you to have a little taste of the beach. They hope you'll enjoy Loretta's specialty.*

*Serves 4*

Ingredients:

*2 Russet potatoes, peeled and cut into bite-sized pieces*
*1 stalk celery, finely chopped*
*¼ cup finely chopped onion*
*1 10.5 ounce can of New England clam chowder*
*1 cup small cooked shrimp (if frozen, thawed)*
*1 14 oz package smoked salmon, with the skin off and cut into bite sized pieces*
*½ cup cream or half and half*
*Dill weed to taste*

Directions:

Cook potatoes, celery and onion in just enough water to cover them until tender. (Put in celery and onion first as they take longer)

When cooked, add chowder, shrimp, salmon and cream. Cook over medium heat until hot. Serve with hot garlic bread or cheese bread.

Dear Reader,

Writing this tale brought back so many memories of the days when I was taking frequent trips to Nashville, trying to make it as a songwriter. The music world is a fascinating one, to be sure. Hearts can get broken in that world, but dreams can also come true, and my cowgirl hat is off to all those songwriters who've made a home there and written songs that have made a home in our hearts. Like my characters, I hope you find your happy place and see your dreams come true.

Honest reviews of my books are appreciated, and I always love to hear from readers, so feel free to connect with me on my website: www.sheilasplace.com.

Happy reading!
*Sheila*

# *Acknowledgments*

As always, thank you so much to my fab editor, April Osborn, my matchless agent Paige Wheeler, and the amazing team at Mira, who work so hard to turn my tales into a book I can be proud of. Thank you to my Nashville friends, especially Chuck Whiting, who gave me a peek into life in the new Nashville.